Praise for *Valknut: The Binding*

"The author mixes mystery, railroads, railroad cops, and the tramp subculture, then throws in Norse mythology...which sounds like an improbable addition. But as in Kevin Hearne's Iron Druid series, the result is a delightful and coherent whole." -- Lee Killough, author of the Blood Hunt vampire cop series

"Loughin has brought to life an underworld few are aware even exists and mixes it deftly with Norse mythology into a fast moving story of love and loss, betrayal and loyalty, family ties and prophecies." -- J.W. Manus, e-book guru of Ebooks = Real Books

"Set aside some time, cause once you start, you won't want to put it down." -- Shannon Mayer, author of The Celtic Legacy Trilogy

Valknut: The Binding

Marie M. Loughin

Valknut: The Binding

An Ottertail Publishing Book

PRINTING HISTORY

Ottertail First Edition/May 2013

For more information, contact the author at
marieloughin@gmail.com or visit http://marieloughin.com

ISBN-13: 978-0615817521

ISBN-10: 0615817521

DEDICATION

*My love and gratitude go to
Leonard Bishop*

(1922 – 2002)

for giving me the tools,

*and to Tom for taking me
seriously (at the right times).*

CHAPTER 1

The diesel engine rumbled. Lennie Cook felt it through the ground under her feet and convinced herself that she shook from vibrations rather than fear. The roar escalated as the train drew near.

Too fast. She glanced nervously at the shabby old man beside her. "It's coming too fast."

The man squinted into the westerly sun and waited, dragging on a hand-rolled cigarette. A warm breeze lifted his shaggy hair. Fine lines creased his cheeks, forehead, chin, even his lips, as though the sun had baked away the inessentials beneath. One eye was a sunken lid of puckered flesh. The other glowed crystal blue in the sunlight. He waited a moment more, two clouds streaming from his nose. Then he pinched the burning end of his smoke and dropped the stub into his pocket.

"Run."

So Lennie ran, racing along the tracks, chasing the old man in a spray of cinders. The train gained speed as it left the yard, and her feet flew and her heart filled with the reckless joy of the child she had been. Then a branch caught her leg and she stumbled. The train loomed closer. The old man ran on, swift as a young athlete. Doubt jittered through Lennie's mind.

I must be insane to follow this guy.

But he knew something about her father, maybe even knew where he'd gone. She might not get a better lead. She followed.

The train caught them and pulled ahead. Two engines on this one. Hot air whipped her face as they went by. Then came the cars— grainers, refrigeration cars, boxcars — avalanching past.

"This one," the one-eyed man yelled. He dropped back and drew even with the front of an open boxcar. In one fluid motion, he leaped, caught the door latch, and swung inside.

Air burned down Lennie's throat. Her aching legs churned. She thought of her father and mustered a final burst of speed. *You sure as hell better be out there, you son of a bitch!*

Then she caught the door latch, felt it jerk her shoulder, and her feet lost the ground. She grabbed hold with the other hand and swung toward the opening. She missed. Her legs banged against the doorframe and fell back into open air. Wheels thundered a few feet away. Sweat slicked her palms and she pictured her body tumbling, rolling under the train, cut in half.

Stupid, stupid, stupid. Her legs careened over a pile of rubble. One hand broke loose. The wheels loomed—giant, crushing circular saws. Her other hand somehow stayed hooked on the door latch. Pain screeched through her arm as her body swung and twisted. Her feet clipped the ground and her hold slipped. Before she could fall, a hand shot from the doorway and caught her wrist. She was dragged aboard with agonizing slowness, the hard lip of the doorframe grinding across her ribs and hip bone.

She huddled on the floor, sides heaving. Shudders ran through her body. Gasping sobs tore her raw lungs. Unable to shake the image of those wheels, spinning and shooting sparks, she curled tightly and wrapped her arms around her head.

"Easy, there," someone said. She felt a reassuring pat on her shoulder. The thunder faded to a muted rumble under the metal floor. She was safe inside the boxcar, warm in a patch of sunlight. She forced herself to take a few deep breaths. Pain lanced her strained arm as she pushed herself upright. How had that old man boarded so easily when she, once a star sprinter for her track club, had nearly ended up under its wheels?

Grimacing, she squinted into the boxcar's shadowed corners, looking for the one-eyed hobo. "There are easier ways to kill me," she rasped, rubbing her shoulder. Her bruised legs ached and blood seeped through a new hole in the knee of her jeans. "I might even cooperate, as long as I don't have to go through that again."

"Actually," came the mild reply, "I think I saved your life."

The voice was clearer, younger than the voice of the hobo she had followed. A stranger sat in shadow near the door. She glanced around the boxcar and didn't see the one-eyed man at all.

Great. She curled shaking fingers around the canister of pepper spray she carried on a belt loop. Just great. Virtually unarmed and trapped with strange men on a moving boxcar. She hadn't been this stupid since she tried to follow her father the morning after he had disappeared. An idiot kid with nothing but a book bag stuffed with clothes, chewy granola bars, seven dollars, and her favorite CD.

She eyed the man, hoping he wasn't unfriendly. Or too friendly. Maybe she should use the pepper spray now, before things could get ugly. But the wind gusting through the doorway might carry the spray into her own face. She flexed her numb hand and found she could make a fist, though the torn skin on her palm would hurt when feeling returned.

"Who are you?" she asked. The tremor in her voice made her wince.

In answer, the stranger slid into the sunlight. He was a little older than she. Or maybe younger—the rails had a way of aging people. He met her eyes, then looked down and rubbed the back of his neck. "Name's Junkyard Doug. Most call me Junkyard."

Lennie relaxed a little. Just a hobo. She had met several while searching train yards and hobo jungles for her father. At worst, they were caustic and reclusive. Some were helpful, even friendly. This one looked better than most, though dust had collected in the creases around his mouth. His face was smooth shaven with a pair of long sideburns. An orange bandana covered brown hair worn in a short ponytail. Metal buttons covered his faded jean jacket, including a smiley face pinned to the breast pocket and a rusted button on the sleeve that said, "Gore in 2000." Only a little behind the times, Lennie thought wryly.

The guy seemed shy, probably harmless, and he had saved her life. Nevertheless, she kept her fingers around the pepper spray. "I guess I should thank you. You might have gotten killed right along with me."

"No problem."

He said nothing more. Just sat quietly, arms draped over crossed legs. She was about to ask where the one-eyed hobo had gone when Junkyard thrust his hand into his jacket pocket and leaned toward her. His face loomed too close, a collection of hard angles that seemed harsh, even sinister. She gasped and pulled away. Her hand convulsed around the pepper spray.

Junkyard froze, his gaze fixed on the canister. Slowly, he sat back and drew his hand from his pocket. In it were two Twinkies. He held them out to her. "Have one. Sorry I don't have more to offer you."

Lennie stared at the packages and tried to remember how to breathe. Her face burned with embarrassment. She looked up and saw friendly amusement in his eyes. Still, she hesitated before taking one. These Twinkies might be his whole dinner. But then, he might be insulted if she didn't accept it.

"Thanks." Her fingers closed on a package. She flinched at the touch of his calloused palm. "My name is Lennie."

The dust that covered the floor of the boxcar now coated her hands as well, so she peeled the wrapper back and ate the Twinkie like a banana. Junkyard ate his cake in three large bites before she could even swallow her first. Then he stuffed the crumpled wrapper in his jacket pocket and resumed his relaxed, cross-legged pose, eyes fixed out the open door.

The train, which had been paralleling a line of trees, broke into an open field of buckwheat. Millions of tiny flowers blurred past, creating the illusion of a solid white blanket spreading into the distance. It made Lennie think of bees and beehives as she licked the filling out of her Twinkie.

When the last bite was gone, Junkyard took her wrapper and put it with the other in his jacket pocket. In a noncommittal voice, he said, "Crazy thing you did, trying to catch onto a moving boxcar."

"You're telling me! It's probably the stupidest thing I've ever done."

Yes, she wanted to find her father. But she had only intended to flash his photo around to hobos and yardmen, not throw herself onto a speeding train. "I never would have tried it, except that one-eyed man seemed to know what he was doing."

The man—what was his name? Rollin' Red? Something like that. He'd made it sound so reasonable, like hitching a ride with no idea when or where the train would stop was completely sensible and logical. She struggled to recall what he had said that was so convincing, but her memory of him was hazy, as though she'd met him years ago instead of less than an hour. She couldn't even remember what he looked like, just an impression of fading red hair and a single eye, as clear as sapphire. It seemed the sum of all human wisdom could be swallowed in its depths.

He had been in the train yard, sitting on the steps of a locomotive as if waiting for her. She remembered trying to show him her father's photograph. He hadn't even glanced at it. "I know who you're lookin' for—and I'm thinkin' it's about time you found 'im."

He'd lifted a closed hand in front of her face and dropped something metallic, round, and heavy that bounced at the end of a silver chain. Tarnished almost black, the object spun slowly for a moment before she recognized it.

It was her father's pocket watch.

With a painful flash of memory, she'd seen her father in navy blue dress pants and a pinstriped oxford shirt, pressed and neat, smelling of dryer sheets as he kissed her goodbye for the last time. The watch was tucked as always in his front pants pocket, leashed by its silver fob.

And years later, the same watch dangled from the hand of a red-haired, one-eyed hobo. She reached out tentatively and cupped it, felt its solid weight, the cool metal against her skin.

"Where did you get this?" she whispered, rubbing the tarnished engravings. But the hobo jerked the watch from her hands. Her fingers knotted around the sudden void. "Hey—give it back!"

She grabbed for it, but he calmly gathered the chain and shoved the watch into the front pocket of his jeans. A short silver loop stuck out, taunting her. She had never wanted to hit someone so much in her life.

"It's your father you're lookin' for, ain't it?" he said. "Well, you jus' follow me if you wanna find 'im."

"Follow you. Right. How dumb do you think I am?"

But her hands ached where the watch had rested. She wanted it back. Now. She glared into his one shining blue eye.

Something had happened, then. Something she couldn't quite remember, and suddenly it had seemed reasonable that she should follow the one-eyed man. In fact, she had no choice. She had to find her father, before it was too late...too late...for what?

The next thing she knew, she was hanging from the side of a speeding train.

Junkyard's voice pulled her out of the memory. She blinked and found him looking at her expectantly. "Uh, sorry," she said. "I guess I zoned out. Did you say something?"

"No problem. I was just asking about this one-eyed man. Where did he go?"

"Didn't you see him? He climbed on board ahead of me."

Junkyard frowned. "Didn't see anyone else. I was taking a nap. Thought I heard a bird squawking, but it was you yelling."

"Well, he must be here somewhere."

Lennie leaned into the shadows and let her eyes adjust. Cardboard and scraps of packing material littered the floor. A hand-truck lay on its side against one wall. Nearby sat a thick, six-foot roll of packing paper, crooked and lumpy, as though it had been rolled by a drunk. There was nothing else in the car. Yet she remembered watching the old man swing on board as easily as stepping into a parked truck. Deceptively easy.

"Where the hell did he go?"

Junkyard glanced around the boxcar. "Like I said, never saw anyone, one eyed or otherwise. You sure there was someone else?" He eyed her suspiciously. "You don't look the type to be drinking Sterno."

"No, no—there was this old fellow with one eye and wild pink hair. Well, not pink. It was faded red, almost white. Anyway, this guy was going to help me find my dad—" She hesitated. Babbling wouldn't convince him of her sobriety. "Well, it's a long story."

"We've got time. This train doesn't stop again 'til Minneapolis."

"Minneapolis!" She gaped at him. "But my classes start tomorrow! I'll never make it back on time."

She leaned her head out the door. Maybe she could still jump off. She would only have a few miles to walk back.

"Whoa, there." Junkyard snagged a belt loop and hauled her back. "Don't even think about jumping. Try it and you'll lose more than a little skin. Train's going near sixty by now."

Lennie watched corn blur by. He was right. After postponing college for years to support her mother, she was going to screw up her first semester. She groaned. "How the hell am I going to get back? I left my purse locked in the car. I don't even have my cell phone."

Not that there was anyone she could call for help. Not anymore. She thought of her mother and swallowed hard against the sudden ache in her throat.

Junkyard shrugged. "I suppose you'll get back the same way you're getting there."

"Not *quite* the same. I'll never try to catch a moving train again." She slumped against the doorframe. What a mess. And all for nothing—the one-eyed man had vanished as if he never existed.

Dejected, she stared out the door, watching the miles pile up behind her. The cornfield had ended, and a half-mile of fence strobed by. Then a farmstead swung into view. She smiled at the triangular pig shelters that so delighted her as a child. "Look, Daddy!" she used to squeal from the back seat of the old Ford station wagon. "That farmer is so nice, he's given each pig his own house!"

Her father would do a lousy imitation of Porky Pig thanking the kindly farmer, and then bellow his huge belly laugh. Her mother would smile indulgently at the well-worn joke, knitting needles clicking at an afghan that never seemed to get any longer.

That was before he had deserted them. Before her mother had begun to drink herself to death.

That ache in her throat wasn't going away. She blinked back tears and glanced at Junkyard. He had resumed staring out the door as if she weren't there. What sort of man would leave his family to follow such a dirty, uncomfortable life?

She dug into her back pocket and pulled out a sealed plastic bag containing a faded photograph of her father, taken during their last family fishing trip. He stood at a lakeshore, extending a small walleye toward the camera. His face looked plumply middle-class and happy.

He had taught her to bait her own hook during that trip. She had felt so proud. And he had taken her swimming, throwing her high into the air, a fountain of giggling girl rising in the bright sun to plunge, bubbling, to the sandy lake bottom.

She couldn't reconcile that image with the man she had grown to hate.

Junkyard was studying her when she looked up. She flushed, wondering what he saw. Probably nothing complimentary. She pushed back the tangle of caramel hair that was always falling in her face and met his eyes. "I know what you're thinking."

He raised an eyebrow and the corner of his mouth twitched. "Oh?"

She plunged ahead. "You're thinking, what's this scrawny, defenseless, fool of a woman doing riding the rails? Does she think she's some kind of rail kid?"

"Well, something like that. You don't exactly look the part."

She bristled at first, but decided to take it as a compliment. "Thanks. And I have no intention of taking up the hobo lifestyle. This was all a big mistake. I was only going to...I just wanted to...uh."

There was no sensible explanation for jumping onto a moving train. She wished she had never brought it up. To her relief, Junkyard didn't comment. Instead, he eyed the photograph in her hand. "That your father?"

She nodded and handed it to him. "His name's Jarvis Cook."

He smoothed the plastic bag to get a better look. After a moment, he shook his head and handed it back. "Picture's pretty old. A man could change a lot in that time."

"It's the most recent picture I could find. It was in my mother's things, along with a letter he wrote the day he left." She looked at the photograph again and wondered what sorts of lines life had put on her father's face, whether his transience had made him thin, whether his laugh was still the same. "The letter said he was taking the iron road, like his father before him. My mom never showed it to me. I think she was afraid I'd follow him. He's been gone ten years."

Junkyard whistled. "Long time. How do you know he's still out there?"

"I don't. But I..."

Lennie hesitated, uncomfortable discussing her life with anyone, especially strangers. Junkyard didn't push. He seemed content to wait, unlike that school counselor she had been forced to see when her anger got away from her in middle school. She had despised the counselor's by-the-clock sincerity and never told him anything. But somehow she found herself wanting to talk to Junkyard.

"For all I know, he died under a piece of cardboard ten years ago. But there's a chance he's alive, so I have to try to find him. It sounds corny, but we were so happy together. I know he loved me. At least, I thought he did. And it seemed like he loved Mom. But then he left and everything fell apart. Why would he do that? How could he leave us like that? My mother..."

The words still came with difficulty. She pressed her lips together, fighting the tightness building in her chest. Junkyard looked away until she began to speak again. Her voice sounded bitter in her ears. "My mother died a few weeks ago. She's been dying by degrees for years. I think she started to die the day he left, like...like he took some piece of her with him. Pulled the plug and all the life started draining away. How could he do that to her?"

How could he do that to me? But she couldn't say that out loud.

She turned on Junkyard. "And you! Do you ever consider what you're doing to the people you left behind? How much they worry? All the pain and loneliness? How can you live with yourself?"

He jerked as if struck and his face went blank. Lennie sucked in her breath. Good going, big mouth—tear into the guy you'll be trapped with for hours. Tensing, she waited to see what he would do.

He answered in a low voice. "There is no one else."

"Oh." She stared at him stupidly. "Oh. I'm so sorry. I'm such an idiot. I shouldn't have assumed—"

Anything else she might have said was lost when the boxcar lurched, throwing her against the roll of packing paper. The floor shook wildly. Bits of grain and gravel bounced and skittered across the floor. She clung to the paper roll, which didn't feel like a paper roll, but she was too jounced to worry about it. She closed her eyes tight, certain the train was about to derail. Junkyard shook her arm and she cracked an eye open, reading his lips to understand him over the din. Rough track, he said. It felt more like a major earthquake.

She tried to relax, but her bones bounced in her skin, awakening every strain and bruise. Junkyard swayed easily, like a sailor rolling with the waves. She envied him. The Twinkie was starting to rest uneasy in her stomach.

When the track eventually smoothed enough so she could raise her voice above the noise, she shouted, "Does that happen often?"

"Yes," he said, "only sometimes worse."

Lennie looked for—hoped for—a grin, but his expression didn't change.

"Oh, man," she groaned, still clinging to the packing paper. "I've gotta get off this train. Are you sure it doesn't stop before Minneapolis?"

Now Junkyard did grin, but in sympathy. "Afraid not. It's a hotshot with right-of-way clear through. Unfortunately, this old boxcar's a rattler, but it was the only one that wasn't locked."

Lennie swallowed hard. "If I get my hands on that one-eyed hobo, I'll..."

She wasn't sure what she'd do. Kick him in the shins, maybe. She sure wouldn't be taking his advice.

"Funny about that," Junkyard said. "I've been traveling the rails for nearly a year now, and I know a lot of the full-time 'bos that ride this Midwest route. Don't remember any with pink hair. Did you catch his name?"

"It's strange. He told me, but somehow I can't remember it. I think it was something like Rattlin' Red, or—"

The roll of paper bucked underneath her, nearly knocking her on her face. She thought they'd hit another patch of bad track until she heard a muffled shout. "Hot dog! I knew it! I knew it was him!"

She scrambled back from the roll as it came to life. It inched and flopped and began to unroll in place. Yards of paper bunched up against her until a hobo finally appeared. Unlike the one-eyed man with his road-wise manner, or Junkyard, who seemed like a regular working guy, this hobo looked the romanticized stereotype. He wore a shapeless felt hat and an old, dark suit patched with squares cut from brightly colored bandanas. With two-day's growth on his chin, dirt smudges on his face, and overlarge shoes, he only needed a red ball on his nose to pass as a circus clown.

As soon as he was free of the paper, he began jumping and jigging around the boxcar, yodeling like a bad cowboy singer. Suddenly the car swayed and he stumbled, teetering in the doorway. Lennie lunged to pull him in, but he swung around and staggered back into the car before she could touch him.

"He's crazy!" she yelled. "We've got to stop him before he kills himself!"

Junkyard watched the older hobo, a wide grin stretching his face. At first, Lennie thought he hadn't heard her over the yodeling, which out-decibeled even the train noise, but he shook his head. "Naw, that's just Jungle Jim." He watched the comic figure rebound off the far wall and laughed. "Hey, Jim! Why don't you sit before you throw yourself off the train."

Jungle Jim didn't seem to hear. "I's right!" he shouted, doing a touchdown dance. "I's right, wasn't I? It was Ramblin' Red! Old One-Eye, himself. No doubt about it!!"

Junkyard reached up and tugged on Jungle Jim's arm. "Can't say I know who you're talking about, Jim," he said, winking at Lennie. "But why don't you grab a piece of floor and tell us about it."

Jungle Jim stopped dancing and stared at Junkyard as though he hadn't noticed him until that moment. "Well, whaddaya know! Hi there, Dougie. Here we are, on the same train—imagine that! There I was, all rolled up in that paper, sweatin' and about to suffercate, all for nothin'. It was no one but you and that girl." He paused, panting a little, and nodded at Lennie. "Hello, Missy. It was just you two all along! I could of been airin' out by the door, watching the scenery go by, doggone it!"

He shook his head, his face drooping in exaggerated sadness. Then he brightened and plunked down on the floor next to Lennie. The odor of stale sweat wafted over her, making her wish Jungle Jim had kept dancing, preferably on the other side of the car. She edged closer to the door.

"Don't worry," Junkyard said, misunderstanding her reaction, "Jungle Jim's as safe as a puppy. A big, flea-bitten puppy with a bit of mange. Eh, Jim?"

Jungle Jim took off his hat and ran fingers through a thinning patch of woolly, brown hair. "That's right, Missy, don't you worry about me. It's ol' One-Eye you should be worryin' about."

"Ramblin' Red didn't seem dangerous to me," Lennie said, though that wasn't exactly true. More that he didn't seem to have harmful intent. "Is he some kind of criminal?"

Jungle Jim tipped back his head and laughed, kicking his legs like a little kid with the giggles. Lennie couldn't help but smile.

"No, no," he gasped. "Not a criminal. Ramblin' Red is outside the law. Some say he's outside humankind, but I don't know nothin' about that." He pulled a filthy handkerchief from his pocket and dabbed his eyes.

"But I do know one thing," he added, suddenly serious, his eyes clear and locked on hers. "He wouldn't of brought you to us for no reason. I'm not too sure I want that kind of attention from ol' One-Eye."

The comic hobo looked ridiculous and was obviously a little simple, but something about the way he spoke those words sent a chill through Lennie. "Why? Who is he? What's he done?"

"Well, now, those are mighty big questions, Missy. Bigger'n you know. See, Ramblin' Red's been around for at least a hunnerd years. He always seems to show up when somethin' big is goin' on. They say he was there at the St. Francis Church Fire of '42. They say he was there before that, at the Wellington Avalanche of 1910. Why, they say he showed up as long ago as the Pullman Riots, an' that was all the way back in 1894."

Jungle Jim stopped talking and grew still. He cocked his head and stared into the corner of the boxcar as though he heard something far away. Lennie couldn't say how it happened or why, but he changed somehow, though he hadn't shifted a muscle. His dopey smile became serene, almost beautiful. Lines of wisdom parted the middle-aged looseness of his face. His eyes closed and, in a sing-song voice, he began to recite:

An' the black bird o' sorrow
lay his blue eye upon you
an' you fall
an' you fall
an' no one catches you
at all...

He pulled his knees to his chin, hugged his legs, and began to rock forward and backward, humming to himself. Lennie didn't know what to think. She looked at Junkyard, who shrugged.

"He does that sometimes. You get used to it."

"Oh, sure I will." She snorted. "Just like I'll get used to this earthquake on wheels and having Twinkies for dinner. Not that I'm not grateful," she added hastily when Junkyard raised an eyebrow. "It's only that, well, I'm not supposed to be here. I'm supposed to be at home, getting ready for classes. And the guy that lured me here isn't even on board. Almost makes me believe Jim's story. I get tricked by some interfering ghost and he doesn't even stick around to keep his promises."

She kicked at the pile of packing paper that was still bunched up against her. "It's all a big waste of time."

The end of the paper slid into the open doorway, flapping noisily. Jungle Jim shrieked and fumbled after it, too late. Before anyone could catch it, the entire length was sucked out the door like yarn caught in a vacuum cleaner. Jungle Jim stuck his head out to watch it twist and tumble away in the fading sunlight. He clung to the doorframe and began to sob. Junkyard crawled over and pulled him a safer distance inside. "What's the matter, Jim? It's only a bit of packing paper."

"Yeah, but now how'm I gonna *hide*? I'm dead for certain, like Tin Can Petey. Dead, dead, dead." He wrapped his arms around himself and moaned, then added wistfully, "I tell ya, ol' Petey could cook better'n Julia Child, and him using nothin' but an old tin can and a little bitty fire. I haven't had nothin' but pork 'n' beans since he died."

To illustrate, he leaned to one side and passed a loud explosion of gas. Settling back, he started rocking again, chanting, "Pork 'n' beans for breakfast, pork 'n' beans for dinner, pork 'n' beans, pork 'n' beans—"

Junkyard gripped his shoulder. "Hold on, Jim. You saying Petey's dead? What happened?"

Jungle Jim stopped rocking. He blinked vacantly, mouthing Junkyard's last question. Then his eyes came alive and his face twisted in anguish. "Petey's dead," he wailed. "Someone killed him, that's what happened, and him not ever hurting anything, not even the flies that landed in his stew. He'd just fish 'em out and set 'em on a branch so they could dry their wings."

He started bawling like a three-year-old, gulping air between words. "No, sir," he snuffled, "Petey never deserved what happened to him, and neither do I."

He shrank down into his baggy suit coat and resumed rocking, moaning and sobbing in rhythm with the movement. Junkyard patted his back and made soothing noises.

Lennie watched them anxiously. She knew there was violence on the rails, but she had never been this close to it before. She admired Junkyard's patience. She wanted to grab Jungle Jim by the lapels and shake the story out of him, and she didn't even know this Tin Can Petey. Perhaps, she thought wryly, it would be better to let Junkyard handle it.

It wasn't until Junkyard promised a package of Ho-Ho's that Jungle Jim stopped his rocking and opened his eyes. He straightened up and blew his nose on a dirty handkerchief. His voice shook as he began to speak.

"Me an' Petey, we caught out of Topeka about three days ago. About halfway to Ames, our ride went into the hole for some repairs. We sat there on that side track for maybe five hours and still no sign of movin' on. It was getting to be dark, so I chanced a little look-see. Petey stayed with our stuff. I couldn't of been gone more than twenty minutes—honest! But when I got back, there he was..."

He tried to go on, working his jaw up and down, but only

strained whimpers came out. Junkyard waited silently until Jungle Jim continued. "It was terrible. He was all tied up with some kinda string. Yards and yards of the stuff, like a bug wrapped up by a spider or somethin'. And he was dead, a knife poked right up through the roof of his mouth, clean up to the handle, his eyes starin' an' starin', like they were beggin' me to take it out. *Take the knife out, Jimmy,* they said, so I tried. I really, really tried. But the knife was stuck in there good, an' there was blood all around, an' ol' Petey—he just lay there, his pack sittin' right next to him, and mine was still there, too."

Jungle Jim began to wail. "Oh, why'd they do it? They didn't take nothin'! Not even the roll of money Petey taped to his ankle. An' the train kept sittin' there, with me in the dark and ol' Petey starin', an' I couldn't stand it no more. I jumped off and hitched my way to Ames. I had to leave him, you know. Aw, but I shouldn't of left him."

As Junkyard listened, his face grew hard and his eyes darkened. He started to speak, then swore instead and slammed his fist on the floor.

Jungle Jim cried out, covering his head. Lennie jumped, gasping, and remembered how little she knew about Junkyard. He shot to his feet and glared down at her as if she had done something wrong. Without speaking, he turned away and leaned, hunch-shouldered, against the doorframe, his back a solid wall.

Jungle Jim settled back into his rhythm of rocking and sobbing. Lennie looked uncertainly between him and Junkyard. Someone should comfort Jungle Jim, but it didn't look like Junkyard was going to move from the doorway. She sidled closer to Jungle Jim, hesitating to speak. For ten years, she never found words to comfort her despairing mother. What could she say to a total stranger?

"It's okay, Jim," she tried.

He didn't respond, and why should he? It was a moronic thing to say. Frustrated, she touched his shoulder and tried again.

"You had to leave him there, Jim. It wasn't safe to stay. I'm sure your friend would understand that."

"I kn-know." Jungle Jim hiccupped and wiped his nose on his sleeve. "It's just that, where'm I g-gonna hide?"

"Don't worry, you don't need to hide," Lennie said. "There's no one else here. We'll be fine." As long as the train keeps moving, anyway.

Jungle Jim didn't seem reassured. He curled on his side and began whimpering. Lennie could think of nothing else to say. More than anything, she wanted to go home. The house might be empty, and so was her life, but at least she would be safe.

She left her hand on Jungle Jim's shoulder and watched the setting sun flash between evergreens in a windbreak. Eventually the whimpering faded. His rocking slowed and finally stopped. Certain he was asleep, Lennie got up and joined Junkyard at the door.

She didn't say anything at first. She was still afraid of the change in him. Tension poured off him like sweat. It was clear he knew something about Tin Can Petey's murder that wasn't included in Jungle Jim's story.

The sun was a pink ball bleeding into the horizon. A cool wind whistled into the boxcar. It would get cooler. Rubbing her arms, she said, "I don't suppose we can close this door."

Junkyard grunted. "Not unless you want to risk getting locked inside for a few days. Or weeks." He pointed to a railroad spike jammed into the bottom runner of the door. "Whatever you do, don't take that out."

Stuck in a smelly boxcar with two strange men and no food or water—not a pleasant prospect. "Uh, I guess I can stand a little wind."

She settled to the floor inside the door and watched the sun sink out of sight. Junkyard hadn't moved or spoken by the time the first stars appeared. She wondered if he planned to stay there with a scowl cemented on his face all night.

"Did you know Tin Can Petey well?" she finally asked. "Or is something else bugging you?"

He didn't answer for a long time. His gaze flicked along a grey-cloaked stretch of farmland, but, judging from his harsh expression, his thoughts were somewhere far less pleasant. When the response came, she barely heard his voice over the wheels and wind. "This isn't the first time I've seen...heard of this sort of murder."

Before she could say anything, Junkyard turned back into the train, leaving her at the door. He dragged a piece of cardboard next to Jim and sat down on it.

"First thing tomorrow," he said, "I'm calling Jim's sister. She'll reserve a ticket, and I'll put him on a bus and send him home."

Awake after all, Jungle Jim yelped and sat up. Tears had left muddy trails through the dirt on his face, but now his eyes were dry and wide with alarm. "Oh, don't do that!" He crushed his felt hat to his chest. "Please don't make me go back! I haven't missed the Festival in twenty years, an' I'm not about to start now. The kids'd be too disappointed."

Junkyard shook his head. "You shouldn't be on the road after a thing like that happens, Jim."

"Aw, but them kids are all I got left! I can't hold a job, an' my buddy is gone—heck, there's nothin' else that matters." Jungle Jim folded his arms over the hat, his face set in a stubborn sulk. "If you put me on that bus, I'll just hop right off at the first stop and hitch back."

Junkyard held up his hands. "Okay, okay. We'll wait until after the festival. And then I'll put you on a bus. And you better plan to stay close to me at night."

Jungle Jim frowned and muttered to himself, but didn't protest.

Junkyard turned to Lennie. "As for you, as soon as Jim is on that bus, you and I are catchin' out for Ames. You're going home. This is no time for some cherry woman to be riding the rails."

Lennie stared at him, too astonished to be angry. It didn't matter that she had already been thinking of going home. She wasn't about to let him order her around. She left the doorway to stand over him. "Listen, guy, I've been taking care of myself since I was eleven years old. I don't need you or anyone else to tell me what to do."

He scowled up at her. "Oh, and I suppose you face down jack-rollers and gangbangers every day. How are you in a knife fight? Are you bullet-proof?"

He was right, but she resented the sarcasm in his voice. She glared at him and wished she could think of some sharp reply.

"I didn't think so," he said when she didn't answer. "You'll have to find your father some other way."

The boxcar floor jumped as the wheels hit a bump. She sat down hard, sending a painful jolt through her strained shoulder. Her temper flared. "Then how the hell do you suggest I find him! I can't leave him out there. I don't desert people just because things get a little rough."

She stopped, realizing she was shouting at him. None of this was Junkyard's fault. He wasn't her father. She rubbed her shoulder and tried to control her voice. "Look, I have no other way to find him. I have no money for detectives. I live on student loans and part time waitressing—"

She stopped, wide-eyed, and smacked her hand to her head, "Damn—my job! I'm supposed to work lunch tomorrow!"

Disaster piled on disaster, all because of this compulsion to find her father. She grimaced. "Scratch that, I now live solely on student loans. My grandparents are dead, my mother is dead, and there is no one else. So if anyone is going to find my dad, it's me."

Lennie glared defiantly at Junkyard. His gaze was equally fierce, his expression as stubborn as she felt. The wheels rattled over track joints with the steady rhythm of a clock. The wind swept through the open door, pushing Lennie's hair into her face, but she refused to blink.

Then she felt a nudge on her arm and found Jungle Jim looking at her, his face sad and serious, and his eyes had gone clear again. "Like Dougie said, ten years is sure a long time. Long enough for a man to do a lot of changin'. Now don't be takin' this wrong, Missy, but are you really sure you want to find your dad?"

"What? Of course I do!"

But those gentle eyes waited, not letting her hide behind glib words. She knew what he meant. Her father could have turned into one of those human derelicts, like those she had seen while searching the hobo jungles along Iowa railroad tracks. Vacant eyed, smelling of urine and ancient sweat, they hardly moved and barely responded to anything. She shied from the thought of bringing something like that home and calling it father.

If only Ramblin' Red hadn't shown her the pocket watch. She remembered its cool, metallic weight in her hand. It had made her father seem more real, like he could still be alive.

"I can't just give up on him," she said, as much to herself as to Jungle Jim.

Junkyard groaned and sandwiched his head in his hands as though trying to keep it from exploding. "You have no idea what's out there. I do. Petey is only one of a dozen murders on the trains over the last year, and they all happened the same way. There've been three in the last two weeks—all of 'em on the FRC Railroad. And those are only the ones I've heard about!"

Her insides ran cold, but this time the fear wasn't just for herself. "All the more reason to get my father off the rails."

21

Junkyard lifted his head and studied her, his lips pressed together in a tight frown. Finally he sighed. "Okay. It's your skin. But you've at least got to go home and get some gear. The hobo life doesn't take much, but it does take something."

He lay back on the cardboard and, rolling so his back was to her, said nothing more. Jungle Jim settled down beside him and began snoring immediately. Lennie watched them for a moment, feeling alone and frightened.

Her original plan had been to visit hobo jungles and rail yards on weekends to show her father's picture around. But now she realized this would never work. The rail system was too vast. It swallowed people without leaving a trace. If she truly wished to find her father, she would have to track him from the inside. The prospect terrified her.

Both men lay as though sleeping on feather beds rather than cardboard on a hard floor. Time to learn from the masters, she figured.

The boxcar had grown dark. Too dark. She tried to remember where she had seen a piece of cardboard big enough to sleep on, but instead her imagination supplied an image of a spider-like serial killer lurking in a corner, ready to pounce and wind her up in a mile of silk.

"Cowering at shadows," she muttered. "I'm sure Junkyard would be impressed."

Wincing in pain from banged up legs and a wrenched shoulder, she crawled deeper inside, feeling ahead until her hand brushed cardboard. Hopefully it wasn't covered with grease. Or worse. She lay down and tried to convince herself that she was comfortable, that a million eyes weren't watching her from the shadows. She couldn't imagine actually sleeping. The noise, the rough track, the strong scent of manure on the breeze, not to mention Jungle Jim's story, would keep her awake.

In the dark, the cardboard felt like a tiny raft on a sea of metal. The train hit a bumpy stretch and she clutched the cardboard's edges, irrationally fearful of being thrown off. Dust floated thickly around her and she sneezed. Something skittered over the floorboards nearby. Was it an animal? A rat? Or shifting debris? She wanted to move the cardboard closer to Junkyard and Jungle Jim, but a strange lethargy overcame her. The wheels settled into a rhythmic clickity-clack. The cardboard drifted farther into the metal sea, taking her with it, until the smells and noises faded away and she was asleep.

The dream came, and it was like no other she had ever had.

She was floating.

She no longer felt the train and its infernal vibrations. Her bones rested easy in her skin. She heard the train, with its banging and clanging and eternal clickity-clack, but—there! Now that, too, faded away.

Something rough curled around her neck, loosely, like the touch of her night-tangled hair. She opened her eyes.

She was floating.

Her hair drifted about her head as if alive. The rough thing about her neck was a rope. Its lazy, snaking length tethered her to a thick branch above her head.

She was floating, but she did not float free.

The branches of a great ash tree stretched all around. She looked for their twig-fingered ends but couldn't find them. The limbs reached for the horizon, curling over it as though cradling the world in a leafy bower. Deer and goats leaped among the branches, nipping young leaves and tender sprigs. Wasps hummed all around, taking their fill of dripping sap. An eagle cried far above, its perch lost in the tree's distant crown.

She floated among them, but apart. She was not of this world.

Whirling wings and black feathers exploded through the branches. Two ravens danced and tangled in the air before her. One landed on her right shoulder. It cocked its head as though listening to her thoughts. The other settled on her left shoulder. It turned its eye on her and she could feel it leafing through her memory.

A squirrel raced its tail up the tree trunk as if running from the devil. He scrambled to a nearby branch and smoothed his red fur, attempting to regain some dignity. Then he hopped closer, nosing his face into hers. One eye shone vivid blue. The other was nothing but a puckered hole. The hair rose on Lennie's arms.

The ravens croaked and launched from her shoulders, their claws drawing bright dots of blood. They fluttered to the branch, flanking the squirrel like bodyguards.

The squirrel plucked a twig and used its splintered end to trace a symbol on Lennie's left hand.

"With this Valknut, I bind you to me in service against the Wolf," it said in a deep voice. "You be not king nor warrior chief, yet I claim you. In this battle, you shall prevail or perish."

She thought it was a silly statement coming from a squirrel, but before she could say so, its one eye began to glow. The twig writhed in its paw, lengthening, straightening, its ragged end growing sharp, until it became a spear so large the squirrel couldn't possibly hold it in its tiny paws. Yet it lifted the spear and threw. A sharp pain lanced Lennie's side. Before she could cry out, her weight fell hard on the rope about her neck. Her spine cracked with a red bloom of agony. The air burst into flame around her, and the tree, the ravens, the squirrel, even the very light were gone.

She dreamed no more.

CHAPTER TWO

The knots in Junkyard's shoulders eased when he heard Lennie crawl into the dark interior of the boxcar. He rolled to his back, stretched, and resumed his cross-legged position by the door. Despite what he had said, he had no intention of sleeping.

Another murder. The victim, Tin Can Petey, was an old hobo with a dopey, gap-toothed smile and sheepdog hair. A bit eccentric, maybe, but harmless.

As harmless as my brother.

Junkyard tried to picture Tin Can Petey as he had last seen him, playing spoons by the fire in an Owatonna jungle, but he couldn't separate Petey's face from his brother's, murdered the same way a year before. He closed his eyes, succumbing to the memory that had looped endlessly through his head on so many sleepless nights since Austin's death.

Back then—a lifetime ago, it seemed—there was no Junkyard Doug. Just Captain Douglas Harding on his last day of leave. He could still hear the ring of the early-morning phone call that had started it all. He had reached for the phone, certain the caller was Lieutenant Matthew Patterson, who had stopped by for a few beers the night before. Doug had just found Matt's wallet behind the toilet.

"Hey, Matt," he said, smiling. "What exactly were you doing in my bathroom last night?"

The other end was silent for a moment. Then a deep voice said, "Captain Harding, this is Colonel Norton. I have some bad news, son. Can you be at my office at 0830 hours?"

An hour later, the Colonel's adjutant showed Doug into a large, sparsely furnished office. As soon as Doug saw the somber face of the Chaplain seated next to Norton's desk, he knew.

Something had happened to Austin.

The Chaplain told him that an FRC railroad detective had called. They'd found a man's body on a freight train, on the platform of a grain car. The wallet was still in the back pocket of his jeans. Austin's wallet. Doug had put Austin on a train just two days before.

Doug moved through the next few hours in a stupor. He felt gutted, robbed of the ballast that had given him a sense of place, of duty. After his father had died years before, Doug had tried to be as much a father as a brother to Austin. It was for Austin that Doug had forgone college scholarships and signed with the army, sending his paychecks home to give Austin the childhood Doug never had. Where Doug had spent high school working at a scrap yard, Austin played sports, went on dates, even ran for school president. Doug had shaved his head, survived basic, and got his butt shot at, all so Austin could grow a ponytail and join the flannel and denim brigade at the University of Minnesota.

And now Austin was gone. Murdered. Doug was to fly to Topeka to ID the body.

Doug packed without thinking, shoving a mismatched assortment of army and civilian clothing into his duffle bag. Out of habit, he stood before the mirror to don his dress greens for the flight. Cleaned and pressed, pants tucked neatly into his jump boots, the uniform looked perfect. But the face that looked back at him belonged to a stranger—too pale, already too haggard to fit the uniform.

When the Humvee arrived to drive him to Pope Air Force Base, he grabbed his bag and reached for the beret hanging on the coat rack. Next to it, his brother's jean jacket hung from a hook, forgotten in Austin's rush to catch a train. Doug lifted it down and held it like a baby. It clinked with buttons that encrusted it like barnacles, a lifelong collection obtained anywhere from science fiction conventions to political rallies to garage sales.

The Humvee's horn blared. Doug ignored it and fingered a stark, black button pinned to the jacket's collar: *My brother jumps from perfectly good airplanes*. He had given it to Austin on his eighteenth birthday. Doug's fingers moved on, touching other buttons—the rusted California Raisin button that had gone an inch into Austin's foot while he swam in Lake Josephine, the *Resistence is Futile* button signed by Patrick Stewart himself at a Star Trek convention. Every button had its own story, which Austin would tell to anyone who listened. Doug unzipped his duffle bag and stuffed the jacket inside.

As Junkyard Doug, he had worn that jacket so much over the following months that he sometimes forgot that it wasn't his. But never for very long.

The train bumped over rough track, rattling the old boxcar. Junkyard opened his eyes and lifted his chin to let the cool, night air stroke the heat from his face. Light spilled from a three-quarter moon, glinting off Austin's collection. Sometimes the jacket was the only thing that kept him from giving up on the hunt—and on his own life. Without its constant reminder, his disguise would have become reality. As it was, he had nearly forgotten what it was like to have a bed, daily showers, and regular meals. Or to meet the eyes of strangers without their gazes sliding away as if he didn't exist.

If he didn't find Austin's killer soon, even the jacket might not be enough to save him.

A woman's scream pierced the boxcar's steady rumble. Junkyard swore and scrambled out of the moonlit doorway. Jungle Jim still lay sleeping on his cardboard bed in a patch of moonlight, but Junkyard couldn't see Lennie in the boxcar's dark interior. No one could have swung inside from the roof and gotten to her while Junkyard was in the doorway. Could they? He had only closed his eyes for those few seconds.

He waited, listening, but heard no voices or sounds of struggle above the drone of the wheels. He felt around, found his pack, and yanked a flashlight from a side pocket. The light would make him a target, if someone had managed to enter the boxcar from above. He wouldn't turn it on until he had to. For now, he held it like a club and began to worm across the dirty floor in the direction of the scream.

In the dark, every noise seemed amplified and full of threat. He paused, listening, ready to launch to his feet. Dust irritated his nose but his hands were too gritty to rub it. He sneezed into the jean jacket's sleeve, rattling Austin's buttons. Cursing silently, he lifted his head and waited. Nothing happened. He moved on.

After what seemed like a month, his fingers brushed something warm and yielding. He gasped and jerked his hand back. The clean smell of soap and lavender reached him through the odor of rotting apples that stained the floor. No self-respecting hobo or thug would smell like lavender. He came to a crouch, pulled a knife from his jump boot, and switched on the flashlight.

It was Lennie. She moaned and turned her head away from the light. Knife ready, Junkyard swept the beam around the boxcar. Jim had rolled off his cardboard and lay wedged against the wall by the door. There was no one else. He returned the light to Lennie and looked for anything that might have made her scream.

She lay unmoving on a piece of cardboard, arms and legs rigid, fingers clutching its edges. Her face twisted in fear, but her eyes moved under closed lids.

A nightmare. Junkyard stared at her, working his jaw. He had dragged himself through dirt and who knows what else, terrified of finding her mutilated corpse, expecting a knife in his own back at any moment, all for a lousy nightmare. Disgusted, he straightened his cramped legs.

He was about to return to his post when Lennie groaned and rolled to her side. Her t-shirt rode up, exposing flesh above the waist of her jeans. A dark stain glistened on her skin. Junkyard leaned closer and drew a sharp breath. Blood pooled in a puncture wound the size of a fifty-cent piece. The injury looked deep and fresh—the skin around it was clean and there was not yet blood on her t-shirt.

An injury like that hadn't sprouted on its own.

He whipped the flashlight around and searched the boxcar again, this time methodically examining every inch. An attacker had nowhere to hide and Junkyard saw no object that could punch a hole like that. A puncture wound that big could be serious, especially if it went as deep as it looked.

"Upper right side...right side," he muttered. "Uh, spleen...no—no, liver. Could have hit the liver. Damn it! Lennie, wake up."

He patted her face, but she didn't respond. He directed the flashlight at her eyes and pulled back first one lid, then the other. Pupils responsive—at least until her eyes rolled back into her head. "Come on, Lennie, you gotta wake up."

She didn't move. Abandoning caution, he strode back to his pack in a fraction of the time it had taken him to crawl across the floor on his face. He tore through clothes and gear until he found the first aid kit. By the time he returned to Lennie's side, blood was beginning to well out of its neat circle. Better staunch it fast, or she'd never make it to Minneapolis.

Wedging the flashlight between his knees, he pressed his palm down hard on the wound. His hand slipped over skin made slick with blood. He fumbled the kit's lid open with his other hand and spilled half of its contents onto the floor. The train lurched and his only roll of gauze took off for the door.

"Shit!"

He let go of Lennie and scrambled after it, but the wind caught the roll's trailing end. Before he could catch it, a streamer of gauze fluttered into the night. Swearing fervently, he returned to Lennie's side, ripped the bandana from his head, and wadded it into a ball. Her shirt had fallen over the injury again. He pushed it back, ready to apply pressure.

A wound the size of a dime stared up at him like a mocking red eye, so shallow he could see a layer of skin under the blood.

"What the hell?"

He sat back, stunned. As he watched, the blood seemed to evaporate and the hole slowly closed. Nothing remained but a red splotch on her shirt and a small white dimple on her side. He reached a hand toward it—a hand sticky with her blood—but the dimple disappeared under his fingers. He couldn't bring himself to touch the smooth space where it had been.

He ran the flashlight along her body, half-expecting her to sprout wings or disappear, but she just lay there, snoring lightly. The scrapes and bruises on her arms and face from boarding the train were gone as well. Blood stained the edges of a tear in the knee of her jeans. That injury had been particularly raw. He scooted closer and directed the light at it.

Smooth, fair skin. Not even a scar.

That just wasn't right. He had seen a lot of strange things on the rails, but nothing came close to this. An eerie, vulnerable feeling came over him, as if the shadows of the nearly empty boxcar suddenly held an extra pair of eyes that watched him when the flashlight pointed the other way. Fighting panic, he swung the light around again, but there was nothing.

"Jeez," he muttered. Next, he'd start spinning in circles trying to shine the light everywhere at once. He snorted at the thought.

Still, the blood on his hands had come from somewhere.

He directed the light on Lennie again, half-hoping, half-dreading it would wake her up. She stirred and muttered something about a squirrel, but continued sleeping. He examined her for some oddity, some hint to explain what had just happened. There was something different about her. He had sensed it from the moment she had boarded the train.

Slender, almost boyish, she wasn't beautiful. At least, not by the usual standards. Her features, half-hidden under a tangle of gold-brown hair, were soft and rounded with a sharp little chin. She looked much younger than he had first guessed, but the two deep, vertical lines between her eyebrows made her look angry, even in her sleep.

That was it, he realized. The difference. He had never felt that kind of intensity from anyone before. Except maybe from himself. He had felt it even before she had started talking. That couldn't explain why her wounds closed up as if they had never happened, but the anger did give her another kind of power. A pissed-off pit bull kind of power. Enough to get her into trouble, but not enough to get her out of it again.

He understood that sort of power. It had nearly gotten him killed, more than once. Somehow, he had to convince her to go home and stay there before some gangbanger found her. Or worse, the serial killer. But he knew she wouldn't listen to him any more than Austin had. He clicked off the flashlight and left her blanketed in the dark, but he could still see her face, fair skin damp from nightmares, her delicate lips parted in sleep.

If the serial killer took her, those lips would be cut and crusted over with blood, her face forever twisted by terror.

He could see it as clearly as if it had already happen. That was how his brother's face had looked, between the zippered sides of a body bag. He shuddered at the memory. The sight had nearly unhinged him for good. But then he had met Detective Harcourt Briggeman and everything had changed.

He had still been in shock when a police officer had taken him from the morgue to the police station. No one had answered his questions beyond the obvious. They wouldn't even tell him if there was a suspect.

He was taken to a room containing a table and two chairs. A box of tissues sat in the middle of the table, along with a pitcher of water and some Styrofoam cups. The room was otherwise devoid of furnishings or decoration.

A broad-shouldered man in his early thirties sat in one of the chairs. His denim shirt was grease-stained and coming untucked from his jeans. Mud flaked from scuffed work boots. He slouched, elbows on the table, his head propped up in his hands, one long leg stretching lazily to the side. He might have been asleep but for the nervous jiggle in the other leg.

The officer escorting Doug strode into the room, leaving Doug in the doorway. "Hey, Briggs." He dropped a folder on the table. "The report's in there, along with duplicates of the pictures, like you asked."

Briggs opened one red-rimmed eye, then the other, and dragged himself upright. "Thanks, Sam. I've been up all night with this case. Again. What a goddamn mess, eh?" He rubbed his face, making waves in the worry lines that creased his forehead.

"Nasty business, and the hell of it is, it'll take a miracle to—"

Briggs spotted Doug in the doorway. "Captain Harding! I didn't see you there." He shot Sam an annoyed glance and stood up from the table. "You are Captain Harding, right?"

When Doug nodded, Briggs thrust out a hand and said, "I'm Detective Briggeman with FRC Railroad."

Briggs's hand was as dirty as the rest of him, with broken, black-rimmed nails. Doug accepted it, saying, "This isn't Fort Bragg. Just call me Doug." The handshake was brief but firm. "FRC Railroad—you're the one who called my C.O. Can you tell me what happened?"

Briggs pulled the other chair out from the table and motioned Doug to sit down. "We'll get to that. First, can you tell me what Austin was doing on that train?"

Doug stared down at his hands and rubbed absently at a dark smudge left by Briggs's handshake. "I got promoted. Just last week. There was a party Friday." He rubbed harder, but the stain only smeared. "Austin never misses a party. He cut two days of classes to get there on time. Hopped trains and hitchhiked all the way from Minneapolis to North Carolina in two days. He tapped the first keg himself.

"I told him not to come, but he did anyway. To surprise me, he said." Doug smiled bitterly, remembering Austin's triumphant grin when Doug answered the door. Guests were due to arrive any moment, and Austin was all greasy hair and diesel fumes. Doug had made him take a shower.

"He left the next morning, maybe ten o'clock. He was still drunk when he got on that train." Austin never would have forgotten his jean jacket, otherwise. The idiot was probably half frozen by the time he...

"That stupid sonofabitch. I told him I'd buy him a bus ticket, even a plane ticket, but he wouldn't let me. He said he hated that recycled air, that it contained more germs than oxygen." He remembered Austin laughing at his arguments, calling him Dad. Doug's voice broke. "Damn kid said he didn't want to get sick."

He could still see the train pulling out of the yard and Austin's arm emerging from the grainer's cubbyhole to wave goodbye. "I should have dragged him onto that bus."

Lost in those final moments, Doug hardly noticed when Briggs pushed back from the table and walked Sam to the door. Their voices murmured for a moment and the door closed. Doug looked up and realized he and Briggs were alone in the room.

"I sent Sam to check train schedules. It should take him a few minutes," Briggs said. "Before we continue, you want some coffee?"

"No. Thanks. Look, let's just get on with this." Restless, Doug was hardly able to stay in the chair. It was time to do something.

Briggs sighed and returned to his seat. "So, you're stationed at Fort Bragg under Colonel Norton, right?"

"Can we just skip the formalities? I've been getting the run around all morning and I've about had it. Now, either you can start giving me some answers—or I'm gonna start getting noisy."

Briggs picked up the file folder and tapped it on the table, straightening the pages within. He went on as if Doug hadn't said anything. "My father served with Colonel Norton years ago. Norton is like an uncle to me. In fact, he just gave me a call this morning." He looked at Doug across the top of the folder. "He spoke very highly of you and suggested you might be able to help us. Unfortunately, we can't tell you much without risking compromising our investigation."

A hollow ache filled Doug's stomach. They weren't going to tell him a thing. "Come on, that's a load of crap. This is my brother we're talking about. My only family. I was supposed to take care of him. What a great job I did of that." His voice cracked and he swallowed hard before continuing. "And now his killer is running around loose out there. You can't expect me to crawl back to Fort Bragg like a good boy and wait for answers."

Briggs hesitated. He pursed his lips and looked as if he wanted to tell Doug something. Then he sighed and said, "I'm sorry. I wish I could give you the details. I could use any help you might be able to give. But all I can tell you is that a serial killer got him. He was tied up, knifed, and left to die sometime before he got to Topeka." He shook his head grimly. "That's a lot of territory to cover, even with the help of the local P.D. and the FBI."

"Dammit, you gotta give me more than that. I got that much from the morning newspaper."

Briggs gave Doug a speculative look and seemed to come to a decision. He placed the folder at the center of the table. "Are you certain you wouldn't like that cup of coffee?"

"What? Damn it, no. I don't drink the stuff."

Briggs leaned closer, looking at him intently. "Now would be a good time to start."

He raised an eyebrow, waiting. Doug let his gaze drop to the file folder between them. Coffee suddenly seemed like a good idea. He drew a deep breath. "Uh, yes, thanks. Cream and sugar, though."

Briggs gave him a grim little smile. "I think the crud in the pot is a bit old. I'll brew some fresh. Be back in say...fifteen minutes?"

As soon as the door closed, Doug reached for the file folder.

Inside, a dozen photographs of the crime scene told him a story that he could never have learned from a visit to the morgue. Image after image fired into his brain. Austin had been cocooned in white string. Yards of the stuff pinned his arms and legs to his body in a fetal position. His eyes, frozen wide with terror, stared from a mask of blood. Out of his gaping mouth protruded the black handle of a knife.

His stomach churned. How could that be his brother? He shoved the pictures away and launched to his feet, knocking his chair over with a crash. He stared at the chair wildly, wanting to pick it up and smash it against the wall, to smash everything in sight. But one thought stopped him.

Someone had done this to Austin.

The idea hit him like ice water. His jumbled up mind fixed on that one thought. Someone had done this to Austin.

With deliberate care, he righted the chair, sat down, and pulled the pictures close. One by one, he paged through them again, slowly this time, memorizing every injury, every clot of blood, every fear-twisted muscle locked in eternal paralysis. When he was finished, he stacked the pictures with precise, controlled movements. Then he began to read.

Ten minutes later, he shuffled the pages neatly into place, closed the folder, and returned it to the center of the table. There were no suspects. The police had found nothing but a collection of useless facts and no leads. The only thing Doug had learned with certainty was that, even with the help of every police department in his territory, Briggs couldn't track a killer who could be hundreds of miles from a crime scene in a matter of hours. By the time Briggs returned to the interview room, steaming coffee in hand, Doug knew with cold certainty what he must do.

The next day, he hopped his first train. That night was the first of many spent in a hobo jungle. His forty days of leave flew by and he resigned his commission. His disguise became a way of life as he joined the hobo community. And after nearly a year, he was no closer to finding the killer.

Meanwhile, rumors of new murders reached him through railroad gossip. And they seemed to be growing more frequent.

He looked down at Lennie, now curled in sleep and shivering against the night's chill. Her naiveté was likely to get her wrapped in a cocoon, a knife ventilating her palate. He couldn't let that happen. He took off his brother's jacket and laid it over her, then settled next to his pack for a long sleepless night.

A moment later, a raven burst from a hidden perch overhead and flew out the open door.

CHAPTER THREE

September 1893
Big Horn Mountains, Wyoming

Walter "Red" Galloway poured a charge of mica powder into a round hole in a granite boulder, lit the fuse, and ran like hell for the shelter of a rock outcropping. He barely had time to throw himself down next to his partner, Angus Cook, before the charge blew. The blast shook the mountain. Fragments of granite ricocheted like bullets off the surrounding rubble and trees. Pebbles and sand showered down on the two men, and a rock the size of a boot dropped between Angus's feet. Angus jerked his legs back and huddled tighter against the outcropping.

"Damn, Red," he said, eyes popping. "Yer makin' them fuses shorter'n my mornin' shit! One of these days it'll be yer head bouncin' at my feet, and I'll be scrapin' the rest of ya off a rock."

Stuck laying track in the wilderness, with no women and not enough whiskey, Red had been amusing himself by cutting fuses shorter and shorter just for the fun of seeing that look on Angus's face. But that last one was a bit close even for him. Not that he would admit it. He took off his hat and casually shook the granite flakes from it. "And I s'pose you'd rather be back in Homestead, rioting at the steel mill again and havin' your head broke open by the Pinkertons."

Angus's hairy, sunburned face knotted up in chagrin. "You lousy piker! I hadn't thought of those dirty finks in months. If it weren't fer them, I'd be workin' reg'lar hours, makin' love to Maggie every night."

"And raisin' a handful of brats, probably none of 'em your own. Any woman that would have you couldn't be too particular."

Angus scowled and cracked his knuckles. He could do it by tensing his fingers and curling them into a fist one at a time. It was a favorite trick of his, and it gave Red the willies. Angus grinned when Red winced. "As if any woman'd let you in her bed, ya scraggly, ol' flea-bitten drifter."

"I am what I am. And same for you." Red plucked a blade of grass and nibbled at the white end. "You wouldn't have stayed with Maggie more'n another week before a train'd choo choo into town, spoutin' steam, and you'd follow its whistle like a dog."

Angus scowled and picked at a callus on his thumb. He was a big man, younger than Red. Where Red was rangy, sun-baked, and topped with fading red hair, Angus was tall, broad-shouldered, and covered with dark, wiry hair. Red liked to tease him, saying that if it weren't for his sun-burned nose, someone might take him for a bear and shoot him. Red liked to tease Angus about everything, but this time he feared he had gone too far. Angus loved trains, but he loved his woman more. Between the Pinkertons and the Depression, he couldn't support her or the child in her belly. Not if he stayed in Homestead. So he found work where he could and sent his paycheck home.

Red opened his mouth to apologize, but heard the crunch of heavy boots on scree. He scrambled to his feet and saw the other workers already laboring to clear the debris from the blast. A burly, red-faced man was coming toward them.

"Heads up, now," Red said. "Here comes the Bossman."

The look on the straw boss's face made Red wish he had stayed hidden behind the outcropping. The yelling started when the straw boss was still twenty yards away. He was wild-eyed and raving by the time he stood before Red.

"What kind of lunatic are you?" Spit flew and his thick arms flapped like the wings of a disturbed chicken. "If you get your lice-ridden carcass blown to smithereens, then I've got to use Anderson over there—" he jerked a thumb at a slow, wall-eyed man working nearby, "—to set the charges, and he's likely to bring the whole mountain down. From now on, your fuses better be regulation length, or I'll tan your hide and wear you as boots. You got that?"

Without stopping for air, he turned on Angus. "Why are you sitting on that fat ass of yours? Company says the road in this pass has got to be ready by 1894. That leaves us less than four months. If that track isn't down before snow flies, I'll send you out in your long johns with nothing but a garden spade to keep the pass clear."

Red and Angus fidgeted, waiting for him to wind down.

"Now get your flatulent asses into that gap and drive some steel," the Bossman finished. "If you set the charge right, you'll take out that knuckle of rock and leave a nice, solid shelf wide enough to run track on."

Red grabbed his kit and hurried to the protrusion of rock before the Bossman could remember something he'd forgotten to say. Angus followed, carrying a hammer and a steel rod.

"Damn, Red. I know layin' track in this here butt-crack of the Big Horns ain't so great, but it keeps the food comin' and keeps us outta them workhouses." Angus paused while Red figured where to set the charge. Red chalked an X on the stone and set one end of the steel rod on the mark. Angus raised his sledge hammer and added, "Just lay off the jokes fer a bit, okay?"

"Sure, Angus." Red flinched when the heavy iron struck the rod. "I never argue with the man swingin' the hammer."

When the hole was deep enough, Angus pulled the rod and ran for shelter behind a ridge. Red joined him after setting the charge, this time using regulation fuse.

The echoes from the blast seemed to go on forever. They could hear the Bossman yelling before the last rumble died away. Red and Angus exchanged uneasy glances as a cloud of dust settled over them. Far more dust than warranted from such a small charge. Puzzled, Red pulled his bandana over his mouth and nose and peered around the ridge. At first, he couldn't see anything. Slowly the air cleared. Instead of a smooth, wide shelf, he saw a deep pile of rubble.

"One little knuckle of rock!" the Bossman yelled, stomping toward them. Red wondered if the man would pass out from all the blood rushing to his face. "What in the hell were you thinking? All I asked was that you take out one stupid chunk of rock and you bury the ledge in five feet of scree. Get your asses over there. You're going to clear out that rubble if it takes you the rest of today and all night besides."

He turned and started shouting at the other workers. "The rest of you, get those ties out of the wagons. The FRC isn't paying you to lie about!"

Angus groaned and hefted his hammer. "My pa always said trains'd get me into trouble someday. *Son,* he'd say, *it ain't right to get so darned worked up over a machine.* But did I listen to Pa?" Hammer on his shoulder, he rubbed his lower back and grimaced. "No, sir! I got a job with the Company, didn't I? Gandydancin' and whatnot, just to be near 'em. And you know somethin'? Pa was wrong. Trains ain't just gonna get me in trouble—more'n likely they're gonna *kill* me." Angus shook his head and trudged off toward the debris.

Unconcerned, Red chuckled and grabbed his shovel. It would take him and Angus a week to clear the shelf by themselves. He knew the Bossman would send help soon enough.

They had been working for over an hour when Red saw something thin and white poking up through the debris. He drove his shovel under it and lifted it out. The thing slid free and clattered on the ground. It looked like a bone.

"Hey, Angus—I found somethin'!"

Angus set his hammer down and winced as he straightened, pressing the small of his back with both hands. "Whatcha got?"

He shuffled over, rolling a cigarette. He started to light it, but stopped short when he saw the bone. "Well, will ya lookit that. S'pose it's human?"

"It's big enough, but there's only one way to know for sure."

Red planted his shovel where he had found the bone and began to dig. Angus watched for a moment, then put the cigarette away and joined in with his hands. They found more bone fragments, but nothing conclusive until Red found part of a jaw. Looked human. He held it up to the light for a better look. Angus kept digging.

"Whoa, I think I got somethin', Red. Somethin' big!" Angus stood over a patch of white that gleamed through the dirt. "And hooo-wee—it sure smells bad."

It didn't look like bone from where Red stood. Too big. He hunkered down next to Angus to help dig. After a few minutes' work, they had uncovered something as large as a horse and wound in white string. Dirt-crusted tufts of dark fur poked through the bindings.

"Maybe it's some kinda art-ee-fact," Red said. "I hear them collectors pay good money for old Indian crap."

Angus shook his head. "Nah, that string looks too clean to be that old. And it smells deader'n a skunk in a beaver trap." He waved a hand in front of his face. "Phew! Maybe we should let it alone."

"Don't go all knock-kneed on me, Angus. Whatever it is, it might be worth somethin' to someone." Red glanced nervously at the wagons, half-expecting to see the Bossman coming toward them. "Let's have a look. We can always hide it and come back for it later."

Red tugged at the string, trying to break it. It felt flimsy and soft, but it held firm. He braced himself and pulled harder. The string bit through his skin and pain shot up his arm. He swore and let go, staring at his bleeding finger. "What the hell?"

"Here, let me." Angus dug in his pocket and came up with a buck knife. He opened it and slid the blade under a few strands. They parted easily. Angus grinned. "I guess my knife's a mite sharper'n yer finger. Now, lessee if—"

Angus's eyes grew large and he jerked the knife away. The cut ends of the string hissed and crackled, shriveling away. The sight chilled Red, though he couldn't say why. He touched one end and jerked his hand back in pain. A blister formed instantly on his fingertip.

Not shriveling—burning! Like a lit fuse. How could a steel blade do that? He staggered back, shouting a warning to Angus. The thing didn't explode, but the ground shook and a roaring filled Red's ears. The remaining string loosened and fell away. Before him, in a slaughterhouse reek, stood a gigantic wolf, its head on level with his own. Its jaws gaped, propped open by a black-handled knife with a long, bronze blade. Its eyes glowed yellow in the sun. Red cried out, backing away. He tripped and sprawled on the ground under its cancerous gaze.

Through his fear, he heard Angus laugh. "Why, it ain't nothin' but an ol' statue."

Red watched in horror as Angus stepped closer to the wolf and slapped it on the flank. He grinned. "Whaddaya so scared of?"

The Wolf swung its head around and fixed Angus with its yellow eyes. Angus froze, bug-eyed and open mouthed.

"Run!" Red shouted, forgetting his own danger. "Run, you stupid bastard!"

But Angus didn't move. The Wolf braced its paw against the bronze knife's hilt and pushed downward. The blade came out with the sound of a shoe sucking free of mud and clattered on the rocky ground.

The Bossman's furious voice shouted at Red from behind. "What the hell is going on here?"

Afraid to move, Red tried to whisper a warning. The Bossman ignored him. Flushed, neck veins throbbing visibly, he stumped over to Angus and began yelling as if this were just another regular day of work. "What's the matter with you? The snow's already flying in Montana and you're just standing around. And as for you, Red, I see you over there taking a nap. If you think I won't dock your pay, you're sadly mistaken—"

The Wolf uttered a growl so low Red couldn't hear it. But he felt it through the rocks under his back. The Bossman felt it, too. He turned, his mouth still flapping, and his words became screams. The Wolf leaped and buried its muzzle into the Bossman's neck, ending his life as he lived it—mouth wide open and making noise.

Red stared, unbelieving, as the Bossman's twitching body hit the ground. He knew he should run, but didn't want to leave Angus. Besides, he wasn't sure his shaking legs had enough strength to stand.

The Wolf turned back to Angus. Its mouth hung open in an obscene parody of a smile, tongue lolling out over its teeth. Angus still hadn't moved or even changed his expression. The Wolf licked the blood-soaked fur around its mouth and stepped closer. Red found he could stand after all. He picked up his shovel, uncertain whether to attack or run while the wolf's attention was on Angus. Not liking either option, he screamed at the other workers for help.

The Wolf looked at him. *They will not hear you.*

Red heard the words in his fear-crazed mind and screamed again, waving the shovel in the air, but the workers unloaded ties as though nothing were amiss.

The Wolf's head swung back to Angus. *You, I shall not kill.*

As though to make a lie of its words, the wolf's mouth opened wide. To Red's fear-crazed mind, it seemed as though its upper jaw touched the sky and its lower jaw scraped the ground. It engulfed Angus, swallowing him whole.

This, thought Red, would be a good time to run.

But before he could move, the wolf sat on its haunches and began to howl. The sound rose in the air so thick and full that Red could almost see it. And as it howled, the wolf began to shrink. Fur sloughed from it in great handfuls, disappearing before it hit the ground. Its muzzle shortened. Its ears turned inside out and flattened to its skull, the points becoming rounded, tufts of fur thinning to a few wiry strands. Its body thickened in some places, shrank in others, reshaping itself, until the wolf was gone. In its place crouched Angus, naked and feral.

Exhausted by fear, unable to accept what he had just seen, Red wanted to believe the man before him was Angus, that it had all been a dream or a bad joke. But the lifeless body of the Bossman told him otherwise. And so did the rim of blood matting the beard around Angus's mouth.

The Wolf who was now Angus examined its new body, flexing muscles, working the joints. Then it picked up the sledgehammer and turned on Red.

Nothing of Angus remained in its eyes.

Angus's face was open, friendly, and quick to laugh—though perhaps not so quick of thought. The same face worn by the wolf was hard, sly, and dangerous. Where Angus's eyes had been warm, wide, and brown, this creature's eyes were as yellow as bile. But the thing that terrified Red the most, that made his insides run like warm bacon grease, was the smile. Unnaturally wide, its sneering curl revealed long, pointed teeth that could never grow in a human mouth. And they dripped with the Bossman's blood.

Get away! Red's mind screamed. *Run, run, run, run, RUN!* But his eyes were trapped in a yellow snare, and that other voice whispered in his head. *Stay*, it said. *Stay and feed me.*

Red found that he didn't want to run after all. In fact, he wanted to be eaten by this monster wearing his friend's face. He couldn't think of anything that could be more pleasant. The shovel dropped from his limp fingers and clattered on the rocks. He took a step forward. The Wolf-Angus's tongue ran over its teeth in anticipation. Smiling, Red cocked his head back, pulled his collar down to expose one side of his neck, and waited for death.

Before teeth touched flesh, a black flurry of wings swept into the wolf-Angus's face. The wings separated into two ravens cawing raucously, gouging at wolf eyes with beaks and claws. The yellow haze retreated from Red's mind. He back-pedaled, clutching his collar closed, as if flannel could stop those dagger teeth.

The Wolf-Angus howled and swiped at the birds. Snarling, he caught one by a wing and swung it hard into its mate. They tangled, fluttered frantically, and hit the ground. The Wolf-Angus again fixed his yellow gaze on Red.

Loose rubble shifted under Red's retreating boots. He staggered back, slamming into the pile of rock he and Angus were supposed to clear from the ledge. The Wolf-Angus closed on him, cutting off his escape.

"Sheeeiit." Red tried to scramble backward up the pile. "Angus, it's me—your ol' friend Red! Whatcha wanna kill me for?"

The Wolf-Angus paused as though considering. "Well, I guess...because I'm hungry."

And he laughed, a growling animal sound that tore the remaining will from Red's body. He went limp and slid to the ground, waiting for sharp teeth to end his life. As the wolf-Angus approached, another raven dropped from the sky, bigger than the other two—the biggest Red had ever seen. A king grandpappy of ravens, with one eye shriveled shut and the other a startling blue shining from its black head.

A desperate hope fluttered in Red's chest. Maybe three birds could succeed where two had failed. The Wolf-Angus snarled and grabbed for the great raven. It dodged him easily, slashing a bloody gash across the wolf-Angus's arm.

Red eased to his feet, ready to run when the raven next attacked. The bird wheeled over the wolf-Angus, uttered one long, echoing cry, folded its great wings, and dove straight at Red's head.

Surprised, Red forgot to move. The raven struck his face like a blast of wind, spraying a wide circle of black feathers that evaporated before they hit the ground. Red's eye ruptured in pain and something filled his head to bursting. He screamed and slapped at his face, feeling warm, thick streams oozing down his cheek. Something stirred in his brain, as if the raven had curled up to nest inside his skull.

A snarl rang through the agony in his head. The Wolf-Angus. How could he fight it now? Still cupping his punctured eye, he blinked and squinted at the approaching monster.

"Come on, Red, ol' buddy," the wolf-Angus growled. "Just gimmee a li'l taste."

The voice was Angus's. A cajoling Angus, as though he had merely asked him to pass the whiskey. Red backed against the rubble, knowing he couldn't escape. As the grinning wolf-Angus reached for him, Red leaned back and kicked his booted toe into the thing's crotch. But the wolf-Angus caught Red's leg and lifted, dropping him onto his back. He leaned over Red, lips curled, and his teeth looked as big as pickaxes. The air in Red's throat felt too thick to breath. Strange thoughts crowded his mind, babbling uselessly, as if in a foreign tongue. One thought rose to the top—he was going to die.

King Grandpappy stretched and swelled in Red's mind, crowding out his thoughts, stifling his will. It forced him to tip his head back to see through his one good eye, though this left his neck fully exposed. Words that weren't Red's own roared from his mouth. "*Huginn! Muninn!* To me!"

The two ravens returned, carrying a heavy, rough-hewn spear between them. They swooped low and dropped the spear on Red's chest. His fingers curled around its coarse shaft. His one good eye, now blue as sapphire, met the yellow eyes of the wolf-Angus and began to glow. The Wolf-Angus's predatory grin became a scowl. He jerked upright and backed away.

"You!"

King Grandpappy grinned with Red's mouth and brought him to his feet with the spear leveled at the wolf-Angus's chest. The two men who were once wolf and raven watched each other warily.

"So, One-Eye, are you here to greet me, to welcome me into this bright new age?" The Wolf-Angus paced, eyeing the head of the spear. "I see you've brought Gungnir—perhaps you have you have come to kill me, as you should have done all those millennia ago."

The one called One-Eye ran a stolen hand down the coarse shaft of the spear. "As much as I might wish to, Wolf, I will not. The prophecy that compelled me to have you bound and buried under the earth still holds."

"Prophecy." The Wolf spat and his yellow eyes burned brighter. "I was a mere pup. I had not destroyed the smallest village, eaten the tiniest human, or even sampled one of their sheep. Yet at the word of the Norn, you came to me in friendship and—" his lips peeled back from pointed teeth, "you betrayed me."

One-Eye tightened his grip on the spear, but the wolf only snorted, nostril's flaring. "Such comedy. I bore you no ill will those thousands of years ago, but now..."

The Wolf's voice became a terrible roar. "Now I will kill you, as your laughable prophecy predicts."

The ground quaked at the sound. The workers stopped unloading the carts and lifted their heads, some looking to the sky for thunder clouds, others looking anxiously at the mountainside for the spill of loose rock.

One-Eye held his ground, waiting for the tremors to pass. "Yes," he said. "Perhaps. But not today. And you will die in the final battle, as well. You must submit to your bindings and wait."

"Never. I have no intention of falling under the heel of the three hags. I make my own prophecy. You will die and the world will be razed by chaos and fire. But it is I who will rise from the ashes to rule the new beginning."

"You have spent too long in the ground, Wolf. Look around you. See what these human have become? Soon they will have weapons that not even your great strength will be able to withstand. They will not fear you."

Fenrir smiled, a sight that would fill his minions with dread over the next century. "It matters not, foul betrayer. There are other ways. They can be made to defeat themselves. And you cannot stop me. Not without risking the end of all things, yourself."

Faster than human agility should allow, Fenrir vaulted from the rock shelf. For a moment, he looked like the wolf he was. Then, as a man, he ran naked into the mountain wilderness.

But in the moment of escape, distracted by the elation of long-awaited freedom, Fenrir's mind opened. One-Eye glimpsed his plan and knew that it could succeed. But in that same moment, One-Eye saw the seed of Fenrir's defeat.

"Huginn," One-Eye called, and a raven flew out of a tall pine to settle on his left shoulder.

"Muninn." Another abandoned the leavings of a cougar kill and settled on his right. One-Eye stroked each and started down the mountainside. He would go to Homestead, where the seed grew even now, in the belly of a woman.

Somewhere under that red hair, smothered under the eons that were the Allfather, a small voice belonging to Walter "Red" Galloway screamed.

CHAPTER FOUR

Daylight drove the shadows deeper into the boxcar where Lennie slept, caught in a nightmare. She ran through the dark, fleeing a pack of wolves with glowing eyes, their snarls growing closer. A boxcar pulled alongside her and she dove inside. Wolf teeth caught her jeans and dragged her back. She clawed at the floor, finding no purchase. Then she was falling, falling. She kicked out just before she hit the ground and awoke with a beam of sunlight across her face.

She cracked her eyes enough to see a dirty metal ceiling. A distant crash of couplers and hiss of venting air brakes suggested she was on a train, but it wasn't moving. Her mouth tasted like she'd been using her tongue to clean the boxcar floor. Grimacing, she squeezed her eyes shut, counted to five, and opened them again. Same dirty ceiling, same nasty taste. *Yep, I'm really here.* A noise escaped her throat, sounding suspiciously like a whine.

Sometime during the night, Junkyard had covered her with his jean jacket. Its collar stuck up in front her face, smelling of campfires and diesel. A black button pinned to the jacket's lapel said, *"My brother jumps from perfectly good airplanes."* She studied the button curiously. A brother. But Junkyard had said there was no one to miss him.

A low, mellow voice began to hum a mournful tune somewhere outside the boxcar. She found it soothing and closed her eyes, not wanting to move. Then she remembered Junkyard's warnings and a vision of tomorrow's headline flashed before her eyes: *Singing Serial Slayer Strangles Stowaway.* She snorted. But she sat up—just in case.

Her hands had gone completely numb while she slept. One still clutched the edge of her cardboard bed as if she might fall off. Smiling wryly, she let go and her fingers began to tingle.

The other hand rested palm up, fingers wrapped around something shiny. A loop of silver chain dangled across her thumb. It couldn't be...

She forced her stiffened fingers to open. On her palm lay her father's pocket watch.

Shocked, she poked at it, hardly believing it was real. She raised its cool, smooth metal to her cheek and remembered how her father used to let her wind it. "Careful," he'd say, winking at her. "If it's wound up too tight, it'll have a nervous breakdown."

She popped it open to read the inscription, though she already knew what it said.

For Jarvis—
May there always be enough time.
With all my love,
Kathleen

Ramblin' Red had taken the watch with him, wherever he had gone. How had it gotten into her hand?

The humming outside turned to song, though she couldn't make out the lyrics. She crawled to the door and peered out, expecting to see Junkyard. He wouldn't have gone far without his jacket. But she saw only Jungle Jim. He stood near the doorway, eyes closed, swaying to his song. She watched him, amazed that such a rough, simple man could sing so beautifully. Then she frowned. Could Jim have put the watch in her hand while she slept?

She tried to picture it, but couldn't make it work. He'd been inside the roll of paper when she boarded the train. Maybe Ramblin' Red had given the watch to Junkyard. But how had the older hobo gotten off the train without Lennie seeing him? And why wouldn't Junkyard have given the watch to her right away? None of it made any sense.

In any case, she was determined not to lose the watch again. She forced her numb fingers to wedge it into the front pocket of her jeans and noticed a dark smudge on the back of her hand.

"Oh, hey!" Jim said, finally seeing her. He trotted over, frowning in concern. "Did I wake ya? I should of waited until you were up, but I gotta get my song ready for the Poetry tonight."

Lennie didn't answer. She was staring at her left hand as though some alien thing had fastened to it while she slept. The smudge was actually a stark, precisely-drawn design of three interlocking triangles.

Really the opposite of smudge, she thought dazedly, her mouth hanging open.

Ugly possibilities of how it got there crawled through her mind, but only the disjointed image of a stick scratching across her hand persisted like a true memory. She traced the design with her finger. Something held the stick, she knew. And that something was a...was a...squirrel?

The dream exploded on her with all its bizarre detail. She had been tethered like a balloon to an enormous tree, and there had been a one-eyed, talking squirrel. And at the end of the dream, there had been fire, and she had fallen...

Her hand went to her neck, feeling for rope burns, but her skin felt undamaged. The dream couldn't have been real. How could a dream squirrel draw a real design on her skin?

The creeping gooseflesh reserved for ghosts and bogeymen prickled down her arms. She spit on the design and rubbed furiously.

Jungle Jim said, "You're never gonna get it off like that, Missy.

Startled, Lennie nearly fell out the door. She had forgotten he was there. "It's just a—um—an ink stamp." She faltered, unsure where the lie was heading.

Jungle Jim shrugged and hopped up to sit in the doorway beside her. He had changed his suit. This one looked cleaner, though it was as patched as the other and even baggier. He smelled better, too, and had combed his hair.

He leaned over the design. "Looks more like a tattoo, to me. An' they don't come off with spit."

A tattoo. Great. What was it that squirrel had said? *With this...thingamajig...I bind you to me.* Wonderful. Now I'm bound to a one-eyed rodent who wants me to do battle with some wolf. Somehow she didn't think this was one of the dangers Junkyard was trying to warn her about. But then, maybe Junkyard was the one who had put the design on her hand. Maybe he had drugged that Twinkie and...and...

"Would you happen to know where Junkyard is?" She tried to sound casual, but her voice came out higher than usual. "I'd like to return his jacket."

"He went to get us some grub a while ago. But don't you worry, Missy. He left me to watch over you. *Jim*, he said, *don't you leave her 'til I get back.* And I didn't go nowhere, not even for a second. Even though you just laid there the whole time. You sure do sleep good."

"Not usually." She usually woke up three or four times a night, disturbed by her mother's moans when she was still alive, disturbed by the silence after she had died. "I guess I was tired out from all the excitement."

It seemed odd that she had slept through the night in such a noisy place with nothing but cardboard for a bed. She thought of the Twinkie again, but the package had been unopened. Besides, Junkyard didn't seem the type to drug total strangers just to decorate them with tattoos. She checked herself over for other unwanted marks that might have sprouted overnight. There was nothing. Just smooth, pale, unmarked skin everywhere she looked.

But that wasn't right, either. Yesterday, she had been covered with cuts and bruises. She inspected herself again, fighting a growing panic. There was a bloody tear in the knee of her jeans, but no scrape underneath. Yesterday, her palms had been torn and bloody, almost too stiff to move. Today, they were covered in smooth, unbroken skin. And, now that she thought about it, her strained shoulder didn't hurt at all.

A chill settled over her. Had she only imagined her injuries? Was she going mad?

Hysterically, she attacked the tattoo, scratching at it, hoping it would peel away along with the skin, as if removing it would set everything back to normal. A thick-fingered, callused hand stopped her. Breathing hard, she met Jim's gentle gaze. Once again, his eyes were infused with a clarity that was normally absent. Her panic faded away.

"I'm thinkin' you should see Urdie," he said.

He nodded twice, firmly, then his eyes let go of hers and he started swinging his legs. One shoelace had come untied and the aglet ticked rhythmically against the boxcar.

Confused, Lennie stared at him. "What's an Urdie?"

"Urdie is Urdie. She's a person. She always comes to the festival." He experimented with swinging his legs one at a time, his head bobbing up and down as the shoelace flapped. "She can tell you 'bout Ramblin' Red, and maybe 'bout your new tattoo."

"Really? And what makes her so wise?"

"Oh, she knows," Jim said with certainty. "She knows everything. She'll come 'round for the Poetry, tonight."

His feet stopped and he looked up, eyes childlike once more. "You're comin' to the Poetry, aren't ya? I'm makin' one up to sing."

Lennie hesitated while Jim waited with wide-eyed earnestness. Despite her brave words to Junkyard the night before, all she wanted to do now was go home. Before she could think of an answer, she heard feet crunching on gravel, getting closer. She ducked inside the boxcar, irrationally certain the tattoo bandit had returned. Jim's newspaper blanket lay on the floor beside her and she pictured herself hiding under it. How brave. She drew a breath and leaned out to see who was coming.

Junkyard strode down the narrow alley between their train and a long string of cars parked alongside on parallel track. He carried a plastic grocery bag and a cardboard beverage holder. She sighed with a sense of relief that surprised her. Possibly, he had been playing tricks on her, but she couldn't make herself believe he meant her any harm. And she sure felt safer with him around.

He raised the bag when he saw her. "Thought you might like something to eat."

Her stomach rumbled. She hadn't had anything but that Twinkie since lunch the day before, and that could hardly be called food. She longed for something more substantial, like bagels, fruit, maybe an egg sandwich. And coffee, definitely coffee.

"You bet. Thanks!" She took the tray of drinks from him, hoping he didn't notice her still-shaking hands. "I'm starving. I could eat a—"

He tossed the bag into the boxcar and an assortment of snack cakes spilled out. Breakfast. Her stomach sagged. She eyed the paper cups with fading hope. "That wouldn't happen to be coffee, would it?"

Junkyard grimaced and shook his head. "Nope—that stuff'll kill you." He hauled himself on board and sat next to her. "Orange juice."

At least it wasn't Kool-Aid. Lennie picked up a so-called cherry pie, but couldn't bring herself to open it. She wondered how long it took for a person to starve to death. Then she spotted a Banana Flip in the pile. "Whoa!" She grabbed it, tossing the pie aside. "I didn't think they made these anymore!"

Junkyard shrugged. "Always seem to have them at the Day Old Bakery here."

Lennie decided not to check the expiration date. The things contained enough preservatives to keep them fresh through a glacial winter. She tore the package open and took a bite. The cake was wonderfully soft and the filling had that artificial banana flavor she remembered so well.

"My dad used to buy me one of these every time I placed in a track meet," she said around a mouthful. She swallowed and grinned. "Good incentive. I got a lot of medals."

Junkyard raised an eyebrow. "Track, eh?"

"Yeah. I started when I was eight. Dad went to every meet."

She used to find him in the stands before she ran, looking out of place in his too-tight Ames Track Club t-shirt. He always gave her a thumbs-up. Her smile faded. Where would she find him now? In a hobo jungle, or maybe a homeless shelter. If she found him at all.

If he was even still alive.

A dull ache settled in her chest. She preferred the sharper, physical pain of her vanished cuts and bruises. Those, at least, would heal with time.

Junkyard rummaged in the grocery bag, coming up with some Ho-Hos for Jim and a package of hair bands for Lennie. She took them gratefully, forgiving him for the lack of coffee. She finished the snack cake and began finger-combing her hair, pondering her next move.

She had no reason to trust Ramblin' Red, but she could search for a dozen years and never find such a strong lead again. She had to follow through on it now, before the trail went cold. If she didn't find her father in Minneapolis, well, maybe then she'd go back to Ames for some gear.

Sighing, she gave up on her hair and tied it back, tangles and all, ignoring the few stubborn curls that refused to be contained. The problem was, she had no idea where in Minneapolis to look.

Or did she?

Ridiculously happy, Jungle Jim unwound his Ho Ho and licked at the white frosting inside. Lennie watched him speculatively. "So, what's this festival I keep hearing about?"

"It's the Greater Midwest Railroad Days—" Junkyard began.

Jungle Jim interrupted with a flood of enthusiasm. "It's the best, is what it is! They got a carnival, an' a flea market, an' art shows, an' a parade—but that's just the tourist stuff. The real fun is seein' my friends. Langford Leftie always comes, an' the Kentucky Kid. Bones O'Riley is a hoot an' a half, an' Too Long Soo sure can bang on her guitar. And of course there's Tin Can Petey..."

Jungle Jim stopped as though he had hit a wall. His mouth dropped open and his eyes emptied. Then, as though the necessary connection had been made, his mouth twisted downward and he blinked tears onto his cheeks. Lennie shot a concerned glance at Junkyard, whose face remained rigidly calm.

"Jim," he said.

No response. Junkyard laid a hand on his arm.

"Tell Lennie about the kids, Jim."

Jungle Jim lifted his head and looked at Junkyard with puffy, red eyes. "Kids?"

He sniffed wetly, and then a smile lit up his face. Lennie was amazed, not only by Jim's lightning mood swings, but by Junkyard's ability to counter them. Jim started babbling like a happy child.

"The kids! They're the very best part of the festival." He jumped to his feet and started pacing. "There's Tyler. He's always lookin' for candy in my pockets. An' Jeffy likes to toot my nose. Little Nick is terrible shy an' I like to make him smile. But best of all is Ashley

Sutter." He hugged himself. "Last year, she brought me cookies! Can we go see 'em, now? Please, Dougie?"

Junkyard laughed. "It's a little early, but I don't see why we can't take a look around." He dug into the grocery bag again and handed Jim a bag of peppermints. "You better take these. You don't want to disappoint Tyler."

While Jungle Jim hid the candy in the many pockets of his suit coat, Junkyard gathered their gear and jumped from the boxcar. Lennie slid down next to him. She resisted the urge to wipe her grimy hands on her jeans, though her clothes were already dusty and a streak of black grease ran across her white t-shirt. She needed a bath, or at least a public restroom where she could wash in the sink. Maybe that tattoo would wash off with a little soap, too.

They started down the alley between the two trains, Junkyard with a pack on his back and Jim carrying a duffle bag held together with duct tape. The thick smell of diesel and rust hung in the air, taking the shine off the morning sun. Lennie shivered and wished she had kept the jean jacket a while longer.

They followed a long line of maroon boxcars just like the one had they traveled in. When Lennie looked back, she could only find their car because the doors were closed on all the rest. Jim wandered a crooked path behind them, bending to examine every bit of trash with a hopeful look on his face.

As they reached the tail end of the train, they came to a half dozen decrepit gray hoppers. Amoeboid patches of rust had eaten through much of the paint on their sides and graffiti covered the rest—obscenities, tags, and faded hobo signatures. A sporadic hiss drifted toward them as they approached the last car. The sound was familiar, but Lennie couldn't place it among the usual train yard noises. Junkyard slowed and glanced back at Jim, who had found an old sweatshirt two cars back and was shoving it into his bag. Without speaking, Junkyard signaled Lennie to stay behind him and rounded the back end of the train. Lennie turned the corner after him and almost plowed into his back.

"Hey, what—" she began. Junkyard waved her to silence, but it was too late. A young man turned from the hopper, a can of spray paint in one hand and a rag smudged red and yellow in the other. Lean and taut, like a whip ready to crack, he watched them through slitted eyes.

Junkyard eased his pack to the ground and held a hand out, palm down. "*Ése*, man. Wazzup?" He spoke in a relaxed voice, but Lennie felt heat pour off his back.

The "man" was just a kid in his late teens, though anger had already chiseled hard lines into his face. He wore a white tank shirt that glowed against his cinnamon skin and showed off a tattoo of happy-sad theater masks on his upper arm. Blood-crusted stitches closed a four-inch gash on the other arm. He tossed the paint can to the ground and tucked the rag into his back pocket, where it hung like a mottled tail.

"*De dónde eres, gabacho?*" he said, openly hostile. "You gotta show me your card."

Junkyard shook his head slowly and let his hands drop to his sides. Metal glinted from his palm, hidden from the gangbanger. Lennie realized with a chill that he held a switchblade knife.

The kid stepped closer. "You walk the Brotherhood's *barrio*, man. You and the *güerita*—" Lennie flinched as his gaze scraped across her face, "—you want to ride the trains, you got to pay the dues."

"Sorry, *amigo*. We're tapped out," Junkyard said in an amiable voice. "Can't you let it go, this once?"

Lennie was close enough to feel an almost indiscernible shift in Junkyard's balance. His thumb rubbed the handle of the knife. Eyes wide, she fumbled at the pepper spray hanging from her belt loop, trying to release it without attracting the kid's attention. She didn't like where this was going. Not at all.

Especially when the kid pulled a gun from the pocket of his baggy jeans and leveled it at Junkyard's chest.

"You sorry?" he said in a low, tense voice. "Too bad. I'm sorry, too."

Lennie's head swam and the gun seemed to swell to cannon size. The gangbanger saw her fear. His lips curled in a half-smile. He raised the weapon and looked down its barrel at her face. "How 'bout I do the *chica*, first. *Sí?*"

Junkyard flicked the knife open. Lennie's breath caught, certain he was about to get himself shot. And her, too. She gave the pepper spray another tug and it came loose in her hand. Before anyone could act, Jungle Jim rounded the corner and plowed into Lennie's back, knocking her into Junkyard.

"Sorry, Missy," he said, "Didn't know you'd be standin' there." Then he saw the gangbanger and his eyes got big. "Hey, Dougie! That guy's got a gun!"

The kid sneered at him and opened his mouth for some snide remark. Junkyard blurred into action, kicking the weapon from the kid's hand. It flew onto the tracks, took an odd bounce and clattered to rest under the end car.

But the gangbanger was quick. Before Junkyard could recover his balance, the kid swung a foot through his planted leg. Junkyard fell awkwardly and rang his head on the iron rail. His knife dropped from his hand and rattled across the gravel. Lennie gaped at it, frozen by the sudden violence. The kid scooped up the knife before she thought to move. Dismayed, she found her voice. "Dammit! Junkyard, he's got your knife!"

The kid rushed at Junkyard. Fresh blood seeped through the

stitches on his arm. "I'll teach you to mess with the Ragman."

Junkyard rolled to his back and blinked up at him, eyes unfocused. The kid grinned and fingered the blade. "This'll be easy, no?"

"No!" Lennie lunged forward, stretching the pepper spray toward the gangbanger. Her hand shook so badly she was afraid she'd drop it. "Back off. Just-just back off, Ragman—or whatever you call yourself."

The Ragman turned toward her. His eyes narrowed on the canister. He spread his hands and let the knife dangle, as if surrendering. What now? Tell him to leave? Then he exploded toward her, snarling. She screamed and back-pedaled. Aiming wildly, she triggered the spray.

Nothing happened.

Aghast, she shook the canister and banged it on her leg. He was on her before she could fire again and caught her forearm with fingers like steel cable. He held the knife casually in his other hand, as if she posed no threat.

"Too bad, *chica.*" His mouth twisted in a vicious grin. "Now maybe we can have a party, just you and me."

She struggled against his grip, panting, every nerve on fire. Over his shoulder, she saw Jim tug at Junkyard, who sat up groggily. She needed to stall and give him time to recover. The Ragman yanked her close, trapping the pepper spray between them. Her finger found the nozzle. It had to work this time. She closed her eyes and whispered, "Please, please, please."

"Hey, I like it!" The Ragman tickled her ear with his knife. "Beg some more, little *chica.*"

"I wasn't talking to you." She triggered the pepper spray, not caring if she caught herself in the blast as well. The canister sputtered pathetically, barely making her eyes water. "*Chingao!*" The Ragman coughed and wiped at tearing eyes, his face contorted with fury. "Fuck, bitch—you gonna pay for that."

Red-faced, he twisted her arm so hard that cords stood out on his neck and she thought her bones would break. She resisted, refusing to let go of that useless spray.

Where the hell is Junkyard?

Sharp pain shot through her wrist and her fingers sprang open. The spray fell to the ground and the pain stopped, but she saw her death in the Ragman's contorted face. He raised the knife. Screaming, she shielding herself with her free arm and waited for the slice of the blade.

But the blow never came. A harsh laugh erupted from the Ragman. She lowered her arm and found him staring at the tattoo on the back of her hand.

"Shit, man!" Grinning unpleasantly, he touched the design with the knife. "Looks like you gonna be no fun, after all. I gotta save you for El Lobo."

Lennie met his feral gaze and her breath caught. He twisted her hand into her face, as if she needed a reminder of what was branded there. But she couldn't look away from his eyes.

His animal yellow eyes.

They burned like acid into her brain. An answering burn flared in her tattoo—an electrical charge that radiated through her hand and prickled up her arm like a column of fire ants.

Then Junkyard tackled the Ragman and Lennie stumbled as his grip tore from her arm.

Dazed, she straightened slowly, still seeing those yellow eyes, full of alien malice. El Lobo—didn't that mean "wolf"? Like in her dream.

The Ragman yelled somewhere nearby. There was a loud smack, a fist striking flesh, and the thud of something large hitting the ground. A knife bounced to her feet. She looked at it stupidly, then scooped it up with a foggy idea of helping Junkyard. But the Ragman was already flat on his back. Blood streamed from his nose, and Junkyard's booted foot pressed down on his throat.

Blood ran from Junkyard's temple and smeared his chin. He glared down at the Ragman, the whites showing around his eyes. Mouth twisted in a snarl, he drew a harsh breath, ready to bear down on the Ragman's neck.

Lennie shook off her stupor. "No, Junkyard! You'll kill him!"

Junkyard didn't look up. He was going to do it. Lennie started toward him, but Jungle Jim got there first and laid a hand on his arm.

"Let it go, Dougie."

They stayed that way for a moment: Junkyard's foot pressing down on the Ragman's neck, Jim's hand on Junkyard's arm. Then the wildness drained from Junkyard's face. His shoulders slumped as if he were the one who had been defeated. He released the gangbanger and nudged him with his boot.

"Get up," he said dully.

The Ragman lay as if still pinned, chest heaving, looking up at Junkyard with wide, terror-filled eyes. Brown eyes.

Junkyard waved his hands as if shooing a fly. "*Ya estuvo.* It's over. Go home."

Watching Junkyard suspiciously, the Ragman scrambled to a safer distance before climbing to his feet. He backed away, rubbing his throat. His smirk returned.

"Pay now or pay later." He shrugged, grinning. "It's all the same to El Lobo."

Irritation crossed Junkyard's face. "I said go!" He stomped a foot toward the Ragman, who jumped like a startled dog and ran.

Junkyard sighed and worked his jaw. Wincing, he probed his bruised and bleeding temple. Reaching into an outer pocket of his pack, he took out a wet wipe and dabbed at his injury. Lennie watched, nervous about him all over again. He might look harmless, but she would never forget how he took down that streetwise punk so thoroughly.

Still, she had been with him for more than twelve hours, and he had done nothing but protect her.

"Here." She reached for the wipe. "Let me do that. You can't see."

"You might want to put that away, first."

She looked down and realized she still held the open knife. The blade looked sharp enough to cut herself just thinking about it. She tried to figure out how to close it, fumbled, and let it drop to avoid slicing her thumb off. Junkyard picked it up and folded the blade away, showing her how the mechanism worked. To her surprise, he handed it back to her. She held it between finger and thumb like a dead fish. "Aren't these illegal?"

"Probably. Some places, anyway. But death is more unpleasant than a little jail time."

She shook her head and tried to hand it back. "No thanks—I'm more likely to cut myself than someone else."

His lip twitched. "Yeah, I know." But he closed her fingers on the weapon. "Take it. The threat alone might be enough to stop a fight."

Under his firm touch, she realized her hands still trembled. She met his eyes. "What you did to that guy—I've never seen anything like that before. You saved my life. Twice, now."

He reddened and looked away, withdrawing his hand. "So bake me a cake when I get you back to your house. I like chocolate."

An awkward silence followed, and he avoided her eyes as she cleaned the blood off his face. She was on her third wet wipe when Jungle Jim gave a yelp and bent close to the ground.

"Hot dog, Dougie! Lookit what I found." He scooped up the Ragman's spray paint. "Just the thing I need."

He wandered off behind the train, shaking the can and chuckling to himself. The hissing Lennie had heard earlier began again. Baffled, she stared after him. Junkyard grinned and shrugged.

"You want that?" He pointed at the pepper spray lying near the track.

"That stupid thing!" She picked it up and thumped on its impotent nozzle. "Do you know how long I've been carrying this piece of crap? Going on midnight runs through the park? Walking home from work after dark?"

"Too long, maybe," Junkyard said.

The amused glint in his eyes irritated her beyond tolerance. With a yell, she heaved the canister as far as she could. It bounced on a stretch of empty track and came to rest in the gravel. A stream of pepper spray fountained high into the air. Lennie watched it stonily.

"Perfect."

Behind her, Junkyard cleared his throat and said in a flat voice, "I hate to rush you, but we should probably get going."

"Right." She didn't move.

"Don't want to get caught standing right under the Brotherhood's logo."

"True."

She gave the canister one last, dark look. As she turned to go, her gaze caught on the fresh graffiti emblazoned in red and yellow on the side of the hopper. Three interlocking letters, BRR, were laid out in a rough triangle that was much too similar to the tattoo on her hand. Her head swam at the sight of it and she had an urge to run far away from anything to do with trains, gangs, and spontaneous tattoos.

Junkyard touched her arm. "You okay?"

"No—yeah." She thrust her tattooed hand into her pocket. "Just shock setting in, I suppose."

She smiled to show she was joking. He didn't look convinced. She tried to match his casual calm, but her voice cracked when she spoke. "So, do you think the Ragman'll come back?"

"Maybe. And if he does, he'll bring friends." Junkyard raised his voice. "Hey, Jim—time to go."

The hiss of spray paint stopped and Jungle Jim's voice drifted around the corner of the hopper. "Be there'n two shakes, Dougie."

The paint can rattled exactly twice, and then hissed one more time in a staccato burst. Silence followed. Lennie and Junkyard exchanged puzzled glances. Jungle Jim came out from behind the hopper. He was wearing bright yellow shoes.

He looked from Junkyard to Lennie and then down at his feet, a big grin on his face. Gravel stuck to dripping laces and yellow spattered the cuffs of his baggy pants. "What d'ya think, guys?"

"Uh," Lennie said. She looked at Junkyard, hoping he could do better. He was laughing.

"I think the kids are going to love 'em." He patted Jim on the back. "Grab your bag and let's go try them out."

CHAPTER FIVE

The back of Lennie's neck prickled with the feeling of being watched as she followed Junkyard and Jungle Jim through the train yard's exit. She glanced back, half-expecting to see a pack of gangbangers charging after them, led by the Ragman.

His eyes haunted her. Brown eyes. She had seen them clearly before he had run away. Had they ever been a different color?

And who was this El Lobo that was supposed to be looking for her?

Lennie's feelings of unease faded as she reentered the everyday world of cars, commuters, and well-kept buildings. The return to mainstream seemed to have the opposite effect on Junkyard. He slowed as the sidewalk grew more crowded, letting Jungle Jim rove ahead. Signs of strain lined his face, as though ordinary people made him more nervous than a train yard full of gangbangers.

"Is something wrong?" she asked.

His jaw muscles worked under his long sideburns. He didn't look at her.

"No."

His tone ended the conversation. They walked in silence along a street lined with red brick buildings and crowded bike racks. A pair of girls came toward them on the sidewalk, backpacks hanging from their shoulders. Though the walkway was plenty wide, Junkyard kept his head down and stepped onto the grass to let them pass.

Lennie watched him uneasily. What was wrong with him? Less than an hour ago, he had dismantled a punk carrying a gun and a knife, but now he couldn't handle a couple of sorority girls.

Jim bounded back to them with his duffle bag half unzipped. "I gotta start getting ready," he said. "We're almost there!"

He plopped down on the sidewalk and dug through his belongings. Junkyard slouched against a lamppost, chin tucked under his jacket collar, hands deep in his pockets. He looked like a vagrant who planned to loiter all day.

He looked completely unreliable.

The low thrumming of heavy machinery vibrated the air. Lennie glanced around, but couldn't find the source of the noise. They had stopped in front of an enormous building with a high, arching facade. It looked familiar. The sign out front said Williams Arena.

"Hey, isn't that where the Gophers play basketball?" she asked. "We must be at the University of Minnesota."

Junkyard gave an indecipherable mutter. Jim looked up from his duffle bag, a sock in one hand and a plastic snake in the other.

"That's right, Missy. They hold the Festival right over there, every year." He pointed the snake at a large oval building across the street. "That's the Marr—ee—ooo—chee Arena."

"Right." Lennie had been here before, for an invitational track meet at the end of her high school career. She had done well, placing third in the 300-meter hurdles and first in the 800-meter dash. But it wasn't a happy memory. Her mother had gotten sloppy drunk at a team dinner.

"Hey, Dougie, which hat d'ya think I should wear?"

Happy for the distraction, Lennie looked at the two hats in Jungle Jim's hands. They were possibly the ugliest she had ever seen: a red-and-green checkered tam with a yellow pompom and an old bowler so dented it was more of a lopsided cone than a bowl. Junkyard gave a furtive glance up and down the sidewalk and pushed himself from the lamppost. He bent over the hats.

"Definitely the checkered one." He grinned, looking more like the man Lennie had met on the train. "The pompom matches your shoes."

Oh, yeah—the pompom tipped the scales for me, too, Lennie thought. She winced when Jim put the hat on. Of course, she would have winced at either choice.

Jim stuffed the bowler back in his bag and jumped up. "C'mon! The tents oughta be up by now. Ashley'll be with her dad, I bet."

As they started toward the Mariucci Arena, Junkyard resumed his unresponsive posture. Lennie walked beside him in awkward silence, while Jim alternately ran ahead and jogged back to hurry them along. The rumble of machinery grew louder as they rounded the building's curved side. A large parking lot lay before them. They had reached the Festival.

The noise came from carnival rides in varying stages of assembly at the far end of the lot. The long, black arms of the Whirling Octopus were already in place. That ride used to make Lennie sick as a child. A kiddie roller coaster in the shape of a snake biting its tail idled next to it. Behind them were the usual pods, arms, cylinders, and tracks guaranteed to make weak-stomached customers hurl. She had never been fond of carnival rides.

Closer to the road, tent canvases flapped in the breeze as vendors and show-casers readied their displays. Jungle Jim skirted the crowd control barriers, bobbing and leaning to see into the tent village. Junkyard smiled and seemed to relax as he watched Jim's antics.

"Is this the whole Festival?" Lennie asked. "It seems small."

Junkyard shook his head. "Just the carnival and vendors, out here." He hooked a thumb back toward the arena. "The bigger exhibits are inside."

Encouraged by this relative explosion in conversation, Lennie asked another question. "I've been wondering, what did that graffiti stand for, back there? The BRR, I mean."

She tried to sound casual. Even so, he frowned and took so long to answer that she feared he had gone back into his paranoid vagrant mode. "It stands for 'Brotherhood of Rail Riders,'" he finally said. "You'd do best to stay away from them."

He looked away and didn't seem interested in elaborating. Lennie was beginning to think sucking strawberry gelatin through a straw would be easier than trying to get Junkyard to talk. She didn't have that kind of patience. "Look, it's not like I was planning to ask the Ragman on a date. I just want some information. If I'm going to find my father, I need to know what I'm facing."

Junkyard stopped abruptly. "They're criminals—that's what you're facing," he said with unexpected force. Lennie flinched and stepped back, but he wasn't finished. "Haven't you been paying attention? Catching on to freight trains has never been safe, and it's getting worse all the time. Drifters aren't exactly known for self-discipline. You might be dead or...let's just say, it's no place for a woman."

His eyes traveled to Jim, who was hiding behind a tree to spy on the festival. Junkyard's face softened. "It's no place for any decent person."

Justified or not, his attitude rankled. "So then what makes you a hobo? Are you saying you're not decent?"

"You're damn lucky it was me. I could have been a jack roller or a drug addict. Hell, the rails are littered with scum and criminals who just haven't been caught yet."

"And my father is out there!"

A woman passing by looked at Lennie sharply and she realized she was shouting again. She didn't care. She glared, daring Junkyard to say something—anything at all. The blood throbbed in her temples, and she was dimly aware of an answering tingle in her tattooed hand.

Then Jim trotted between them, hopping from foot to foot with excitement. "She's here! Ashley's here!"

A huge smile lifted his fleshy cheeks. He dropped his bag and ripped the zipper open. "Your pardon, Missy, but I gotta finish gettin' ready before we get too close. Can't be lettin' the kids see me like this."

It was impossible to stay angry before this onslaught of happiness.

An odd assortment of junk piled up on the sidewalk as Jim ransacked his belongings. Some items didn't surprise Lennie— rumpled boxers, a matted cardigan, a toothbrush, and other items he might need on the road. But plastic flowers? And bright red canvas high tops? At least size 12, by the look of them. And what did he need with pristine white evening gloves?

Frantic, Jim rummaged through the pile, muttering to himself. At last, he found what he wanted. "Hot dog! I knew I had one to match!"

He took off his hat and pulled an elastic band over his head, letting it snap around his neck. A purple bow tie with yellow spots dangled from it, slightly off-center. He didn't bother to tuck the elastic under his shirt collar. She wasn't sure how he thought it would improve his appearance.

Junkyard nodded. "I like that one, Jim. It really stands out."

Feeling like the sane minority, Lennie didn't comment. Jim rooted around and fished out the white gloves. He slapped them together a few times, picked off invisible lint, and pulled them on. Recognition set in when he fitted a red super-ball on his nose. Lennie burst out laughing.

"You're a clown!"

Both men looked at her as if she were the one whose caboose

had derailed. Embarrassed, she laughed a little too hard. "I thought...I thought..."

Jim looked hurt. "Ya didn't think I dressed like this all the time, did ya?"

Still laughing, Lennie shook her head helplessly. Jim shrugged and gave his nose an experimental toot. It made a sound like a squeaky duck. He took the ball off, spread a thin layer of adhesive inside, and replaced it. Settling the checkered hat on his head, he climbed over the barrier and trotted toward the tent village. Lennie watched him through tear-filled eyes and decided Junkyard was right. The yellow pompom bouncing on the hat did match the spray-painted shoes. Not to mention the polka dots on the bow tie. Laughter gripped her like a bad case of hiccups. It felt good after the last twelve hours of craziness.

Junkyard gave her a quizzical smile. Still giggling, she wiped her eyes and tried to explain. "He always acted so...um."

Junkyard waited for her to finish. She tried again, looking for the most polite phrasing. "I didn't know he was a clown. I thought he was, uh," she tapped her head, "mentally..."

"Handicapped?"

She nodded, feeling stupid. Somehow, she always ended up feeling stupid around Junkyard.

Jim bounced to the middle of the tent village, tooting his nose and yelling, "Halloo, halloo, halloo!"

He didn't have to wait long. A blond girl around eight years old burst from an exhibit tent, yelling, "Jim's here! Jim's here!"

She threw herself at Jim. He caught her under the arms and swung her high in the air. A boy about the same age flew out of another tent and Jim bent low to let him crawl onto his back. The boy hugged Jim's neck and reached over his shoulder to search the handkerchief pocket of his jacket.

"I can see why they call him Jungle Jim," Lennie said.

Junkyard smiled. "That's Tyler Carpenter—he's looking for candy."

The girl grabbed Jim's hand and pulled him toward the tent. "And that's Ashley Sutter. She's probably got a bag of cookies stashed in her father's tent. He's a bull from the University yards. Collects railroad detective badges and has an exhibit every year. He and Jim are old friends—known each other since before Ashley was born."

Lennie considered Jim's belongings at her feet. Holes in the bottom of an old shoe watched her like beggar's eyes. He might be a clown, but that didn't explain his mood swings or weird personality shifts.

A burst of childish laughter rose over the thrum of machinery. More children had joined Ashley and Tyler. Jim took off the checkered tam and his hair frizzed up like tufts of brown cotton candy. He waved the hat through the air, knocked it against his hand, and dropped it on Tyler's head. Peppermints showered around Tyler's ears and bounced on the ground. As a unit, the children dove for the candy. Jim's grin was so large Lennie could almost count his teeth from a block away. She couldn't help but grin back.

Whatever else he was, Jungle Jim was a good clown.

She knelt and began putting his belongings back in the duffle bag. She had begun to think of them as props rather than junk. Junkyard squatted beside her to help.

"Nothing makes Jim happier than a swarm of children. We can leave him here while we show that picture of your dad to some friends of mine."

He pulled the zipper closed and stared after Jim, his hand still on the bag. He smiled at the boisterous scene, but his eyes were somber. "Jim's been clowning at railroad festivals around the Midwest for maybe twenty-five years. Every year, he does his hobo bit in Boone, Britt, Topeka, and sometimes even at the Pullman Historical Reenactment. He used to work for the FRC Railroad, repairing trains at the University yard."

He tucked Jim's bag under his arm and stood up. "About five years ago, Bill Sutter—Ashley's dad—was inspecting a train that had just rolled into the receiving yard. He swung up onto the platform of a hopper to have a look in the cubbyhole. A jack-roller dove out and knocked Bill onto the track between cars. Control tower didn't see him and signaled the unit to move. Jim was an air monkey at the time, doing brake repair. He saw it all and pulled Bill out of the way, but a snag hanging off the side of the train caught him in the head before he could get clear. Laid him flat. Bill says Jim hasn't been right, since. Couldn't do his job anymore, so he went to live with his sister in Illinois."

Jungle Jim's act ended and the kids started playing freeze tag between the tents. Ashley was "it." She had frozen three of the kids and was after Tyler. Jim danced out of reach whenever she came close. Lennie watched him with an odd mix of sadness and amusement. He had lost so much—but he hadn't lost everything.

Junkyard touched her arm and she turned to him. The worry in his eyes surprised her.

"Listen to me, Lennie," he said softly. "You really shouldn't be riding the rails. Not now. It's just too dangerous—"

"Not that, again. I told you—"

Closing his eyes with a pained expression, he raised his hand to cut her off. "I know—you're going to do it anyway. Just wanted to be clear so you don't get confused and think I've accepted the idea." He pulled his wallet from his pocket. "As long as you insist on going through with this, you'd better get one of these."

He flipped the wallet open and showed her a white, laminated card. It bore his name, a date, and the letters BRR watermarked in red, laid out in a triangle. Like the Ragman's graffiti. Like her tattoo. Lennie stared at the card, aghast.

"You're a *member*?"

"No, but I'm not a fool, either. The real members don't pay dues. They collect them. And if you don't carry a card, they'll collect everything you own, including your life."

"Then why didn't you show it to that punk instead of fighting?"

Junkyard shrugged and put the card away. "Would have ended the same way. You don't have a card. I doubt Jim has one, either. At least this way, the punk didn't get my name."

Lennie didn't know what to say. How many times should she thank him for saving her life?

Fortunately, she was saved from saying anything by a shriek of childish laughter. She and Junkyard turned to watch Ashley chase Jim, her shoulder-length, white-blond hair whipping around her face. Everyone else was frozen, but Jim ran with high-stepping strides just out of her reach, racing in tighter and tighter circles until Ashley finally reached out and touched him. He made a great show of freezing on one wobbly leg and fell to the ground.

Lennie laughed. "If I were him, I wouldn't get back up. He's a little old for playing tag."

Chuckling, Junkyard waved at Jim and dropped the clown's duffle bag over the rope barrier where he could get to it easily. "That's Jim for you. Shouldn't be riding trains any more, either, but he can't seem to stay away. Rail workers up and down the line all know him and look after him. The 'bos look after him, too. He helped more than one of them before the accident."

"Is that why you take care of him?"

She winced as soon as she said it. Hobos don't like prying questions. He watched Jim without answering, frowning at some inner thought. Then tension drew his mouth in a hard line. He rubbed his closed fist as if his knuckles hurt. "I need no reason to look after someone like Jungle Jim."

He stalked away, leaving her alone on the sidewalk.

CHAPTER SIX

Detective Harcourt Briggeman climbed rusty metal stairs and stepped into the retired caboose that served as his office. He threaded his way through an obstacle course of stacked files and cleared a space in the center of his desk. Normally the clutter gave him a jaw-clenching headache, but he didn't notice it today. He tossed a fresh, new file folder onto his desk.

There had been another murder. Number fourteen. And all of them on *his* line. Exhausted, he dropped into his chair. The seat listed hard to the left. He gasped and clutched the armrests, fighting to stay upright. "Damn!"

He shifted his weight and his seat leveled tentatively. It had been so long since he sat down that he'd forgotten the chair was broken. He had also forgotten to file a requisition for a new one. He eyed the stacks of paperwork rising like tenements from his desk and office floor. The requisition form lived in one of them. No point in digging it out; the Company would undoubtedly turn down the request. FRC Railroad was a bankruptcy waiting to happen.

He sighed, flipped open the file folder, and paged through its contents. The Hobo Spider's latest victim, another transient, had been found during the night. The coroner estimated that he'd been dead at least three days. Fingerprints identified him as Peter Olson, a.k.a. Tin Can Petey. He was fifty-seven years old, had no known relatives, a long list of vagrancy charges, and one count of shoplifting, later dropped by the store owner. Harmless, according to the few hobos willing to talk to Briggs.

The photos were gruesomely similar to the other thirteen sets.

Briggs hardly needed to look at them. After the first three or four murders, the images all started to run together. Sometimes when he closed his eyes he saw them all at once in some sort of sick collage. He forced himself to examine the pictures carefully. The killer was bound to screw up sooner or later and Briggs wasn't going to be the one to miss it.

The phone rang. Briggs picked it up absently, still studying the photos. The nasal voice of Henry Willowbe, the Company's Director of Safety, filled his ear.

"Briggeman, about time you showed up. Where have you been hiding? There's been another murder."

Oh, really? Briggs wanted to say. I'm always the last to know.

But Willowbe was the man who signed his paycheck; Briggs kept his voice level. "Sorry, sir. I was at the crime scene until dawn and just got back from interviewing the victim's acquaintances."

Willowbe didn't even pause. "And why didn't you call me when the body was found?"

"It was called in at 2:00 a.m., sir. I figured you—"

"Never mind. There've been, what, nine murders on my line, now, and I want to know what you're going to do about it."

"Fourteen. And I—"

"What's that? Fourteen? Good God, Briggeman, I don't need tell you we can't afford to have some serial killer scaring off any more clients."

Or getting blood all over our nice, clean, freight cars, eh, Hank? "Trust me, sir, I don't want any more people killed, either. But there's not much to go on. This murder looks just like the others—same white string, same kind of black-handled bronze knife. The string's on its way to Los Alamos by now, but I'll bet you a dozen donuts those coneheads'll be as stumped by the stuff as they were the first thirteen times. And I don't hold out much hope for the knife."

There had been no latents on the knives from the other crime scenes. No manufacturer's markings, either.

"I'm doing the best I can with what I've got, sir. And so's the DMPD and the FBI." He added that last bit hoping Willowbe would get the hint that Briggs wasn't the only one who was stymied.

"Obviously your best hasn't been good enough. You're going to have to expand your limitations."

Briggs suppressed a snort. And here I was, trying to go beyond them. "Frankly, sir, unless the killer slips up bad, we're going to need a lot more resources to nail him."

"Like what? You said yourself that the police up and down the line are involved, not to mention the FBI."

"Yeah, but they can't inspect every train car that passes through every yard. Even if they could, the killer can get on and off a train without ever going through a yard. He can kill and be hundreds of miles away before we ever find the body. What we really need are people on the inside."

"On the inside," said Willowbe.

"Yes, sir. Decoys—lots of 'em."

With a pang, Briggs thought of Douglas Harding. He had all but given that very assignment to the young captain a year ago and no one had heard from him since.

The sound of Willowbe's pencil tapping on his desk traveled down the phone line.

"Where are we going to get decoys?" The belligerence left his voice, exposing poorly controlled anxiety. "I don't suppose you'd volunteer?"

"Love to. I'll just let those smuggling and theft cases slide for a few weeks—or months—while I hunt the killer down—"

"No, no. That won't be necessary." Willowbe was suddenly businesslike. "I'll make some phone calls, see what I can do. Let me know if you find anything more."

More than what? He hadn't found anything, yet. Hanging up, he pushed away from the desk and paced the three steps of available floor space. If he thought it would help, he'd have gone undercover months ago, smugglers be damned. But the odds of one undercover agent—two, if you counted Harding—tracking the killer were painfully low. He had ruined Harding's career, and probably his life, for nothing.

"Man, I don't need this crap."

That's what his brother Hammond had told him when he had urged him to take that Northfield P.D. job. "You don't need that crap, Harry. Settle down. There's plenty of college chicks in Northfield—get a wife or something while you still have most of your hair."

Briggs had passed a hand through his short, thick brown hair and eyed his brother's receding hairline. "Right, Ham—I figure I got more time for that than you do."

In truth, he liked the challenge of his position. Vandalism, drug smuggling, theft, arson, murder—as the sole detective for a shrinking regional railroad, it all fell under his purview. But now he wished he had listened. Over the last year, the BRR had become a real power, swallowing or destroying any competitive gangs along the line. The crime rate had risen from a steady trickle to a tsunami flood. And these serial killings…

Fourteen murders on *his* tracks and he had no leads whatsoever.

The idea of having nothing worse to think about than speeding tickets, a few drunken students, and the occasional cow-tipping incident was sounding damn good. But he couldn't quit until he got this mess cleaned up. *If* he could clean it up.

Restless, he returned to his desk. A stack of files blocked his computer monitor. He moved it to the floor, sat down, grunted, got up again, wheeled the broken chair out the door and pushed it down the stairs. There was a lot of banging and clanging, and a satisfying crunch when it hit the gravel below. He shoved the folding chair he kept for guests in front of his desk and turned on his computer.

He made a point of searching the Internet periodically in case the killer was psycho enough to start a blog or website about his activities. A stretch, but checking made Briggs feel like he was doing something. He tapped in the keywords "hobo" and "killer." The usual crap appeared—games, music, hobo spiders, and an ever-growing clutter of irrelevant, self-indulgent blogs. He refined his search and found links for Robert Silveria, who bludgeoned hobos in their sleep, and Resendez-Ramirez, whose victims lived near the tracks. Solved crimes, unconnected to the current slayings. There were historical references to the Mad Butcher of Kingsbury Run and current references to the Brotherhood of Rail Riders. The Mad Butcher was ancient history—no connection there. And the BRR was just a glorified street gang on wheels. Typical gang violence, obviously unrelated to the bizarre killings.

He scrolled through dozens of links, looking for something relevant. Something he hadn't seen before. Then he spotted a title that made him pause: *Hobo Spider Claims Another Victim*. He clicked on it and sat back, stunned. Austin Harding's bloody face filled his screen, the black handle of a knife protruding from his mouth.

Outrage crackled through Brigg's brain. This was a confidential police photo. Some greedy bastard had leaked it.

He wrenched his cell phone from its case, ready to chew some ass, but forgot to dial when he read the photo's caption. *Another bizarre murder claims a traveler of the iron road. Could the Butterfly Killer be at it again?*

What the hell? He skimmed the article, at first hopeful, then incredulous. The author tried to claim a supernatural connection between the Hobo Spider and some old murders. The website, an online tabloid, was hardly a trustworthy source.

Even so...Butterfly Killer.

He set the phone down and entered keywords for a new search. A fresh set of links filled his screen, all of them irrelevant except for one: "Butterfly Killer Cocoons 10th Victim."

An old newspaper article appeared. The accompanying photo showed a body wound in stark white string. The scene bore an uncanny resemblance to the crime scene Briggs had visited during the night—body curled within its cocoon, wedged against the wall of a boxcar. The coat draped over the victim's face didn't hide the pool of blood underneath. The article indicated that a knife had been thrust through his mouth. Just like the victims of the Hobo Spider.

The cases were never solved, but the last murder took place in 1942. The killer was undoubtedly dead by now. Even if he weren't, he'd be too old to commit these crimes. So, what? A copycat? Or some weird family thing, son inheriting from father?

Briggs sent the page to print and sat back, gnawing an abused thumbnail. There had to be a connection. He picked up the phone and speed-dialed the FBI contact for the case.

"Parker. Briggs, here. I got something for you to check into and you're not going to believe it."

CHAPTER SEVEN

Junkyard strode away from Lennie, too agitated to deal with her questions or even her presence. She might have good reasons for riding the rails, but that wouldn't stop her from getting killed. He didn't want to go through that again.

He should get away. Leave Lennie, Jim, and this whole damn city behind. The killer wasn't going to strike in broad daylight in the middle of a crowded city. Junkyard should be on a train somewhere, moving on. Alone.

But he had lied to Lennie. He did owe Jim, though not for money or food, the way she might have thought. He couldn't leave the simple hobo unprotected. Once you started taking care of someone on the road, you might as well adopt him for life.

The first time he had met Jungle Jim, Junkyard was still Douglas Harding, the photos from his brother's police file fresh in his memory. Doug had only to blink to see Austin's face stained black with blood. Absolute terror lingered in those lifeless eyes; Austin might have died of it before the knife ever touched him. When Doug slept, Austin's dead face pleaded with him, lips moving around the blade until the blood ran fresh.

So Doug didn't sleep. He grew hag-ridden and wild with rage, stalking through hobo jungles like a mean drunk looking for someone to pound. Most hobos avoided him. The few who got in his way never challenged him a second time.

One cold November night, Doug crashed a riverside jungle near Fergus Falls. Beet harvest was over and the last of the temporary help waited to catch out for a place to winter over. The rage was bad that day, swelling in Doug's chest until he thought his rib cage would burst. In the dark, he saw a lone man hunched over a trashcan fire to warm his hands, his jacket collar pulled up and hat pulled down so only a bushy black beard showed between. Doug snarled something at him, he couldn't remember what, and hoped the man was the sort to fight back.

The man lifted his head and glared at Doug across the fire. He drew himself straight, slowly, so that Doug could appreciate the full extent of him. The long shadows cast by the firelight made him look seven feet tall, but Doug figured he couldn't be more than six foot six. Red and black plaid flannel hugged a pillar of a neck. The fabric of his jacket strained around broad shoulders and thick arms. If he had an ax, he might be Paul Bunyan.

Doug nodded. Should be a good fight.

The man crossed his arms over his chest and looked Doug over. No doubt he saw Doug as some scrawny upstart, not even six-foot tall—easy meat. Doug smiled. Then boots crunched over the frozen ground. A beer can clattered and rolled to a stop at his feet. Tall shadows stepped into the dim circle of light.

"Got a problem, Blackie?"

Three men lined up next to the first. They might all have come from the same litter—broad-shouldered, barrel-chested, neck circumferences matching their hat sizes. The one who spoke smacked a crowbar into his palm and sneered at Doug. Most of his teeth were missing. He growled an order and the others spread out to surround their prey. Doug figured he could take two, maybe three, before the fourth caught him from behind. He swallowed. For the first time since starting hobo life, he felt something besides rage.

He backed away, hoping to escape into the dark. The skin between his shoulder blades tingled a warning. A hairy hand slapped down on his shoulder and shoved him back into the circle. A deep, coarse voice above his head said, "Not leaving before the dance, are you?"

Doug looked up at the speaker. If grizzly bears could talk...

The circle closed behind Doug. Sweat prickled under his arms and his flesh twitched in anticipation of pain. He didn't try to apologize to Blackie. The mood had shifted. His attackers sensed sport. Any sign of fear would only add to their fun. Ignoring the icy wind, he shrugged off his jacket so he could move better.

The toothless man poked at Doug with the crowbar and laughed when Doug jumped away. "Hey, Blackie, looks like we got us a chicken to pluck."

The others chortled as if it were a good joke. Their jeers echoed across the river. Doug's insides churned with fear and self-disgust. After they'd finished with him, whatever remained would probably wash away in the next rain. His brother's killer would go on killing.

Grinning, Toothless hefted the crowbar. "Let's see how well this chicken can dance!"

He swung the crowbar like a baseball bat. Doug ducked and it whistled over his head, ruffling his hair. Dodging the backswing, he swept a leg through Toothless's ankles. Toothless crashed down and the crowbar flew out of his hand. Doug pulled his knife and turned on the others before the crowbar hit the ground.

The pack closed ranks. They weren't smiling any more.

Then a weird apparition bounded from the shadows, landing between Junkyard and the beet pickers. "A dance, didjya say?" it yelled, sounding ludicrously cheerful. "Jungle Jim can dance, yes siree. Jus' watch me!"

It was a crazy thing to do. A Jungle Jim sort of thing to do. In the weeks that followed, Doug saw him do the same thing in half a dozen similar situations. The simple hobo did it on impulse, without a clue that he was stepping into a pack of rabid dogs. But intentional or not, if Jim hadn't been there, Doug might have died that night.

Jim hopped into the circle next to Doug and stuck his arms up in the air like an arthritic ballerina. He attempted a pirouette, stumbled, caught himself, and leapt with bent knees and cocked feet. Distracted, the men seemed to forget about Doug. He should have been edging toward the woods, but he could only watch, as bemused as the rest of them, as Jim pranced with the grace of a three-legged goat, yodeling *The Dance of the Sugar Plum Fairy.*

I gotta get out of here, Doug thought. But he couldn't leave this goofy simpleton to be pulverized in his place.

After one particularly energetic display of elbows and knees, Jungle Jim tumbled spectacularly and landed on his back, legs stuck rigidly in the air. One of the men began to grin. Another laughed and said, "Di'n't he say he's Jungle Jim? I heard of him. Arizona Stu said he saw 'im pull a whole wrench from his nose, one time."

The men started telling Jungle Jim stories, each more outrageous than the last. They hardly seemed to notice that the man himself was lying at their feet.

Doug's mouth dropped open. The odd hobo should be flat on his back, all right, but beaten bloody, with Doug stretched out beside him. Instead, the violence had gone out of the pack. Doug reached down to help Jungle Jim up. "That was amazing. I've never seen anything like it."

Jungle Jim flashed a big, happy smile. His eyes held no guile, no hint of relief. "So ya think they liked my show?"

Blackie waved his arms, demonstrating a particularly wild stunt, and a burst of laughter swept through the men.

"Yes, Jungle Jim," Doug said. "I'm sure they liked your show. And so did I."

"Hot dog!" Jungle Jim whooped and did a happy dance. Doug shook his head, wondering how the simple fellow had survived so long.

"Come on." He took Jungle Jim by the arm. "Let's get out of here before those beet pickers remember they wanted to turn me into fertilizer. I know a place where we can jungle up."

They sheltered near the river in a pocket carved from the steep embankment by a past flood. Doug started a small fire and nestled a can of beans at its edge to warm. Sheltered from the wind, wrapped in his bedroll, he felt almost comfortable. He shared out some jerky to Jungle Jim and settled back to stare into the night.

The clash with the beet pickers had shaken him. Since Austin's death, he had wandered the rails in a red haze. With a shock, he realized that he hadn't thought about his brother's killer in weeks. Not in exact terms, at any rate. He rubbed his face with his hands. Tangled strings of uncut, greasy hair flopped over his fingers and oily dirt flaked from his ragged beard.

The familiar, futile rage welled up in him. He had become his disguise, a purposeless vagabond shaking his fist at life's injustice and doing nothing at all to stop it.

He dropped his hands and looked across the fire at Jungle Jim. The bozo held two spoons back-to-back in one hand and began clapping them between his knee and the palm of the other hand. The clackity-clack drummed on Doug's nerves. "What the hell are you doing!"

Jungle Jim paused the spoons. "Oh, hey! Glad ya woke up!" He pointed at the fire. "Your beans is boilin'."

Juice bubbled over the lip of the can and sizzled in the embers. Doug ground his teeth and snarled something unintelligible, but the moment of uncontrolled fury had passed. Leaning forward, he wrapped a gloved hand around the can and found himself looking across the flames, straight into Jungle Jim's face.

"You're doin' it all wrong, Douglas Harding."

Confused, Doug looked at the can and back at Jungle Jim, wondering where he could go wrong in warming beans.

"Listen, Doug. Jus' listen." The simpleton was gone from Jungle Jim's eyes and a new gaze, sharp and wise, reached deep into Doug to touch his soul. A shiver spread down Doug's back.

"Ya gotta stop what you're doin'. You're not gonna catch the killer by beatin' up every ham-handed hobo on the road."

Hot bean juice soaked through Doug's glove, unnoticed. He felt cold—colder than the snow that had begun to fall. Somehow this guy knew his name, though Doug had never mentioned it. Knew about his brother…his quest.

An ember popped in the fire. Light and shadow danced over Jungle Jim's face. Doug felt dislocated, lost in the surreal. Maybe the beet pickers had knocked him on the head, after all.

"The bait don't go after the fish, son." Jungle Jim sat back on his blanket. "An' you, Dougie, are the bait."

Doug's head rang with the obviousness of Jungle Jim's statement. A serial killer wouldn't go after a badass punk with plenty of fight in him. He'd wait for an easier target. The clackity-clack resumed. Jungle Jim grinned crookedly and met his gaze across the fire. His eyes were as vague and guileless as before. Doug wondered if the exchange had happened at all. But it didn't matter. He had his answer. The focus for his rage. He was not the hunter. He was the bait. He had only to lay himself open and wait.

And when the fish finally came, it would find that this bait had teeth.

Months rolled by. More hobos died. Doug changed his name and perfected his disguise, wearing dirt and sweat like other men wore aftershave. Sometimes he splashed Thunderbird on his clothes, though he never drank the stuff. He learned to draw into himself, to stand with slumped shoulders and avoid eye contact, one hand out for loose change. Over time, his disguise became automatic, until he came to think of himself as Junkyard Doug—Junkyard to his friends. He went for days without a thought for Captain Douglas Harding. All the while, the rage never left him and he never forgot his mission.

But the killer sure as hell wasn't going to target him here, in the middle of a university campus. Especially not with Lennie and Jim sticking to him like burrs. Junkyard growled in frustration, and a plump girl in a too-short skirt veered wide around him on the sidewalk. Disgust flashed across her face as she passed by.

Screw her.

A group of frat boys filled the sidewalk ahead, laughing and giving each other friendly shoves. They didn't seem to notice Junkyard. He stiffened and slowed to a shuffle, finding it harder to breathe as they approached. Then they were on him. He lowered his head to avoid their eyes. One of them shouldered him off the sidewalk. He stumbled and leaned against a tree to catch his breath. A film of sweat coated his face. He shoved cold, clammy fists into his pockets and squinted at his worn jump boots, struggling to find the line between himself and his disguise.

If he didn't find his brother's killer soon, he might lose Douglas Harding altogether.

Lennie watched Junkyard stride away, uncertain whether she should follow. He obviously wanted to be alone, but what was she supposed to do? Hang out with Jungle Jim and the kids all day?

She hesitated, then started after him. He could at least point her to the nearest hobo jungle so she could show her father's picture around.

A crowd of young men blocked the sidewalk ahead. They carried backpacks and wore jeans and hoodies. One wore a sweatshirt sporting a fierce-looking gopher. College boys.

Junkyard saw them, too, slouching and ducking his head between hunched shoulders as they approached. It was like he became a different person. Lennie might have walked past without recognizing him if she hadn't seen him change. The group engulfed him. His orange bandana bobbed in the sea of heads for a moment, and then disappeared.

"Hey, Junkyard—wait up!" She picked up speed, not wanting to lose him.

The students continued toward her, pushing and jostling each other as they laughed at some joke. Unable to find an opening, Lennie stopped in the middle of the sidewalk and crossed her arms. She wasn't about to lose Junkyard because of a bunch of frat boys.

"Ex*cuse* me!"

Startled, they nodded amiably and crowded aside, filing around her. She snorted softly. Dopey puppies.

She found Junkyard off the sidewalk, leaning on a tree with his head down. His face was gray and damp. He didn't notice her until she touched his arm. "Hey, are you all right?"

His head jerked up, exposing raw panic in his eyes. With visible effort, he straightened and put on the calm, more confident version of Junkyard, as if pulling on a shirt.

"I'm fine," he said shortly. "Just needed to get away to think."

About what? she wanted to ask. She knew so little about him. Instead, she said, "If I said something to offend you, I'm really sorry."

His gaze brushed her face and he looked away. "No, no. It's just...no."

There was an awkward pause, then he said, "I was thinking, some of the more sociable hobos hang around the jungle exhibit during the festival. A couple of them are already here."

He pointed across the parking lot. A cluster of large cardboard boxes and tarps huddled under a maple tree at the edge of the pavement. Among the boxes, a tall, thin figure stirred a pot suspended over a portable fire ring. "You could show them your father's picture. But first, I'd like to talk with Bill Sutter, Ashley's dad. I expect he's setting up his badge exhibit."

He started walking toward the tent village. Lennie followed, relieved that he was talking again.

"You could show Bill the picture, too," he added. "He's been a bull with the FRC railroad for almost twenty years. Probably met every hobo to pass through Minneapolis."

The festival wasn't open, yet. Hobbyists and vendors bustled with last-minute activity, unpacking boxes and setting up exhibits. As Lennie and Junkyard threaded between rows of tents and tables loaded with memorabilia, they caught a glimpse of Jungle Jim through a gap between exhibits. He saw them and waved, then pounced on a bouncy ball as if it were an elusive frog. Ashley and her friends mobbed him, jumping for the ball in his upraised hand. Lennie smiled, wishing she were that uninhibited.

Junkyard headed for the middle of the village and stopped in front of a tent sporting a sign with a railroad detective shield painted on it. The door flaps were tied back. Inside, a man in a blue work shirt and jeans was setting up a display case. Its glass top was propped open and it contained a number of shiny, metal badges.

Lennie knew instantly that the man was Bill Sutter. He had the same white-blond hair as Ashley, though his had gone thin and limp, with a comb-over that couldn't hide the pink scalp underneath. There was nothing thin or limp about the rest of him, though. He was built solid and square, with a hint of pudge around the middle.

Bill squatted to dig through a box at his feet. When he saw

Junkyard approaching, he stood up holding a double handful of detective badges. "Doug! Glad you could make it!"

Junkyard smiled. "Wouldn't miss it. How've you been?"

"Great, great. Just let me put these down." He dumped the badges into the display and shook Junkyard's hand. He let his gaze turn pointedly to Lennie. "I see you brought a date to the festival this year, eh?"

Junkyard's face turned a red that clashed horribly with his orange bandana. "No—I—she—"

"Good, good." A smirk twitched at the corner of Bill's mouth. He offered his hand to Lennie. "Let me introduce myself while the lad unties his tongue. Name's Bill Sutter."

Lennie tried not to wince when he ground her finger bones together.

"So have you two been over to the jungle, yet? They got the stew bubbling away, already. I had my first bowl an hour ago." He threw a wink at Lennie. "Nothing's as good as a mug of mulligan stew first thing in the morning, eh?"

"I wouldn't know," said Lennie. "I've never had it."

"Oh, well, you're in luck. Bones O'Riley's the chef this year. He'll put a burn in your ears, but his stew is balm on your tongue. Tell you what, I'll get someone to watch my collection for a minute and go with you. I can always use another bowl."

With an anticipatory grin, Bill closed the lid of the display case. Junkyard laid a hand on his arm. "Wait a minute, Bill. I want to talk to you first. I assume you know Tin Can Petey is dead."

Bill's smile vanished and he nodded, his eyes growing hard. For the first time, Lennie could picture him as a train yard bull. "Word is, the Hobo Spider got him."

"That's right. Well, here's something you might not know," Junkyard said somberly. "Jungle Jim was there."

The pink drained from Bill's face. "My God. I thought there were never witnesses. Did Jim actually see the killer?"

"No. He'd left Petey alone for a few minutes. When he came back, Petey was—well, you know how this killer operates. Jim's pretty upset about it. I thought you should know."

Bill nodded, but it seemed to Lennie that he hadn't really heard. His eyes glazed, as if he no longer saw them or the display case, or even the tent village. Then he blinked and his hands clenched into thick-fingered fists.

"That's fourteen, Doug. And we're no closer to catching the guy. Unless…"

Sweat glistened on his large, amiable face. He glanced at Lennie, then back to Junkyard, lowering his voice. "Did you learn anything new?"

"No. But I'm sure as hell not going to let Jungle Jim be number fifteen. Look, Lennie and I have some things to do. Can you watch over Jim, make sure he gets to the poetry reading if we don't get back before then?"

"Sure. Yeah. I can do that. He can stay at my house tonight, too. That's the least I can do." He dragged a sleeve across his forehead. "Jeez, he might have been killed! Maybe I should go check on him."

"Wait—Mr. Sutter?" Lennie hated to interrupt, but she didn't want her father to be number fifteen, either. "Junkyard tells me you're with the railroad police. You've probably met a lot of hobos, right?"

Bill looked at her with mild surprise. "Yeah, quite a few over the years. Not all of them were glad to meet me, though—eh, Doug?"

Junkyard's face went deadpan. "Whatever you say, Mr. Sutter, sir."

A hint of Bill's earlier smile returned. "Why do you ask?"

"My dad disappeared ten years ago. When my mother—"

Damn, would she ever be able to talk about her mother without her throat closing up? She swallowed hard. "I recently found out that my father might have become a hobo. Maybe you've seen him?"

She handed Bill the photograph. He studied it a long time. For so long, he didn't seem to be seeing the photo anymore. The odd, glazed look returned. Finally, he blinked and she could see fear in his eyes, but he said nothing, just let his gaze roam nervously over her face. Then he seemed to reach a decision.

"That's—" He paused and took a breath. "I think he's—"

The wails of an injured child cut him off. He froze, listening, but the crying stopped. "That sounded like Ashley!"

He looked so alarmed that Lennie felt a stab of sympathetic fear. He brushed past her and rushed around the side of the tent. "Where did she go?"

He took a couple of steps and hesitated, looking frantically around. Tents blocked the view in every direction. A hint of panic entered his voice. "She could be anywhere."

"We saw her just a couple of minutes ago, back the way we came. I doubt she went far." Junkyard cut through a row of exhibits and looked down the next lane over. "In fact, here she comes now," he called. "Jim's giving her a piggy back ride."

"Thank God." Blinking rapidly, Bill ran a hand over his balding scalp. An odd mixture of relief and pain crossed his face. He pulled a handkerchief from his pocket and mopped his forehead, then wiped his nose. Jungle Jim arrived a moment later with Ashley on his back. He let her slide down to the ground and she clung to his hand, her face red and scrunched up to hold back her tears. At the sight of her father, she began to cry again.

"Daddy! I hurt my knee!"

She let go of Jim and rushed to Bill, wrapping skinny arms around his waist. He stroked her hair. "Uh oh," he said gently.

"You're not supposed to do that! Let's see the damage."

Ashley let go and stepped back, displaying an ugly scrape just below the knee. Blood trickled down her shin and into her white ankle sock. Bill bent over the injury and frowned. "Now, Ashley," he said in mock disapproval, "how many times have I told you, the blood's supposed to stay on the *inside* of the skin. This calls for strong medicine."

Then he kissed her knee above the scrape and gathered the half-giggling, half-sobbing girl in his arms. He held her, eyes closed, like he felt her small pain a hundred times over.

Lennie watched impatiently. She didn't want to interrupt the father-daughter moment, but Bill seemed to have forgotten her father's photograph and she was sure he had recognized it.

As if sensing her dilemma, Jungle Jim said, "Say, Missy, did you show Bill your daddy's picture yet? 'Cause he knows just about everyone from here to Mississippi."

Lennie gave Jim a grateful smile. "Yeah, I did. He was just about to tell me something."

"What about it, Bill?" Junkyard said. "Do you know where he is?"

The fear returned to Bill's eyes. He kissed the top of Ashley's head and didn't respond for a long time. Finally, he thrust the photograph at Lennie.

"Sorry, never saw him before." He didn't meet her eyes.

His voice was bland, but his hand shook when Lennie took the picture from him. He knew something. She was certain of it. "But you—you..."

What could she say without accusing him of lying?

"Look, I'd love to talk some more," he said, still avoiding her eyes, "but I've gotta get Ashley cleaned up. Bandages, Neosporin— you know. Jim, would you mind staying with my display for a few minutes?"

Without waiting for an answer, he strode off through the tent village with Ashley in his arms.

Lennie watched him, stunned. No one spoke until he was out of sight. Junkyard looked as baffled as she was. "What the hell was that?"

"I don't know, but I'm gonna find out." She started after Bill, but Junkyard stepped in her way.

"Not now. He's obviously upset. Let's come back later and talk to him someplace more private." His eyes narrowed at her speculatively. "Bill's as solid as they come, though. I'd like to know what's got him so spooked. Is there something you're not telling me?"

What could she say? You know that mythical character, Ramblin' Red? The one that magically disappeared? Well, somehow he put my Dad's pocket watch in my hand while I was sleeping right under your nose. Or maybe you'd like to know about this new tattoo of mine, or the way that gangbanger's eyes glowed yellow. Yeah, that could be important.

"No," she said, dropping her gaze. She felt like crying. "No, there's not."

The doors opened at Mariucci Arena, where fragile model train dioramas and the more valuable, easily damaged, or less mobile displays of railroad memorabilia were housed. Railroad buffs streamed inside for a glimpse of the old railroad days and to add to their collections. Across the street, security removed the sawhorses from the carnival entrance. The rides groaned to life, gears crying for lubrication. People trickled through the entrance, dispersing throughout the tent village or crossing the lot to reach the rides before the lines grew too long.

The Greater Midwest Railroad Days were officially open.

And amidst the noise and bustle, invisible to human eyes, a shadow erupted like an oozing boil in the blacktopped pavement of the parking lot. A vague sense of revulsion imbued those who approached the apparently vacant area, and they automatically veered around it. Children straying into its aura ran to their mothers, crying from unknown fears. Even the birds and insects would not fly over the shadow.

Within its depths stood three figures—two human and the one who made the shadow. One of the humans, a gangbanger with a freshly stitched injury on one arm and a tattoo of a happy-sad theater mask on the other, fidgeted uneasily and rubbed his arms as though the clinging darkness burned his skin.

The other human, an older man, was bent nearly double, as though someone had punched him in the stomach. The top of his head was as smooth as a tonsure, with a fringe of gray hair drooping from his temples in lank strings. He stared at the ground with hollow eyes, his face locked in an expression of abject horror. He would not move unless ordered to do so.

The shadow maker himself looked as human as the other two. He looked like a businessman in his tailored suit, high-collared white shirt, and narrow tie. The black curls on his head were cut short and neat, and a trim black beard covered his broad face. But his eyes glinted yellow as he studied the carnival grounds, and blackness streamed from him like smoke from a fire.

He made the shadow, but that was all he made. In all else, he was a destroyer.

He was also immortal, or nearly so, though this body was human. The original owner had been called Angus Cook, a name lost decades ago. The shadow maker who now owned this body was Fenrir, Hrodvitnir of old. In this time and place, he was called El Lobo.

The body would not grow old or die so long as he inhabited it, though it could be killed, releasing Fenrir in his true form. But humanity was not ready for that. For now, he preferred to remain a man.

Fenrir touched the minds of any who passed. Ordinary minds for the most part. But a simple twist turned admiration into envy; a small push turned anger into rage or hatred into murder. Those he touched would take home small bits of violence. By the end of the day, pockets of chaos would break out around the city.

All to the good. His lip curled, exposing unnaturally long, sharp teeth. The festival attracted thousands of tourists, but more importantly, it attracted railroad workers from all over the country, from all levels of the industry. A push here and a twist there would create chaos on a broader scale, perhaps not as economically crippling as it would have been decades before, but damaging nonetheless.

The festival also attracted a darker type. The hobos came for the free meals and the chance for glamour in an otherwise grim life. The homeless and bums came to beg, their minds weak with hunger or booze. The drug addicts and gangs came to deal, to fight, to steal anything that could be sold.

Fear came easily to such. They were his slaves. They and others like them had spread from city to city, where they fed like termites on the pillars of civilization.

But such minor destruction was more of an afterthought. It was not why he had come to the festival.

He was nearly ready.

One or two small details to attend to, and then he could destroy the fate that had imprisoned him in prophecy. He awaited one of those details, now—One-Eye's latest pawn. He felt his pockets and pulled out a pack of cigarettes. If the body was now his, so were the body's habits. He sucked down a mouthful of smoke and studied the festival's activities with a hint of a frown.

Once before, he had been nearly ready. If not for the interference of one insignificant human—a soft and weak specimen, at that—he would have brought this world to ruin years ago. He turned baleful, yellow eyes on the shriveled man beside him and drove a spike of shadow deep into his mind. The man's limbs spasmed, but his expression didn't change.

There would be no such interference, this time.

The Ragman, as the gangbanger liked to call himself, laid a hand on Fenrir's arm. Fenrir stiffened, suppressing an urge to turn on his presumptuous underling and feed on his flesh. The burning yellow of his eyes tinted the Ragman's face. The gangbanger jerked his hand away, but he didn't cower as others might. "It's them, El Lobo. The girl with the tattoo, like I tol' you."

Fenrir forced back the blood lust and studied the woman and man crossing the parking lot. The man wore a bandana and a jean jacket studded with buttons. His mind sizzled with intense emotions barely held in check by an iron will. But even the stoutest will could be broken.

Ordinarily, Fenrir would have found use for such a mind, but he was far more interested in the woman. Slender and small, even for a human female, she didn't look like much of a threat. Signs of strain showed in her face and a confused tangle of emotions rode the surface of her mind. One-Eye must have grown desperate, sending such a champion against the Wolf. He sent a dark tendril of shadow toward her. She would be crushed as easily as her predecessor.

CHAPTER EIGHT

Lennie slowed and looked back toward the tent village. "What if Bill leaves?"

Junkyard kept walking toward the Festival's jungle. "He won't. He looks forward to this festival all year. It's his best chance to pick up new badges for his collection."

"Besides," he added, smiling, "I know where he lives."

His assurances gave Lennie little comfort. After ten years of wondering what happened to her father, she had finally found someone—a *real* person—who knew something about him. It was frustrating to have to walk away.

As they approached the jungle, a pressure began to build behind her eyes, and her tattooed skin began to prickle again. She rubbed the marks uneasily, wondering about dirty needles and infections. She stuffed the suspect hand in her pocket and her fingers found her father's watch.

"Dammit." She had no time to get sick, now. And she certainly had no time to coddle thickheaded railroad cops. Her father could be looking down a bronze blade right now.

She rubbed her eyes. The pressure in her head had grown into a dull pain, casting a yellow pall over everything. And something was watching her. She could feel it getting closer. The hairs on the nape of her neck lifted as though tickled by hot breath. She whirled around, but no one was behind her. A slick film of sweat coated her face. She licked her lips, tasting salt.

Junkyard had moved on without noticing she had fallen behind. Two children crossed his path, screeching like blue jays as they raced for the carnival. She tried to focus, but her thoughts kept turning back to Bill. Why couldn't he just tell her what he knew? She had to find her father before the serial killer got to him.

She had to find out why he'd abandoned her.

Bill was the key, and he was deliberately holding back. She was certain of it. And the more she thought about it, the angrier she became. She wanted to hit him, make him hurt, feel the pain that she felt.

He'd talk. She'd make him talk.

The world blurred yellow and she pictured herself shouting at Bill, tearing down his tent, smashing his meaningless display. What could a collection of police badges mean to a coward? If Bill knew something, she'd get it out of him.

A woman herding a group of chattering school children toward the carnival looked into Lennie's face and gasped. Pulling the smallest child close, the woman hustled her charges away. Lennie hardly saw them. A memory came, unbidden, from the day after her father had disappeared—the first time she saw her mother drunk. She'd come home from school to find her mother passed out on the floor, a bottle of amaretto leaking into the carpet beside her. Lennie had tried to move her, but she couldn't. And there was no one to help her.

She was eleven years old. Only eleven.

She remembered sitting on the couch and staring at the sprawled body of her mother, crying until her eyes and nose grew hot and puffy. Drained, hiccupping, she wiped her face on her sleeve, covered her mother with a blanket, and mopped at the carpet with a beach towel. The sweet alcoholic stench stayed in the house for a week.

That was her father's fault. It was *all* his fault. And he would answer for it, every last pain and humiliation. But to find him, she had to make Bill talk.

She took an uncertain step back toward the tent village. Her body trembled with a growing need for violence. She wanted to give in to that need, but part of her knew something was very wrong.

The tattoo burned as though building an electrical charge. Hardly aware of what she was doing, she pulled her father's watch from her pocket and flipped it open. *For Jarvis*, it said. She tried to remember her father's face. Not faded and frozen in time, as it was in the photograph. Not the haggard transient she imagined he had become. A living, breathing face that smiled at her. One that loved her.

Electric fire surged from the tattoo. Her fingers convulsed on the watch. The small bones in her hand vibrated as though they caged a thousand wasps. The vibrations swarmed up her arm.

The pressure in her head vanished.

Light-headed, she swayed with the sudden release. Her vision cleared. Everything looked so ordinary. Not yellow at all. The Ferris wheel clattered and groaned, slowly rolling nowhere. The sweet, greasy smell of funnel cakes wafted on the light breeze. Her stomach rumbled, but that was all she felt. The anger had faded and the tension of restrained violence was gone.

The tattoo had returned to normal, as well. Just a thing of skin and ink. With wonder, she traced a trembling finger around its three interlocking triangles. What the hell just happened?

A hand closed on her shoulder. She jumped and twisted away. It took her a moment to realize it was just Junkyard.

"Sorry, didn't mean to startle you. You all right?" He looked into her face more closely and frowned. "Jeez, you're sweating. You'd better sit down."

"No, that's okay. I'm just, uh…" Her stomach rumbled again. "I'm—I'm just hungry. I guess that snack cake didn't quite do it for me."

"Easy enough. We'll get you a bowl of Bones's stew. Then you can show your dad's picture around."

Lennie nodded and let him lead her toward the jumble of boxes that made up the jungle exhibit. Her legs felt shaky. Sitting seemed like a fine idea. So did the stew. Good thing it wasn't a long walk.

Deep inside the carnival, the giant snake came to life and chased its tail around its track.

At first glance, the festival's jungle exactly matched Lennie's image of a real hobo jungle: a warren of makeshift cardboard hovels, reinforced with plastic.

A huge maple tree growing in the nearby landscaping provided shelter from the sun. A blue plastic tarp hung over a branch, anchored by cement blocks. A cook fire burned underneath. A log had been dragged next to the fire to act as a bench.

The jungle seemed believable, but something was off. It took Lennie a moment to realize what. Everything was clean. The cardboard boxes and the wooden crates had never been touched by rain. The fire burned in a rust-free rod-iron fire ring, and the ends of the log bench were freshly and evenly cut. Even the asphalt looked recently swept.

Still, the expected smells were there. Faint whiffs of stale alcohol, old sweat, and wood smoke mingled with the usual parking lot odors of motor oil and tar. Someone had left a battered guitar leaning against the log bench. Its face was scarred and dull. A dirty, red wool blanket draped over the log beside it. Otherwise, the jungle seemed deserted.

"Where is everyone?" Lennie said.

Junkyard shrugged. He seemed more interested in the pot hanging over the fire. "They're around somewhere." He leaned over the pot, rubbed his hands together, and picked up the ladle. "Want some stew?"

A steamy, onion smell drifted above the less pleasant odors. Her mouth began to water. Before she could answer, a husky voice roared at them. "Hey, git your grubby mitts outta that stew. Payin' customers only!"

A woman unfolded from an ancient pick-up truck parked on the other side of the boxes. She fixed Junkyard with a hard gaze and stretched upright, so skeletally thin that Lennie thought she might rattle when she walked. She was several inches taller than Junkyard and her maroon down vest didn't reach the top of her jeans. A purple t-shirt pooched out between the vest and a tightly cinched macramé belt. A fedora sat on her bleached-blond hair like a turtle on a hay-mound.

Junkyard ignored her. He gave the pot a stir and lifted the ladle toward his mouth. The truck door slammed, releasing a shower of rust and dirt.

"Tetch any o' that stew and die, Junkyard," the woman said, except "die" came out as "dah." Wherever she came from was way south of Iowa.

Junkyard stiffened and dropped the ladle, which missed the pot and hit the pavement with a bounce. He raised his hands high and turned with exaggerated slowness. "Easy, now. You're not gonna shoot me, are you?"

A corner of his mouth twitched.

The woman frowned. "Oh, hush-up and give me a hug, scoundrel." She crossed the jungle in three long strides and wrapped vine-like arms around him.

"Hello, Soo," Junkyard said, his voice muffled by her shoulder. "I swear, woman, you could take a nap on a rail and have room to roll over. Why don't you eat something for a change?"

"Just killed me a possum this mornin'." Stepping back, she slapped her concave belly and smiled in satisfaction. "Ate the whole thang m'self."

Junkyard looked her over. "You should have eaten two. And what the heck did you do to your hair?"

"Nothin'. Ah heard y'all were comin' and it turned this color all on its own."

They grinned at each other like cats eyeing a favorite toy. Watching them play, Lennie felt some of her tension and fear ease. That horrible spell in the parking lot began to fade like a hazy, yellow nightmare.

"Glad y'all could make it, Junkyard," Soo said. "Ah git tired of the usual crowd. All spit an' no polish."

Lennie couldn't resist. "If he's the polish, I'd hate to see the spit."

Bad impulse. Both heads swiveled in her direction. Junkyard's eyes widened and he gave a little whistle that made her wish she could turn invisible. Grinning too wide for her comfort, he said, "Lennie, I'd like you to meet Too Long Soo, the best guitar player and biggest mouth on the FRC Railroad. Careful you don't cut yourself on her wit."

Soo ignored Junkyard and eyed Lennie critically, taking in her dirt-streaked shirt, staring especially hard at her thin canvas shoes. Lennie felt like a frog in the shadow of a blue heron.

"Interestin' choice of friends, y'got there, Junkyard. You didn't take 'er on the road dressed like *that*, didja?"

"Nah, she caught onto a moving train all by herself, wearing those. I'm just trying to get her home in one piece."

Now Lennie was irritated. He had made that point one time too many. "Quit talking about me like I'm lost luggage. I keep telling you, it was an accident!"

Soo raised an eyebrow and pursed her lips, taking her time to respond. "You *accident'ly* caught onto a movin' train? What, y'all were just standin' by the tracks, mindin' yer own business, and next thing you knew…"

"That's not what I…" Lennie began, but there was too much to tell, too many reasons, and none of them made sense, even to her.

Junkyard took pity on her. "Hey, don't mind Soo. She treats everyone like dirt." He reached up and bumped the back of Soo's hat, knocking it over her eyes. "I'd be more worried if she were nice to you."

"It's not that. It's just all…"

Words wouldn't come. Suddenly she felt tired. Ten years' worth of tired, and the last day had nearly put her over the edge. She just wanted to do nothing, think nothing, for at least a week. She looked at the ground, letting loose curls hide her face.

Frowning, Soo shoved her hat back on her head. "Never you mind, sweetie. My mouth runs like a monkey after a banana wagon."

She took Lennie by the arm and led her to the makeshift bench by the fire. "Are y'all hungry?" She rolled her eyes toward Junkyard. "Ah bet y'ain't had nothin' but Ho-Hos an' Twinkies since you got on that train."

Junkyard looked offended. "Hey, they've got nutritional content—"

"Fat, sugar, and preservatives cain't keep the blood flowin' smooth. Now sit down, girl, and Ah'll dish y'up some of Bones O'Riley's finest mulligan stew. We'll hear your story all in good time."

Lennie sat gratefully and leaned closer to the flames, finding their warmth comforting. Soo retrieved the ladle from the ground. Grit caked its bowl. She shot a dirty look at Junkyard, but he was studiously examining the company logo on the side of a refrigerator box.

"Lucky fer you, I got another," she grumbled.

A moment later, Lennie held a steaming Styrofoam bowl in her hands. The beef-broth aroma of French onion soup filled her nose. The stew was loaded with meat cooked down to strings. She stirred it. Chunks of carrot and potato surfaced like sluggish fish. She burnt her mouth on the first spoonful.

Junkyard and Soo set up a folding table as she ate. She watched Junkyard move around the jungle, working efficiently, confidently, and with an easy, athletic grace. Nothing like the man she had followed through the University campus. Which one was the real Junkyard?

A spark popped in the fire, startling her, and she realized she had been staring. She looked away and found Soo's intense gaze centered on her. Embarrassed, Lennie's face grew warm. She pointed at her bowl.

"Stew sure is hot."

Soo's expressive eyebrows gave a visual snicker. "Fire does have a way of warmin' things up."

"It tastes really good, though," Lennie said, trying to distract her. "Bones O'Riley must be some kind of gourmet chef."

"Bones? A chef?" Some of the toughness left Soo's face and she chuckled. Unlike her speaking voice, which was hoarse and dry, her laugh sang out in a rich, musical alto. "Oh, that's a hoot. Ah think it's time y'all met the boys."

She rang the ladle against the pot like a dinner bell. "Hey, Bones! Hotshot! Git out here!"

A hollow thump shook a dryer box lying on its side nearby. A muffled voice grumbled, "Yeah, yeah, whaddaya want, already?"

"Come on out, boys, Junkyard's here."

There was no further movement. Soo winked at Lennie. "He brought a girl with him, 'n' she's got a story to tell us." She paused, listening to the silence, then added, "She's purty."

Junkyard stopped working and watched the box with a grin. It shook and swayed with a lot of thumping and scraping sounds. Finally, a bald head popped out of the open end. Frowning, the man blinked blearily at Lennie and wormed out on his hands and knees. Still frowning, he brushed himself off and headed for the fire. Lennie made room for him on her log, but he chose to stand with his eyes down, flicking furtive glances that didn't quite reach her face.

"This here cue ball is Hotshot Bob," Soo said. "He comes all the way from Oregon."

He glanced up, like he expected Lennie to say something.

"Hello, Bob," she tried. "Or, um, Hotshot. Hotshot Bob."

He gave a brief, weak smile, then his face fell back into a frown. That must be his natural expression, Lennie decided. His cheeks just sag that way. He scooped the red blanket from the log and headed for the stew pot. As he passed by, his foot caught the guitar. It toppled with a jangle.

"Woody!" Soo flung the ladle at the pot and dove for the guitar as if Hotshot Bob had dropped a baby. The ladle hit the lip of the pot and rattled on the pavement behind her, forgotten.

"Shee-it!" She examined the guitar with her long nose so close she might have been sniffing for blood. Her pencil-like fingers stroked the battered wood as if to comfort it. Finding no new dings, she sat back on her haunches and looked Hotshot Bob up and down.

"Yer one lucky sonuvabitch, ye didn't hurt 'im. This ol' guitar," she pronounced it *GEE tar*, "has been played by the hand that wrote some of the greatest road songs ever. Mr. Woody Guthrie, himself. His signature's right there, near the end of the fingerboard."

Behind her, Junkyard lip-synced her words as if she had said the exact same thing a hundred times before. Soo turned on him sharply. "As fer *you*…"

He was saved when the side of the wooden crate nearest the fire fell open with a loud smack. A heavily bearded man with dark, matted hair crawled out.

"Woody, my ass," he growled. "More like wood scrap. You ask me, that piece of junk looks like it's been beaten more than played."

"Nobody asked you, ya big galoot." Soo gave the guitar a final pat and set it down. "Lennie, this here's Bones O'Riley, the Happy Chef. No one goes hungry when he's around."

"Especially himself," Junkyard added. He looked pointedly at Bones's midsection, which spilled out the sides of his grimy overalls.

Bones labored to his feet and stumped over to the stew pot. Lennie thought he might help himself to a bowl. Instead, he leaned close, waved the steam toward his nose, and sniffed. Apparently, he didn't like the smell. He gagged, letting his tongue hang out. "Who threw their stinking socks into my stew?"

"Stew's fine, Bones." Junkyard assumed an innocent expression that Lennie didn't trust at all. "In fact, Lennie thinks you must be a gourmet chef. What do you say to that?"

The little bit of skin showing between Bones's beard and eyes turned red. He glared at Junkyard and then at Lennie.

"Ignorant bitch."

Lennie flinched. She began a sharp response, but Junkyard's wink stopped her. Bones paced between them and the pot, grumbling and throwing his hands up.

"Damn meat's too tough. Not enough onions, either. And I'll crap up a tree if there's any fresh sage to be found in this butt-hole of a town. Potatoes as wrinkled as my grandma's ass. Carrots as flaccid as a castrate's dick…you call that stew good, and you deserve to have your taste buds peeled."

The more Bones talked the more agitated he became, and the more colorful his word choice. Lennie stared at him in amazement.

He was literally frothing at the mouth, yet somebody actually considered him presentable enough to include in the festival's hobo exhibit.

Soo and Hotshot seemed unaffected, but when he drew a breath for another round, Junkyard stepped in and took him by the shoulder. "I know it's not your best effort, my friend, but those citizens—" Junkyard swung an arm toward the potential customers wandering among the exhibits and rides, "—they won't know the difference."

Mollified, Bones's grumbling faltered. He dropped down on the other end of Lennie's log and nearly jolted her from her seat. Crossing his arms over his belly, he stared at her as if she were a vegetable too rotten to add to his stew. Hotshot sat on a cement block near the fire and draped the red blanket over his shoulders. He sat motionless, staring at his feet.

"I think they're ready to hear your story," Junkyard said. Soo nodded and settled cross-legged on the ground next to the guitar.

"Oh. Right." Lennie dug the photograph from her pocket. Her throat tightened a little, as it always did when she looked at the photo. Her father grinned toothily, holding that little walleye out like it was the biggest fish in the world. The picture had been taken just one month before he left.

She passed the photo to Soo and folded her arms to hide her tattooed hand. It might be best to concentrate on her missing father and leave out the more...fantastic events.

"My father disappeared ten years ago," she began, and she told them the barest facts. They didn't need to know about the whiskey her mother added to her morning coffee and the half-pint of gin that finished her day, or the repo man and the unpaid medical bills. They certainly didn't need to know about the hours Lennie had spent in front of her bedroom mirror, thinking that, if she had been a boy,

vanish. His tailored suit and pressed shirt collapsed, disappearing before they hit the pavement. He felt the Ragman's astonishment, for a falcon sat on the ground where Fenrir had been. It fixed the Ragman with yellow eyes and opened its hooked beak. Then it stretched its wings and took flight.

The shadow dissipated with Fenrir's departure.

"What the fuck?" The Ragman had seen a lot, working for El Lobo, but this shit was the craziest, yet. Feeling exposed and uneasy, he eyed the hollow man, whose face shone with snot from nose to chin. All the stupid burro did was stare off into space. His brain had done a ghost long before the Ragman had ever seen him. In some ways, the sight of him put more fear into the gangbanger than El Lobo himself.

"What the hell you do to make El Lobo hate you so bad?"

The hollow man only blinked. One eyelid stuck, opening a few seconds after the other.

"*Chingao!*" The Ragman shuddered. "*Vato loco.*"

He set off at a fast walk to do as Fenrir ordered. He had no wish to earn himself the same fate.

A moment later, the hollow man's limbs came to a stilted, haphazard form of life. Face slack, eyes unfocused, he shuffled after the Ragman, moving as if powered by cogs and levers.

CHAPTER NINE

Briggs hung up the phone. Adrenaline slogged through his sleepy veins like an infusion of amphetamine. He had a name.

The Des Moines police had fumed a clean partial off the knife that killed Peter Olson. They'd found a match on AFIS. No guarantee that it belonged to the killer, but at least he had a name: James Tuttle. After almost a year of doing little but counting bodies, it was a start.

James Tuttle. The name nagged at Briggs's memory, but he couldn't place it without more information. He checked his e-mail impatiently. Nothing yet. He thumped the screen, willing a message to appear. The police were supposed to send him whatever NCIC had on the guy. He hated being at the mercy of other people's priorities, but his caboose office wasn't considered secure enough to house its own NCIC terminal. He'd have to wait.

He took a swig of coffee and reached for the nearest stack of files, thinking he might as well catch up on some paperwork. His cell phone rang before he could get started.

"Briggs here."

"This case has just gotten a whole lot weirder."

"Parker?"

"Yeah, it's me." The FBI agent sounded agitated. "I checked into that Butterfly Killer case you told me about. It's real, all right. Unsolved, too. The killer didn't leave any more evidence back in '42 than the Hobo Spider gives us now."

"Damn." As if this case wasn't slippery enough. "It can't be the same guy. An old geezer might have been able to catch one person by surprise, but we've got fourteen victims, here. Some of them are young guys."

"Yeah, well that's not all. That article you found didn't tell you everything. Guess what kind of knife the Butterfly Killer used."

Briggs blinked away images of a black handle protruding from Peter Olson's bloody face. He grimaced. "You gonna make me say it?"

"Black-handled, bronze blade, just like our friendly, neighborhood Hobo Spider. I put in a request for evidence on the Butterfly Killer case. If they kept any of that cord around, I'll get it tested."

Something thumped on the roof of the caboose. Briggs started and looked at the ceiling. Idiot squirrels. "What if it comes out the same? It's going to be hell cross-referencing our case against events that happened seventy years ago."

"Yeah, I might wish you'd never made the connection, but it's not like we have so many leads."

"There's that. But we do have one other. AFIS came back with a name on that latent."

Whatever had landed on the roof seemed to be hopping around, scratching at the metal. It left the roof with a scrape and something black fluttered past the window. A bird, then. A big one. He returned his gaze to the computer screen. An e-mail had arrived from the DMPD. "I'm about to check his criminal records. I'll let you know where they take me."

"Somewhere better than this, I hope."

"No shit."

Briggs hung up and leaned close to the screen. "Okay, Mr. Tuttle—let's see what kind of history you have."

Tuttle was in the system, but barely. No outstanding warrants, no convictions, not even a parking ticket. But his sister had reported him missing and mentally handicapped two days ago.

And there was a photograph.

Briggs sat back and whistled. He did know the guy. He called himself "Jungle Jim." A gentle fellow, though a bit goofy and definitely on the slow side. The expression "toys in the attic" might have been invented just for him. But Briggs had liked him. No way in hell could he be the killer. It just didn't fit. And yet…

This was the second time Jungle Jim Tuttle had been at the crime scene of a Hobo Spider murder. What were the odds of that, if he wasn't connected in some way?

Briggs remembered the day he had met Jungle Jim. It was early last fall. Summer had made a comeback, and the sun beat down on the Des Moines yards with enough heat to grill a hotdog on a rail. A foreman had called Briggs at the end of a long shift. He had found a body. From the sound of it, another victim of the Hobo Spider. Briggs was the first lawman on scene.

A slaughterhouse smell met him before he reached the boxcar. He gagged and held his handkerchief over his mouth and nose after he climbed on board. He stayed just inside the door and studied the scene, taking care not to move his feet or touch anything.

FBI reports from earlier cases had called the Hobo Spider murders "vaguely ritualistic." To Briggs, alone in the boxcar, staring at the thickened, red trails flowing from the victim's mouth like a macabre stream of consciousness, it looked like a blatant attempt to communicate with some grotesque god.

Blood coated the victim's chin and neck, but the cord that wrapped the body remained pristinely white. Flies covered the pool of blood drying on the floor and buzzed around the head, but not one landed on the cord.

Sweat stung Briggs's eyes. He wiped it away with his sleeve. The inside of the boxcar was even hotter than the outside and the body was degrading rapidly. Even so, it didn't seem possible that a fresh corpse could stink so much. His stomach churned. The smell reminded him of the time his dog had gotten loose and rolled in the carcass of a dead raccoon.

When the singing started outside, he gladly jumped out to see who it was. The hot breeze felt cool on his face. He pulled the handkerchief away and gulped air, clearing the smell from his nose.

A man wandered toward him down a siding, his cheeks rosy from the sun. He wore a battered fedora and an ill-fitting suit. His worn leather shoes looked much too large. He belted out his song in an absurdly beautiful tenor, adding a skip to his walk in time with the music. All he needed was a bindle on a stick and he might have stepped out of a Norman Rockwell painting.

The innocence of the man and the pure joy in his song contrasted jarringly with the horror inside the boxcar. There was a sense of evil and light in such close proximity that Briggs felt an irrational fear that darkness might ooze from the boxcar and overwhelm the guy. He knew with sudden certainty that he had to keep this one safe, at least.

The hobo strolled past Briggs, whistling now, with his hands stuffed in his pants pockets. His shoes had bicycle reflectors duct-taped to their heels.

"Hey, wait a minute." Briggs hurried after him. The hobo turned, unsurprised, though Briggs could have sworn the hobo hadn't seen him.

"Oh, it's you." The hobo smiled as though he had known Briggs all of his life. Normally, Briggs would have written the guy up for trespassing. Hobos were a danger to themselves and to others. But this time the idea never occurred to him. Instead, Briggs brought him back to the office to cool off, and fed him a Coke and a day-old donut. The man said his name was Jungle Jim and started babbling about his "kids."

"Oh, they just love my tricks," he said. "They come from miles all around, they do, when they hear ol' Jungle Jim's in town."

He went on, listing the children he had met and the cities they lived in. Briggs listened, puzzled, until Jungle Jim hauled his duffle bag onto his lap and began demonstrating an amazing array of props. There was a garish, over-sized bow tie that twirled at the tug of a string. There were silk flowers that disappeared into a narrow tube. There was a fake hand, presumably for handshaking, a rattlesnake that looked distressingly real, and a jar of Mexican jumping beans. Jungle Jim was either insane, or he was a performer of some kind. Possibly both. Either way, Briggs found that he liked the hobo a great deal. He couldn't let him ride the trains.

"So, where are you heading, Jim?" If it wasn't too far, Briggs could spring for a bus ticket.

"On up to Minni," Jungle Jim said around a bite of donut. Powdered sugar ringed his mouth. "My friend, Bill—he's a bull up there in that University yard. It's Ashley's birthday. She's his daughter. I got her an itty bitty doll house with ittier bittier people inside."

Suddenly it all made sense. Briggs had heard about the Minneapolis yard worker who got his brains scrambled saving a bull's life. He had become sort of an unofficial mascot to the FRC Railroad Company. This had to be the guy—there couldn't be two like him. Might as well let him ride the train and save the bus fare. The engineer would probably let him sit up front. He'd be safe enough up there.

Briggs escorted Jungle Jim to a train bound for Minneapolis, made up and ready to leave. The engineer grinned when he saw Jungle Jim and offered him a seat. The roar of the idling engine made conversation difficult, so Briggs just waved and turned to go. A tap on his shoulder stopped him. He looked back into Jungle Jim's face. Something about the hobo's eyes had changed, grown clearer, and his expression had grown serious.

"Don't feel bad, Harcourt." Briggs heard him clearly over the noise, though Jungle Jim didn't appear to be shouting. "I know you're gonna do your best. There's just nuthin' you or anyone can do."

And then he was gone, back inside the unit. Briggs considered following him up the stairs to find out what he meant, but the engine shifted louder, shaking the ground beneath his feet. Briggs stepped back and watched it pull away, but all he could think about was the strange stillness in Jungle Jim's eyes.

He hadn't seen Jungle Jim since. The presence of his fingerprints on a murder weapon worried him. If he wasn't the killer, he could be a witness and therefore the next target. Briggs had to find him, and quickly. Assuming he was still alive.

That left one problem: How to find Jungle Jim. People vanished on the iron road every day, intentionally or otherwise. It could take weeks to track him down. He might never find him at all.

Briggs reviewed everything he knew about the hobo, starting with the fact that he wasn't really a hobo at all. He was a clown. If he remembered rightly, Jim's "kids" came from Midwestern cities in FRC railroad territory. A company man, even after he quit working for the company.

He pulled his keyboard closer. After a quick search, he found three festivals occurring this weekend in FRC Railroad territory: The Britt Draft Horse Show in Iowa, the Greater Midwest Railroad Days in Minneapolis, and Pioneer Days in Altoona, Kansas. All three had web sites, none of which listed Jungle Jim as an attraction. But that didn't mean he wouldn't show up.

Briggs ignored a growing sense of futility and studied the FRC Railroad map plastered on his office wall. Thirteen red pushpins dotted the map. He added a fourteenth close to Topeka. Not that the location of the victims meant anything. Most of them were found on train cars and may have traveled for days before discovery.

But it was clear that, like Jungle Jim, the Hobo Spider showed a preference for FRC Railroad.

Britt, Minneapolis, Altoona. Which one?

Britt was popular with the hobos, but it seemed unlikely that a clown would perform at a horse show. So…Altoona or Minneapolis?

Six of the bodies had been found in Minneapolis—two of them off-train in rail yards. Minneapolis was the biggest hub for the FRC Railroad. Maybe it was the Hobo Spider's personal hub, too.

He reached for the phone, ready to call the Minneapolis police. Then he sighed and let his hand drop to the desk. He drummed his fingers. This was ridiculous. There could be a dozen festivals within 90 miles of Minneapolis that weren't advertised on the Internet. Jungle Jim might not even be performing this weekend. Maybe he was shacking up in a cardboard box in Missouri, doing a little fishing on the Mississippi.

He ought to give Parker a call and make use of FBI resources. He should contact the officials of all the likely festivals. He should notify the police departments of cities in the FRC territory…put out an APB on Jungle Jim throughout the region. He should—

"You'd be wastin' your time, boy."

Briggs jerked upright. "What the hell?"

He hadn't heard the door open, hadn't heard footsteps on the hardwood floor, but a strange old man stood close enough to his desk to brush it with his fingertips. He wore a peaked, wide-brimmed hat over faded red hair. A dark blue overcoat draped over his shoulders like a cloak.

Definitely eccentric. Briggs didn't have time for this.

"Look, I'm busy. Why don't you step over to Human Services."

Briggs waved vaguely to the south. "I'm sure someone there can help you."

The stranger didn't move. Briggs sighed. So much for the friendly approach. "Scram, Grandpa. I've got important phone calls to make."

The man answered as calmly as if Briggs had politely asked him for clarification. "I said, you'd be wastin' your time. You wanna find Jungle Jim, there's only one place t'look."

Startled, Briggs pushed back from his computer and glowered at the stranger. "How the hell do you know about that?" He didn't wait for an answer. "I haven't known about Tuttle for five minutes and you waltz in telling me you know where he is? Look, buddy, I'm in no mood for games. Who are you? What do you know?"

"Enough!" The air crackled around the stranger. His overcoat billowed as if lifted by a stiff wind.

Briggs's mouth snapped shut. The door must have blown open—it *had* to be open. He shot a glance at the door. It remained stubbornly closed. Yet the stranger's coat flapped and his hair fluttered around his face in the perfectly still air.

Reluctantly, Briggs felt his gaze drawn to the man's heavily lined face, to a single, clear blue eye. He felt its touch like ice on his brain and tried to look away, but couldn't make his eyes work right. He tried to stand, to reach the phone, to do anything. He couldn't move. He could only stare into that terrible blue gaze.

"They call me the Wanderer." The stranger's voice changed, growing deeper and more formal. "All I ask is that you listen."

As if Briggs had a choice. He focused all his strength on his right hand, just inches from the upper right desk drawer. He kept a gun there in case someone he was questioning did something unexpected. He couldn't think of anything more unexpected than this. Except he couldn't get his hand to move.

"Nice trick, Gandalf," he growled, "but if you don't knock it off, I'll—"

The stranger's eye flared like blue lightening, stunning Briggs into silence. A blue haze bathed the caboose, softening the file cabinets, the stacks of paper, and the hard edges of Briggs's desk. It seemed to seep into his very thoughts, softening those as well. Briggs stopped fighting. His muscles relaxed and he forgot whatever empty threats he was about to make.

"Your first instinct was correct," a voice said. "Jungle Jim is at the festival in Minneapolis. He will be at the hobo moot. If you do not seek him there tonight, he will pass out of your reach forever."

Caught by that bright orb, Briggs no longer saw the stranger. Memory of the visit evaporated in a blue mist. When he spoke, he was talking to himself.

"Jungle Jim did say he had a friend in Minneapolis." His tongue felt thick and heavy. "That bull at the University yards. Might be worth checking, anyway."

The blue faded and disappeared. Briggs was alone in the caboose. As far as he could remember, he'd been alone all morning. He grabbed his train schedule and scanned it for a ride to Minneapolis. There was only one train going out today, slated to leave in twenty minutes. He vaulted from his chair, then clutched his head, suddenly dizzy. He was more exhausted than he had realized.

"Got no time for that." He grabbed his thermos and, grimacing, chugged the cold dregs of his morning coffee. Poor substitute for a nap. A shower might be nice, but he would have to settle for a clean shirt. He undid the top two buttons of the sweaty, coffee-stained denim shirt that he'd been wearing for forty hours straight, pulled it over his head and threw it in a corner. The bottom drawer of his desk held more clothes than his closet at home. Some of them were even clean. He yanked it open and found a denim shirt, pre-buttoned except for the top two buttons, and gave it a sniff. Not too bad. He pulled it on.

Unlocking another desk drawer, he drew out a .40 caliber semi-automatic. Good, but good enough? He hesitated, then selected a .38 revolver and strapped it to his ankle.

It took him a full minute to find his Kevlar vest, which was hanging on the coat rack under his windbreaker. Ransacking his office, he shoved everything else he might need into a leather grip.

Seven minutes to make the train. That clock had better not be slow.

Outside, wheels shrieked against air brakes. He shoved the grip under his arm and burst through the caboose door. As he turned to lock up, his keys tumbled from nervous fingers and rang down the metal steps to the ground. He stared at them, unmoving.

Wasn't he going to call someone? Parker?

And hadn't there been someone…a man in his office?

He turned the handle and slowly opened the door. The room was empty. The phone lines were quiet. But he felt like he was being watched.

A harsh scream sounded behind him. He whipped around and the world flashed blue. A wave of vertigo hit him. He leaned against the doorframe and shook his head to clear it. I must be more tired than I thought. Guess I can sleep on the train.

He scanned the tracks near his caboose. The yard's grounds were deserted. The cry came again, sounding less human this time. Just a crow or something, he decided, rubbing his temples. Must be nearby, or he would never have heard it over the train noise.

He poked his head back into the caboose. As he had thought, the lights were still on. Good thing he'd checked–they might have stayed on for days. His gaze fell on the wall clock as he reached for the switch. Less than five minutes before departure. He would have to run. He took one last, bemused glance around the room, flicked off the lights, and closed the door.

As he sprinted toward the tracks, a raven took off from the roof of the caboose and began its own journey north.

CHAPTER TEN

Junkyard played pinball as if he were wrestling a steer. He yanked the machine back and forth, bumping and straining against it. The pinball table shook and two of its legs jumped from the floor. Lennie leaned on the bar behind him, wondering if he intended to flip it on its back. She sipped her beer and grinned. She wasn't sure what effect he was having on the ball, but she sure enjoyed the show.

"You're lucky that machine's got a high tilt threshold—if it has one at all."

She had to shout to be heard, even though she stood less than five feet behind him. A group of college students had gathered around a nearby table to play some kind of drinking game involving dice, a cup, and lots of laughter. Junkyard ignored the noise and slammed his hip against the machine.

"Don't bother me. I'm playing multiball."

He had brought Lennie to the Dinkytown bar to kill time until the poetry reading, though she suspected he had chosen this particular place to avoid the Ragman and the BRR. Gangbangers would stand out like sharks in a goldfish pond in a college bar. After a night in a boxcar and a morning spent in the company of hobos, entering the bar felt like crossing into another world. Feeling safe for the first time in twenty-four hours, she let herself relax, though she couldn't stop herself from glancing back at the door whenever it opened.

Junkyard's head bobbed as he tried to follow several balls at once. The balls flew wildly around the table, pinging off bumpers and each other so quickly that he could do little more than keep them in play. A drop of sweat rolled down his cheek. He hunched a shoulder against his face to wipe it away. In that instant, four balls shot dead-center for the exit. Expletives peppered the air over the tabletop. The last of the balls drained despite the heroic wrench he delivered to the machine.

"Damn!" He slammed a flat hand down on the glass top. "I really hate it when that happens. I was only fifty thousand points from a high score, too."

Lennie chuckled. Good thing he didn't panic like that around gangbangers. "Not much glory there, anyway. I bet they unplug the machine every night and wipe out the top scores. Some drunk freshman probably posted high score half an hour ago."

He glared and waved her toward the machine. "Okay, bigshot. If that's such a crummy score, let's see if you can beat it."

She brushed past him and planted her hands on the front corners of the table. She made a great show of studying the score. "I don't know," she said slowly, "I'll have to score more than twice my first two balls put together to beat you. Still—" she shot a glance over her shoulder, "–would you care to make a little wager?"

He raised an eyebrow. "Such as?"

"Breakfast tomorrow." Her stomach gurgled pathetically and curled in on itself at the thought of the fruit pies and snack cakes waiting in his duffle bag. "Something healthy. Grapefruit, maybe. Some cereal—or better yet, some eggs."

Junkyard made a sour face. "Okay, whatever you want. But if I win, you have to sit in the Laundromat and watch my clothes spin while I go take care of a few things."

"Deal!"

She turned back to the machine. Lights blinked all over the table. Another strike in a number of places would send her score climbing. She put her hand on the plunger. Junkyard crowded behind her, looking over her shoulder. She fidgeted, uncomfortably aware of his presence. "Do you mind? A little room please?"

"Oh. Sorry, Maestro."

He moved to the side of the machine and watched her expectantly. That wasn't much better. She frowned. She wasn't usually so easily distracted. *Out of practice, I guess.*

Sticking a pinky out like a lady drinking tea, she pulled the plunger back a measured distance. Junkyard's snickers penetrated the din. Then she let go and the ball raced up a chute that had eluded him throughout the game. The ball dropped into a pit and rattled off points. His snickers died with a grunt.

"Hey, how'd you do that!"

Lennie smirked. She wiped her hands on her jeans, rested her palms on the edge of the machine, and waited, feeling the familiar buttons under her fingers. The ball popped back into play, rebounded off the walls, lost speed, and rolled toward the exit. She caught it neatly on a flipper.

"Maybe I should have mentioned," she said, letting the ball ease down the flipper, "the girls from my track club liked to hang out at malls between events at out-of-town meets. I spent all my time in the arcade instead of shopping with everyone else."

After her father had gone, there had been no money for extras. She could play for a long time on fifty cents and no one expected her to buy anything.

With a snap of the wrist, she flicked the ball through a lighted gate. A knock sounded from inside the table. Extra ball. A few well-placed shots sent the ball circling around the track. The multiball light flashed on. She nailed it first try and smiled. Multiball was good.

Balls streamed onto the table in a mercurial flood. Junkyard hovered over the glass top watching the score climb by large increments, his moans of dismay almost lost in the noise of a boisterous pack of university students pouring into the bar. Lennie shut out the noise and worked the controls with the precision of a racecar driver. She had never tilted a machine in her life. When it was over, the display boasted high score and the *free game* indicator blinked an invitation at her.

The bar erupted with cheers—a guy in a Minnesota Gophers hoody had won the drinking game. Lennie turned and bowed as though the applause were for her. When she straightened, Junkyard glowered at her with his arms crossed.

"You were sandbagging."

She pointed at herself, wide-eyed. "Me? Oh, no. It just takes me a while to warm up."

He scowled. "Come off it. I never would have agreed to that bet if you'd played like that the first two balls."

"I know. So it's eggs for breakfast tomorrow, right? And maybe a bran muffin. Fresh."

"Yeah, yeah. And would you like it served on a silver platter, with a rose in a bud vase? Maybe a little espresso?"

"You're cute when you sulk, you know that?"

Someone bumped her from behind, knocking her into the pinball machine. The bar had become uncomfortably crowded while her back was turned. She watched, irritated, as the last table was taken. The after-dinner crowd was starting to arrive.

"This place is getting packed," she said. "Is there someplace else we can go?"

Junkyard didn't answer. His face had become a mask of barely controlled panic, worse than his reaction on the crowded sidewalk earlier in the day. Dismayed, she picked up his duffle bag and tugged his arm gently.

"Come on, Junkyard. Time to go."

His arm felt rigid through his jean jacket, but he began to move.

She forced a path through the throng, pulling him behind her. When they reached the door, he stumbled into the open air and leaned against the side of the building, blinking against the daylight.

"Sorry about that," he said after a few deep breaths.

He didn't offer an explanation. Looking at his pale, sweating face, Lennie didn't push. Maybe this explained why he lived in boxcars. Feeling exposed, she kept nervous watch on sidewalk traffic while his breathing slowed and the panic faded from his eyes.

"What now?" Lennie said before the silence could get awkward. "Go back and talk to Hotshot Bob?"

He glanced at the sun sinking toward the horizon and shook his head. "Nah, we can catch him at the poetry reading tonight. I want to find someplace to grab a shower. But first," he took his duffle bag from her hand, "well, I've still got laundry to do. The Laundromat is just down the street."

Lennie winced. The bet was more unfair than she had intended, given he must have been fighting a panic attack through the whole game. She thought of volunteering to watch his laundry, after all. Then a large, black bird flapped on the sidewalk behind him. Too large to be a crow. A raven, maybe? It uttered a low, long croak that Junkyard didn't seem to hear and fluttered up to a neon sign a couple of doors away. The sign said *Ozzie's Tattoos*. Below it hung a smaller plaque of painted plywood: *Welcome to Hell's Parlor.*

The raven cocked its head and looked at Lennie with a shiny, black eye. She ran a thumb over the design on the back of her hand and felt a sudden urge to visit the shop. Maybe the resident artist could tell her something about the tattoo—like, how to remove it.

"I'll meet you at the Laundromat in a few minutes," she told Junkyard. "There's something I want to do first."

Hotshot Bob huddled in his box, shaking and muttering to himself under his blanket. Bones's comment about him peeing his pants had reached him through the cardboard walls. It hadn't come to that, but it wasn't far from the truth.

El Lobo was back. He was back and his shadow ate at Hotshot's brain like cheap wine. *I shoulda lit outta here the minute that girl flashed that damn picture.*

Instead, he had crawled back into his box, thinking he would hide until dark and then catch out. After all, no one knew where he was except Too Long Soo, Bones O'Riley, Junkyard, and that blasted girl.

El Lobo found him anyway.

A familiar yellow haze filled Hotshot's mind full of shadow. He crouched, wanting to tear through the cardboard walls and run away, but the shadow in his mind grew fangs, biting and gnawing until he writhed in head-splitting agony.

"No—stop! I won't tell. I'm yours—yours 'til the end…I swear it."

Bones O'Riley's voice bellowed back at him through the cardboard. "Hey, I never said I wanted ya, Now shut the hell up, you festering pustule. You'll scare the customers away."

Hotshot whimpered and rocked back and forth, banging his head on his knees as though that might relieve the pressure.

I'm gonna die, I'm gonna die, I'm–

The jaws of shadow inside his head clamped down and his eyes shot wide, unseeing. His back arched, arms drumming the sides of the box, and a new fear was born, that he would not die after all, not ever, and the torment would go on and on.

Just kill me, he tried to beg, but his teeth clacked madly around wordless whimpers. Then suddenly the pain was gone. The shadow withdrew.

The aftershock hit and Hotshot wet himself, after all. He curled tightly around the stain, as though the smell could drive the fouler stench from his soul. He huddled that way, panting, a rabbit hiding from dripping teeth. At last he slept, and the jaws followed him into his dreams.

Hours later, sunlight cut across his face through a tear in a cardboard wall. He blinked and turned his head away from the light, but the rancid air of the sun-warmed box wouldn't let him escape back into sleep. He wormed his way outside, the still-damp fabric of his pants pulling stiffly at his thighs.

The sun hung low in the west. Oncoming storm clouds blotted out much of the sky. The sunlight reflected off them, casting an eerie yellow glow over the festival grounds. Like seeing through El Lobo's eyes.

Gotta get me outta here.

A shadow flickered across him. He flinched and lifted a protective arm, but it was only a hawk soaring high overhead.

"Lucky bastard." The rail yards would be a short flight for a bird, but Hotshot would have to reach the trains the human way. If he got there at all. He rubbed both hands across his face, pulling his sagging cheeks tight. For a moment, his younger self peered between his fingers. Then he dropped his hands and his flesh fell back into bloodhound folds.

The parking lot swarmed with people crossing between the tent village and the carnival rides. Some gathered in the jungle, slurping hot stew and laughing at the shenanigans of Too Long Soo and Bones O'Riley. No one was looking at Hotshot Bob. No one he could see, at least. He draped the red wool blanket over his shoulders, slung his pack, and began walking.

Regular people usually didn't see Hotshot. He was just another invisible, grate-sitting obstacle that must be skirted on the way to work. But they saw him today and a path opened before him. He was too grateful to wonder why, but if he had thought about it, he'd have figured it was because he stank like an outhouse. He couldn't see the stain of horror on his face.

At last he eased through a break in the train yard fence. Sweat coated his bald head despite the cool, rain-scented breeze. He leaned back against the chain-link, breathing hard, and scanned the nearest string of cars for a ride.

This part of his escape was the easiest and most dangerous. He had only to cross a hundred yards of open gravel and he could lose himself in the trains. But if anyone from the BRR saw him, he'd be dead before nightfall. He needed to find a ticket to ride, and quick.

Then he spotted a boxcar on the main line with one door open. He could roll up in some thousand-mile paper and hide until departure. Then he would ride a bit, maybe jump out when the train slowed for a hill. Lose himself in farm country. Use the last of his cash to catch a Greyhound for Santa Fe. He had a nephew there.

And he'd stay away from the trains for a while. Maybe forever.

First, he needed a drop of courage. He tucked himself among the spindly shrubs that grew along the fence and pulled a flask from his pocket. His face twisted reflexively as he took a swig. It had to be the worst hooch he had ever tasted. It was wonderful. He took another drink to keep the first from getting lonely.

When the festival people had hired him to play the part of a hobo at their little fake jungle, they'd said, "no drunks." What a joke. But the money was too good, so he hadn't touched a drop in a full twelve hours. Not his longest stretch, but it seemed an eternity when the dry spell was supposed to last three days.

As he raised the flask again, a ragged black ghost dropped into the branches above his head. Startled, he threw his arms over his face, sloshing whiskey everywhere. The ghost cawed and folded itself into a large, black bird. Hotshot sputtered in irritation. Nothing but a damn crow. The thing had made him spill half of his drink. He swung at it, missing. It cocked its head and looked at him with one bright, beady eye as if to say, *Sorry, man, I didn't know you were there.* Mollified, Hotshot muttered to himself and nestled back to finish getting drunk under the bird's commiserating gaze.

Sober hobos in a jungle. Ha. Those festival people would have a conniption if he showed up at their jungle with some real 'bos. Too Long Soo and Jungle Jim were about as hobo-like as Bozo the Clown.

"Yeah, get some real 'bos in there, suckin' down the sterno, pissin' themselves," he told the bird, forgetting the state of his own pants. "Maybe a coupla derelicts passed out on that nice, clean festival pavement, choking on their own puke. Yeah, Bob, that'd bring the tourists running."

He took another hit from the flask. The stuff was going down much smoother now, and that stretch of gravel between him and his ride was looking wider with every drink. He was just thinking it might be better to wait in the bushes until dark, snooze a bit, maybe even go back to that so-called job, when a shriek tore the air above him. The hawk was back, circling overhead. He squinted at it, trying to straighten his eyes. Might be a falcon.

Then the raven exploded out of the bushes like a tattered cannonball.

The falcon wheeled and screamed a challenge. Bending its wings, it dove at the raven. The two collided in a tangled ball of black and brown feathers and plummeted toward the ground. The ball split open just before it hit. Four wings beat the air; four claws scrabbled for purchase in flesh. The raven slipped loose, but the falcon rolled and slashed. Black feathers fluttered down. Hotshot winced in sympathy and watched the raven fly off, bobbing through the air on its injured wing. The falcon resumed circling over Hotshot's head.

Hotshot belched and tried to relax, but he felt edgy without the raven's companionable presence. The falcon overhead made him feel exposed. Sooner or later, Junkyard or one of El Lobo's lackeys—or worse, El Lobo himself—would root him out of the bushes. Any way he thought about it, staying here would end badly, and he sure as hell couldn't go back to the festival.

If only that damn girl hadn't come along. Jeez. He hadn't minded looking at her, not a bit, until she pulled out that wrinkled picture of Jarvis Cook. Hotshot shuddered. The last time he had seen that sorry bastard, El Lobo had carried him kicking and screaming into his lair. Had him under one arm, like a little kid. Hotshot had never seen El Lobo so mad. He was like an animal about to bust out of that three-piece suit he always wore. Cook must've stuck it to him good, to rile him up so much. Too bad for Cook.

It had happened a long time ago, when Hotshot was still in the inner circle of the BRR. His memory of the events was eroded by alcohol and fear, but he remembered one part clear as yesterday. He had followed El Lobo and Cook into the lair and taken his usual place just inside the door, ready to be of service. To his surprise, El Lobo ordered him out. Uncertain what else to do, Hotshot stood guard outside the door.

Then the noise began.

Hotshot could take the screams. He had heard these things often enough to feel boredom. But then the screams changed, as if drawn from some deep, dark well...cries of horror torn from the very roots of a man's soul. The hair rose all over Hotshot's body and the horror seeped through his pores to take anchor in his own soul.

That was the day he began to drink. He fell from El Lobo's inner circle soon after, becoming nothing more than an errand boy.

When that girl started waving Cook's picture around, that was enough for Hotshot. He didn't want to know what happened to Jarvis Cook, and he did *not* want to live through it again with this girl. He sure as hell didn't want to come up against Junkyard Doug, either. Now that was one scary sonofabitch. Not as bad as El Lobo, but he'd seen Junkyard take out a brace of the BRR with his bare hands, a few months back. And them with chains, knives, and all. No, Bob, not gonna get crunched between El Lobo and that crazy bastard.

He drained the flask. "Just one thing to do. Get my sorry, boney, old ass out of here."

He peered through the branches at the open gravel. Nothing moved. He popped his head out and took a more careful look. Still no one. He crawled out of the bushes, panicking a moment when their woody fingers caught at his shirt. Sweating and trembling, he clambered to his feet. The ground seemed to heave beneath him and he lurched drunkenly into the fence. He clutched at the chain link, his head swimming so wildly he thought it might spin on its axis.

Come on, Bob, nothin' but an ethanol earthquake. Can't expect to drink this shit lyin' down and then get up and do a jig.

He closed his eyes and held onto the fence until the earth's movements slowed to a roll. The falcon screeched overhead, circling lower. Hotshot had to go *now*, or he might never make it any farther than these bushes. Letting go of the fence, he stumbled toward his ride. But the boxcar kept moving on him, first off to the left and then to the right. Half-expecting the full membership of the BRR to come charging down on him, he ran the last few yards to the train, falling down twice.

And then he was there. Home base. Safe. He tossed his pack inside. It took him several tries to scramble in after it, and then he collapsed on the floor, his heart highballing in his chest. The only noises were the usual rail yard clashings and bangings. He began to relax and daydream about Santa Fe. His nephew's wife was a pretty good cook, if you liked Tex-Mex. But he would have to deal with that mutt. What was its name? Calvin or Cowboy, something like that.

"Hey, Hotshot, how's it goin', eh?"

Hotshot sat up and stared wildly at the open doorway. The sudden voice was cheerful, friendly...and it terrified him. He scuttled away until his back was against the closed door on the opposite side.

"Who's that?" His voice shook. He squinted at the backlit face in the opening. "That you, Bill? 'Cause if it is, please don't kick me off."

"Yah, sure, it's me."

Relief warmed Hotshot like good rum. Even a regular bull would be welcome just now, considering the alternatives, but Bill Sutter was something better than regular. Ever since Jungle Jim pulled him from under that train, Bill had been soft on hobos.

"I know you're supposed to throw me off, but can you let it go just this once?"

The silhouette shook its head. "I'm afraid I can't do that, Hotshot. See, there's a problem."

Bill planted his hands and heaved himself inside, landing with a soft grunt. A smell like something dead and rotting followed him. Hotshot hugged his legs to his chest and watched Bill uncertainly. The boxcar felt more like a trap than home base.

"You don't have to come after me, Bill. I'll get out, if that's what you want." Hotshot cringed at the thought. He did not want to go back to the festival's jungle, especially with that falcon circling overhead. "But can't you let me stay? Please, I just gotta get out of town. They're after me, Bill."

"I know they are, Hotshot." Bill climbed to his feet. "I'm sorry.

This is just the wrong place for you to be."

Bill moved forward until the light was no longer behind him. Hotshot could finally see his round, fleshy face. The normally pleasant features were pulled tight, reminding Hotshot of a dog with its ears laid flat. Bill's eyes looked swollen and he blinked rapidly. The tears running into the creases around his mouth frightened Hotshot more than anything else that had happened that day.

But the coiled cord in Bill's hand frightened Hotshot even more.

"I'm sorry, Hotshot." Bill's voice broke as though he truly were sorry. "El Lobo wants you gone."

The soft, thin cord glinted white in the filtered light. Bill pulled something from a pocket with his other hand. A furtive ray of sunlight flashed across it as he swung his arm forward. It was a knife. A bronze-bladed knife. In a gloved hand.

The evidence was clear even for Hotshot's ethanol-soaked brain.

"It's you! You're the one that killed Tin Can Petey—and all those others, too!"

Bill took another step. He said nothing, but the anguish in his face told Hotshot everything.

Oh, bad! Hotshot rolled and drove his shoulder into the closed door. *Bad and worse and worse!* His feet scrambled for leverage on the worn, dusty floor. *Worse than Junkyard.* He clawed at the unmoving door, driving flaked rust under his nails in little previews of pain. *Worse than the BRR.* Grasping the edge of the door, he rammed his shoulder against the metal, driving so hard that he raised his entire length from the floor. He strained until his fingers ached and his shoulders cracked in their sockets. But no matter how much he struggled, he could not alter one fact: boxcar doors can't be opened from the inside.

I'm gonna die.

Hotshot slumped under the waiting knife. Sobbing, he looked

into Bill's haunted eyes.

"Why, Bill?"

"I think you know the reason."

Hotshot recognized the torture and self-loathing in Bill's eyes. He had seen that look on too many faces from his post inside El Lobo's den. Somehow El Lobo could reach into a guy's thoughts and jerk them around like a puppeteer yanks on strings. Next thing you know, the guy's doing all kinds of ugly things—beating his wife, shooting up the office pool, knifing a total stranger. Things he would never do on his own. Things he can't explain to the police, or even to himself.

When the guy *knows* what's happening to him...when he knows and still can't stop it, well, then he wears an expression just like the one on Bill's face.

"Yeah, Bill, I get it."

"It's Ashley, see." Bill lifted the cord and knife on upturned palms and stared at them as if they already ran with blood. For a moment, Hotshot thought—hoped—he would throw them to the floor.

"If I don't do what he says, he'll go after Ashley." Bill lifted his eyes and Hotshot's last hope died. The anguish, the doubt, even the fear were gone from Bill's gaze. Only a fierce determination remained.

"I have no choice."

"No. No, I guess you don't."

And then the pain began. Somewhere far away, Hotshot heard the screams of Jarvis Cook. They came, he realized, from his own mouth.

Bill Sutter stood over the corpse of Hotshot Bob, gasping through his tears. Blood ran down the spattered door and collected in the crack at the bottom. Soon it would begin a slow drip to the ground.

He should go. Someone might see the blood. He should leave and change his clothes, fill the gloves with sand and throw them in the river. But he couldn't make himself move.

He had known Hotshot for eight years.

No more. He closed his eyes, squeezing tears onto his cheeks. I can't do this anymore.

Even as he thought this, he knew he would do it again. And again, and again. Whatever El Lobo wanted, just to keep Ashley safe. Who would be next? His boss? His brother? Thank God my wife is already dead, he thought, and hated himself a little more.

A falcon shrieked outside the boxcar. Bill lifted his head, understanding. A new assignment, his next victim. The image of a face formed in his head and dismay filled him. He had thought this nightmare couldn't get any worse. But how could he stop it? There was Ashley, though he could hardly look at her anymore. He couldn't meet her eyes at all.

How would she feel, if she knew?

Something hardened inside him, the last bit of courage, perhaps, or maybe just desperation. He had thought all his choices were taken from him, that there was nothing he wouldn't do, no one he wouldn't kill, but he was wrong. He slid out of the boxcar and faced the sky.

"No. Not him. Never him."

The falcon swooped low and he ducked, but not before sharp talons grazed his scalp. He straightened, ignoring the blood that already streamed into his face. "I won't kill him. He saved my life and nearly died for it. You can't make me do it."

For the first time in a year, those words had meaning.

Lennie paused at the door of the tattoo parlor. She had never been in one of these places before. The idea of enduring minutes, even hours, of pain to permanently engrave some cheesy artwork on her flesh didn't appeal to her. Besides, she couldn't shake the image of tattoo parlors as dirty, back-alley sleaze pits frequented by bikers and gangs. The small print on the welcome sign didn't help: *40% Discount with Parole Card.*

Lovely. Just my sort. She pushed her way into the store.

The scene before her left her feeling foolish and vaguely disappointed. The room was large, well lit, and the tiled floor glistened with recent waxing. An antiseptic smell with chemical overtones hung in the air. Potted plants decorated the reception desk and a lush Norway pine grew in a wooden tub in a corner.

A counter ran along one wall, crowded with neatly arranged bottles and tools. Two reclining chairs were stationed before it, bright lights mounted overhead on jointed metal arms. A college-aged girl lounged like a centerfold in one of the chairs, her blouse half-unbuttoned and one shoulder exposed. She chatted with a friend, flashing perfect, French-manicured nails with each gesture. A heavy, middle-aged woman bent over the bared shoulder and touched a corded tool to a button-sized pattern on the skin. The girl flinched.

"Ouch! Hey, Ozzie—"

The older woman lifted the tool and raised an eyebrow. "Did you think it wasn't going to hurt?"

"Yeah, but—" The girl glanced at her smirking friend. "Oh, go ahead."

"Right. But you'd better hold still, girl, or I might accidentally connect the wrong dots." Ozzie glanced at Lennie, blinking under the bright work light. "Be with you in a moment, hon. This won't take long."

The artist's tool whirred like an anemic dental drill. Lennie's teeth ached sympathetically. Hopefully tattoos didn't come off the same way they went on.

While she waited, she studied the sample tattoos covering one wall. There were patterns of eagles, snakes, even a skunk. Skulls, roses, and skulls with roses in their teeth. Jesus portraits, Hellfire, Celtic knots, unicorns, Bugs Bunny, and even a Buddha. Anything conceivable could be tattooed on flesh. The real question was how easily it could be removed.

As she moved down the wall, the patterns gave way to photos of finished work. Some of the designs were fantastically intricate and vivid. Even beautiful. One photo made her pause. It showed a tattoo of an elaborate tree that completely covered a man's back. Its tangled branches curled over his broad shoulders and around his heavily muscled upper arms. It seemed familiar, somehow.

"What's this one?" she asked.

"That's the World Tree," Ozzie said, glancing up from her work.

"It's amazing." Lennie leaned closer, taking in the detail. Was that a squirrel on the tree trunk? Reeling with déjà vu, she traced the design lightly with her fingernail. Bees filled the gaps between the leaves. Deer leaped from branch to branch and at least one slit-eyed goat peered through the foliage.

Just like in her dream.

But she had never heard of the World Tree before, or seen pictures anything like it.

Ozzie finished the girl's tattoo and came up behind Lennie. "I think that's one of my best," she said, nodding at the photo. "It took a long time, though. I had to do it in stages." She looked at Lennie doubtfully. "You might want to start with something a little smaller."

The door jingled as the two girls left the parlor. Giggles drifted back through the closing door. "Man, Mom's going to *kill* me. But I can't believe how much that *hurt!*"

Ozzie rolled her eyes and shook her head. "Some people ought to stick to the tattoos that come out of gumball machines. So, what can I do for you, hon?"

From the tone of her voice, Lennie suspected Ozzie had pegged her as a gumball chewer. She couldn't argue. "I'm not here to get a tattoo. I was hoping you could tell me what it would take to remove one."

"I don't do tattoo removals any more. Not since they came up with lasers. These days, they got that IPL therapy, too. Expensive as hell, but it works pretty good."

Lennie sighed. She couldn't afford to pay someone to rub her hand with a pencil eraser—forget a more expensive treatment. But it was nice knowing it could be removed, some day.

Seeing her disappointment, Ozzie added, "I still do cover-ups, though. Maybe I can change it to something you like better. Let's see the tat."

Lennie held out her fist to let Ozzie examine the interlocking triangles. "I'd really rather get rid of it altogether, but I guess altering it might..."

She stopped, alarmed, when Ozzie swore and grabbed her hand, bringing the tattoo closer to her eyes. "Where the hell'd you get this tattoo?"

"Well, I was...I just..." Lennie stammered uncomfortably. She pulled her hand away. "I just woke up this morning, and there it was."

Ozzie raised an eyebrow. "You're telling me you really have no idea how you got this tattoo?"

Lennie's face grew warm. She knew what Ozzie was thinking. Embarrassing, but easier than explaining the real story. "No, I don't. Why? What's wrong?"

"I've seen that pattern before." Ozzie gave Lennie a long, hard look. "Maybe five, ten years ago, this guy came into the shop with a tat just like that on his hand. He wanted it off, too. Said he tried laser therapy, but it didn't work. I found that hard to believe, but he wanted me to do a cover-up, so what the hell."

She shrugged. "I'm not sure what the fuss was about. It's not a devil symbol or anything. But I told him, it's your dollar. He hardly cared what the design was, as long as I did it fast."

Her nostrils flared as she eyed the tattoo, as if it gave off a bad smell. Uncomfortable, Lennie pulled her hand away. Ozzie's gaze followed the tattooed hand as if she were afraid to let it out of her sight. "Here's the weird part—the ink wouldn't take. Damned freaky. I probably spent three or four hours, switching patterns, switching colors, but the new tat always washed off easier than kids' watercolors. Damnedest thing I ever saw."

Lennie listened with growing excitement. It couldn't be a coincidence. She pulled the photograph out of her pocket and handed to Ozzie. "I'm looking for my father. I know this is an old picture, but do you think this could have been the guy?"

Ozzie brought the photo close to her nose. "Yeah, that could be him. I remember, he was balding and had a round face, like that."

She squinted at Lennie, suspicious. "Are you telling me that you woke up with a mysterious tattoo just like your missing father's, and you have no idea where it came from?"

Oops.

"Well, see, it's complicated."

Both eyebrows went up, and Lennie could feel a downturn in Ozzie's mood. She tried to think of some reasonable explanation, but she had never been a good liar and Ozzie didn't give her time to make something up.

"You're not involved in some kind of cult, are you?" Ozzie growled. "Because I don't truck with cults."

"No! Not me." Though that could explain a few things. "Never. Absolutely not."

Ozzie's posture changed, definitely more hostile. Lennie winced. Damn—too much protesting. She plucked the picture from Ozzie's hand. "Thanks for the information. I'd better go. I—I'm supposed to meet someone."

She hurried from the tattoo parlor, feeling Ozzie's hard stare on her back.

The Laundromat was a few blocks from the tattoo parlor. Lennie hurried down the sidewalk, uneasy at being in the open alone. But it had been worth the risk to learn that someone had seen her father, even if it had been years before.

For ten years, she had believed her father had simply run off. Her mother had never explained, never laid blame, even in her most drunken state. In fact, she had never mentioned Jarvis Cook again. If Lennie tried to question, her mother responded sharply—it was not to be discussed. Lennie had always thought her mother was too bitter or sad to talk about it. But maybe that wasn't the issue. Maybe her mother was afraid.

Lennie glanced back nervously. Still no sign of gangbangers. Even so, she quickened her pace, reaching an intersection as the light turned red. She pushed the walk button impatiently. The Ragman had recognized the tattoo. Somehow, his boss—El Lobo—had something to do with it. But what?

She thought again of the letter her father had left behind all those years ago. After her mother's death, Lennie had unearthed a trunk stored at the back of a closet. It was full of baby clothes, a crumbling bouquet of dandelions, photographs, some baby teeth and other treasures from Lennie's childhood. At the bottom of the trunk, buried under those lost pieces of childhood, was an envelope addressed simply, "Alice."

After all those years of wondering, the letter had been Lennie's first clue to where her father had gone. And, more importantly, why. Time had yellowed the paper. She'd read it so often over the days that followed that the folded edges grew thin and dirty. The words themselves became imprinted in her thoughts.

My Dearest Alice,

The dreams have gotten worse, though I told you they had gone away. Elements from them are manifesting in my waking life, even affecting me physically. I fear that the story my father told me is true. I must leave before the curse of my forefathers falls on Elena, my little Lennie. If it's not already too late.

Even now, I want to set this pen down, burn this note, and return to bed, never to leave your warmth. But I can't. I'm a fool and a coward for having stayed so long. I'm taking the iron road. You won't see me again.

Be strong, and know that I'll always love you,

Jarvis

The first time Lennie read the letter, the relief was almost physical. He hadn't left because of anything she had done. He had never stopped loving them. Her guilt evaporated.

But her anger hadn't gone away. Nothing could excuse those destitute years after he had left them. No mysterious curse, no vague reference to danger. Nothing.

Or so she had thought. Now, she wasn't so certain.

The light turned green. She pondered the contents of the letter as she crossed the street.

"*Affecting me physically,*" it had said. Had her father awakened to find the same tattoo on his hand? A final sign that it was time to go?

Go and do what?

"Damn it, Dad," she whispered. He might have thought to protect her by running off and leaving her out of the story, but she was in it just the same. And where his father had given him explanations, she was left completely unprepared.

She hesitated when she reached the Laundromat door. Through the window, she could see Junkyard sitting with his feet up on a table, paging through a magazine. She wished she could tell him everything, but he would probably think she was crazy.

The only one who seemed likely to tell her anything was Ramblin' Red. If she couldn't find her father, maybe she could find him and find out what he knew.

If she could get him to talk.

If she could trust him.

CHAPTER ELEVEN

Fenrir bent his wings, backstroking air to slow his descent. He stretched out his talons and settled neatly on a railroad tie next to a dilapidated building. Under the cover of shadow, he let go of the falcon shape stolen from Freyja decades ago. Feathers fell away, vanishing before they touched the ground. The small, hunched figure lost its shape and roiled upward like a dark wall cloud. It assumed a shaggy, long-muzzled form before coalescing into the broad-shouldered, wiry-haired man that was once Angus Cook. Light from the setting sun angled sharply across the rail yard, but it didn't penetrate the shadow in which he stood.

The end was near. He stared into the red sun, envisioning the burning destruction that would engulf the world. His nostrils flared, almost smelling the salt air of the sea that would rise up and wash away the blackened ruins. Prophecy said the world would be born anew. It also said that he and all other Jotnar would perish, leaving the last surviving Aesir to rule alone.

So said the prophecy.

Fenrir had never liked that prophecy.

From the time of his imprisonment by the Aesir, he had plotted against the Norn, devising ways to change or destroy fate, to create his own destiny. Now his plans neared fruition. Only the Norn stood in his way. And a woman named Lennie Cook.

Fenrir walked to the door, pausing to check his Rolex. Twenty minutes to 7:00. He was early. Good. His nose wrinkled at the cloying smoke that drifted from the building. It would not hurt to be early for his appointment with Monte.

The building seemed an unlikely headquarters for the Brotherhood of Rail Riders. It stood at the edge of the departure yard, far from the control tower. The sliding door gaped open, off its track. Rust stained the siding like spattered blood, the metal so thin in places that it would take little effort to punch through.

No one bothered the building. Fenrir had made certain of that. If any of the yard workers noticed it at all, they would vaguely remember that it had been rented for storage. Tramps and thieves would see glistening walls of corrugated steel, a solid core door sealed by a heavy lock, and they would look for easier targets.

Members of the BRR would see the building as it was, the audacity of its condition a testimony to their master's power.

Fenrir ran a hand over his head to smooth his short, dark curls. A futile gesture. That aspect of this body would not submit to his control. He tugged his shirtsleeves, straightening them under his suit coat. Gold cuff links flashed at his wrists. He pushed the door open and stepped inside.

The usual smells hit him: iron, oil, and gunpowder. A bare bulb hung from a rafter at the end of an orange power cord, its light dulled by the sweet, drifting smoke. Wide metal shelves lined the walls, holding everything from knives and handguns to automatic assault weapons and grenades. Packages of caked cocaine and blocks of black tar heroin were stored on the topmost shelves. Donuts of compressed marijuana were stacked like spare tires on the cement floor. Someone had broken open the marijuana, which explained the source of the smoke.

Fenrir's lip curled in irritation. He would have words with Monte. But first he stopped before a long, thick skein of white cord hanging on the wall to perform what had become a ritual.

Here was Gleipnir, the ribbon that had bound him when the largest iron links could not. Its coils stretched to the floor from a hook set higher than his head. He rolled a hank of it in his fingers. Hundreds of string-thin strands slid loosely within the twisted length. He remembered how the ribbon had once cut into his flesh. The feel of it set his fingertips afire with the ghost of agony, yet he gripped it firmly, letting the pain feed a hatred more ancient than the oldest human city.

"May the cowards rot with Hel for eternity."

The curse should have been empty, worn flat from countless repetition, but it resounded with the fury of its first utterance.

He cursed himself as well, for his naiveté those thousands of years ago. With uneasy trust, he had accepted the Allfather's challenge to test his lupine strength. He stood like a ruminating cow while the Aesir bound him with Gleipnir. Tyr rested his hand between Fenrir's teeth as collateral against his release should he fail the test. Tyr, whom Fenrir trusted and called friend.

Tyr, whose blood Fenrir still tasted—a bitter payment for the loss of his freedom.

The Aesir laughed at his struggles. "Gleipnir is made of the sound of a moving cat, of a woman's beard and the roots of a mountain," they said, mocking him even as he devoured Tyr's hand. "It has the strength of bear sinew, the weight of fishes' breath, with bird spittle to keep it supple. It cannot be broken, even by you."

Fenrir howled at his betrayal, bucking and straining, but Gleipnir only grew tighter until he could no longer move.

Still, the Aesir were not done with him. They anchored him to the ground and, as he lay panting, drove a sword into the roof of his mouth, jamming the hilt against his lower jaw so he could not bite.

"Why?" he howled as they did this to him.

"The prophecy."

Then they told him the words of the Norn, foretelling the day when Fenrir, who had never ventured near the smallest village nor taken a farmer's weakest stock, would swallow the Allfather and bring forth the flaming end of the world. Thus justified, they bound his head so they need not see the agony in his face. And when his whimpers became more than they could bear, they drove him far under the ground.

For thousands of years, Fenrir dreamt of the Allfather's death and vowed that this much of the prophecy would come true: The Allfather would die. But he, Fenrir, would survive to rule the new world.

Almost reluctantly, Fenrir dropped the strands of Gleipnir from his fingers. The memory of its bite fed his need for vengeance. Without that focus, he would lack the will to maintain this ridiculous human facade and would rampage the earth in wolf form, destroying, killing, until these new humans found a way to destroy him.

No, he thought, running a hand down the length of a rocket launcher. It was better to help the humans destroy themselves.

A beer can ricocheted off the far wall and clattered to the floor. Muffled giggles burst from a king-sized mattress sprawled in the farthest corner of the building. Fenrir lifted his head, nostrils wide, confirming the musky scent of sex in the melting pot of odors. Monte had brought a woman into the lair. Another rule broken. A growl rose in Fenrir's throat and his eyes narrowed to yellow slits.

It was time for his meeting with Monte.

He approached silently. A thin stream of smoke rose from a joint smoldering in a hubcap near the bed. A crumpled pile of cans added the stench of stale beer to the polluted air. Humans fouled their surroundings with their every action. A mound of stained pillows and uprooted blankets squirmed on the mattress. A bare ass, hairy and muscular, bobbed in and out of the heap, accompanied by grunting and feminine moans.

"Monte." A ridiculous name, well suited to the man. "I need to talk to you."

The bobbing continued.

"Monte." Fenrir put the snarl of the wolf into his voice. Blankets flew. Monte's shaggy head and pale shoulders appeared. His eyes widened in surprise. Fenrir had not yet taught him enough fear.

"El Lobo!" His gaze darted to the joint and back to Fenrir. He smiled nervously. "You're early."

"This is unacceptable, Monte."

Fenrir noted the glint of defiance in the gang leader's eyes. A soft arm tipped with gold-lacquered nails reached out of the blankets to pull Monte back. He shook it off. The girl sat up, not caring when the blankets slipped off, leaving her naked. Her gaze fell on Fenrir and widened with interest. She was round of thigh and belly and large-breasted, yet slender of waist. She might have been of the Jotnar, the people of Fenrir's father, but for the sun-browned skin and thick, black hair. She arched her back and smiled invitingly. When Fenrir didn't respond, she sneered and bit Monte's shoulder. From the red marks on his torso, it seemed she had done so before.

Monte winced. "Later, Loralee," he said, flinching away.

"Hey, baby," the girl said in a voice both petulant and teasing. "Don't leave me hangin'." She ran a gold-tipped finger up her body and plunged it into her mouth.

Monte watched her, licking his upper lip. "Not *now*, Loralee. I'm talking to El Lobo, the big guy himself." But his gaze fixed on her breasts.

Loralee pouted and rubbed her leg across Monte's thigh. "But, Monte, you said *you* were the boss."

She slid her hand under the blankets on his lap. Monte's eyes shot wide, then lost focus. He reached for the girl's breast.

A low growl rumbled in Fenrir's chest. Monte didn't seem to hear, or perhaps he didn't care. Snarling, Fenrir grabbed a handful of

Monte's hair and yanked him off the bed. Loralee screamed and tried to run, but Fenrir caught her by the neck. She clawed at his arm and tried to twist free. "Let go of me, you bastard!"

The rage of eons threatened to burst from Fenrir. He saw himself as wolf, with blood-matted fur, bodies piled around, crushing those smelly cars and stale houses the humans so loved. It would be so...good.

Then he saw himself dead, the Allfather walking free on the earth.

Focus.

Gold flashed, and the girl's fingernails laid open his face.

Control.

Fenrir squeezed just enough to shut her up and make her concentrate on breathing. Then he turned to Monte, who dangled from his other hand, kicking and thrashing, his forehead stretching visibly. Something gave way with the sound of weeds tearing from the earth, and Monte jerked closer to the floor. He screamed and grabbed Fenrir's arm, trying to pull himself up. Blood trickled past his hairline and down his neck.

The blood scent inflamed Fenrir, weakening his control. Drool ran from the corner of his mouth and his breath hissed through bared, pointed teeth. He thrust his face close to Monte's.

"I told you, I need to talk to you."

Monte's eyes rolled back into his head and he stopped struggling. "I'm sorry!" he cried. "I'm sorry, I'm sorry..."

The urge to bite off Monte's face was almost irresistible, but Fenrir listened to colder thoughts. He had hand-chosen Monte to lead the Brotherhood of Rail Riders. The gang leader had the instinctive intelligence, the connections, the charisma to unite urban gangs all over the United States, regardless of colors. Unfortunately, the very qualities that made him valuable also made him difficult to control without ruining him. But perhaps Fenrir had coddled him too much.

He dropped Monte to the floor. The gangbanger huddled where he fell, holding his bleeding head. Fenrir pulled Loralee closer, savoring the stench of sweat and sex and fear. She fought for air, her eyes round, her arteries throbbing under his fingers. An answering heat pulsed from his loins. He ran his tongue over dagger-sharp teeth, wishing he could tear into the soft flesh under her chin. Saliva filled his mouth. He could almost taste the warm blood, feel it running down his throat.

But, said the cold part of his mind, that might be too much for Monte. He wanted to inspire the man with fear, not render him useless.

With great effort, he controlled the madness. Instead of ripping the girl open, he lifted her by the neck. She made satisfactory gagging noises. Her tanned skin turned darker, taking on a purple tinge. Her tongue protruded, bleeding, cut by her own teeth. She rolled bulging eyes toward Monte and managed a plaintive squeak for help. Monte watched in slack-jawed horror, never moving.

Fenrir brought her face close to his. "Don't worry, baby," he said. "*I* won't leave you hanging."

He began to squeeze. She struggled and clawed at his hand. One gold-lacquered nail lodged in his wrist and broke off. His fingers tightened, crushing muscle and tendons, rupturing arteries. Blood oozed through his fingers, hitting the floor in bright circles. She kicked wildly, missing him. Something snapped with a resounding crack, deep in her neck. She went rigid, back arching, then drooped in his grip like a wet towel. He held her long after the twitching stopped, feeling her life bleed away even as the blood lust drained from his eyes.

At last, sated, he threw her into the pile of empties, sending cans skittering across the floor. Turning to Monte, he pulled a silk handkerchief from his breast pocket and carefully wiped his hand.

"Like I said, I need to talk to you."

Monte sat unmoving, his hands still pressed to his head. His mouth still hung open and his eyes were glazed with shock.

"Hmmm. Perhaps I overdid it, after all."

He grasped Monte and lifted him to the bed.

"Monte."

The gangbanger's expression didn't change

"Monte, listen to me."

Slowly, Monte's head swiveled and his gaze fixed vacantly on a spot of blood on his master's lapel.

"Listen carefully." Fenrir said each word slowly. "I'm not going to kill you."

Monte swallowed hard. He let go of his head, but kept his hands out as though he expected a blow. "You–you're not?"

Fenrir patted him on the shoulder. "No. You see, I need you."

Monte met Fenrir's gaze and his pupils dilated, reflecting yellow. "You do?"

Fenrir spoke to him patiently, like a father explaining a difficult concept to his child. "Yes. You are still part of the great plan. In fact, you have a starring role." He paused, watching hope seep back into Monte's maddened eyes.

"But there are rules. You remember the rules, don't you, Monte?"

Monte nodded, apprehensive again. His gaze wandered to the hubcap next to the bed. It had overturned in the struggle. Loralee's blood-spattered arm lay across it. He shuddered and looked away.

"The rules apply to you, too. Is that clear?"

Monte nodded again, this time more eagerly. Good. His mind was broken, but he would still prove useful.

"Very well." Fenrir looked around the floor as though it were littered with dirty clothes and broken toys. "Now get this mess cleaned up. And then—"

He thought of the Valknut. And the woman who wore it. "Summon the Ragman. I have a job for you both."

CHAPTER TWELVE

The ride to Minneapolis seemed interminable to Briggs. He hadn't slept in more than forty hours and his eyes felt like dusty marbles. He leaned against the bulkhead and tried to nap. The dull, steady roar of the engine lulled him, but every time he drifted off, he was jolted awake by the nagging feeling he had forgotten something back in his office. He started rummaging through his grip for a third time and noticed the engineer smirking at him.

Briggs grinned wryly. "Must be getting obsessive-compulsive in my old age, eh, Squibb?"

Herbert Squibb was old enough to be Briggs's grandfather and had been completely deaf for as long as Briggs had known him. Squibb nodded as if he'd heard and grinned a mouthful of oversized dentures.

"You look like a fella on a hot date who done lost his condoms." He chortled, obviously pleased with his own wit, then stopped abruptly when something shifted behind his lips. He slurped, stuck his thumb in his mouth, and gave his denture plate a little shove. Smacking his lips, he squinted at the track ahead. Random tufts of gray hair on his head quivered with each bump.

Briggs chuckled. Some people strove for eccentricity. Others had it thrust upon them.

The grip still lay open before Briggs. A third search wouldn't change its contents. He zipped it shut and slumped back against the bulkhead. Every muscle ached with exhaustion, but the nagging feeling wouldn't leave him alone. He tried to retrace those last few minutes in his office. No matter how hard he concentrated, the memory slid from focus, leaving him with vague impressions obscured by a blue haze. He didn't even know what had made him so certain James "Jungle Jim" Tuttle would be at the Greater Midwest Railroad Days.

Aggravated, he shifted position. Maybe his brother was right. A quiet job in Northfield sounded pretty good, just now. Maybe some beautiful, blond Ole from St. Olaf College would think he wasn't too old. A leggy music major with a thing for cops…

The daydream deepened into sleep. Random images flitted through his dreams. He was in his office, but the computer desk was replaced by an elegantly set dinner table. A plateful of steak and potatoes steamed before him. A cold beer appeared, dripping condensation on the tablecloth. His mouth watered, but as he reached for the fork, the table disappeared. Now a beautiful blond girl stood before him, singing "Ave Maria" in a pure soprano. She wore a black leather cat suit, neckline plunging to her navel. He could see her abdomen tighten as she sustained the crescendo.

He had always liked "Ave Maria."

The girl's crescendo stretched impossibly long, her face darkening with exertion. The color washed down her cleavage, covering her arms, deepening her skin to an even tan. A wave of thick, black hair overwhelmed the blond curls. That lovely, round note rose to a piercing shriek, and then cut off with the sounds of choking. Her eyes bulged, their whites flushed red. Her gold-tipped fingers tore at her throat. A false fingernail snapped off and landed at his feet, gleaming like a gold coin. A shadow fell across Briggs from behind. He spun around—

—and rammed his face into the iron bulkhead of the diesel unit. The shriek of braking wheels made his ears ring. The floor rumbled under him as the diesel unit rolled to a stop on uneven track. Briggs rubbed his face and tried to focus his eyes. Hell of a dream.

Squibb worked the controls, powering the locomotive down. "That'll do," he said. "Welcome to Minni, boy."

"Thanks," Briggs mumbled. Why was he in Minneapolis? He forced his sluggish brain to work. James Tuttle. Right. There was a festival and Tuttle might be at it.

He stood and gathered his grip and jacket. He could smell Squibb's breath from across the cab. Or maybe it was his own breath. He brushed passed the old man and started down the steps.

"Better grab yerself a shave before you go see that girlfriend of yours, heh heh. And maybe a breath mint, too."

Squibb's cackling rang too loudly in Briggs's stressed ears. Briggs turned back, ready with a retort, but the face grinning down at him from the doorway didn't belong to Squibb. The hair was too thick, and faded-red rather than grey. A single, blue eye glowed in the shadow of a floppy-brimmed hat.

The spot between Briggs's shoulder blades prickled. He had seen that face before, though he couldn't remember where. The apparition spoke, its gruff voice echoing in Briggs's mind.

"You'd best hurry, boy, or you'll be too late."

The eye flashed like a camera bulb. Briggs flinched and fell backward, dropping his grip. The bag bounced down the steps and hit the gravel below. He blindly flung out an arm and caught the rail, or he might have bounced down after it. Shaken, he eased himself to the ground and rescued the bag. When he looked up into the cab, the strange face was gone and Squibb's big teeth glinted down at him.

"Here, boy." The old man tossed him a small, square packet. "You better take this."

Feeling numb, Briggs caught it automatically and started across the train yard in a daze. The after-image of the blue flash hung in his vision, casting an otherworldly pall over the tracks. What had just happened?

The ring of his cell phone gave his nerves a good kick. He swore and pulled it out of its holster.

"Briggeman, here."

"Hey, Briggs. This is Campbell at Minneapolis security. We've got another murder."

Briggs's hand tightened on the phone. *You'd best hurry, boy...*

"Briggs? You there, Briggeman?"

Briggs swallowed dryly. He really didn't want to hear any more. "Yeah. Go on."

"They found a woman's body in the dumpster behind the control tower at the University yard. It looks nasty."

Not Tuttle, then. Briggs bowed his head, allowing himself a moment of relief. Not likely a Hobo Spider victim, either. Those bodies were always male and were left on a train car or near the tracks.

"We have a problem." Campbell sounded stressed. "Willowbe's having kittens over another murder in his territory. He says he'll come up and handle this one himself. You know what that means."

"Yeah. Might as well hand the case over to Daffy Duck. Look, tell Willowbe I'm already in Minneapolis. Maybe that'll satisfy him and he'll stay home."

"Thank God. We owe you one, Briggs. The crime scene is still intact, if you want to check it out."

Briggs got what information he could and ended the call quickly. He was completely awake now. Adrenaline worked so much better than coffee. As he put the cell phone away, he remembered the packet Squibb had tossed to him. He opened his hand and read the label. Trojan, it said. The ribbed kind. He laughed. Same old Squibb.

By the time he reached the control tower, the last of the retinal burn had faded from his vision, along with all memory of the one-eyed stranger.

January 2, 1942
Atchison, KS

Little Herbie Squibb shivered on the steps of the St. Francis Episcopal Church and folded his arms over his mittened hands. He thought about following his pa inside, but those union meetings were long, boring, and sometimes scary when the men turned red-faced and started yelling. No, he'd rather stay outside, even in winter. It wasn't much below freezing and there was enough moonlight that he could see just fine. He reached into his pocket and pulled out his new yo-yo, a Big "G" Genuine. He got it for Christmas and had to learn at least one trick before school started up again.

Two more of his pa's friends from the rail yard arrived, their coat collars pulled up almost to their hat brims. They were so busy talking that they didn't notice him standing right there.

"…still don't know. Them wildcat strikes are dangerous," one of them was saying. Herbie perked up. Had someone gotten himself bitten by a wildcat? Now that would be news.

The other man was new at the yard. He was big, dark, and mean looking and Pa said he had funny yellow eyes. Herbie didn't like him, but his pa said he was important. The man growled and stuck a cigarette in his mouth. "It's settled. Nothing will stop the strike, now."

The cigarette bobbed when he talked. It should have been funny, but somehow it only made the mean-looking man creepier.

Herbie wanted to hear more about the wildcat, but the men went into the church and the door closed with a puff of warm air. He was left alone with a wildcat on the loose. Heart beating fast, he looked up and down the deserted street, staring especially hard at the shadows around the trashcans. There, did something move in that alley?

Moving as little as possible, he slipped one hand free of its mitten and threaded the yo-yo string onto his middle finger. He thought about what his pa said on Christmas morning. A yo-yo was more than a toy. Philippine natives used them to hunt. Herbie wrapped his fingers tight around smooth, hard wood. If that wildcat came anywhere near him, he'd bean it on the noggin a few hundred times. That ought to do it.

He crouched by the church wall and watched, still as Father Paul in silent prayer. At least a full minute ticked away. Nothing moved. His neck started to itch under his wool scarf. Then his leg started to itch, right behind the knee. Cold snot ran down his upper lip, but he didn't dare wipe it away.

Then he remembered: Pa said wildcats were afraid of people and wouldn't come into town. Those men must have been talking about somewhere else.

Disappointed, he scratched his neck and leg, then wiped his nose on his scarf. Oh, well. He still needed to learn a trick. He'd start with "Around the World." He stuck his icy hand, yo-yo and all, inside his coat to warm it up in his armpit.

A shiny, new Packard pulled up in front of the church, its spotless chrome glinting under the streetlight. A big truck coasted to a stop behind it. Some men got out and milled around, talking their grown-up talk.

"...wouldn't come to this if they'd just follow union rules," one of the men said. "Damn wildcat strike. Don't they know the country's at war?"

The others grumbled in agreement. They sounded angry, but

Herbie had more important things to think about than wildcats. Ignoring the angry men, he got the yo-yo going good, up and down and up and down and LOOP. The yo-yo sailed around in a big circle, but the line went slack and the yo-yo came down dead. Herbie sighed and wound it back up.

"Here, pile some more under this window," someone called in a loud whisper.

Up and down and up and down and...

"...screw them boards in tight. No one gets in or out..."

LOOP.

Herbie wrinkled his nose. Someone's car was sure leaking gas bad. Pa said that could be real dangerous.

ZING. The yo-yo sailed over his head. The string was tight. It was going to work, this time.

"...really soak it..."

SNAP!

The string whipped back, yo-yo-less, and hit him in the face. The stringless yo-yo shot through the air, hit the cobblestone with a sharp, sickening crack, and bounced down the street.

"No!" The beautiful, perfect, green paint would be chipped for sure. Herbie's whole world seemed to shrink down to that small, bouncing wonder, his only present that wasn't socks or long underwear or hand-me-down books. He followed it down the street.

Somewhere behind him, beyond the edge of his world, a man's voice bellowed, "Now! Run!"

There was a great *whomp* and something walloped Herbie in the back. He flew through the air, passed over the wobbling yo-yo, and hit the cobblestone with a dull crunch. Stunned, he lay on his back, listening to the ringing in his ears and watching his steamy breath waft into a glowing orange sky. Slowly, his hearing came back, and with it came the sounds of shouts and booted feet, and a crackling roar that sounded like a fire popping in the fireplace. Only much, much bigger.

Suddenly scared, even scareder than when he thought a wildcat was after him, he sat up. Smoky, too-warm air hit him in the face. He blinked his eyes clear. All the horrifying details came to him at once: the burning kindling stacked all around the church, piled highest at the exits, the boards nailed across the door, and windows too high, oh, much too high for anything but a bird to escape. Greedy fingers of flame clawed at the stone and wood building. Stained glass figures danced, lit up by fire inside.

Wooden pews, Herbie thought. It's all wood and cloth and candles inside.

"Pa!"

Shrieking, he ran for the church. A bucket line had already begun throwing water on the inferno. That would do as much good as spitting on a forest fire. Doors opened on neighboring houses and more people rushed out. Some pulled the burning kindling away from the building as if that could somehow take the fire back. Herbie dodged through them, trying to reach the door. Stained glass shattered outward, raining down in colored bits of scorched Apostles. Herbie's heavy boots crunched on them as he took the steps two at a time.

"Pa!" He reached out to tear the flaming boards away with his bare hands, but he was yanked backward. An arm wrapped around him, lifting him off the steps.

"No! My pa's in there."

He kicked his feet helplessly and beat at the wiry arm, but it heedlessly carried him away from the church. Frantic, he sunk his teeth into the flesh.

A man's voice snarled in his ear. "Sheee-it, boy! I'm jus' tryin' to save you from yerself."

"But my pa! He's in there and I gotta let him out!"

"Boy, whoever is in there ain't comin' out alive."

"Yes, he will. I just have to—"

The man spun Herbie around and fixed him with one blue eye set in a wrinkly face. He held a roughly carved spear decorated with black feathers and his cloak billowed around him like a sheet drying in the wind. He looked so strange that Herbie forgot to struggle and stared.

"Your pa's dead, boy. Now, you might never understand, but this fire had to happen and it had to happen tonight."

All at once, Herbie knew this man had done it. Those other men had set the fire, but this man had told them to do it. Maybe he was going to kill Herbie, too, but Herbie was too mad to care.

"I hate you. You're evil!" he screamed, and he pulled his arm back and threw his small fist into that wrinkly nose as hard as he could. It crunched nicely under his knuckles.

"Shee-it!"

Herbie kicked the man's shin and threw himself backward. The man dropped the spear and grabbed Herbie's collar with both hands, pulling him up until they were nose to nose. Herbie glowered into that single eye and the eye glared back, fierce, almost glowing. And then it *was* glowing, brighter and brighter, staining Herbie's thoughts forever. The man's grip slipped from Herbie's collar and he fell, lost in an endless sea of blue.

Down the street from the fire, the sleeping owners of a Queen Anne mansion would have been astonished to find three weird women watching the church burn from their upper balcony. The oldest, a grandmotherly woman in a big-buttoned coat with molting fur trim, leaned over the rail. "I'm disappointed in young One-Eye. Couldn't he have found a less destructive way to stop the strike?"

The youngest, a little girl with Shirley Temple curls, looked up from her spool knitting. "Don't worry, Urdie. He'll pay for being so bad."

The third figure joined the old lady at the rail. A cold wind tossed her frizzy black hair around her dark face. "How do you mean, dear?" She adjusted her silver-rimmed spectacles and peered at the blaze across the street. "What happens next?"

"Yes, tell us, child," said Urdie. Her hat, overburdened with faded silk flowers and a wooden partridge, started to slide. She clamped it onto her head and stepped back from the rail. "Does he succeed in stopping the wolf's plans, at least?"

The girl knitted three more stitches. "Won't tell. It would ruin the surprise."

Nearing its end, her ball of yarn disintegrated into a tangled knot. The girl frowned and yanked at the yarn. Her knitting slipped off the nails and pulled halfway out of the spool.

"Dratted thing," the girl shrieked. She tore at the yarn, unraveling a row of her knitting. The old lady smacked her hand and glared at her.

"Stop that, Skuldi! You know what happens when you don't finish. Now, tell us—what's going to happen to young One-Eye?"

"Won't." The girl crossed her arms and stuck her lip out.

"Hush, you two." The frizzy-haired woman leaned so far over the rail that her necklace dangled in the firelight. Its crystal beads shone like fireflies on a leash. "Something's happening."

The flames had reached the roof of the church. Sirens wailed and the bucket line parted to let the town's only fire truck ease closer to the blaze. Men piled off the truck and began running out hoses and ladders. Amidst the chaos, One-Eye struggled with a small boy.

"Verdandi, my old eyes don't see so far ahead. Who is that boy?"

"He isn't important," said Verdandi. "Just wait."

The boy kicked One-Eye in the leg. One-Eye dropped his spear, which clattered on the cobblestones and rolled away.

Urdie gasped. "That's no way to treat Gungnir! What's One-Eye thinking?"

Water streamed onto the burning roof as the firemen fought to keep the flames from leaping to nearby buildings. Two firemen climbed a ladder to reach the broken window with a hose.

"Oh, they're very brave," said Urdie. "But surely there's no one alive—oh!"

Just as the first fireman reached the window, a falcon exploded out of the church. It wheeled high in the air, smoke and shadow streaming from its wings. Firelight turned its speckled white breast orange. Its head darted, its overlarge eyes searched the teeming street. With a cry, it dove straight at One-Eye's back. One-Eye turned, his one blue eye aglow. He threw up an arm to shield his face, but the falcon swerved and skimmed the cobblestone.

"No!" One-Eye dropped the boy and charged after the bird, but he was too late. The falcon snagged the fallen spear in outstretched talons and flew into the air.

One-Eye raised both arms. "Huginn! Muninn!"

A pair of ravens exploded out of the trees and circled One-Eye's head. "Follow. He's taken Gungnir."

The little girl giggled, her knitting forgotten for the moment. "They'll follow, but they won't catch him!"

Urdie held her hat firmly to her head and stared upward at the black sky where the birds had disappeared. "Oh, dear. This is bad."

Verdandi straightened her glasses and gathered her shawl tight around her shoulders. "Very bad, indeed."

Tall clouds gathered to the west, promising a storm. Briggs stopped walking for a moment to judge their speed. Rain would come sooner rather than later.

Golden-pink bars of sunlight knifed through the clouds over the train yard, lending a red-gold cast to the control tower's dirty walls. Yellow tape marked off the area surrounding a dumpster at the foot of the tower. A pair of investigators worked methodically over the ground inside the tape. They seemed to move slowly and carefully, but Briggs knew they were rushing to collect evidence before the rain washed it away. A man stood on a ladder that leaned against the dumpster, holding a camera and an evidence bag. By the sour expression on his face, Briggs guessed that the air he breathed was none too fresh.

Briggs flashed his badge at the uniform stationed at the crime scene's perimeter. "I'd like a look at the body, if it hasn't been removed."

The officer nodded and jerked his head toward the dumpster. "Go ahead—she's in there, all right. Some damn hooker. I brought her in for solicitation just last week." He sneered and rolled his eyes. "Called herself Loralee."

Briggs gave him a sharp look. "Got what she deserved, eh?"

The officer blinked, looking chagrinned. "No, I didn't say that. I just—"

"Right. Just tell me where I can walk."

Flustered, the officer looked like he wanted to say something more. Then he shrugged. "Straight to the ladder. They're almost done with the grounds."

The stench hit Briggs as he strode toward the dumpster and his lip curled reflexively. How long had the body been in there? But there was something more to the smell than decay. Something familiar...

A woman popped up from inside the dumpster as Briggs got to the ladder. A mask, eye shield, and baseball cap obscured her features, but the lock of blond hair straggling from under the cap suggested that Briggs was looking at Marybeth Simms from the Hennepin County Medical Examiner's Office. He had worked maybe a half dozen cases with her and had been impressed by her intuition. He had also been impressed with her thick, blond hair and easy-going manner and had taken her out to dinner more than once.

"Here's the last of it." She handed the man on the ladder a baggie and brushed her gloved hands together. "How about going on a White Castle run while I pack her up? I'm starved."

It was Marybeth, all right. Same cheerful voice, recognizable even through the mask, and same penchant for greasy burgers. She spotted Briggs and waved. "Grab some gloves and booties and climb in here. You gotta see this."

She disappeared into the dumpster before Briggs could answer. He smiled ruefully. "Hi, Marybeth."

The man on the ladder tossed him a pair of booties and left for his burger run so fast that Briggs didn't have time to say thanks. Briggs donned the booties and pulled a pair of latex gloves from his grip. As an afterthought, he added a paper filter mask, hoping it would block the smell.

The dumpster was mostly empty. Good—less garbage to wade through. Maybe this wouldn't be so bad. He climbed the ladder and lowered himself inside. The putrid odor pierced through the mask before his feet hit the floor.

"Christ!"

He threw a hand against the wall and waited for his lunch to decide whether to stay or go. Slowly, his sense of smell dulled and his lunch decided to stay where it was. Eyes watering, he stepped between a spilled box of packing peanuts and a fly-covered, half-eaten pizza to reach the body. Marybeth squatted near the head, speaking in a low, rapid voice into a recorder. Briggs crouched near the feet.

From the smell, he expected the corpse to be rotted and covered with flies. He was wrong. The woman's body lay sprawled across a burst trash bag. She was naked, so he could easily see that her skin was still smooth and intact. No bloating had occurred. The blood on her neck, the only open wound, was still wet and red.

"Where the hell is that stench coming from?" The only organic matter he could see besides the body was the fly-covered pizza.

"I don't know," said Marybeth, her voice muffled by her mask. "But that's not the only weird thing. Look at that wound!"

Marybeth made room so Briggs could get a closer look at the woman's neck. Her throat was flat and misshapen. Puzzled, he leaned closer. It took him a moment to understand what he was seeing. He sat back with a grunt.

"It looks like it's been crushed. What did it?"

"Someone's hand," Marybeth said matter-of-factly.

"Come on, be serious."

"I am. Look." She traced a dark indentation on the left side of the neck. "And see? Four more bruises on the right side. Exactly where a thumb and four fingers might wrap to squeeze a victim's throat."

Briggs checked again. She was right. And the blood had come from punctures at the ends of the bruises, where the attacker's fingers might have dug into the flesh. "You're saying some guy did that with one hand?"

That would certainly shorten the list of possible suspects.

"Yeah, and not only that—look." She used a pencil to lift long, black hair away from the victim's face. The discolored skin, hemorrhages around the eyes, and protruding tongue were typical signs of strangling, but her head lay at an odd angle.

"Looks like her neck is broken," he said. "Might've happened when she was dropped into the dumpster."

"Don't I wish. I'll have to verify, but I see no sign of damage to her head. It looks to me like she landed on her ass on that trash bag. I suppose someone might have twisted her neck after she was dead, but I don't think so."

She pushed the hair clear of the body's neck and pointed at the spine. "There are more bruises here. It looks like he crushed her throat, then adjusted his grip to encompass her spine. Big hands."

She sat back and drummed her pencil on her thigh. Her eyes blinked rapidly behind her eye shield. "I'll be able to say more after the autopsy, of course, but my first guess is that we have a psycho superman on the loose."

Just what he needed. "Could the guy have been hopped up on PCP or something?"

"Maybe. Even Superman needs a little help, once in a while." A note of clinical admiration entered her voice. "I can't wait to see the samples from under her nails. Maybe we'll find out that he's some sort of genetic weirdo."

"She scratched him? Then maybe some of this blood is his."

He bent close to her hand to check her fingers for blood. Four long, manicured nails glinted back at him in a familiar shade of metallic gold. The fifth nail was missing.

"It couldn't be," he whispered. His gaze traveled to the victim's face. He hadn't looked that closely at her features before. Now he looked past the death contortions and swore.

He knew that face.

He closed his eyes and saw her as she was in his dream. Blond at first, then dark haired, singing "Ave Maria." And then she started screaming...

"Hey, Briggs! Wake up!"

How could a girl he'd never seen before show up in a dream and then end up dead in a dumpster an hour later?

Marybeth shook his arm. "What's wrong? Did you know her?"

"No." Briggs blinked stupidly. What else could he say? "Uh, no. Not really."

"Okay. Then try to stay focused." She pointed at the victim's neck. "You notice anything weird about those wounds?"

He took a shallow breath, almost grateful that the stench gave him something else to think about. "What, you mean besides the fact that they were made one-handed by someone with more hand-strength than an orangutan?"

"No need to get sarcastic," she said, folding her arms.

"Sorry, it's been a very long, very strange day. What am I missing?"

"No flies."

"Huh?"

"There are flies buzzing all around us." A smug note entered her voice. The girl liked to show off. "They're coating that pizza over there like a double order of olives. Look, one just landed on my eye shield. Why aren't flies going after that nice, fresh blood on her neck?"

"Good question." And a familiar one. He had seen something like this before. But where?

And then it hit him. Briggs had asked the same question months ago, in a boxcar, the day he had met Jungle Jim Tuttle. The stench had been awful. The boxcar was hot, but the body had not degraded enough to explain the smell. And there were no flies on the body, though they swarmed the blood pooling on the floor.

"Oh, shit. I gotta go."

"What's wrong?"

"I've got a hunch."

This murder was connected with the Hobo Spider. He couldn't prove it, but he knew it as surely as if he had witnessed the killings, himself. He was also certain that James Tuttle did not have the size or strength to murder Loralee. That made him a witness—their one and only. Not an enviable position.

"Well, don't keep it to yourself!" Marybeth said. "What is it?"

"I'll tell you later. But right now, I've got to find someone before he becomes the next victim."

CHAPTER THIRTEEN

Lennie squirmed on the hard bench seat, impatient for the so-called poetry reading to end. She didn't see why Jungle Jim had been so excited about it. The performers were just that—performers. And not very good ones. None of them had recited poetry. Jungle Jim hadn't even shown up.

She and Junkyard sat front and center on rickety bleachers that might have been dragged out of a high school gym. It had gotten cold once the sun had set. A gust blew Lennie's hair into her face. She shivered, grateful for the jacket Junkyard had bought her, though she felt a bit conspicuous in it. It was a black, second-hand letter jacket with leather sleeves and a giant, gold K on the chest. Between that and the bleachers, Lennie was having flashbacks to night football games in high school. Come to think of it, she'd rather watch football than the current performer, who told Internet jokes while he juggled.

She leaned closer to Junkyard. "I thought there was supposed to be poetry. And where are all the hobos?"

"Poetry?" He looked puzzled, and then seemed to understand. "Oh, that's later tonight. This is just part of the festival. I thought you might like it."

"I see," she said, trying not to show her irritation. She'd rather be somewhere warm, but she didn't want to offend him. "It's, um, it's great. Thanks."

"No problem."

The performer finished and bowed to anemic applause. Junkyard went back to watching the stage as if he were eager for the next act, but a hint of a smirk twitched the corners of his mouth. Lennie eyed him with suspicion. "This wouldn't be revenge for the pinball game, would it?"

"What? No." He looked at her with wide-eyed and completely fake shock. "No, of course not. Well, maybe. But it has the side benefit of being around a lot of people. Seems like a good idea after our run-in with the Ragman."

A drop of rain hit Lennie's face and a gust of wind tore some hair loose from her ponytail. "Okay, you've had your fun. Surely there are places *inside* with a lot of people. I think this metal bench has siphoned all the heat out of my butt."

"Just a little longer. The best is yet to come. I promise."

"That wouldn't take much," she muttered. Junkyard didn't seem to hear.

The next performer was introduced as a hobo poet, though his poems sounded more like bad song lyrics than actual poetry. Some were supposed to be funny, others romanticized portrayals of adventure. All were loaded with clichés and self-justifying crap about life on the open road. Finally, the performer tucked his bindle under an arm and sauntered toward the stage's side exit.

"*I'm catchin' out / On liberty's trail,*" he intoned, giving a wave which Lennie desperately hoped meant his act was drawing to a close.

> "*Happy and free*
> *Is my life on the rail.*
> *Don't try to tie me,*
> *No strings can bind me,*
> *'Less'n I end up in jail.*"

A weak chuckle rippled around the audience. Lennie's hands curled into fists inside her jacket sleeves. "Try writing a poem telling how happy and free the ones who were left behind feel."

Junkyard leaned closer. "Did you say something?"

She shook her head. If she opened her mouth again, she might heave boiling outrage directly onto the stage.

The poet bowed to scattered applause and several people got up to leave. Lennie envied them. The MC came on stage and the worry on his face was visible from the bleachers. His voice cracked as he began the next introduction. "Right, yes, uh...hang on, folks, I have a special treat for you. Here, all the way from Little Yellow Banks, Kentucky, is Too-Long Soo and Woody, her bangin' guitar. Give 'em a chance, folks. You won't be sorry."

Surprised, Lennie forgot her anger and applauded as Soo strode onto the stage. She wore the same purple shirt and fedora as that morning, but had swapped her maroon down vest for one of black leather. Her battered guitar hung from her shoulder, string ends sticking out from the pegs like cactus spines. She perched on a stool that was almost tall enough for her and settled the guitar on her knee. Winking at Lennie and Junkyard, she started to play.

The MC wasn't exaggerating—Soo really did bang on her guitar, on the strings and on the wood. The result was energetic and percussive. She hunched over the guitar like a human question mark, head down, isolated in a circle of light, as if she played privately in her living room while uninvited listeners pressed their noses to the picture window.

As she thumped and stomped her way through a lively, bluesy-sounding tune, the bleachers began to fill and a crowd gathered in the periphery. Eventually her hands slowed on the guitar. She leaned toward the microphone. "I'm gonna play a Woody Guthrie song for y'all that'll make ye want to either write to Congress or go on vacation. Me, well, I play this song a lot, so my Congressman asked me not to write 'im anymore."

Her fingers climbed the fingerboard like a spider. "He asked me real polite-like, too. Sent out a man in a nice black suit and some kinda radio stuck in his ear." She banged out a single chord and let it ring. "Made me feel special."

The audience laughed and Soo launched into the song. Recognizing it, Lennie hooted in delight. Her father used to sing the same song every time they had gone fishing together, even before she could bait her own hook. The verses were a little different than Lennie remembered. Thinking back, she realized the words had been a little different every time her father sang it. Likely, he made them up to fit the moment. That was how she needed to remember him. Gentle, jovial, fun. The time for anger was gone.

The song ended and Soo launched directly into another. By Billy Bragg, she said. Lennie had never heard of him, but it didn't matter. Soo's rusty contralto could make the alphabet song sound good. A little star-struck, Lennie leaned close to Junkyard. "She's amazing. Who'd have thought it? Next you're going to tell me that Bones O'Riley has his own show on the Food Network, and Hotshot Bob is a NASCAR driver. Where are all the *real* hobos?"

He looked at her sharply, frowning. "What's a real hobo? It's not like you have to pass a test and wear a uniform to be a—"

He glanced past her and stiffened, his eyes widening in recognition. She started to turn.

"Don't look," he said. He returned his own gaze to the stage. "It's the Ragman. Along with a couple of his homies. Just act normal and watch the show. It's dark—maybe they won't spot us."

Lennie caught her breath, remembering the Ragman's creepy eyes, his breath...his iron grip on her wrist. She tried to keep her gaze fixed on the stage, but couldn't stop herself. She glanced back.

The Ragman's eyes were waiting for her. Not human brown, as they should have been, but animal yellow, shining bright in the shadows at stage left. The sting of a thousand electric mosquitoes answered in her tattooed hand and she slapped her other hand over the triangles.

"Um, he spotted us, all right."

The Ragman's mouth twisted in a slow, ugly sneer. He nudged his companions and pointed. Lennie was suddenly glad they were front and center on the bleachers, surrounded by at least a hundred people. But the show wouldn't last forever.

Oblivious, Soo was telling a story to the audience. "—and Charlie had the winning numbers, but he couldn't hear too good. He threw that lottery ticket down the port-a-potty. When his buddies found out, they crammed into that john like they's goin' for some kind of record. Well, it started to shake, then it started to wobble—"

"What are we going to do?" Lennie whispered. She braced her hands on the bench, every muscle tensed and ready to run. But Junkyard stayed where he was. He gave a loud cough. Still talking to the audience, Soo glanced his way and Junkyard jerked his head toward the Ragman. Soo's gaze slid from Junkyard to the gangbangers. She gave a little nod and continued her story.

"—that john tumbled down the hill, them boys hollerin' and carryin' on inside like a bunch o' fifth grade girls in a Tilt-O-Whirl. It finally came to rest upside down in the middle of the road. Y'all don't want to know what was leakin' out the air vents."

Soo paused to let her listeners wince appreciatively. The gangbangers mounted the bleachers and began working their way through the audience. Lennie elbowed Junkyard frantically and leaned forward, ready to shoot off the bench, but he held her back.

"Wait," he mouthed.

"Are you crazy?" She glanced at the gangbangers. Her heart pounded as if she had already sprinted a mile. "We can't stay here!"

"Everyone gathered 'round that port-a-potty," Soo continued, "waitin' fer that door to open. That's when my Uncle Charlie yelled, 'Why, here it is. It was in my pocket the whole dang time!' "

She banged a riff out on the guitar while the audience laughed and clapped. The gangbangers were nearly behind Lennie and Junkyard, two rows back. Lennie's legs twitched with an hysterical desire to run.

"And now, folks," Soo said over the applause, "I'd like to direct yer attention to the center of the bleachers. Hank, can y'all give us a spotlight on them three boys?"

There was an awkward pause. Then a small halo of light swung around to the audience, exposing naked surprise on the hard faces of the gangbangers.

"*Now* run," said Junkyard.

Lennie launched from the bench before he'd finished speaking, with Junkyard close behind. Soo's amplified voice followed them as they plunged into the darkness behind the stage.

"I know these here boys don't look like much, but they have an act y'all wouldn't believe. Come on up, boys, and do your thang."

There was silence, then the Ragman swore. "You dead, bitch. Walkin' dead."

Lennie and Junkyard dashed toward the parking lot. Most of the festival had shut down for the night, but the neon glow of the carnival shone like a beacon at the far end. Shouts of surprise and anger erupted behind them. Lennie pictured the bangers scrambling from the bleachers, trampling anyone who got in their way. She ran harder, but the pavement between them and the carnival seemed to stretch into a great asphalt ocean. They'd never make it.

Then the white display tents mushroomed out of the darkness just ahead. Junkyard veered sharply and dodged behind the nearest tent. Surprised by the unexpected move, Lennie overran the turn. Catching herself, she turned back on time to see the gangbangers stride from the bleachers, into the darkness behind the stage. She willed herself invisible and sprinted the last few steps to the tents.

"There she is!"

Lennie swore and darted out of sight. The Ragman's harsh shouts followed her into the canvas maze. The tent village was dark, deserted, with door flaps tied closed for the night. Lennie and Junkyard wove between tents, dashing through patches of stark light painted by streetlights on the white canvas walls. The gangbangers' curses grew louder. Fear tightened Lennie's throat and she began to wheeze. Junkyard bumped her arm and pointed at a sign over a doorway. It was painted with a railroad detective shield.

Bill's tent.

They ran for the door. Its flaps were tied back, but there was no light inside. Surely Bill had gone home. Then something dark moved inside, like a figure made of solid shadow. Lennie stopped.

"Someone's in there," she whispered.

"It's just Bill. Get inside before they find us."

The dense shadow seemed to evaporate as he spoke, revealing the dim, ordinary form of a man. She blinked. What had she seen?

The slap of running feet rang like gunshot behind them. Junkyard yanked her into the tent and dropped the door flaps over the opening. Trying to quiet her breathing, Lennie bent to help tie the door shut. Wind shook the canvas, yanking the strings from her fumbling fingers. The sounds of pursuit stopped abruptly. She could hear the gangbangers' voices clearly.

"Shit, man, we lost them. Not good. Not good at all. El Lobo wants the *chica* real bad."

"Maybe they went into a tent."

"*Si*, I thought I saw something move over there."

Lennie froze, her fingers still on the strings. Slowly, silently, Junkyard moved to the side of the door, his knife already in his hand. He motioned Lennie to do the same, so she dug into her pocket for the Ragman's knife. Then the voices moved off, growing faint. Junkyard held one hand up, waiting for what seemed like an hour before he relaxed and put his knife away. He bent to finish tying the door flaps closed.

Lennie nearly screamed when a camping lantern flickered on behind her. A man straightened from the lamp and stared at her bleakly. He hardly looked like the Bill Sutter who had pointed her toward Bones O'Riley's mulligan stew that morning. His fleshy cheeks sagged, pale and glistening with sweat, and a dark clot of blood showed through his thin, blond hair. Lennie nudged Junkyard.

"Hang on," he grunted. He finished fastening the last tie without looking up. "That'll hold 'em. For about five seconds." He let his head droop and braced his hands on his knees like a winded basketball player. "I feel like I'm breathing fire."

Bill leaned on the display case unsteadily. A duffle bag dangled from one hand and he clutched a railroad police badge in the other. His disheveled, blood-streaked face had a look of desperation that Lennie didn't like. She thumped Junkyard's back harder.

"Ouch!" Junkyard straightened and rubbed his back. He looked at the man and frowned. "Jeez, Bill, you look terrible. What happened?"

Bill's shadow-haunted eyes flicked between Junkyard and Lennie. He seemed to have forgotten the duffle bag in his half-raised hand. Then he shook his head as though to clear it and breath exploded from him.

"Holy crap, Doug." He dropped the police badge into the duffle bag and swept a hand through his hair, laying some of the longer strands over the bloody spot. "I thought you were—" he hesitated, swallowing, "well, someone else."

"Who—" Junkyard began, then shook his head. "No, tell us later. Right now, better turn off that damn light before—"

"*Vatos!* Look, a light in that tent!"

"Shit!" Junkyard met Lennie's eyes. They were trapped.

"That's gotta be them," another voice said. It sounded like the Ragman. "Save the *chica* for El Lobo, but leave the man for me. *Lo chingaré!*"

"Dammit, Doug." Color washed into Bill's face. He frowned, looking more like the bull Lennie had met that morning. "I thought you stopped picking fights. I can't keep bailing you out."

"Hey, he started it."

The scuff of running feet reached through the tent walls. Bill grabbed his jacket from the back of a chair and pulled a gun from its pocket. "Never mind, tell me about it later. Pull up the canvas and run. This, I can handle."

Junkyard shook his head. "You can't face them alone, Bill," he said in a low whisper. "Between the three of us, we'll scare them off."

Lennie backed away from the door until she bumped into the rear wall. "It's nice of you to include me, but I doubt any gangbangers would be scared of me."

"She's right. Just keep quiet and get her out of here," Bill whispered. He stuck the gun in the back waistband of his pants. "As far as they need to know, you were never here."

The sounds of running stopped outside the tent. Bill, Junkyard, and Lennie fell silent, listening to the harsh breathing at the door. The tent flap shook violently.

"Shit, man," a voice said. "Double knots."

"Cut it. Just cut it."

Something snicked. A knife poked between the flaps and sawed into a tie at head-level. Junkyard pulled his own knife and started toward the door, but Bill caught his arm.

"Who's out there?" Bill called in a stern voice. He motioned Junkyard and Lennie to the back of the tent.

The blade paused for a heartbeat. "Let us in and find out."

The voices laughed and the knife slid once more across the tie, parting it. Junkyard dropped silently to the ground, pulling Lennie down with him. Wind battered the walls, widening the gap in the door. Arms crossed, Bill stepped in front of it to block the view.

"Hello, Ragman. You don't need to slice up my tent. If you want in from the storm, all you gotta do is ask."

"*Lo siento*, Bill. We didn't know it was yours," the Ragman said, but he didn't sound apologetic. "We were jus' looking for two *amigos*, *sí*? A *gringo* with sideburns and a skinny woman with wild hair."

"Friends of yours?" Thunder rolled, almost obscuring Bill's voice. "From the description, I'd say they don't sound like your type."

"Me and my *compadres*, we like all types."

The gangbangers laughed. Not a pleasant sound. Lennie wanted out. Now. Carefully, quietly, she sidled to the back wall. Junkyard did the same.

"Tell me, *mi amigo*." The Ragman's voice turned hard and humorless. The knife went to work on the next set of ties. "Do you know where they are?"

"Now stop that." Bill sounded genuinely irritated. "Don't you know how to untie knots, boy? Here, let me do that."

Bill went to work on the double knot, still blocking the gangbangers' view of the interior. The wind struck again, hard, and the tent shuddered violently. Under the cover of flapping canvas, Junkyard lifted the back wall and they rolled through the opening. The wall dropped closed behind them, muffling Bill's voice.

"Now, do you see? No one in here but me."

Rain splattered down. Lennie pushed to her feet and tried to look in all directions at once. The gangbangers hadn't thought to send someone to check the back of the tent, but she felt as if the very shadows were watching her.

"Carnival," Junkyard whispered, and Lennie forced her stiffening legs to move.

The storm was almost on them. Carnival music blasted at full volume, but the rides had shut down and the few remaining customers were heading for their cars before the sky truly opened. Lightning flashed overhead, followed seconds later by a loud rumble. Lennie ran, half-expecting to hear gunshots at their backs, but there was nothing—no angry shouts, no firecracker pop—just carnival noise and the rush of wind. She slowed and trotted backward to check for pursuit. The lot between them and the tent village was empty.

Then she looked up.

Shadow billowed above the tents like black smoke against the night-darkened clouds. But where smoke would dissipate in the wind, this shadow reached across the parking lot, an oily black snake driving all its malevolence onto the single point that was Lennie.

She stumbled backward, barely keeping to her feet. Pressure swelled in her head, like the morning's attack, only faster and stronger. Her tattooed hand began to burn and the hairs lifted on her arm. A memory arose in her mind, blocking the storm, the parking lot, even blocking the music from the carnival. She saw her mother lying in a puddle of vomit, unconscious and not breathing. She tried to push the memory away, but the images came anyway, their edges bleeding into yellow haze.

The smell had been the worst. Stale beer and bile. She had opened the front door to it after school on her thirteenth birthday and had wanted to run away without stepping inside, pretending not to see her mother on the floor. But her father had been the one to run out, not Lennie. So she dropped her book bag and addressed the situation as though following a checklist: 1) call 911, 2) clean out victim's mouth, 3) administer CPR.

When her mother coughed back to life, Lennie found a blanket to keep her warm until the ambulance came. Just another day at the Cook's residence.

But had it really happened that way? She had found her mother passed out many times, but had she ever stopped breathing? Had it ever happened on Lennie's birthday?

Real or not, the memory was now hers. Forever.

Electric fire surged in her tattooed hand, clearing her head for a moment. But the pressure returned, worse than before. A new image came—her father's face, sneering and ugly in the thickening yellow haze. She wanted to claw at the face, tear it away...

Instinctively, she focused on the burning tattoo. A prickling radiated from her hand with an almost audible hum. Her fingers convulsed, but she forced them to spread. The charge built along her lifeline, throbbing, threatening to split the skin. She could feel its power, could sense the potential, but had no idea what to do with it.

Above her head, the shadow recoiled as though sensing her efforts. She thrust her palm toward it, fingers splayed. She could almost picture what she needed to do.

Then Junkyard was there, pulling on her arm. "What're you doing, Lennie? They'll see us."

She yanked her arm free and desperately tried to regain her focus, but the charge faded, leaving her hand cold and numb. "Damn it!"

Still breathing hard, Junkyard scanned the parking lot. "What's wrong? Did you see them?"

She looked at him, incredulous. "What do you mean? Can't you see it?"

"See what?" He pulled the bandana from his hair and wiped his face with it. He looked younger, more vulnerable without it. "Lennie, we have to go."

"There." She pointed into the sky above Bill's tent and watched

Junkyard's reaction. His gaze trailed upward, but he looked puzzled. Lennie looked past her still-pointing finger and saw only the ordinary matte black of a stormy night sky. She let her hand drop.

"Never mind."

She rubbed her tattoo like a talisman, the one solid piece of evidence that she wasn't hallucinating. Maybe she should tell Junkyard about the mental attacks, the tattoo, everything. If all of it was real, he should be warned. If it wasn't, if she was crazy, well, maybe he should be warned about that, too.

"Uh, Junkyard?" She hesitated. What approach would make her sound the least insane? "I've been—"

"Can it wait? We're vulnerable here. Not enough people around."

As if to punctuate his statement, the loud music cut out, leaving them in sudden, ominous silence. The shadows seemed to press closer, as if listening to their plans. Junkyard must have felt it, too. He started walking fast enough that Lennie had to trot to keep up. He kept his voice low when he spoke again. "Let's get to the poetry reading. Some of those 'bos are pretty tough. The 'bangers won't want to tangle with them."

"Uh, sure. But—"

"Besides, I'm a little worried. Jim was supposed to be with Bill. If he's not at the poetry reading—"

Lightning crashed overhead, so close that there was no lag before the thunder. The sky opened and water came down in wind-blown waves. Junkyard took off at a trot. Frustrated, Lennie followed.

CHAPTER FOURTEEN

Running again. This time, through a wall of rain. Lennie wiped at the water streaming down her face and tried not to think about how tired she was. Junkyard seemed ready to run all night, but she was a sprinter, not a marathoner.

Lightning tore the clouds to the north, then again to the south. Thunder rolled across the sky. She cringed, feeling exposed.

"The gods are going bowling," she murmured, feeling a little delirious. Her father used to say that during storms. Another flash blinded her for a moment, followed by a sharp crack. She ducked, her nerves crackling in response. *The gods are going bowling, bowling, bowling.* She hated thunderstorms.

"This is...just a little...dangerous." She didn't have enough air left to infuse irony into the statement.

Junkyard only grunted and slogged through another puddle. His ponytail had fallen out and the hair-band, knotted at the end of a thin lock, bounced on his shoulder as he ran. Her own hair clung to her neck in wet strings, and her canvas shoes flopped and squished with each step. She hoped the poetry reading was someplace that had a roof. And central heating.

Junkyard slowed when he reached East River Parkway and stopped to study the steep embankment below. A faint odor of dead fish wafted up from the river and mixed with the wormy smell of rain on pavement. Cones of rain-muted light radiated from the streetlights, deepening the surrounding shadow. Lennie leaned over the guardrail. In the weak light, the tangled, leafy mass lining the slope below might have been shrubbery or the tops of tall trees.

"What are we looking for?"

Junkyard answered without turning. "A path. It leads down to an abandoned boathouse."

"A b-boathouse?" So much for central heating. The old letter jacket had kept Lennie's arms and torso mostly dry, but her rain-soaked jeans chafed like sandpaper across her thighs and her teeth had started to chatter.

"Hobos've been using it for decades, though not so much anymore. In the old days, there might've been fifteen, twenty 'bos looking for a place to stay on a night like this. The boathouse was big enough to hold 'em, and the river was handy for cooking and washing. Now, they'd rather jungle up closer to the track than go all the way down to the river. But it's perfect for the annual poetry reading."

Junkyard paused as a lone man crossed into the halo of a streetlight. Lennie tensed until she saw that the man wore a cowboy hat and gray coveralls stretched over a large gut. No gangbanger could survive looking like that. Hitching up the legs of his overalls, he climbed over the guardrail and disappeared down the embankment.

"Ah, that must be the path." Junkyard started toward the spot as two more people stepped into the light. They saw him and waved before following the first man over the side. Junkyard waved back. "The fellow with the forked beard and yellow slicker is old Slim Dandy. Thinks he's the next Pete Seegar. He'll probably sing something at the poetry reading." He swung a leg over the guardrail. "Careful, this mud is slippery."

Lennie hesitated, uncertain what she was getting herself into. Attending a poetry reading had seemed reasonable enough in the daylight, when Jungle Jim had suggested it. But going to a secluded, abandoned building with a bunch of rough men she didn't know wasn't so appealing.

Still, she *knew* what the gangbangers would do if they caught her. And the poetry reading was her best chance to find out something more about her father. Besides, where else could she go? Exhausted, teeth chattering, she forced her stiff legs to move. Maybe there'd be some coffee boiling over a campfire, like in the movies.

Before she could follow Junkyard over the rail, she heard the scrape of feet on pavement. She looked around, expecting to see another hobo heading for the boathouse.

The street was empty.

But the footsteps continued, and the jingle of coins joined the cadence—*shuffle-jingle-shuffle....shuffle-jingle-shuffle*. A lot of coins. Someone had deep pockets.

Lennie stood transfixed, caught by the rhythmic duet. Slow and steady, *shuffle, jingle, shuffle*, Frankenstein's monster out for an evening stroll.

"Junkyard?" she whispered, but he had disappeared down the trail. She peered into the shadows. Did monsters carry pocket change?

A form distilled out of the mist, dark and undefined at the rim of the streetlight's world. Another sound joined the cadence, like the faint, steady clicking of squirrel's teeth on a walnut shell. The figure stepped closer and the streetlight unveiled an incongruous straw hat with a full bouquet of artificial flowers clumped on one side.

The obscured figure became a short, fat old woman laboring down the sidewalk in three layers of mismatched flower-print dress. *Shuffle-jingle*—the shuffle from an ancient pair of snowmobile boots, the jingle from a luggage-sized purse hanging from the crook of her elbow. Knitting needles clutched in her knobby-knuckled hands clicked at green wool like chopsticks fighting over spinach noodles.

Lennie exhaled. Muscles she had unknowingly clenched ached as she allowed herself to relax. No monster, no mummy, not even a gangbanger. Just a little old bag lady. Who had caught her staring.

The woman stopped in front of her, so close that Lennie could see the dirt imbedded in the straw weave of her hat. An odor wafted from her, strong but not unpleasant, like damp moss growing at the foot of a tree. Small, bright eyes met Lennie's out of a wrinkled face. Lennie wanted to look away, but she could hardly pretend she hadn't noticed a person two feet away on an otherwise empty street.

The corners of the bag lady's eyes crinkled at Lennie's discomfort. She spoke in a cheery grandmother voice. "Can you spare some change for a hungry old lady?"

The bag lady ran her fingers down a length of green yarn. A shiver ran down Lennie's spine.

"I'm sorry," Lennie said with an apologetic smile. "I don't even have fifty cents to call my mother for a ride."

Lennie's voice caught as she realized what she was saying. It was only an expression, a way of saying "I have no money for you," but it hurt nonetheless. Her smile tightened against sudden tears.

"Oh, dear. That won't do." The woman fussed at her purse's latch. "I think I can spare some change for *you*."

The purse's hinged mouth sprang open, spitting coins to the ground. Distressed, the bag lady put a hand to her mouth. "Oh, my!"

Her eyes darted to follow the bouncing and rolling money. When the last coin settled, she lowered herself to her knees, leaving the purse open at Lennie's feet. It was filled to the top with coins: copper and silver, large and small. Spare change, indeed. The purse must weigh at least thirty pounds.

The bag lady gathered her coins along the curb, hunched on all fours like a gaudy, over-stuffed ottoman. "I'm saving for the future, you know." She picked up a penny. "It's never too soon to start."

Lennie stooped to help, but the bag lady was surprisingly quick. She scraped up the coins by the fistful, dumped them into the purse, and clambered to her feet before Lennie could retrieve more than a handful. Lennie tried to return the coins, but the bag lady folded Lennie's fingers over the money.

"No, child. You keep those. Use them to make your phone call—though it'll take more than spare change to reach your mother, now, won't it."

"What? How did...who—"

The right question would not congeal. Then Lennie noticed that the woman's hands, still cupped around her own, were warm and dry despite scrambling after cold, wet coins on puddled pavement. Impossibly, the layered dresses, the boots, the ridiculous fake flowers on her hat, were all untouched by the weather.

The woman was part of it.

Though Lennie's tattoo remained quiet, though no shadows beat at the doors of her mind, Lennie knew that this woman was no bag lady. She had to be part of the gauzy web of impossibility that had snared Lennie the moment she had latched onto the door of a moving train.

Lennie tried to pull her hand free, but the dry grip of gnarled fingers held her fast. The bag lady turned Lennie's hand over and nodded at the tattoo as if she had expected it to be there.

"Yes, you are the one, aren't you." She tsked and traced a finger around the interlocking triangles. "Poor thing."

"W-what do you mean?" Lennie didn't want to be *the one*, not to little old bag ladies, or one-eyed dream squirrels, and especially not to towering shadows that rained black tar on her soul.

The bag lady looked over her shoulder, then back at Lennie. She leaned in to whisper. "You wear the Valknut, my dear. The rune of binding. Odin's mark."

As she spoke, the air thickened with the rich scent of loamy forest floor. Her voice deepened, growing distant and formal. She straightened and seemed to grow taller, willowy within dark robes, though she never ceased to be a squat bag lady in flower print and straw hat. She leaned closer still, holding Lennie's gaze.

"You are the one who must face the Wolf. Face him to find your father and put things right. Face him, and remember this—*that which can be cut can never be broken.*"

The words rang in the heavy air, echoing deep in Lennie's mind until she knew she would never forget them. Then the woman dropped Lennie's hand and fussed with her hat, just a bag lady again. She picked up her purse and snapped it shut.

"You remember that, child, and do what you need to do." Purse slung over one arm, knitting tucked under the other, the bag lady turned to shuffle-jingle away.

Lennie stood as though paralyzed, a thousand questions piling up in her throat. Finally, here was someone who could answer them. "Wait!"

The bag lady paused. Lennie waved her fist in the air and said, "Do you know where this tattoo came from? And who are you, anyway?"

The woman looked genuinely startled. "Why, don't you know? I'm Urd."

This must be the "Urdie" Jungle Jim had told Lennie about. Urdie would be at the poetry reading, he had said. She *knows* things. Well, if she knows so much, then she can sure as hell answer a few more questions.

"Do you know what's been happening to me?"

"Did your father not tell you?" Lennie shook her head and the bag lady tsked. "For shame. Yes, you should be told—"

Legs hissed through the tall grass on the embankment. Junkyard's voice called for her. Lennie ignored him and waited for Urdie to go on.

"Lennie, come on," Junkyard said, sounding more insistent. "Do you *want* those 'bangers to find you?"

She glanced back at him. He looked worried and a little irritated. "I'm sorry," she said. "I was talking to this lady. She seems to know something about..."

As she spoke, she gestured at the spot where Urdie had been. The bag lady was gone, without jingle or shuffle or clicking of needles to mark her passage.

Lennie ground her teeth together so hard that her jaw ached. "Never mind," she said. "Go on—I'll be right behind you."

She was getting very tired of having things disappear whenever Junkyard showed up.

CHAPTER FIFTEEN

The falcon circled above two figures spotlighted under a streetlight on East River Parkway. The air hung dead in the aftermath of the storm; no wind to catch in feathered sails. Nevertheless, the falcon paused, hovering motionless on bowed wings. Its head pointed downward, a predator assessing his prey.

Lennie Cook, the prey, stooped to pick something up. The other figure flickered like a candle under his yellow raptor eye—now a bag lady, sometimes something else, always Urd. Fenrir hated her in all her forms, for she was the keeper of the prognostication of his death.

He sank lower on the lifeless air. Carnivore blood burned in his breast. Frustrated, he clacked his beak and struck the air with his talon. He wanted to take them both. Now. He would take them both, but not together. Lennie would live her illusion of freedom a few hours longer.

Tonight, everything would change. After tonight, the prophecy that had gripped him in its own taloned feet would be no more.

He marked Lennie with his predator eye. Then, with a few powerful strokes of his wings, he plunged down the embankment into the dark woods below.

The gathering for the poetry reading grew by ones and twos. Hobos ambled down the path, emerging from the trees like lost scarecrows. Soaked with rain, they escaped the bone-chilling mist in the relative dry of the boathouse. Some clambered onto plywood bunks stacked liked track shelving on racks that once held sculls and skiffs. Others hunkered down on the crumbling cement floor, jostling to find space under the leaky roof.

Lennie stopped at the edge of the boat landing. She thought her teeth might shatter from chattering if she didn't find a way to get warm, but she couldn't bring herself to enter the boathouse. The panel door gaped open and she could see dark figures moving within. It reminded her of the Jaycee's Haunted House she had entered as a child, where monsters lurked, dark mounds of unknown terror, grabbing for her in strobing flashes of twisted faces and clutching hands.

She had never enjoyed haunted houses.

But these weren't ghosts and monsters. These were real hobos, men who may have seen her father, would maybe help her find him. She looked back toward the woods where Junkyard had gone to collect firewood, took a deep breath, and stepped through the boathouse door.

At once, a huge man lunged out of the shadows, snarling like a stray dog. A bulbous nose and broken teeth loomed at her through the dark.

"Yargh—git on outta here, ya scunge." Ulcerous breath sprayed her face. "Ain't enough room for no more!"

He shoved her so hard that her feet left the ground. She landed badly on a jag of broken concrete and tumbled down toward the river. She skidded to a stop just short of the water and lay face down, waiting for pain. There would be blood, too. It was only a question of how much. She groaned and a chorus of harsh laughter erupted from the boathouse.

And this was supposed to be a *safe* place to hole up?

When she opened her eyes, a pair of boots stood before her. Her gaze trailed up patched and faded blue jeans to a jacket covered in slogans. One of them said, *With friends like you, who needs enemies?*

"Oh. Hi, Junkyard."

She sat up, wincing, feeling where every bruise and scab was going to emerge. Junkyard shifted his load of firewood under one arm and leaned over her.

"You okay?" He looked more amused than worried.

"So. These are the poets." Lennie worked her tongue around and spit grit. "Literary giants, all. I can tell."

Junkyard snorted. "Yeah, well, you know these artistic types. Very temperamental." He helped her up and made a show of brushing dirt off her jacket. "Strange, though. Slippery Mick usually behaves himself at these things. Good thing he didn't notice you were a girl, or he might not have let go."

"Oh, now there's a lovely thought." Mick's hulk paced like a caged ogre in the boathouse doorway. Lennie shuddered. It was hard to imagine how a soft man like her father could survive ten years in such company.

"Maybe it's the weather. The crowd seems rougher than usual, tonight. You'd better stick close." Looking her over, he pushed her hair under her jacket's collar and zipped the jacket to her chin. "There. Now try acting more like a guy."

He rummaged in his bag and handed her a wet wipe. She used it to dab the scrapes on her chin and hands. A sharp pebble had lodged in her palm. She picked at it, wishing for soap and water. A hot shower would be even better. Followed by a night in her own bed. The pebble came loose, covered with blood.

The moment it was out, the wound sealed as if zippered shut.

She blinked and rubbed at the spot, then felt her chin. The skin was smooth and unbroken. Just like this morning, her injuries were gone as if they had never existed. She looked at the bloody pebble in her hand and a wave of vertigo hit her.

"You sure you're all right?" Concern entered Junkyard's voice.

"Uh, yeah." She drew a deep breath, fighting rising panic. "Just banged up a bit. I think most of this blood came from this one scrape."

She closed her fist before he could see the perfectly healthy skin underneath the blood. The last thing she needed was for Junkyard to start asking questions she couldn't answer for herself. "Let's go get the fire started before I turn a whole new shade of blue."

If she was going to have to sit through poetry written by these people, she could at least be warm.

Monte squatted like a molting vulture in a dark corner of the boathouse. Dried blood caked his scalp. A sticky clump of uprooted hair clung, unnoticed, to the side of his face. He hugged his legs to his body and stared over the tops of his knees, his eyes red-rimmed and peeled wide. Despite the crowding, the hobos stayed away from his niche, as if in deference for crowning madness amidst the merely unstable.

The girl and Junkyard Doug sat at the edge of the landing, waiting for some hobo to start stammering his poetry in the flickering light of the fire. The girl's hair was tucked inside her jacket, as if that would fool anyone into thinking she was a guy. Monte certainly knew better. He stared at her until his vision blurred. Never blinking, he rolled his eyeballs back into their sockets, then refocused on the girl.

El Lobo wanted that girl. Wanted her bad, he did, and Monte was not going to disappoint El Lobo. Not again. Hell no, not *ever* again.

He sucked a line of drool back into his mouth and stared at the girl's slender neck stretching from a black letter jacket. He could almost see El Lobo's big hand clamped around her throat, squeezing, squeezing, blood welling between the fingers, those searing eyes always fixed on Monte, painting the world yellow...

Monte's eyelids crashed down, blinking El Lobo away. He never wanted to see those glowing eyes again. Not ever. Ever. Again.

He had to get the girl. But not now. He might not get away with it, even in this crowd of losers, and El Lobo would not be pleased, hell no, not at all.

Monte would be patient. Monte would be smart.

He would wait.

Briggs shone his flashlight down the embankment at a dark gap in the trees. That must be the path to the boathouse. One of the bulls from the crime scene had given him the directions. The bull had whistled skeptically when Briggs had told him he wanted to go to the hobo poetry reading.

"Nothing like a little high-risk boredom on such a fine night, eh?" the bull said. "You want some backup?"

"Nah, I'm not going to stir anything up. I just want to make sure Tuttle is safe."

The bull shrugged. "It's your Friday. Just take Oak Street to East River Parkway and head up-river three or four streetlights. Follow the path down to the river—you can't miss it."

Briggs had always found the words "you can't miss it" to be less than assuring, but he thought he could make out a faint trail leading to a gap in the trees. It looked more like a deer track than a proper path. He stepped over the guardrail and started toward it, grimacing as the rain-soaked weeds brushed his pant legs.

An uneasy feeling grew as he walked, as though someone had taped a bull's-eye in the middle of his back. He paused at the tree line and swung his flashlight around. Nothing but trees and weeds. But it would be easy enough for someone to hide. Hopefully his FRC police jacket would make a would-be mugger think again.

The break in the trees looked more like a rabbit hole to nowhere than a trail through the woods. He stepped through the gap, sinking ankle deep into wet leaves. After a few yards, the path turned, cutting off the dim glow of the streetlights. The woods were strangely quiet after the noise of the storm. No wind, no animal sounds, just the drip of collected rainwater. Spooky. The target feeling itched like a fleabite between his shoulder blades.

Now he wished he had accepted that backup. He rested his hand on the cell phone hooked to his belt, but he could hardly ask for assistance, now. What would he say? *"Gee, these woods are awful scary. Could you send someone?"*

He chuckled, feeling stupid. Then the phone jangled under his hand and he nearly knocked himself out on a low branch. Swearing, he rubbed his head and answered the phone. "Briggs here."

Marybeth's voice bubbled around a burst of static. "Pizza or burger?"

Brigg's grinned. Marybeth claimed she could predict what he was going to eat when they worked a case together. She was usually right. "Take a guess," he said, playing along.

"That's easy—burger."

"Bingo."

"I knew it. It was the flies, right?"

"Yeah, I couldn't stomach pizza after seeing them laying eggs on the one in the dumpster." He ducked under the tree branch and picked his way down the path. Damn, it was dark. "Do you have something for me, or are you only interested in my eating habits?"

"Well, you do eat at the most fascinating array of fast food restaurants."

She was baiting him. She must have found something good. "Come on, cough up!"

"Oh, it's nothing much." She grew more serious. "In fact, nothing at all. That's what's really odd. The killer didn't leave a trace. There wasn't even any skin or blood or fabric fiber under her fingernails."

"Maybe he killed her before she could struggle."

"No, remember, she lost a fingernail."

The girl's gold, manicured nails were long and curled, like talons. Probably false. "Don't those things pop off all the time?"

"You should have looked closer. She didn't just lose the fake nail. Half of the real one was torn off with it. A bloody mess, but all the blood was hers. Other nails were chipped and loosened, too—on both hands. If you bother with a high-dollar manicure, you're not going to put up with that for long. I'd say they were damaged in the struggle. Maybe she couldn't reach her attacker's bare skin, but surely she would have torn into his clothing."

Briggs brushed against a sapling and suffered a shower of rainwater from its leaves. "Could someone have cleaned her nails up?"

"No, there's the usual dead skin—her own—plus beer residue, some ketchup, and semen. We're following up on the semen, but remember, she was a prostitute. That won't get us far without some corroborating evidence."

"So maybe the evidence just evaporated along with the flies."

"Or..." Marybeth paused dramatically.

"What?"

"Or maybe there was never any evidence to leave!"

The woods seemed oddly silent. The flashlight penetrated only a few lousy feet. There could be anything out there.

"They pay you to come up with that crap?" he grumbled. He felt anxious to keep the conversation going, but he didn't like the direction it was heading.

"I'm serious." She sounded more sincere than Briggs liked. "Think about it. No latents. No blood except hers, no fibers, not even a glove imprint."

"You saying she got killed by a vampire or something?" This was turning into the weirdest case he had ever worked on.

"Don't be silly. Too much blood left in the body. Besides, no bite marks, and a vampire has corporeal form. Even the undead leave trace evidence. Or so I've heard. I'm thinking some kind of spirit."

"Oh, come on, Marybeth. You telling me a ghost did that?"

"Well, I wouldn't put it in writing, but..."

Briggs began to walk faster, underbrush whipping at his legs. "A ghost. Just for the sake of argument, can you think of any explanation belonging in the real world? You know, the world *I* live in? Because—whoa!"

A wall of bark rushed at him out of the darkness. He was so intent on the conversation that he had nearly run into an enormous elm tree.

"Hello? Briggs, are you there?"

Why was a tree growing in the middle of the path? He swung the flashlight around, turning in a slow full circle. The tree wasn't growing in the path. In fact, it was growing in a patch of moss. There was no sign of a path.

"Briggs?"

"Uh, Marybeth, I'm going to have to call you back." It would not be good to admit to her that he was lost. Not good at all. "Maybe tomorrow. Things have gotten, uh, busy here."

He returned the phone to his belt. "Shit. How the hell can a guy get lost in a ten-acre stretch of woods?"

He gave a vicious kick to a clump of moss, sending it into the trees. The boathouse was somewhere along the riverbank. Find the river and pick a direction. He headed downhill, toward the sound of rushing water.

The bull's-eye feeling was back. Briggs zipped his jacket against a chill that went deeper than his clammy shirt. Joke or not, Marybeth's theory fit the facts. Gangbangers and thieves he could handle, but he had no idea how to deal with a murderous ghost. He followed his flashlight through a maze of tree trunks, feeling as though something large and predatory was hanging over him. But when he directed the flashlight overhead, he saw only a twiggy web of branches. No otherworldly spirit there.

He nearly screamed when a black ghost burst from the weedy floor and swept toward him. It loosed a harsh cry and launched into the sky.

A crow—or maybe a raven, said the logical detective voice in his mind, but he wasn't in the mood for logic.

He began to run.

The poetry reading had no structure, no rules, and no master of ceremonies. Hobos gradually emerged from the boathouse or trickled down the path to the landing, seating themselves on the damp concrete or against trees in nearby shadows. They waited without seeming to wait, muttering and scratching, snarling at anyone who came too close. A half-dozen had gathered loosely about the oil drum that served as a fireplace. They kept their heads down and avoided each other's glances, loitering as if in coincidental proximity.

Lennie studied each face, looking for her father's features, finding no similarities. She and Junkyard sat at the edge of the landing near the path. They were close enough to the front to watch the audience and far enough from the fire to go unnoticed. Junkyard fidgeted and leaned close to Lennie.

"Something's wrong," he whispered. "They usually loosen up at these things and have a good time, but they're all acting like stray dogs without an alpha. Looks like they could turn on each other any minute."

Lennie shuddered. "I don't want to get caught in the middle of that."

"Don't worry. I'm sure they'll settle down once the readings start."

But he didn't look sure. He looked tense, ready to launch to his feet, and his eyes flicked restlessly from face to face. Hardly reassuring.

He glanced over his shoulder at the path. "I hope Jim gets here, soon," he said in a low voice. "I thought he'd be here, already. I'm getting worried—the Ragman saw him with us this morning."

"I'm sure he just went someplace to get out of the storm."

Lennie knew she should be more concerned. Jungle Jim wouldn't stand a chance against the Ragman or his cronies. But the pressure behind her eyes had returned and she couldn't think about much else. The feeling was more diffuse this time, as though the focal point were somewhere else. Feeling exposed, she wished she at least had a tree at her back. And that the tree was somewhere in Hawaii.

Finally, a hobo took a hit from a hip flask and stepped beside the oil drum. He pulled a crumpled paper from his pocket and smoothed it between his hands. Chin to chest, he read in a rusty, halting voice.

Valknut: the Binding

I heard the freedom whistle blow
From miles on down the track.
I kissed my Lady Saturday—
Goodbye, I won't be back.

The poem droned on, expounding on hobo themes of itchy feet and freedom. More lies. Lennie shifted uncomfortably and tried to listen. Junkyard had spread a thick layer of newspaper on the ground, but the cold concrete leached through to chill her still-damp backside. She slouched forward, rubbing her temples.

"This poem is no better than the one at the festival's show."

Intent on the speaker, Junkyard said nothing at first. Then he bent his head closer to hers and said, "It's not the poem that's different. It's the audience."

And he was right. The men who had warily circled each other now turned toward the speaker like a ragged chorus before their director. Tears shone in the eyes of one old man, his face a shriveled prune grown moldy with gray whiskers. A younger man with a bruised eye and split, swollen lip paced the landing as though ready to take to the iron road that very moment. All the hobos bore the same look of intense longing on their faces.

"Somewhere over the rainbow," Lennie murmured. Her anger faded to pity. She fell silent and tried to understand.

One poem followed the next, the speakers with varying amounts of facial hair, dressed in coveralls or frayed jeans. One man mumbled so low that only those in front could hear. Another wore an ancient suit and orated in a deep, singsong voice. "Ah, the wind! The midnight air! Take ease, oh weary feet, in this thunderous chariot of iron!"

Hesitant or loud, spoken or sung, the words were interchangeable, the poetry uniformly bad. It didn't matter. The audience was as rapt as if Jack Kerouac had come among them.

They had no idea they were being watched.

The clouds broke overhead. The light of a three-quarter moon fell upon the river's shore, where it struck a shadow with no visible source. Within the shadow, Fenrir sent tendrils of dark thought through the hobo gathering. They listened to their fellows, unspeaking, unthinking, caught in a hobo past, facing a street person's future.

And as they listened, Fenrir stole their souls.

A twist here: Tonight, the fork-bearded man would find a preteen runaway sulking behind a gas station and convince the boy to go with him to see the world. Then the man would rape him and leave him dead in the river. A jab there: Tonight, the fat one in the tattered rain coat would burn a man's business to the ground, leaving a hundred people jobless. A prod: Tonight, the quiet one at the back would start a fight at a strip club that would send men to the hospital and tie up two squad cars for half the night.

For years, he had sent others like these crawling like fleas across the belly of society, unseen but ever-present, biting the vulnerable, spreading discontent like disease. Now, he did it more out of habit, for his plan was nearly ready. Just a few minor tasks, and the end could begin.

He turned to the two minds that burned most brightly in the dark. His thoughts first snaked over the girl. A powerful anger lay buried within this one, and anger gave him leverage against her, though he did not strike yet. She was not like her father, who was too timid to be more than a short-lived annoyance. Her will had solidified under the pressures of her youth. With each meeting, he had felt her growing stronger. Now the power the Allfather had given her was ready to flower. He must confront her, but not here.

Go on, be the wolf.

Shouts of affirmation rose to the treetops, as though the hobos agreed with the voice in Fenrir's head. The audience wanted a song, and they wanted it from Jungle Jim. The hobo clown shook his head shyly and waved them off. "Naw, it wouldn't be right to interrupt Mackinaw Matty. Not right dab in the middle of his poem."

Think on it, Fenrir. All that nice, hot blood.

And the taste of human blood was on Fenrir's tongue. His human shape slipped and the strength of the wolf filled him.

No! Fenrir shook his head, violently, like a dog with a bug in its ear. He couldn't let his man-shape go. Not yet. He was still too vulnerable. He slammed his full will against the puny essence of Angus Cook. *You will be silent!*

The voice did not answer.

Mackinaw Matty doffed his hat. "It's all right, Jim. I was nearly finished, anyway." He stepped aside, making room for Jungle Jim by the oil drum. "Do you have something new for us?"

"Matter o' fact, I do, Matty."

Jungle Jim picked his way through the audience. As he passed, he leaned on a shoulder: Tonight, the fork-bearded hobo would rummage for food in the garbage behind a restaurant and a pre-teen runaway would return home after an hour of sulking in the empty lot behind a gas station. Jungle Jim brushed a leg there: The quiet man would walk past the strip club and spend a quiet night in a shelter.

With each step, with each pause, with every touch of a hand, Jungle Jim undid all the malicious tinkering Fenrir had affected on these, the foot soldiers of his army.

Fenrir watched, hating the hobo clown. He had waited millennia for his release from Odin's trap, suffered more than a century of patient planning, and now, as the end finally approached, Jungle Jim plagued him with swarm of gnat-like set-backs that seemed likely to drive him mad.

Simple, defective Jim Tuttle must somehow be more than he appeared to be.

For perhaps the hundredth time, Fenrir probed the hobo's mind. As always, he couldn't get past the images of dollar-store magic and small children begging for candy. Pathways to deeper memories and desires, easily accessed in normal humans, were closed off by a wall of damaged tissue. Fenrir had never been able to penetrate it.

The more direct solution hadn't worked, either. The gangbangers he'd sent to kill Tuttle had returned, one after another, not only failing in their mission, but made so useless that Fenrir had to destroy them. Even the normally reliable Bill Sutter refused to kill him. Sutter would be punished for that. And Fenrir would find another way to rid himself of Jungle Jim Tuttle.

A sudden wind ghosted through the trees, dislodging leaf-captured rain. The fire popped and hissed angrily. Jungle Jim bent to the pile of kindling near the oil drum and added broken branches to the fire.

Straightening, he pulled a bright red handkerchief from his pocket and started to wipe his hands. A blue handkerchief followed the red, then a green, and yellow, hanging like garish laundry on the line. A chuckle passed around the audience. Grinning sheepishly, Jungle Jim stuffed the colored cloths back into his pocket.

Then the kindling caught and the fire flared. In that one blink, that small moment it took for eyes to adjust, the happy clown was gone. Jungle Jim wore the same face, but somehow changed, as though another person wore it.

The difference, Fenrir realized, was in the eyes. Before, the murky surfaces of those eyes reflected a cloudy mind. Now, they focused with an intensity that almost glowed. Surely another entity had invaded Jungle Jim's mind, becoming trapped in a defective host.

Only one like himself could interfere so easily with his plans.

Perhaps it was Tyr.

His eyes burned yellow at the thought, for it was Tyr who had baited the trap One-Eye laid for him. He probed Tuttle again. The wall seemed softer now. He pushed against it, feeling it give. The hobo stiffened and lifted his head, as though sensing the invasion. His eyes turned unerringly, staring through the shadow Fenrir wore like a cloak, straight into Fenrir's eyes.

The moment was broken by the muffled thrashing of running footsteps in the woods. The wall in Jungle Jim's mind solidified and his eyes dimmed, just a ridiculous fool once more.

Fenrir withdrew, disturbed. Tuttle had tracked him. That had never happened before. He did not know what it meant. Still, the wall had given way for a moment. It would do so again. And he would be waiting.

Briggs crashed through the woods, berating himself as he ran. There's nothing to run from, you idiot.

A tree branch loomed suddenly out of the dark. He dodged and tried to slow down. But the hill was steep and the wet leaves were slippery and he couldn't seem to stop running, no matter how sensible his thoughts were.

Then, without warning, he broke into a clearing lit by the dim, orange light of an oil-drum fire. More than a dozen pairs of eyes swerved toward him, staring with everything from indifference to open hostility.

It seemed he had found the poetry reading.

Not exactly how he had planned to make his entrance. He hadn't planned to make an entrance at all—just wait in the trees until he could get Tuttle alone. I've got to get over this fear of black birds.

Feeling exposed, he forced his breathing to slow and scanned the motley collection of men gathered in the dim light of the fire. No friendly faces in this bunch. He was sure they could all read the panic on his dripping, wild-eyed face.

Two big thugs stepped closer, looking ready to make a park bench out of him. Briggs forced a smile and kept his hands well away from his gun and nightstick. Clearing his throat, he tried to think of something to say that wouldn't antagonize them more. Before he could speak, a familiar voice hailed him from the direction of the fire. An oddly dressed man jumped up and down in the space that served as a stage, waving an arm at him.

"Hi, there—I remember you, I do."

The cheerful greeting hung oddly in the hostility charged air. Briggs waved, painfully aware that his every move could trigger unpleasantness. At least he had not made the trip to Minneapolis for nothing. Tuttle was here, safe, and possibly saving his life.

"Hello, Jim."

"Hey, everybody! This is my friend, Detective Briggs! He gave me some donuts one time. And a Coke, too! On a day hotter'n a coal furnace. Isn't that right, Mr. Briggs?"

Briggs cleared his throat. This was no time for a nervous crackle in his voice. "Sure, Jim. I remember. Good to see you again."

A smile lifted Tuttle's paunchy cheeks. He made his way to the two glowering thugs and rested his hands on their shoulders. The thugs seemed to relax and some of the antagonism bled out of their faces. The expressions on the hobos closest to Tuttle softened, as well. The effect rippled through the rest of the crowd.

Briggs watched, so amazed he almost forgot his danger. In all his years of policing the railroad, he had never seen anyone have such an effect on a group of ornery, independent, sometimes violent, and always eccentric hobos like these. Briggs still didn't feel safe, but at least the hobos looked wary instead of openly hostile, sullen instead of angry. Better.

But the improvement might not last. Briggs chose his next words carefully, trying to keep from sounding official. "I'm glad you're here, Jim. I was hoping we'd get a chance to chat."

That drew some sharp looks, but Tuttle nodded happily. "You betcha, Mr. Briggs. I's just about to sing a song—maybe we can talk after that."

Tuttle patted the two thugs on the back and returned to the oil barrel limelight. The audience settled onto their seats of cement and damp cardboard. They hadn't accepted Briggs, but they would tolerate him for Tuttle's sake. The thugs lingered, glaring at Briggs in a way that inspired images of park benches wearing Briggs's clothes. He did his best to be invisible and waited for Tuttle to begin.

"You folks are probably wantin' a funny little ditty—somethin' cheerful, I suppose. But I don't have it in me tonight. Not even a little." Tuttle reached into the inner pocket of his patched suit coat and pulled out a carefully folded scrap of packing paper. "Instead, I's hopin' you wouldn't mind me singing a song I wrote for a friend of mine. It's called *The Ballad of Tin Can Petey*."

There was a moment of silence. Apparently the news of Peter Olson's death had spread quickly. A man in a button-covered jean jacket called out, "Sure, Jim. Sing it for Petey. And sing it for everyone who died the way he did."

The man's voice sounded strained with emotion, as though he had personal experience with one of victims. Briggs eyed him, thinking he looked familiar, but he couldn't place the face. He'd have to get a closer look at him before he took Tuttle to the police station.

Tuttle took off his felt hat and tucked it under his arm. There was a brief flurry of movement around the fire as other men did the same. His eyes swept the audience, gathering them into his sorrow. Then he began to sing in a clear tenor, and Briggs forgot all about the man in the jean jacket, the hobos, and the two thugs waiting to rearrange his anatomy.

Me and Petey caught out of Topeka,
Doin' the boxcar slide.
Got stuck in the hole down Elmont way,
Pullin' slivers from my hide.
Petey pulled slivers from my hide.
Ain't nobody give us an easy ride.

Jungle Jim's voice caught and held every hobo in the clearing. They remembered Tin Can Petey as everyone had known him—a soft-hearted little gnome who could make a feast out of gristle and rotting potatoes.

The night fell dark with the devil's own lies.
I shivered from head to toe.
Petey—he said, "Hey, what's takin' so long?
We still have a ways to go."
Petey—he said, "We got a ways to go."
Ain't nobody gonna tell him no.

They saw themselves in Petey, not as the colorful characters they pretended to be or the romantic figures the public wished them to be. They saw their lives as dirty, hard, and as bumpy as a ride on a rattler they could never get off. And while they mourned for Petey, they also mourned for themselves.

I jumped on down to see what's goin' on,
Leavin' Petey all alone.
A mistake, a blunder, a tragedy,
I can't never, ever atone.
Petey—I'm sorry, I can't never atone.
Ain't nobody shoulda left you alone.

Loosened by Jungle Jim's voice, shaken by sorrow, the last of Fenrir's controls fell away from the hobos' minds. Each would leave this place to live his life as he chose, acting for good or evil according to his nature.

Then something new entered Jim's voice—a wavering in his otherwise perfect tenor, or perhaps a wavering that went deeper than that.

> 'Cause when I got back to that dark boxcar,
> It was silent as a stone
> Petey lay still, a knife stuck in his head,
> Done and been, no more to roam.
> Petey took the westbound, no more to roam.
> Ain't nobody gonna bring him home.

The last notes dwindled away. There was no applause. The audience didn't move, hardly breathed. Tears ran down even the meanest of the faces.

Jungle Jim seemed to have forgotten where he was. He stood by the fire, head bowed, his shoulders shaking with grief.

Waiting, watching for his chance, Fenrir slipped into Jungle Jim's mind and found the wall had weakened again, as though softened by tears. He pushed against the crumbling barrier...

And burst into the only human mind he had never been able to reach.

If he had known strong emotion would lower the barriers in Tuttle's mind, he would have started killing the simple man's friends months ago. He braced himself for a struggle, believing that Tyr would be waiting for him. Fenrir hated him nearly as much as One-Eye, for if the great betrayal had been One-Eye's plan, Tyr had used their friendship to betray him.

But when he entered the hobo clown's mind, he found only the ordinary thoughts and memories of Jim Tuttle.

Incredulous, Fenrir ransacked Tuttle's mind. There *had* to be another entity hidden somewhere in this confused clutter. It galled him to think that a mere human had been responsible for hindering his machinations. Yet he found nothing. Jungle Jim was alone in his head. Worse still, the fool was as simple as he seemed. He had no idea what he was doing to Fenrir's plans.

Jungle Jim had done it all without even trying.

It was like rending open the armor of an enemy, one who had nicked him more than once in battle, to find nothing but an insect inside.

Fenrir resisted the urge to tear into the essence of Jungle Jim, to gnaw and worry at it until only shreds remained. This human had caused him considerable irritation; he did not want to destroy him too quickly. He would take his time and pick through the hobo's memories. There must be something he valued, something Fenrir could twist, prod, destroy if need be, to cause the suffering such impudence deserved. He had only to find it.

And once this obstacle was removed, he would set his final plans into motion. The end was near...the end of all. And then, the reign of Hrodvitnir, Fenrir the Wolf, would begin.

He surveyed the somber group of men who sat with heads bowed as a flock before a priest. He would not work his will on Jungle Jim while he remained in this company. There must be no interference from his friends. Fenrir sent dark tendrils of thought into Jungle Jim Tuttle once more.

Briggs surveyed the church-like stillness of the clearing, amazed at the effect Jungle Jim's song had worked on this pack of bums and thugs. The song itself wasn't so special, he realized. It was as if emotion poured from Tuttle and flooded the landing.

Still more surprising was the effect the song had on Briggs, and he hadn't really known Peter Olson. He hoped no one would think anything but rain had dampened his cheeks. Not that anyone was looking at him. Even the two thugs seemed to have forgotten him.

If there had been any doubt before, Briggs was now certain Jim Tuttle had nothing to do with Peter Olson's murder. But he may have witnessed something, and that could endanger his life. Briggs wasn't about to lose sight of him until he got him safely into protective custody. He edged forward, careful to avoid eye contact with the two thugs.

Tuttle seemed to have forgotten where he was. He held himself stiffly and stared over the audience's heads. The other hobos began to stir, blinking and looking around as if the air had suddenly cleared. Briggs got the sense that the poetry reading was over. No one cared to follow Tuttle's song with some trite poem about the joys of the iron road. One by one, they climbed to their feet, obscuring Briggs's view of Tuttle.

Afterwards, as he tried to piece the events together, Briggs was never certain what happened next. He had begun to push his way through the crowd, determined not to lose Tuttle. But instead of forcing his way directly to the oil-drum fire where he had last glimpsed Tuttle, he had somehow ended up at the back of the crowd.

He couldn't guess how that had happened. The memory was gone.

He caught a last glimpse of Tuttle, the firelight flickering over his still face, and then Briggs stumbled over someone's foot and hit the concrete on his hands and knees. The foot he tripped over belonged to the jean-jacked man he had recognized earlier.

The man met Briggs's eyes with a gaze haunted by a private pain. With an almost audible click, his features slid into place in Briggs's memory. Shorten the hair, shave the sideburns and—that's right—put him in a uniform. This was Austin Harding's brother.

The throbbing behind Lennie's eyes had eased during Jungle Jim's song, but now it was back, worse than ever. It was as though the boathouse landing was perched on a geyser, and she was the only one who could sense the pressure building. She wondered dimly if this was how people with precognition felt when they chose not to take a flight that ended in crash, or stayed home from the maiden voyage of the *Titanic*. If only it would be so easy for her to avoid disaster.

She pressed cold fingers to her eyes and huddled against her bent legs, trying to remember what it was like to be warm. Something scuffled nearby, followed by the painfully familiar sound of a body hitting the broken pavement hard. She raised her head to look and winced as the small light of the fire amplified the throbbing. The man with the FRC Police jacket was on his hands and knees, staring into Junkyard's face. He looked both incredulous and incredibly annoyed.

"What the hell are you doing here, Harding?"

Junkyard's mouth twisted bitterly and he looked away without answering.

"Harding? Is that your real name?" Lennie couldn't help asking, though her head hurt worse when she spoke. This was the first solid fact she had learned about him.

He hesitated, looking ready to deny it. Then he shrugged. "Yeah. Sure. Douglas Harding."

He pushed himself off the cardboard and picked up his duffle bag. "Now, if you'll excuse me, Detective Briggeman..."

"Not so fast." Briggeman stood quickly and brushed the dirt off his hands. Junkyard tried to push past, but Briggeman stopped him with a hand on his shoulder. Junkyard stiffened, and Lennie thought he might take a swing at the detective. Great. Maybe when they take you to jail, they can drop me off at the hospital before my eyeballs explode.

Briggeman let his hand drop, but stayed in Junkyard's path. "Easy, Harding. I just want a few answers. Starting with *Are you trying to get yourself bloody killed?*"

Junkyard grunted impatiently, straining to see past Briggeman. Worry creased his forehead. "Love to tell you all about it, but I need to catch my friend before he wanders off. It's not safe for him out here."

Jungle Jim! Lennie had completely forgotten about him. She looked toward the fire. Hobos were milling around it, saying their goodbyes before they—how did they put it? She fought to focus, but her brain had turned to slag. Before jungling up. That was it. Hobos jungled up for the night. Good idea. She let her head drop to her knees and stopped fighting the pain.

Briggeman's voice continued above her. "Dammit, Tuttle's gone! How the hell did I forget about *him?*"

A round of colorful epithets followed, mostly directed at himself. His voice sounded incredulous, angry, and anxious, all at once.

"Tuttle!" He shouted. "Hey, Tuttle! I just wanna talk."

Junkyard's voice echoed him from another part of the landing.

"Jim, where are you? It's time to go to Bill's house!"

Lennie tried to lift her head. She should help look for Jim. He shouldn't be wandering on his own. She pressed her hands to her head, trying to keep her skull from blowing apart. Why couldn't anyone else feel it? Then, with the abruptness of a popped bubble, the pressure was gone.

She gasped and sat up, shocked by the sudden release. Briggs and Harding stood before her, facing each other, both breathing hard. The landing had emptied of hobos. No one had answered their calls.

Jungle Jim was gone.

Briggeman drew a breath that hissed through clenched teeth. "Shit."

Junkyard nodded grimly. "Yeah, no shit."

CHAPTER SIXTEEN

Jungle Jim Tuttle shuffled through the deserted parking lot. The wet pavement spattered his pretty yellow shoes with grit and mud, but he didn't care. He had no heart for clowning, anyway. Not tonight. His insides were too swelled up from missing Tin Can Petey.

He had even skipped the clowning at the poetry and had sung his song for Petey. Sung it as best he could. And at the end, those tears kept running down his face and a voice in his head said, *you just need to be alone, is all.* And Jim knew it was right. Bill wanted him to stay with him and Ashley, and that nice detective fellow wanted to talk to him, and Junkyard hadn't wanted him to go off alone, but it was too hard to stay and be happy for people when he felt so sad. So he had slipped off into the woods before anyone could make him do anything else.

Mariucci Arena hulked to his left, looking like a great big turtle against the night-gray sky. Jim had once heard someone say that the world rode around on the back of a giant turtle. Or maybe that was something he'd gotten from a book before his accident made it hurt too much to read. He looked at the turtle building and tried to imagine what size head might go along with that body. For a moment, he thought he heard its thick under-shell scraping the pavement and knew it was coming after him.

"Don't be eatin' me," he yelled, shaking his fist at the building. "I'm not a giant bug."

But it was only the sound of wind pushing a sheet of cardboard across the parking lot. The turtle blurred and became just a building again, and all the streetlights wore halos. Jim shook his head and walked on. "Now I'm seein' things, Petey," he said. "The whole world looks different without you in it."

He squeezed his eyes and hot tears rolled out. The halos disappeared. He could see the festival's jungle ahead. Then his eyes filled again and he couldn't see much of anything. His foot caught in a pothole and he stumbled to one knee. Sobbing, he climbed to his feet and tottered unsteadily toward the jungle.

Why couldn't he stop crying? Other friends died, friends as good as ol' Petey, and Jim never cried before. It was the way of things, after all. Everybody dies. But this time was different somehow. He couldn't remember ever being this sad, except when his wife left him after the accident, and that was different. She took his two little baby girls—the younger one about Ashley's age—and went away without telling him where.

Someone moved in the festival's jungle. A small campfire cast a warm circle of light that made the night around Jim seem even darker. The fire was tended by a tall, thin person who looked like a fence post wearing a hat. It had to be Too Long Soo. He always liked Soo. The smell of camp coffee and mulligan stew reeled through the wet air and hooked him in. He took a deep breath and put a jaunt in his step. Maybe he could stop crying, now.

But all of a sudden, pictures of his lost family came crowding back, all yellowy, like old newspaper. It felt like someone had opened his head and dropped them in. He stopped walking and pressed his hands to his head, wishing the pictures away. If only he could open his skull and take them out again. A sob built up in his chest. He squeezed his throat shut and wouldn't let it out.

These pictures didn't come from him. He knew it. So he wouldn't let them make him sad. He would ignore them and have some of Bones O'Riley's stew.

Soo leaned over the fire to pour herself some coffee. Then the scene shimmered, like he was seeing it through yellow heat waves over hot pavement. He felt a stirring in his brain and Soo started to change. Her hair shrank and darkened to short brown curls. Her hat disappeared. Her legs and arms shortened, too, and got thicker. She lifted her head from her coffee and looked straight at him as if she could see him there, in the dark. He gasped and staggered back.

It wasn't Soo sitting there. It was Sharon, his wife, plump as ever, especially the parts she sat on. Her cheery face looked like he remembered, only she didn't look so cheerful now. She stared at him funny, like she was scared of him. Scared and disgusted. And her eyes were yellow.

Then all of a sudden he was inside his little three-bedroom house a few blocks north of the tracks. He wandered room to room, just like he had five years ago when he had come home to find it empty. There was the flattened carpet and clean patches in the peeling wallpaper that told him where the furniture had been. There was the melted spot on the kitchen counter where Sharon had set a hot frying pan. There were the girls' empty closets, somehow smaller without the rock collections and dress-up clothes and toys to fill them up. Everything, just like he remembered it.

Only this time, the house wasn't quite empty. Sharon was still in it.

"You can't support us anymore," she said. "You're nothing but a dummy." She had never said these things to him before she left, but the words were there now. And her eyes said even more. *I can't stand to let those clumsy, stupid hands touch me.*

Feelings stirred through him. Bad feelings that made him heat up all over. He fought them, afraid of what they might make him do. A sob shook his body and this time he couldn't swallow it back down.

It isn't real. That's Soo there, not my wife, and this isn't my house. These feelings aren't real, neither. Someone's messing with me.

He stared at his hands, which had clenched into fists all by themselves. He had to get away. Still sobbing, he lurched away from the jungle. The feelings faded as he left the firelight behind. A few more steps, and he couldn't remember anymore why he was running. He just knew he couldn't stay there.

The wind picked up again, blowing right through his worn suit coat. If he couldn't stay with Soo, he'd need some other shelter. The festival had all sorts of hideaways a guy could tuck himself into for the night. Jim tried to figure what place might be best, but his thoughts felt thicker than usual. He shrugged and started off for the tent village.

Halfway there, the sheet of cardboard dragged past him, flapping and turning like a living thing. It seemed to know where it was going. Cardboard was a blanket, or a mattress, or a lean-to against the wind and rain. He pounced at it, missed, and gave chase. The cardboard flew in a burst of wind, scooting past the food vendors' deserted stands. It came to rest in the festival's carnival, pinned against Ashley's favorite kiddie ride, a train that looked like a big snake chasing its own tail on an oval track. Thinking of Ashley, his throat tightened and he thought he might cry again. He had nothing left but her and the other children who knew him as Jungle Jim, the hobo clown.

Jim hurried to the cardboard. He couldn't let it get away again. He was too tired to run after it any more. The wind tried to take it from him, but he grabbed it and held on tight. Air puffed from his lungs like a train whistle and his legs felt wobbly. If he didn't find a place to jungle up soon, he might just go to sleep right where he stood.

He looked at the kiddie ride. In the day, the train would race up and down and around its track with a load of squealing kids. Ashley always rode up front with her white-blond hair streaking behind her like a comet tail. The ride was quiet now. It would make him a fine house, and the cardboard would be his roof.

He climbed to the pavement inside the oval ride and wedged the cardboard between a heavy control box on the ground and the underside of the track. Taking one last look around, he crawled inside his new lean-to and fell asleep before he knew he was lying down.

Lennie hadn't played inside a cardboard box since she was eight years old, when her father had brought home a new washing machine. Her mother had exclaimed over the shiny, white washer, but Lennie was far more interested in its packaging. That box had housed her own private world for months, until the cat turned it into his back-up litter box.

This box didn't seem nearly as large as the one she remembered and the air had the same stifling paper-and-glue odor that had driven her out of her cardboard forts as a child. But it was the best shelter she could get for less than fifty cents. And at least it was clean.

As painful as that pressure in her head had become during the poetry session, the sudden release was almost as bad. The landing emptied of hobos while she sat in an incoherent daze. Junkyard had to prod her into moving. He'd left her at the festival's jungle before going to look for Jim. Too Long Soo took one look at Lennie's dull eyes and led her to the nearest empty box.

"Crawl in, girlie. Yer lookin' more tired than a hound dog after a night of coon huntin'."

But now Lennie felt fine, though exhausted and plagued by a small, completely ordinary headache. She should be out with Junkyard, looking for Jim. But she had no idea where to look. Most likely, she would just get lost.

Soo's voice penetrated the thin cardboard walls as she argued with Bones O'Riley over the ingredients for tomorrow's stew. Bones claimed that the carrots were "so limp they'd have to soak in Viagra for a week to stiffen up." Soo countered that the carrots were fresh bought, that he was being "more ornery than a pit bull with mange," and that she was getting tired of Viagra jokes. The conversation seemed almost ordinary after the bizarre events of the last thirty hours.

Lennie squirmed uncomfortably and poked at the pile of newspapers that served as her pillow. She tried to relax, but it was no use. Tired as she was, her mind wouldn't slow down. Too much had happened, this day. She sighed and switched on the flashlight Soo had given her.

If not for the tattoo, she might believe that she had taken a nosedive into schizophrenia somewhere between Ames and Minneapolis. From the moment she had awakened in the boxcar, she had been sensing things that weren't there and had been assaulted by beings she couldn't see. Her body seemed to have developed a power she couldn't understand. Most distressing, no one around her ever seemed to notice anything unusual.

She pointed the flashlight upward and stared at the circle of light on the cardboard ceiling. There had to be a connection between Ramblin' Red, the tattoo, and the mental attacks, if only she could see the pattern.

The pressure she had sensed at the poetry session had to be related as well. She tried to pinpoint when she had first felt it, but it seemed like it had been there at a low level all day. She had only noticed it after the readings were well under way. During Jungle Jim's song, it expanded like a constipation of the mind, blocking her ability to think or see. And then, magically, it was gone. Why?

Abruptly, she knew with awful clarity the focal point of the attack.

She should get up, find Junkyard, tell him...tell him what? *Something is after Jungle Jim—I could tell by the way my headache went away when Jim disappeared.*

Yeah, right.

Still, she should try. Junkyard had said something about checking Bill's house. Soo might know where that was.

But Soo seemed very far away. In fact, even sitting up seemed like far too much work. She yawned. Her concern for Jungle Jim faded into an almost drunken lethargy. Alarm trembled in the back of her mind. *This isn't right.* She struggled against the unnatural pull of sleep. But her eyes closed anyway. The flashlight slipped from her relaxed fingers and rolled across the floor. Its light cast shadows of nothing in the corners of the box.

The carnival sprawled across the pavement like the skeleton of an abandoned alien city, the wind whispering through its rusting metal bones. From one extremity came the frantic, lonely flap of a loose awning. From the other came the jingle of chains on the swing carousel. At its heart, there was a muttering, a shallow cough, and then the gentle seesawing of Jim Tuttle's snores.

The moon had gone out behind charcoal clouds. Layers of shadow blanketed the carnival. In the lee of a cotton candy stand, the deepest shadow of all swelled and split in amoeboid separation. The blacker portion drifted to the oval of Ashley Sutter's favorite ride, roiling with Fenrir's rage.

Here was Jormungand, Fenrir's own brother, rendered in rusting metal and peeling paint. The colossus of the deep, reduced to a two-dollar ride in a traveling carnival. The yellow in Fenrir's eyes flared, threatening to pierce his cloak of shadow. These humans made mockery of his brother for the entertainment of their children. They would soon learn what a child of Loki could do.

Fenrir climbed to the center of the ride and stood over Jungle Jim's little shanty. The hobo moaned within, his mind a playground where Fenrir toyed with his dreams.

It was not enough to merely kill him, though that would be easy enough to do. Fenrir would tear out Jungle Jim's soul, soil it beyond redemption, and feed it back to the simple man in tortured pieces. He might not kill him at all.

He began his work delicately, peeling back the first onionskin layer of Jungle Jim's mind. His manipulations were subtle at first. Fenrir would not underestimate the clown in his eagerness for revenge.

Jungle Jim was dreaming the memory of a cool fall afternoon shortly before the accident that had changed him. His thoughts were clear, as though his brain had never been damaged.

Sharon had brought Jessie and Alexandra to see him at work. He sat on the open tailgate of a pick-up parked in front of the roundhouse. His wife stood next to him and a child perched on each of his knees. They watched a diesel unit ease forward. Jim was supposed to check the air brakes on the unit before it went out again. The power of the train's massive engine vibrated through them and hot air blew dirt in their faces.

"A tornado in a can," he said, and the girls flung their arms around him in delighted fear. He laughed, holding their warm bodies close, and looked at his wife to share the joke.

Instead of laughing with him, as she had all those years ago, Sharon stiffened, her mouth tight and disapproving. Her eyes glowed yellow.

Jungle Jim thrashed in his sleep, knocking the cardboard aside. Fenrir leaned close, his lips twisted somewhere between a snarl and a grin. He opened a memory of another place and time, and began again.

Jessie, Jungle Jim's little darling, the younger of his two children, had fallen off her tricycle. She sat on the roadside, the skirt of her dress torn and bunched around her thighs. Blood streamed from scrapes at her elbow and both knees, but Jim knew her tears were those of frustration rather than pain. She was his tough girl, his adventurer. He lifted her into his lap, the peach fuzz of her leg hairs soft against his calloused hand. "There, now. Don't cry—you didn't hurt your trike a bit."

She laughed through her tears and kissed his cheek. Then her mother burst from the house. Instead of bringing bandages, the way he thought he remembered, she snatched Jessie out of his arms.

"I saw it," she screeched. "I saw it all through the window. You just stay away from my daughter—don't you ever touch her again!"

She snarled at him, and her teeth had lengthened, each ending in a sharp point. Jungle Jim started, almost waking up, but Fenrir pressed him back.

"Not yet—there is more," he murmured, his voice a low growl. Jim dreamed on.

He was giving the girls a bubble bath. Both girls had sculpted their hair in Dairy Queen curls. He chuckled and filled his hands with colored bath foam, dotting each girl's nose in purple. He rubbed the foam on Alexandra's back, over the washboard of small muscles and ribs. The soap felt slick on her smooth skin.

"Stop that!"

Startled, Jim fell back from the tub. Sharon stood in the bathroom door, her face distorted in outrage.

"You pervert!" She crossed the bathroom in two strides and

swung her open hand at his face. The fingers ended in hard, sharp nails, more dog-like than human. They laid his cheek open with four long gashes. "If you ever come near my babies again, I'll kill you!"

He gaped at her. Why had she struck him? He was only giving the girls a bath. Then he looked down at himself and saw that he was naked. Smears of purple foam streaked his body.

No, it didn't happen like that—it never happened like that!

But he was caught in the dream, his crazed wife standing over him, blood dripping from impossible claws. He fought the false memory, fought to awaken, but the dream wouldn't let him go.

Sharon is doing this to me.

He didn't know where the thought had come from, but he was certain it was true. And now she threatened to keep him away from their children. He kicked out at her, driving her back. Then he was on his feet and charging her, hands outstretched, and he could hear the girls screaming behind him, the fear in their voices, see the hatred in Sharon's eyes, and he knew that this wasn't real, that he would never strike his wife or hurt his children in any way. Someone was doing this to him.

Someone from outside.

He stopped his attack and let his arms drop to his sides. Sharon roared and landed a blow to his head. He didn't move to defend himself. Closing his eyes, he felt her fists bloody his nose and loosen a tooth, but he told himself this couldn't be his wife. This wasn't his bathroom. There was no cold, damp tile beneath his bare feet. Those little girls weren't his daughters. Jessie would be eight now, and Alexandra would be eleven.

This couldn't be real.

The blows grew weaker and disappeared. The screams faded along with the smell of grape bubble bath, and he could feel the shoes on his feet and the hug of a belt and bow tie. He opened his eyes, certain he would find himself under the cardboard, safe within the ring of Ashley's favorite ride. But he was wrong.

He was back in his house. It was empty except for the litter of a hasty move. He bent and picked up a crumpled paper. Straightening it, he saw that it was one of Jessie's drawings—a crazy-looking girl with wild hair and spaghetti legs. There was a turtle in the bottom corner. All her pictures had a turtle somewhere. He folded the paper carefully and put it in his coat pocket. When he looked up again, Sharon stood before him. This time, she was not alone. Bill Sutter stood beside her, one arm draped possessively around her shoulders.

Fat Bill. Jovial Bill. Bill, his friend. The man whose life he had saved.

"Yes, Jim," Sharon said. "I'm leaving you. Can you blame me? Bill has a bigger income, a bigger house. Lord *knows* he has a bigger brain."

She nibbled at Bill's neck. "In fact, pretty much everything about him is bigger."

She stuck her tongue in Bill's ear. It was far longer than it should have been. Sweat broke out on Bill's forehead. He licked his lips and pulled Sharon closer. She wrapped her arms around him and leered at Jim.

"Jessie and Alexandra have a new father now."

She tilted her head and her tongue disappeared into Bill's mouth.

Jungle Jim's hands balled into fists inside his pockets. The back of his neck burned and the air seemed too thin to breathe. *This never happened,* his inner voice insisted. *Sharon left without saying anything at all.* But that small thought was lost in violent emotion.

For years, loss and rejection had sliced Jim's heart with the sharp blade of grief. He wandered town to town, trying to fill the emptiness by bringing laughter to others, laughter that rang hollowly in his chest. But Sharon's betrayal had awakened a dark animal in him, one that sneered at those weaker emotions. One that howled for revenge.

He awoke.

This time, Fenrir allowed it, holding Jim tightly in the prison of his delusions. Jim struggled to his feet. Fenrir stepped back and let him rise. "Yes, Jim. Go to her. Kill her."

It was a long walk to Bill's house, but Jim found he wasn't tired any more. The closer he came to Bill's house, the angrier he became, until his mind burned white-hot. Anyone on the streets that late would have seen a lone man dressed in shabby, whimsical clothes with the look of murder on his face. After his passing, they might have felt a chill, as though Death himself followed close behind.

Bill lived on a street lined with young maple trees and an occasional old elm. His house was a small bungalow with beige stucco siding and trim the color of dried blood. The windows were dark. They were asleep, then. The girls were tucked into the smaller bedroom for the night, and Bill would be in the master bedroom— with Sharon.

Jim crossed the grass and stepped into the front landscaping. The moon broke through the clouds, lighting his way. He found a small resin frog nestled in the mulch between two bushes and bent to pick it up. The mixed scent of cedar and roses stopped him. He loved Bill's roses, with all the different colors and blooms the size of his palm. Ashley loved the white ones best.

He nearly gave it up then. Bill could have Sharon. Jim could go back to the jungle and have some coffee with Soo. But a sharp image of Sharon's leering face intruded, the false memory more real than the smell of any flower.

Jim snatched up the frog, gripping it so tightly that the stone-hard legs cut into his fingers. Then he grasped the upper half, and lifted. The house key lay inside, glinting in the moonlight. The key to hell.

Jungle Jim stood at the front door for a long time.

"Why am I here?"

Why am I here...why am I here...why...why?

For a moment, the layers of memory separated in his mind. Confusing and contradictory images fought for prominence—the sorrow in Sharon's eyes as she leaned over his bandaged head in the hospital...Sharon's snake-like tongue thrusting into Bill's ear...playing elephant with his daughters on his back...the hatred and revulsion in Sharon's eyes as she snatched 3-year-old Jessie from his arms...having dinner at Bill's house and telling Ashley a bedtime story...his own daughters clinging to Bill's legs and looking at Jim in fear.

It always came back to that—his children. His baby girls. They were his, and she had taken them.

The jumbled memories slammed together into one complete set. The contradictions were gone. There were only betrayals and spite and little hatreds. He saw Sharon in bed with Bill...the sneer on Sharon's face...the sweat on Bill's forehead. A furnace burned in Jim's chest. His breath came in short explosions. The house key grew hot in his hand. He reached for the doorknob. And stopped.

"No."

He jerked his hand back as though the knob burned red hot. The key lay in his palm, gleaming innocently in the moonlight. It didn't matter what was real, or why Sharon had left him, or who the girls now called "daddy."

He was Jungle Jim Tuttle and he would not do this thing.

He flung the key into the yard and turned away from the house. The false memories crumbled and fell away. He was whole again, free of the evil that had invaded his mind. He hugged himself and smiled up at the moon.

"We beat it, Petey!" he howled. "There ain't no foolin' Jungle Jim."

Then he clamped his hands over his mouth. He wanted to laugh and sing and do a silly jig, but not here. He didn't want to wake Ashley. Maybe Soo would still be awake back at the jungle. She could play her guitar while he sang. He tried to take a step away from the house, but his feet wouldn't move.

Shocked, he looked down at his stubborn shoes. His hand raised on its own, clenched around something hard. One by one, the fingers uncurled, though he didn't will them to. The house key lay in the palm of his hand.

Horrified, he tried to fling it away again, but it stayed in his hand. His traitorous feet turned him back toward the house. The hand reached for the doorknob. This time, he couldn't stop himself. The key slid smoothly into the lock and the door opened.

Moonlight streamed through the picture window, highlighting the blocky shape of Bill's armchair to the left of the door. A couch ran along the far wall. At its elbow yawned the hallway that led to the bedrooms.

The floor was covered with what looked like a hobo jungle for Barbie and all her friends. Jim's feet threaded relentlessly through the clutter. He fought his rebelling body until sweat stood out on his face, but the dark arch of the hallway loomed closer. That's when the true nightmare began. One after another, hideous images paraded through his mind. Images of himself with Ashley, torturing her, doing unspeakable things, finally throwing her limp body into the Mississippi. He tried to close his eyes, to shut out the visions, but how could he escape pictures in his own mind?

A scream swelled in his throat, but his mouth wouldn't let it out. No! he wanted to say. I never did that! I wouldn't...

Yet these weren't false memories. As sure as he knew his own name, he knew he was being shown the things he *would* do. And, just as certain, he knew this was as much a punishment for Bill as for himself, though he didn't know what for.

He was in the hallway. The moonlight didn't reach this far. He could only see the dim outlines of doorways, the dark rectangle of a painting on the wall. He knew the painting showed a lighthouse on a rocky hillside. Bill's grandmother had painted it from a magazine picture. Jim stared hard at it now, wishing it would light up and burn the darkness from his brain. Then he was past it, and the hallway only got darker.

He was at Ashley's doorway. Drawings were taped all over its surface, obscured by darkness, like windows he couldn't see through. His hand reached for the doorknob. He willed it to stop, and for a moment it seemed to work. He became a statue, unable to go back, unwilling to go forward.

But only for a moment.

Yellow eyes burned in his mind, shredding his will like torn tissue, and he knew he couldn't fight this thing. His eyes grew hot, casting yellow light on one of Ashley's drawings—a crayon bird flying on impossibly small wings. He grasped the door. His trapped screams echoed through his mind, and behind the screams he heard the howl of animal laughter.

He was in Ashley's room. A blue canary nightlight cast a dim light on her sleeping face. The candy smell of a child's perfume hung in the air. Her room was as messy as the living room, her desk and floor littered with toys and dirty clothes. He lifted a pair of leggings from the back of her desk chair and stretched them between his hands. Ashley muttered in her sleep. He froze and watched her roll to her side, her white-blond hair tinted blue by the nightlight. She cuddled around her stuffed bunny, but did not wake up.

The yellow eyes in his mind glowed brighter. Slowly, he wrapped the ends of the leggings around each fist. His feet tread softly toward the bed. Heat spread from his groin and he felt himself grow hard.

His mind gibbered in horrified panic. Tears ran down his face—the only action that was his own. He struggled for control as he leaned over the girl. This was Ashley, the same age as Jessie. Ashley, who ran to him when he came for a visit, who didn't care that his brain didn't work quite right, who loved him in his shabby clothes, who would hug him through the smell of the railroads. A child, a baby, and he loved her more than he loved himself. Anger surged in him, real and all his own.

I am Jungle Jim Tuttle and *I will not do this thing.*

He built an image of himself in his mind, a clown in a bow tie and yellow shoes, with laugh lines around his eyes and a heart that beat in its own time. A man who would die to protect a child. The Jungle Jim in his mind reached into an imaginary duffle bag and rummaged through silk scarves and decks of cards, discarding Mexican jumping beans, a hand buzzer, and a squeaky nose. Then he found what he needed.

He pulled forth a plastic flower and faced the glowing eyes. Foreign, wolfish laughter filled his mind. He ignored it and stepped closer to the eyes, holding out the flower. A tube dangled from it, with a bulb on the end. Gathering all his will, all his need and love, he squeezed the bulb. A thin stream of water sprayed out.

The eyes blinked.

Jungle Jim wrenched control of his body. He had only an instant, but an instant was enough. He staggered backward, crashing into the desk chair. The chair tipped over and fell onto a toy piano, which began to play a tinny version of "Twinkle, Twinkle, Little Star." Before he could move again, the yellow eyes were back. His body no longer belonged to him.

That's all right, he thought. I don't need it anymore.

Ashley sat up in bed and stared wildly around the room. Jim stood next to her desk, a dark figure to the child, face obscured in shadow except for glowing yellow eyes. She gathered the covers to her chin and screamed the thin dog-whistle scream of a child. Jim crossed the room and clasped a hand over her mouth, but the piano played on and on.

The bedroom door burst open.

There was a pause. The piano segued to "Mary Had a Little Lamb." Then there was a man's shout and a flash and a loud noise. Jim's body spun around. A second noise. Jungle Jim slammed into the closet door and slid to the floor.

The laughter in his head became a howl of rage rampaging through his mind like a mad dog. Jim smiled, his face his own again. He was free.

Bill fumbled at the wall next to the door and switched on the light. He kept his weapon trained on the figure sprawled by the closet. The guy didn't move. Good thing. Bill's hands were shaking so badly he'd probably miss if he had to shoot again. He risked a glance at Ashley. She huddled on the bed, sobbing into Bun Bun's matted fur, but she seemed all right. Relief washed through him, leaving him weak. He lowered the gun and sank to his knees.

But in one small part of his mind, the place where Fenrir dwelled with his threatening yellow eyes, Bill knew he would have been almost as relieved if she had died.

The thought sickened him.

"Everything's all right now, baby," he said, though he knew it wasn't. Not for him. "You just stay right there."

The man by the closet groaned and raised one knee as though trying to sit up. Bill lifted the gun, his finger tensed on the trigger. From the clothes, it looked like some kind of bum. He wondered how the guy got into his house. Then he saw the shoes. Bright yellow, from the eyelets to the soles.

"Jim!" He dropped the gun and climbed to his feet. "Oh, my God—what have I done?"

Jim lay still again, his face ashen. His polka-dotted bow tie had twisted so that one loop touched his chin. His jacket had fallen open. Blood bubbled from two soupy patches on his chest, already soaking into the carpet. He looked into Bill's face and smiled.

Bill grabbed one of Ashley's blouses and pressed it to the wound closest to Jim's heart. The blood soaked through it instantly. "Oh, Jim, I'm so sorry. I didn't know it was you. I thought someone was— I thought Ashley was—"

He couldn't even say what he had thought. "I've got to get help—get you to a hospital. They'll make you better, I promise. Just hold on."

Jungle Jim stopped him with a hand on his arm.

"No." The air gurgled in Jim's lungs when he breathed. "I'm catchin' the train to Glory, Bill. Nothin' gonna stop that now."

His eyes were clear, as if he had never had that accident. Maybe more clear than they had ever been. Bill stared at him, not understanding. "Come on, Jim. Stay with me. I'll go call an ambulance."

Jim gripped Bill's arm tightly, not letting him go. The blood flowed so quickly from his wounds.

"I'm not the one that needs savin', Billy boy. You already did that." Jim struggled for another breath. "Now you gotta save yourself."

His hand relaxed and slipped from Bill's arm. A small, wheezing gasp escaped his mouth and his chest did not rise again. Bill knelt next to his friend, too shocked to move or even to cry.

"Daddy?"

He felt a small hand on his shoulder and looked up. Ashley stood next to him, clean and beautiful in a mint green nightgown. She stared at Jim's body, her eyes large and lower lip trembling. "Is–is Uncle Jim dead?"

Bill nodded, unable to speak. Shock had drained the color from Ashley's face. Her gaze didn't move from the body. She had never seen a dead person before. Bill wasn't sure she knew what it meant to be dead. He wrapped his arms around her, shielding her from the sight. Tension had robbed her of softness and she felt like a bundle of sticks. How could he ever explain to her why he had shot her favorite friend?

"He scared me, Daddy." She began to shake. "Why was Uncle Jim in my room?"

He looked down at the body, suddenly blank. Long ago, Bill had given Jim a standing invitation to sleep on the couch, had even told him where the key was hidden. Jim had stayed with them often, but would hardly leave the living room, as though afraid to overstep his welcome. Even after all these years, he wouldn't use the bathroom without asking permission. Jim had never gone into Ashley's bedroom before.

Bill scanned the room with a policeman's eye. The desk chair had fallen on its side. The clothes and books that had been piled on it were scattered wide, as though the chair had been hit with some force. The back of the chair still rested on the toy piano. He had always hated that piano, with its insistent, off-key songs. Now he hated it even more. Without its infernal noise, Jim might still be alive.

Then he saw the leggings clenched in Jim's outstretched hand. Their black fabric seemed to swell in his vision, screaming their horrible purpose. And he knew what had happened—what had *really* happened.

It seemed Fenrir had found a way to make Bill kill Jungle Jim, after all. The punishment might have gone further than that, if Jim hadn't crashed the chair into that god-awful piano.

Bill nestled his cheek in the softness of Ashley's hair and stared at Jim's body. "I think I should be thanking you, old friend," he murmured.

It was time to call the police and put an end to it. Time for it all to stop.

CHAPTER SEVENTEEN

"Can I pinch her awake?"

"Tsk, you're such a naughty thing."

"Am *not*. I just don't want to wait for*ever*."

"Quiet, you two. Look—she's waking up."

Lennie didn't want to wake up. She ignored the whispers and burrowed deeper into her dream, where she soaked in a bubble bath, sipping licorice spice tea while unseen hands rubbed her shoulders. But it was no use. She couldn't convince herself she was warm when sleeping in damp clothing inside of a damp box. She let her eyes flutter open, expecting to see dimly lit cardboard walls. Instead, a triangle of odd faces peered down at her. A bare light bulb dangled from an orange extension cord suspended high above their heads, casting their faces in shadow.

"Who—what is..." Lennie tried to sit up, but only her eyes would move. "Where—"

"When and why," said a creaky voice coming from the figure stationed at the top of Lennie's head. "Those are very good questions."

With a start, Lennie realized it was the bag lady she had met before the poetry reading. She still wore the flower-print hodgepodge and her fingers worked ceaselessly at her knitting.

"That's why we're here," said another voice. It belonged to a younger woman at Lennie's left. She was dark-skinned, dreadlocked and wore wire-rimmed reading glasses at the end of her nose. Enough beads and crystals hung around her neck to decorate a Christmas tree.

"I don't understand." Lennie's head was still cloudy with sleep. "*What's* why you're here?"

"To answer your questions, of course," said a third, impatient voice, belonging to a little girl at Lennie's right. She looked like a normal eight-year-old in the midst of a sulk.

"Some of them, at least," the girl added, then stuck her tongue out at the bag lady. The beaded lady shushed her.

"But before we answer—"

Their expressions became almost predatory. Unable to move, Lennie felt like road kill about to be pecked. The three faces loomed in her vision, one after the other, their features distorting surreally.

"—we need to know if –"

"—you remember –"

"—the words Urdie gave you –"

"—last time we met," Urdie finished.

Lennie's senses reeled as though she lay on a turning merry-go-round. She closed her eyes against a wave of vertigo. "I don't know what you want to hear."

"Yes, you do, dear," Urdie said. "You just need to think."

And Lennie did know, even if she didn't understand. She answered in the same singsong cadence the bag lady had used under the streetlight, just before she had disappeared.

"That which can be cut can never be broken."

The spinning stopped abruptly.

Lennie didn't recover so quickly. The incongruous scents of rust, moldy leaves, and pot smoke filled her nostrils, and her head felt light and strange. She opened her eyes cautiously. The three figures shimmered and transformed. Where the bag lady had been, a tall, slender woman now stood, her face etched with age, sorrow, and joy. A broad-shouldered, plain-faced woman replaced the beaded lady, her hands rough and red with work. Both wore shapeless cowled robes.

This has to be a dream.

The thought brought Lennie such relief that she decided it was true. But it was no ordinary dream. It had the same feel as the squirrel dream from the night before.

"Look, I don't want any more tattoos, so just—"

She stopped, catching sight of the third figure, a creature straight out of a Scrooge movie. Completely shrouded, it stood motionless, as if in an endless wait. *As if waiting for me to die.*

Lennie knew with creepy certainty that nothing of flesh and blood resided under the robe. What would she find if she tore the cloth away? Bones? Nothing at all?

The figure slowly raised one arm within a draped sleeve and pointed at Lennie as though about to pronounce her doom. She cringed and held her breath, not wanting to hear.

"See, Urdie?" the figure squealed, nudging the robed woman beside it. "She remembers what you told her—and she even made it sound like you."

The three robed figures blurred. Lennie blinked, and there was only a little girl sticking an elbow into the ribs of a frumpy bag lady.

"Hush, child," said Urdie. "Now you've made me drop a stitch, and there's so little time as it is."

The beaded lady nodded, her dread-locks rattling her necklaces. "In fact, time is nearly up."

"What time?" Lennie wished she could wake herself from this bizarre dream. "I don't understand any of this."

"Of course you don't, dear." Urdie's kindly smile revealed worn, yellow teeth that barely clung to her gums. She ran her hand along the yarn. A shiver scraped down Lennie's back.

The little girl interrupted enthusiastically. "Yeah, well, see, it all has to do with the end of the world." She held up a small, plastic weaving loom that looked just like the one Lennie had used to make dozens of nylon-loop potholders when she was a child.

The beaded lady rested a hand on the girl's shoulder. "Now, Skuldi, you're telling it all out of order. Past, present, and *then* future, remember?"

The girl scowled and flung her loom away. There was a crash and the sound of plastic skidding over cement. "I *never* get to go first."

The beaded lady stiffened, frowning, and Urdie gasped. "Skuld! You could have broken that, and then what would have happened?"

"I don't care."

"You'd better care, urchin. Pick that up right now, or I'll—"

"You'd have to catch me first, you old cow." The girl disappeared from Lennie's view.

"Stop it, both of you." The beaded lady rolled her eyes at Lennie. "They are so predictable sometimes. Urdie's always telling Skuld what to do, and Skuld...well, she can be so contrary. I'm always stuck in the middle."

She looked across Lennie in the direction Skuld had gone. "All right, Skuldi, have it your way. You go first."

"No."

"We're listening, Skuldi—tell us what the future holds."

"Everybody dies."

Urdie pressed her lips together. For a moment, Lennie thought the old woman might go after Skuld and haul her back by her ponytails. Instead, she smiled around clenched teeth. "That's a little too general, dear. Can you be more specific? Maybe a little more

CHAPTER EIGHTEEN

Briggs surveyed the crime scene, noting the overturned furniture, the toy piano grinding through *Pop Goes the Weasel* on dying batteries, the black cotton leggings gripped in Jim Tuttle's convulsed hand. It looked exactly like the police had said when they called him in—the transient entered the little girl's room with the intent to kidnap or harm. The owner shot him. Cut and dried.

But it didn't feel right at all. Briggs couldn't believe he had been so wrong about the simple hobo—especially after what he'd seen Tuttle do at the poetry reading. He squatted next to Tuttle's body. The peaceful, almost joyful, expression on the hobo's face seemed to say that being shot in the chest had been his last, greatest desire.

And the child's story...she claimed that Tuttle's eyes had glowed yellow in the dark just before her daddy shot him. Probably a dream, but Briggs couldn't help thinking of Marybeth's spook theories. It was hard to see what the prostitute's murder had to do with Jim's death, but Briggs's instincts said they were connected somehow. Just thinking about it made him start to smell that same foul, rotting animal stench here. He frowned. Probably just the reek of sweat and death that rose from Tuttle's body.

He headed for the bedroom door, hoping to clear both his head and his nose. But the putrid odor grew stronger as he drew away from the body. He sniffed uncertainly and stuck his head into the hallway, almost colliding with Marybeth.

"Hey, Briggs—sorry about your star witness."

Her voice was slightly muffled. She was already wearing a mask and latex gloves. He registered her presence but didn't answer.

Instead, he moved closer to her, sniffing.

"This is new." She leaned away, looking puzzled and amused. "A simple 'hello' would work fine."

"Do you smell that?"

Marybeth pulled her mask down. Her nostrils flared. "I smell a lot of things, not all of them nice. Do you brush with garlic toothpaste?"

Briggs shook his head with irritation. Sometimes it was hard to hold a serious conversation with Marybeth. "I keep catching a whiff of that same odor we smelled at the dumpster this afternoon. It doesn't seem to be coming from the body, though."

"Maybe it's coming from me. I was up to my armpits in that prostitute's body all evening."

He took another sniff. Fried chicken and car freshener. He stepped past her, leaving her frowning in the doorway.

She crossed her arms. "Hey, you were supposed to say, 'Don't you ever bathe?' or something. You're getting slow, buddy-boy...oh!" She wrinkled her nose. "Ugh, now I smell it, too—like a dog that found something dead to roll in."

The source of the odor couldn't be the living room or the kitchen, or Briggs surely would have noticed it when he first entered the house. That left the bathroom and Sutter's bedroom. The light to the bedroom was on, revealing an unmade double bed, scattered dirty clothes, and his uniform hanging over a chair.

"I think it's coming from in there." Marybeth had come up behind him to look into the bedroom. "Either something crawled under the bed to die, or—"

"Or whatever—or whoever—makes that smell is still in there. Stay here."

"But—"

"I said stay here." He glanced back toward the living room.

Sutter sat in his armchair, elbows on knees, holding his head. A uniform from the MPD stood over him, writing something in a notebook. The little girl had gone to the neighbor's house for the night. "Better yet, go back to the living room and send Charlie in here."

Without waiting for an answer, Briggs unholstered his weapon and entered the room. It didn't seem likely that anyone else was in the house. Bill had probably already checked, himself, after calling the police. But *something* made that smell.

The sparse furnishings offered few hiding places. The bed was low to the floor. If someone was under there, he wouldn't be going anywhere too quickly. The closet seemed a more likely place for a body to hide—living or dead. Briggs edged toward it cautiously.

The floor creaked behind him. "Nothing under here."

Briggs yelped and jerked around, nearly dropping his weapon. Marybeth was on her hands and knees, peering under the bed.

"What the hell are you doing? I told you to get back to the living room."

"You don't really think someone's hiding in here, do you?" She looked up at him, one eyebrow lifted sardonically.

"It's a possibility," he said defensively, "and I don't want you in the line of fire."

"Well, there's nothing under the bed but dust bunnies and one fuzzy pink slipper."

He glared at her. "Nothing, *this* time. What if one of those dust bunnies had been a man with a gun?" He paused, absorbing what she had said. "Pink slipper?"

She reached under the bed and pulled it out. "Child sized. Whose did you think it was?"

Briggs sighed and let it go. He walked to the closet door, Marybeth close behind him. The stench intensified.

"Whatever it is, it's gotta be in here." He pulled on a glove and reached for the knob. His stomach churned in anticipation. "If it looks as bad in there as it smells, I'm going to start losing weight on this case."

But when he opened the door, they saw only normal closet clutter: sneakers on the floor, spare uniform hanging next to some badly ironed dress shirts, golf clubs, a box of detective novels. Nothing that should smell like hyena's breath.

Then he saw it, hanging just inside the door, so close it brushed his arm—a five-foot skein of white string.

It was so innocuous-looking that at first he had thought it was a bathrobe, but his skin crawled where it had touched him. Leaning close, he took a whiff. Odors exploded in his sinuses, overwhelming his brain. Layer upon layer of smells as ancient as time itself—the reek of betrayal, the sour stink of fear, the acrid burn of hatred, and other smells, more heinous. He stumbled back and gaped at the string through tearing eyes.

Marybeth crowded behind him. "What is it? What's wrong?"

He pulled a pencil from his pocket and lifted a strand of the string. Pristine white. As if dirt—or blood—would never cling to it. "We've found the source of that smell. And, if I'm not mistaken..."

He paused. A polished wooden box rested on the floor below the skein, large enough to hold a pair of boots. The lid was ajar and he caught the red-gold glint of metal inside. Could it be...?

He knelt beside the box for a closer look. The wood was so dark that it appeared black, but the swirls of wood grain were darker still. He shined a penlight into the gap.

Inside the box, eight bronze knives with shiny black handles were laid out like crown jewels on plush green velvet.

Briggs tried to talk, but his throat was suddenly dry. He coughed and tried again. "Marybeth, I think we've found our killer."

"What? Which killer?" Marybeth sounded as dumbstruck as he felt. "What do you mean?"

"The Hobo Spider. It's Bill Sutter."

Lennie woke up. At least, she thought she was awake. She was reluctant to open her eyes. Where would she be, this time? Hanging from a tree? In a boxcar?

Maybe she had never left home in the first place. Her real home, not the cramped, dilapidated house she had lived in since her parents' bank account had run dry. If she opened her eyes, she might see the fake wood fan whirling on her old bedroom ceiling, surrounded by glow-in-the-dark stars.

Right. And she would find her dad in the living room, watching television with her mom. They could all share a laugh at the crazy dream her life had become and analyze the symbolism of squirrels and hobos and weird sisters.

She cracked one eye open. The ceiling hung low above her. Reaching up, her fingers grazed the surface with the hollow whisper of cardboard. She was back in the refrigerator box.

"'Bout time you woke up, girl."

Lennie yelped and tried to sit up, thumping her head on the ceiling. A dark figure stretched beside her. The flashlight lay on the floor between them and cast living shadows on a finely wrinkled face and shaggy, faded-red hair.

"Ramblin' Red?" Her voice came out as a croak. She had almost convinced herself that he didn't exist.

He propped his head on one arm, an unlit cigarette hanging from his lips. His one eye cast a blue light, creating another layer of shadow. "Just call me Red."

The cigarette flared on its own. Neat trick. Must not be so hard—everyone seemed to be able to do it.

"Are you...real?"

He laughed, amused. "Real? Dang, girl. 'Course I am." He frowned a little, considering. "Least-wise, most of the time, I am. I think."

That was close enough to real for Lennie. She shoved him onto his back, and threw herself on top of him. Planting her elbows firmly in his gut, she grabbed his collar and gave his head a shake. His mysterious demeanor evaporated with a gasp of cigarette smoke.

"Just what the hell have you gotten me into, you manipulative, flea-bitten bum!" The words exploded from her in a spray of spit. She shook him again. His head thumped dully against the wall and the cigarette flew out of his mouth. "You and your damn tattoo. You might as well have painted a bull's-eye on me. Did you do that to my dad, too? I ought to rip your one eye out and add it to Bones O'Riley's stew."

He gaped at her. His single eye, now dim and ordinary, stared wide in surprise. She wanted to shake him until his teeth rattled out of his head, but part of her wondered: should she be attacking a guy who could call fire from the air and make his eye glow?

Yes. Under the circumstances, yes.

On the other hand, she needed answers. She eased up, but only a little. It felt good to be in control for once. "I want to know what the hell is going on. So start talking or I'll be feeding you eye-ball soup."

Taking his time, he rescued his smoldering cigarette from the floor and stuck it in his mouth. The cigarette's tip burned as he pulled on it again, but not as brightly as his eye. "A lot's goin' on. Can ya be more specific?"

Lennie gripped his collar tighter to keep herself from going for his throat. No one had given her a straight answer since she began this little adventure. Why should she expect Red to be any different?

"You tricked me onto that train. Why?" She was too angry to wait for his answer. "As far as I can figure, I've been in a narcotic induced delirium ever since. I've had bouts of paranoia, delusions of power, and just now, three hallucinations tried to convince me that the world needs me to save it. How am I doing so far?"

"Not bad, exceptin' you're not on drugs and them weren't hallucinations. They was manifestations."

She grimaced, struggling between her need for answers and a desire to hurt him bad. "Okay. How about the paranoia?"

"Maybe so, maybe no. But I can tell ya this—" he somehow managed to wink, though he only had one eye, "—Fenrir really is out to getchya."

Lennie's anger went cold. Red couldn't know about Fenrir unless he could see into her dreams. Or unless Fenrir were real.

She shuddered, believing him, though everything about him was so unbelievable. "Then I ask again—why?" she whispered. "Why did you drag me into this? None of this has anything to do with me."

"The Norn—your hallucinations—already told ya. He ain't gonna kill you. He can't. Least-wise, not directly. That makes you the only one that can git close enough to stop 'im." His expression turned grim. "You gotta go after him, girl. No tellin' what'll happen if you don't."

"You're crazy." The air inside the box had grown hot and thick with smoke. "I'm not going after anyone but my dad."

Something shifted in his one eye. His face shimmered in the swirling smoke, and then he wasn't Ramblin' Red at all, but some greater presence, with a long nose and broad brow. When he spoke again, it was with a deeper, more resonant voice. But the single blue eye was the same.

"You must go into the den of the Wolf, as Tyr went thousands of years ago—as your father went before you. You must bring about the binding of Fenrir, though it be at sacrifice to yourself. Do not fail, as your father before you failed, or all will be lost."

The power in his voice reverberated through her bones. She swayed dazedly. His effect was immense, relentless, his wisdom vast. It was like sitting at the foot of an ancient redwood, its roots buried in the depths of time. She wanted to comply. Needed to comply...

Except it was so unfair. How was she supposed to fight a magical evil guy?

"You've got to be kidding," she croaked. If he was so vast and wise, he could fight his own damned battles.

The flashlight flickered, and Red was just Red again, with cigarette in hand and Lennie's fingers still twisted in his green plaid shirt. He shrugged, and his voice slid back into its comfortable drawl. "Sorry, girl. That's the way of it. You gotta bind him up, again."

She scowled. The more he talked, the less she liked him. "Bind him with what? My shoelaces? If my father couldn't stop him...if *you* can't stop him, how can I?"

"I'd love ta stay an' chat, but a pack of Fenrir's boys are sniffin' down your trail this very minute. Maybe the Wolf won't hurt ya, but those boys ain't so queasy about it." He pried her hands from his collar and pushed her toward the door. "You better get on outta here, and fast."

Even as he spoke, something crashed outside of the box, like a heavy gong hitting the pavement. Too Long Soo let out a shrill stream of curses. Lennie pushed open the cardboard door.

And found herself nose to nose with the most hideous face she had ever seen.

She yelped and sat back, scraping her head on the ceiling. The wavering flashlight lit a man's red-crusted, snarling face in the doorway. A strip of bloody scalp flapped on his forehead like an ill-fitting toupee.

"Fenrir wants you," he said, sounding too much like Peter Lorre. "Wants you baaaad, he does."

His red-rimmed and wild eyes gleamed with a yellow madness that took her breath like a blow to the stomach. Her tattooed hand responded, burning as though lightning bolts wove around her fingers. Static power, ready to discharge—if only she knew how. She stretched her palm toward him, hoping to zap him into an ozone-scented dust cloud.

Nothing happened.

His arm shot in and caught her ankle. Hard fingers ground into her bones, pulling her toward the opening. She clawed at the smooth floor and screamed for Red to help her. There was no answer. Desperate, she stomped her heel into the man's face. He howled and let go. The box rocked crazily. Sobbing, Lennie slid back against the wall farthest from the door.

That's when she realized she was alone.

There were no other doors, no openings. Ramblin' Red was just...gone. The same way he had disappeared from the boxcar.

"Nice timing, Red," she whispered.

The flashlight flickered one last time and went out.

"Perfect."

Now the box had become a dark trap. She licked her lips. The scrap of light seeping through the cardboard door brought her no comfort. That creep could wait for her outside for the rest of the night. Hell, he could bring in a pick-up truck and haul her away, box and all.

From the parking lot, Too Long Soo let out a primal scream, more angry than hurt. Harsh voices shouted in a mixture of English and Spanish. Feet scraped and scuffled across pavement. The light in the crack danced and flickered with struggling shadows. There was another crash, and Bones O'Riley's foul insults punctuated the cacophony.

Lennie felt for the flashlight, found it, and hefted it in her hand. Not much of a weapon. Sweat broke out on her face as she remembered the insanity in her attacker's eyes. Ramblin' Red was right—that guy wasn't a bit queasy about hurting her.

She pressed herself into the corner, every nerve vibrating under her skin. Any second, that hideous face might reappear in that opening, and she wanted to be as far from it as possible.

But the box was only cardboard. With a hollow thump, six inches of sharpened steel sprouted through the wall a finger's width from her ear. She screamed and recoiled from it. The blade waggled back and forth, withdrawing slowly.

For a moment, she could only stare at the light shining through the new gash in the cardboard. Then she sucked in a breath and threw herself down. In that same instant, the knife struck through the wall where she had been.

She huddled on the floor, trying not to touch the walls, and covered her head with her arms. Hysterical sobs choked her throat. She fought them back, trying to think, but the box shook violently.

"Stop it," she screamed, hardly knowing what she was saying. "Just stop it!"

The box shook again, harder, and an insane shriek of rage penetrated the cardboard. She lifted her head and saw the dull glint of steel. The knife was stuck in the wall, hung up in the cardboard.

Now might be her only chance to escape.

She gathered her legs under her and eyed the door, but she couldn't make herself go through. She wasn't sure she would ever move again. Just sit frozen while that lunatic sliced the box apart around her.

Then Soo howled, in pain this time. The sound struck Lennie

like a starting gun. She launched herself through the opening and hit the pavement on her belly, her lower half still inside. She scrambled free and crouched low, ready to lash out.

The jungle was in chaos—the card table overturned with its legs in the air, bags of groceries dumped on the ground, boxes scattered and flattened. The stew pot lay on its side among scattered embers, a muddy lake of mulligan stew puddled around it. Bones O'Riley stood spread-legged before the pot, swinging a piece of firewood like a club. Beside him, Too Long Soo gripped a pop bottle in one hand and a meat fork in the other. Her hat was gone and her hair fanned out from her head like broom straw. A trickle of blood ran from the corner of her eye.

Three gangbangers circled the pair warily. A paint-stained rag hung from the pocket of their leader. The Ragman. He had almost killed Junkyard that morning. Bones and Soo wouldn't stand a chance.

Lennie crawled through the jungle, trying to stay hidden. Behind her, the crazy man who had attacked her pushed between the boxes, muttering to himself. Every few steps, he cackled and kicked over another box. In just a few seconds, he would find her.

Great. Sandwiched between deadly gangbangers and a homicidal madman. This day just kept getting better and better. She picked up a stray can of beef broth and hefted it. Not much of a weapon, but better than nothing.

One of the gangbangers lunged at Soo. Something flashed in his hand and a gash opened in the lanky singer's down vest. White feathers bled from the cut and floated away in the wind. Soo swore and clouted him with the bottle. The gangbanger staggered back, so close to Lennie's hiding place that she could see the interlocking BRR tattooed on the back of his neck. Lennie surged to her feet and knocked the gangbanger in the back of the head with the beef broth.

He spun around, knife in hand. A snarl twisted his face. "You dead, bitch."

The knife came down. Lennie raised the can of broth in a desperate attempt to block it, but the blow never came. With a high-pitched scream, the gangbanger arched his back and flung his arms wide. Eyes rolling with pain and panic, he lost his balance and fell on his face. Stunned, Lennie watched him writhe on the pavement, twisting his arms to reach the foot-long meat fork buried in his back. Soo stood over the fallen man, brandishing her Coke bottle. She glared at Lennie.

"What're y'all standin' around for? They're lookin' fer you, ya nit-brain. Get the hell outta here!"

Another gangbanger came at Soo's back. Bones O'Riley charged him and cracked the firewood across his head. It worked much better than a can of broth. The thug dropped to the ground, out cold. But that left Bones's back unprotected. The Ragman lunged at him, knife ready.

"No!" Lennie heaved the can of beef broth at the Ragman, then looked around for another weapon. A hand grabbed her shoulder and spun her around. She staggered against Hotshot's box. The madman was on her before she could recover. He shoved her against the heavy cardboard and pressed his crazed face close. One eye had swollen shut with a fresh bruise. The other eye bloomed with yellow madness.

"I told you, Fenrir wants you." He leered hideously and giggled. "And now, Monte's gonna bring you to him."

CHAPTER NINETEEN

Junkyard knelt among rain-dampened bushes and watched the home of the bull who had befriended him over the last hellish year. Floodlights glared across the yard, illuminating the police cars in the driveway all too clearly. They had already been there, cherries flashing, when Junkyard arrived. Crime scene tape marked the perimeter of the yard. Not wanting to get entangled with the police, he had hidden in the neighbor's landscaping and watched a stream of people go into Bill Sutter's house, each checking in with a uniformed officer before entering. So far, no one had come out.

He shifted his weight uneasily, wishing he could see inside. The blinds had been drawn all over the house. The window in the door was too small to reveal much from this distance, but he stared at it anyway, trying to see who moved inside.

It would have been so much simpler if he could have kept both Jim and Lennie with him after the poetry session. But Jim had slipped away, forcing Junkyard to choose one or the other. Now it seemed he wasn't protecting either one. He didn't even know if Jim was inside.

For the first time since he had met Jungle Jim, the rage threatened to take control, urging him to forget Jim, forget Lennie, and get down to the business of finding his brother's killer. He couldn't do that, though. Jungle Jim needed him too much. And, he realized, swallowing against the ache in his throat, he needed Jim just as badly.

As for Lennie...he didn't want to think too hard about her. Not yet.

An unsteady breeze stirred the bushes and he fidgeted

uncomfortably. With a gentle *tink*, collected rain splashed onto one of Austin's buttons—*Home is Where the Heart Is.* He wiped the water from it with his thumb. Usually, he wore a water resistant windbreaker when it rained and wrapped the denim jacket in plastic. But today wasn't a usual day.

The front door opened. Junkyard shifted his position for a better view. Mud squished coldly under his knees. A man in a dark jacket and a uniformed police officer stepped from the house and strode toward a white truck parked among the police cars. Talking in low voices, they opened the back of the truck and pulled out a gurney. Junkyard half rose, clenching his jaw so hard it ached. The living weren't transported to hospital in white trucks.

The wheels of the gurney clattered over the threshold as the men pushed it into the house. Everything seemed to pause after the door closed behind them. Even the wind stilled and the bushes stopped dripping. Junkyard drilled his gaze into the door's small window. He could see movement, someone's back, an arm, but no faces.

One gurney, one body.

Junkyard remembered the first time he had visited Bill. He hadn't been too sure about going to the house of a train yard bull, but Jungle Jim had talked him into it. Bill had come to the door with a smile on his round face and called back over his shoulder, "Ashley—Uncle Jim's here!"

There was a squeal, and a small, blond streak shot out the door and wrapped itself around Jim's waist. Bill chuckled and brushed his daughter's hair with his fingers. "All right, squirt," he said. "Let the man into the house."

Then he turned to Junkyard and offered his hand with a smile. Since then, that same hand had been offered every time Junkyard had passed through Minneapolis.

One body. Whose?

The door swung open and the cop backed out, pulling the now-loaded gurney. It stretched into view, revealing a featureless body bag. Junkyard sat back, frustrated. He would know nothing until Briggs chose to tell him. Or he could read it in the morning paper, with everyone else.

The gurney trundled toward the truck, rattling heavily over cracked pavement. One wheel slipped off the edge of the driveway. The gurney tilted precariously. When the men wrenched it back onto the pavement, the body bag's zipper gaped open at one end. The floodlights shone into the opening, lighting up a shoe as yellow as a small sun.

Gangbangers' paint. A symbol of fear and hate turned into a thing of innocent delight.

Junkyard gaped at it helplessly. Numbness spread through him. He heard the truck's doors slam, the engine start. Had he really seen it? That shoe? Maybe he was mistaken...some other shoe...some other person...

The branches above Junkyard rustled, knocking loose a brief downpour. He looked up reflexively, not really caring. The branches swayed, empty but for twigs and leaves silhouetted against the moonlit sky. Then something thumped at his shoulder blade. He jerked, startled out of his shock, and scrambled out from the bushes. A huge, black raven fluttered into the puddle where he had been sitting. A single BB eye glinted at him under the flood lights. Junkyard waved an arm, trying to scare the bird away. It hopped back a few inches and cocked its head for a better look at him.

A truck's headlights switched on, reminding Junkyard that the bushes no longer hid him. Heedless of the bird, he scooted into cover and watched the vehicle pull out of the driveway, taking Jungle Jim's body with it. He felt nine years old again, watching the ambulance drive off with his dying father. But where his father had kept him safe from the outside world, Jungle Jim had kept Junkyard safe from himself.

Who would hold back the shadows now?

The raven plucked at Junkyard's jacket. Its beak clamped onto one of Austin's buttons and jerked as though trying to pull it off. Junkyard yanked the button away and swatted at the bird. It fluttered a short distance and cocked its head again. The button hung loose, almost freed from the denim. It said, *A friend walks in when the rest of the world walks out.*

An image of Lennie popped into his head, so real he wanted to brush the caramel curls back from her face. The bird blared a crow-like, "Caw, caw." To Junkyard, it sounded more like a harsh, "Go, go,"

Lennie is in danger.

There was no reason to think so, but he knew it, felt it in the petrifying cold that spread through his body. He launched out of the mud and tore through the neighbor's lawn. Vaulting a low picket fence, he stumbled onto the road and took off at a hard run toward the jungle.

Silent now, the bird scratched in the mud beneath the bushes on Bill Sutter's lawn and pretended to look for worms. When Detective Harcourt Briggeman exited the house, the bird uttered a soft croak and took off, its black wings slicing into the darkness.

Bill Sutter's house served as a focal point for more than friendship, murder, or even an oversized raven's sense of timing. The house was a crux where all points, past and future, came together. The unseen were drawn to watch the house, spectators of events transpiring and choices made.

To Ramblin' Red, sitting in a tree, Jungle Jim's defiance was a victory, though small and certainly not final.

To Urdie, handbag jingling and snowmobile boots shuffling a block away, Jungle Jim's death was an omen.

To Fenrir, watching the house from the ink of his own shadow, Jungle Jim's death meant one less impediment in his path. To Fenrir, Jungle Jim's death was a signal.

"Oh, the times, they are a changin'," Urdie sang, getting the melody completely wrong. Her needles clacked as she made her way down the sidewalk, incorporating indigo yarn into the work tucked under her arm. Every few stitches, she paused her knitting to run the yarn between her fingers. When she reached a streetlight, she let the needles hang and fished scissors from her pocket. As she stretched the yarn to cut it, a man broke through the hedge of a nearby yard and dashed across the street in front of her. The buttons on his jacket flashed in the light. She read one—*Earth is Room Enough*—and then he was gone.

Snip. Indigo ceased, replaced by florescent orange. The scissors were deposited in the pocket. The clacking resumed, and so did the shuffling and jingling.

Shadows crowded the streetlight's glow. A piece of the dark parted from the rest and blocked Urdie's path.

"Hello, young pup," Urdie said without looking up. "Come to try again?"

The darkness curled away like steam, unveiling the stolen human form of Fenrir. A cigarette hung from one corner of his mouth. His lip curled.

"Try is such an uncertain word."

"And still an appropriate one, my dear. After all, you tried ten years ago." Urdie stopped walking, but her hands continued to work. She ran her fingers down the orange yarn and wrapped a loop around a needle. "Try, try again, but you still won't be able to kill fate."

Fenrir growled and his eyes flared yellow. Once before, he had come upon Urdie on a similar dark street, intending to tear her apart. One-Eye's champion of the moment had intervened, setting Fenrir's plans back another ten years. That interfering human now served Fenrir in torment, a hollow shell filled with terror, subject to Fenrir's smallest whims.

"There will be no *try* this time, old woman."

Fenrir's voice rang with triumph. Urdie looked up for the first time and saw the seven-foot spear in Fenrir's hands. She stopped knitting. Her oversized purse slipped off her arm and hit the ground with a chink.

"So," she whispered, a hint of a smile at the corners of her mouth. "You brought Gungnir."

Primitive and rough-hewn, the spear spoke of raw power. Hand-carved runes tracked down its shaft. Black feathers dangled from the leather straps behind the knife-sharp bronze head. Fenrir hefted it in one hand.

"I thought that would get your attention. You should never have given One-Eye that prophecy."

He brought the spear to his shoulder, ready to throw. Urdie tucked her needles into her knitting and folded her hands. "You were in the ground too long, young pup," she said, "or you would know this will never work."

"Oh, but I think it will." He stretched his empty hand toward her, a javelin thrower's pose. One by one, he curled his fingers into a fist, each knuckle popping like distant gunshot. Then he threw.

The spear plunged into Urdie's chest, shredding layers of flower print like tissue. The force knocked her out of her heavy boots and sent the flowered hat spinning from her head. She hit the pavement with a dull thud and lay still.

Fenrir approached cautiously, frowning, for she had made no sound. Bending close, he saw the blood, the vacant eyes staring skyward, and knew that the prophecy was broken. All things were now possible. His eyes flamed like small suns, venting the triumph that burned in his heart.

The end had begun.

Calling Freyja's stolen falcon form, he let the visage of Angus Cook fall away, allowed himself to shrink and the feathers to cling. There was one more hindrance in his path. A small one, true, but one with which he must deal.

And then he would stir the waters of chaos.

With a soft rustling of feathers and a fierce screech, he was gone, leaving the remains of Urd on the pavement like abandoned laundry. Then, one-by-one, her body, her boots, her knitting, even the flowered hat, shimmered and disappeared. All that remained of Urd was an oversized handbag, its clasp burst, her savings scattered over the damp pavement.

CHAPTER TWENTY

Monte cackled and pressed Lennie against the cardboard box, his wet lips inches from her face. He stank of defecation and sweat. Blood dripped from his oozing scalp onto her neck. She tried to wrench herself free, but he gripped her forearms hard enough to bruise.

He could kill her easily. He could do anything he wanted. But what frightened her more was that he was no one-eyed spook or undead shadow that only showed up when no one else was looking. He was real...and he knew about Fenrir. Which meant—

"Bones—behind you. The Ragman!"

Soo's warning was followed by a grunt and the sounds of scuffle, but Lennie could only see Monte's face. She jerked her knee up—hard. He twisted and blocked it easily with his thigh. If only she could reach the switchblade, still in her back pocket. She just needed to get one hand free.

But she couldn't break Monte's grip. His eyes burned like candle glow over his sloppy grin, reflecting the fire in Fenrir's eyes. Responding, her tattooed skin prickled with an urge like a building sneeze. She tried to focus on it, but the yellow intensified, filling her vision, choking her will to fight. She closed her eyes, but the yellow tainted even the darkness behind her eyelids. Her struggles weakened until she could only hang limply in Monte's grip.

Something crashed to the pavement and Bones yelped, spewing curses like machine gun fire. Soo's voice rang through the noise half an octave too high. "Y'all better leave him alone, Ragman, or Ah'll show you a whole new meaning fer 'on the rag'."

I should help, Lennie thought dimly. Soo and Bones were in trouble because of her. She heard the smack of fist on flesh and tried to make herself fight, but her muscles barely twitched. Desperately, she focused on the untapped power humming through her finger bones. It was there, the buzz of angry bees. She pictured it flowing from her fingertips and tried to aim it at Monte. Nothing happened.

Useless tattoo. She was going to die with a lightning bolt trapped in her fist. She hoped it would explode in Monte's face.

You are pathetic—like your father before you.

Shocked, she opened her eyes and stared into Monte's lunatic face. The deep, growling voice couldn't have come from him. Was it only in her head? It hardly mattered. Its tone was disdainful. Worse, it was dismissive.

And it was right. She hung powerless, a weakling in this madman's grip, blaming some random tattoo for not rescuing her.

Well, there had been no tattoo when she had won the State Championship in the 400 with a sprained ankle, or when she had worked two jobs her senior year and still pulled a 4.0. No tattoo had given her the strength to strap her crazed mother to the bed near the end, administering meds and cleaning up bloody vomit when they couldn't afford hospitals.

To hell with the idiotic tattoo.

"You bastard," she snarled. "I'll show you pathetic!"

As though feeding on her defiance, her tattooed hand flared with electric fire, burning away the yellow haze. Screaming her rage, she yanked her arms down savagely and broke Monte's grip. Her clawed fingers found his ears and crumpled them like wadded Kleenex. She anchored her nails deep into cartilage and dug her thumbs into his eyes.

Snarling, Monte wrenched at her hands. She felt one of his ears give way. Seeming oblivious to injury, he rammed his head into her face. Pain exploded in her nose. Stunned, she let go of his head and fell backward. The cardboard box slid out from under her and she hit the pavement hard, with Monte on top of her. She fought him blindly as tears streamed and blood flowed into her mouth. He caught one arm, then the other, and clamped her wrists together in a grip she couldn't break. Blood rattled in her throat and she coughed, spraying his face. He licked her blood from his lips and laughed. His eyes blazed.

Had her father died this way?

He, too, thought to fight me, but he was a coward. A nothing.

She was falling, falling through a yellow fog, though she still felt Monte's weight on her arms and the pebbled blacktop beneath her. Within the fog, she saw her father, Jarvis Cook—balding, thick at the waist, just as she had last seen him. He stood a few feet away and smiled at her.

"Dad!" She wanted to run to him like a little girl and hug him around the middle.

Then a huge shadow fell across them both. Her father looked up and gaped at something behind her, an oppressive presence that turned the air suffocatingly cold. His face turned white under a summer tan and he backed away, arms lifted as though to deflect a blow.

I crushed him, as I will crush you.

Her father's mouth stretched open in a voiceless scream. He seemed to shrink, shoulders hunching, chest sinking inwards. His eyes grew unnaturally wide, open windows into the fear that shriveled his soul.

"No," Lennie whispered, horrified. Somehow, she felt it all— everything her father felt as he lost his mind. She felt his muscles go rigid—hot breath panting across his tongue—shirt clinging to sweating back—needles of terror jabbing his skin...no, her skin. And as her own will melted along with her father's, she had a sudden realization. Her mother wasn't drowning her sorrows in a bottle, as Lennie had always thought.

She was drowning her fear.

"You understand, now, don't you." Monte laughed in a voice unnaturally shrill. "Monte knows."

He dragged her to her feet. Her head lolled helplessly and tangled hair hung in her eyes.

"Time to go visit El Lobo."

An agonized scream ripped through the jungle. The dwindling part of Lennie's mind that was still coherent recognized the voice and knew: the gangbanger's knife had found Bones O'Riley. Monte paused to watch the fight. The pall smothering Lennie's mind eased somewhat as those glowing eyes focused elsewhere. Lennie raised her head and gazed blearily at the battleground the jungle had become.

Too Long Soo lay on the ground a few yards away. Bones remained on his feet in front of her, wielding his firewood like Conan the Barbarian in grimy overalls. The Ragman lunged at him, and Bones beat him back with a solid clout to the head. Lennie felt a brief flare of hope, but Bones was a cook, not a warrior, and blood soaked through the clothes on his back. Limping, he dodged once, twice, but his reactions were too slow. The gangbanger's fist connected and he dropped.

"No," Lennie whispered. She pulled weakly against the iron fingers around her wrists. Monte only squeezed tighter.

"Finish him," he ordered.

The Ragman nodded and leaned over Bones, knife readied for a killing blow. Before he could strike, a man hurtled into the jungle, moving so fast that Lennie saw only the flash of buttons on a dark jacket.

Junkyard.

The Ragman saw him too late. Junkyard slammed a fist into the side of his neck and the gangbanger dropped to the ground, quivering.

Monte glared at the twitching gangbanger. "Oh, Fenrir will not be pleased."

He seemed to have forgotten about Lennie. The yellow haze cleared and her strength came flooding back. She drove her knee upward, this time catching him squarely. He buckled and let go of her. She reached for her pocket and pulled out the switchblade.

"*Best not try to use it for anything but show,*" Junkyard had said earlier in the day, after a futile effort to show her how to use it. "*Or it'll most likely end up in your own hide.*"

Maybe. Or maybe not. The knife had heft. Like a roll of quarters.

Before Monte could recover, she drove her loaded fist into his stomach. The breath whooshed out of him and he doubled over, falling to his knees. He reached for her, his mouth working in airless gasps. Wishing for steel-toed boots, she landed a roundhouse kick to the side of his head. He toppled and curled like a stunned wasp.

Lennie stood over him, panting. An unnatural silence fell over the jungle.

"I'm impressed."

She whirled, ready for another attack, but Junkyard was the only other person still standing. He looked her over, raw relief clear on his face.

"When that guy had you like that, I thought he was going to—" He swallowed hard and turned his head away.

"Yeah, I thought so, too." She scanned the wreckage around her, grateful that everything was colored in normal nighttime shades of grey.

Junkyard gestured at her hand and said, "I think you can put that away now."

Lennie looked down. Her fingers were clenched so tightly around the closed switchblade that the skin over her knuckles looked ready to split. She grinned sheepishly. "Never had a chance to open it."

Swearing colorfully, Soo came to her knees. She shook her head, blinking as though trying to focus. Lennie was having a bit of trouble with that herself. Feeling light-headed and twitchy, she stepped carefully around Monte and made her way to Soo's side.

"Are you all right?"

Soo's voice rasped harshly. "Ah feel like Ah been knocked down by a two-ton wreckin' ball."

Bones groaned and tried to sit up. His face was grey above his beard and blood smeared his forehead. Junkyard knelt beside him and gently pushed him back. "Easy there, big guy."

Bones winced and peered up at him. "Oh, it's you. Still uglier than a warthog's ass, I see."

Junkyard's smile couldn't hide the worry. "Good to see you, too, Happy Chef. Looks like someone tried to fillet you, though. Mind if I have a look at your backside?"

"Guess not." Bones's face twisted in sudden pain. He drew a ragged breath and glared at Junkyard through a half-opened eye. "But you have to pay a dollar, just like everyone else."

"Put it on my tab."

Though Junkyard leaned into him, doing most of the work, Bones's jowls bulged with the strain of rolling to his side. A dark stain soaked the pavement where his back had been. He lay panting while Junkyard undid his overalls' strap and peeled back the denim. There was a lot of blood—enough to soak Bones's t-shirt and obscure the actual cut. Lennie's head swam at the sight and her legs felt wobbly.

Junkyard gently pulled the shirt away from the wound. Breath hissed through Bones's teeth. "Damn, that hurts—why don't you just piss on it, while you're at it."

"Quit yer gripin' and let the man work," Soo said. Her gaze flicked worriedly from Bones to Junkyard.

The gash ran like a bloody river from Bones's lower back through the waistband of his boxers. It was easily the worst injury Lennie had ever seen. Her legs buckled and she sat abruptly while Junkyard examined the wound more closely.

"It's a good thing you're so fat," he said. "That knife didn't come close to any major organs. Soo, can you bring your truck around? I want to get him out of here before anything else happens."

"Ah'd like to, but those punk bastards flattened all four tires. We'll have to carry him someplace safe an' go fer help."

Something scraped pavement at the edge of the jungle. The Ragman dragged himself upright. Soo swore and lurched to her feet. Sneering, the Ragman held up a cell phone. Before anyone could move, he staggered away, into the dark.

"Shee-it! Better wrap up that slab o' bacon, Junkyard. Ah think the dogs are comin'!"

Lennie scrambled to her feet. Her arms ached, she could hardly breathe through her nose, her tailbone felt bruised, and pain shot through her pinkie toe like it had been snapped off backward. She had never been less interested in running. But she wasn't interested in staying, either.

Junkyard draped Bones's arm over his shoulders and tried to heave him upright. "Come on, big guy—time to go."

Bones tried to rise, but fell back with moan, his face contorted with pain. Junkyard braced himself to try again and Lennie moved to his other side to help. Harsh shouts echoed across the parking lot. Feeling an urgent, renewed interest in running, Lennie hauled on

Bones's arm. He shook her off angrily.

"Hear that?" he wheezed. "That's the cavalry, and it's not on our side. Now, leave me and get the hell out of here."

Junkyard shook his head. "Can't do. They'd split you like a roasted hot dog."

"Only if they think I'm alive, and right now, there's nothing I'd like better than to play dead."

Bones shifted his bulk back onto the stained pavement, let his arms flop ad hoc, and locked his eyes open, unfocused. He looked very dead. Then he winked up at them and said, "Laying here beats the hell out of trying to out-run a bunch of teenaged punks. Now go."

The voices were getting closer. Junkyard stared into Bones's eyes. The fat man gazed back calmly. "It's all right, Junkyard," he said, his voice uncharacteristically gentle. "I'll be fine. Go."

Junkyard nodded once and turned away. Soo gave Bones a long, worried look. Then she ran to her truck, flung the door open, and grabbed her guitar off the seat. Junkyard frowned and started to say something, but Soo cut him off. "Ain't no way I'm leavin' Woody for those punks."

With a growl of exasperation, Junkyard took off across the parking lot. Soo followed, Woody banging discord on her back. Lennie hesitated, looking back at Bones. "But we can't just leave you!"

Bones lifted his head. His eyes blazed at her above a bristling beard. "I'm safer if you leave, dimwit! Their coming after *you*, so put a rabbit in your ass and hightail it out of here."

He dropped back into the dead position. Looking past his sprawled body, Lennie could just make out dark forms emerging from the carnival at the far end of the parking lot. Swearing to herself, she turned and ran.

Halfway to the tent village, she heard a shout and slowed to risk a look back. The streetlight at the center of the pavement lit the jungle like a stage. Monte was on his feet amid the wreckage. Two new gangbangers had joined him. One of them leaned over Bones and prodded him with his foot. Monte turned his back on them and stared out into the dark. Nose in the air, he rotated his head slowly, as though trying to catch a scent. Two pinpricks of yellow light stared from his face, tracking across the pavement. They stopped when they reached Lennie, fixing on her in the dark. He pointed.

"She's there."

He didn't raise his voice, but Lennie could hear him perfectly. The gangbanger standing over Bones straightened and pointed an arm at her. Something metallic glinted in his hand. The hairs at the back of Lennie's neck prickled. "He's got a gun!"

She was in the middle of an empty parking lot, without even a tree for cover. The gangbanger aimed down his arm.

And the fat body lying at his feet jack-knifed, taking his legs out. Gunshot cracked wildly overhead.

"Don't shoot them, you idiot," Monte screeched. "El Lobo wouldn't like it if you hit the girl."

"Lennie, get moving!" Junkyard and Soo had stopped a few yards ahead. Before Lennie could follow them, there was a loud pop of gunfire.

"Bones!" Soo's face twisted in horror. She started back toward the jungle, but Junkyard wrapped his arms around her, guitar and all.

"No, let me go." Woody rang hollowly as Soo tried to wrench free, but Junkyard held her tight.

"You can't go back there, Soo." His voice was soft, but urgent. "Bones's best hope is for us to draw them away from him."

"Uh, seems to be working." Lennie fought panic as the three men charged into the shadows. "They're coming."

Junkyard didn't let Soo go until she stopped struggling. She stared back at the jungle, anguish clear on her face.

"Soo—"

"All right, dammit," she snarled. "Let's go."

CHAPTER TWENTY ONE

They didn't stop running until they reached the chain link fence bordering the train yard. Gasping for air, Lennie clasped her hands behind her head and forced herself to take a few long, slow breaths. Soo was in worse shape. She lowered her guitar to the ground and crouched beside it with her head down. Her bleached hair hung like mop strings around her tear-streaked face.

They had lost the bad guys in the tent village, but Lennie knew it wouldn't take them long to show up. She scanned the train yard while Junkyard searched for a break in the fence. Exhaust hung heavy in the air. A diesel unit idled somewhere in the iron forest, hissing and popping, full of metallic complaints. Flood lights created pockets of deep shadow between cars. Anyone could be hiding there. Or any thing.

"What are we doing here?" Lennie said, still breathing hard.

"Hear that train?" Junkyard wiped sweat from his forehead and pushed aside the shrubbery along the fence. "It's all hosed up and ready to go. There's a break in the fence somewhere around here. As soon as I find it," he tugged at a section, "we're getting on board. You're going home."

"What? No—I've got to find my dad!"

"Not this trip."

"But you don't understand—"

He waved her off. "We don't have time to argue. Those 'bangers'll be here any minute."

"Dammit, my dad is—"

Junkyard turned on her, his fists half-raised. She shied back.

"Don't you get it? Those 'bangers are looking for *you*. People are getting hurt because of you—good people." He slammed the fence with an open hand. The chain link shook loudly and she almost missed his next words. "I'm not letting you hang around until you're dead, too."

She understood, then; it wasn't just "people" that needed her to leave. *Junkyard* needed her to leave. That realization stung more than she expected.

But people might get hurt if she left, too. Her father. The whole world, if she wanted to believe Ramblin' Red. *Fenrir ain't gonna kill you*, he'd said, *but you can stop him*.

She had a deep lack of desire to meet up with Fenrir. But did she have a choice?

"Oh, fer cryin' out loud. We cain't go." Soo rose to her full corn-stalk height. Her face was pale and grim. "What about Jungle Jim? Ah cain't believe yer leavin' him behind."

Junkyard's back stiffened and he said nothing for a long moment. Then he slumped and pressed his forehead against the chain link.

"Jim's dead," he said in a flat voice. The air seemed to die around his words. "I saw them carry the body from Bill's house. Place was crawling with police. They don't show up like that for a heart attack."

For a moment, the only sound was the steady grumble of the diesel unit. Then Woody slipped from Soo's fingers and hit the grass with a hollow bong. The strings rang unpleasantly until the sharp hiss of air brakes swallowed the noise.

Lennie felt faint. That sweet, innocent man. "And Bill?"

"They only brought one body out." Junkyard shot an angry look at Lennie, as if he thought she were to blame. He yanked roughly at a section of fence. The chain link whipped back, almost hitting him in the face. He caught it and held it open. "Time to go."

The diesel unit began to ease forward. Couplers stretched and rattled as freight cars jerked to life. Soo bowed double and squeezed through the gap in the fence, but Lennie shook her head. "Uh-uh. Not happening. I told you last night, I'm never catching onto a moving train again."

The air throbbed as electric motors struggled to gain momentum. Soo slung the guitar over her shoulder. "Don't be silly, girl. It's pokin' along slower than a dead armadillo." She nodded toward the street behind Lennie. "Besides, the bad guys are here."

Instinctively, Lennie crouched behind the shrubs and peered back the way they had come. A pack of shadowy figures paused between streetlights, two blocks down the road. She could make out the glint of chain on denim, the flash of a white tank shirt under an open jacket...and the faint gleam of yellow where eyes should be.

Monte.

Even in the dim light, he looked ready to come apart. The torn flap of scalp stood out like a feather in his hair. Blood stained his puffy face and his head twitched with a spastic rhythm. Yet there he was, running the pack, his nose in the air as if sniffing her out.

And, with uncanny accuracy, he found her.

He turned toward her slowly, deliberately. One eye had swollen shut, but the other glowed pus yellow, transfixing her through the shadow. Lennie's tattooed hand flared and stretched toward Monte under its own power.

"*Ese!*" Monte called to the pack. He pointed at Junkyard. "Smoke that bastard. Leave the girl to me."

Lennie watched her hand with trance-like focus. Her fingers splayed wide. The skin on her out-thrust palm burned with an electric fire that demanded release. This time, something would happen. Let them come a little closer, and the power would discharge, and then—

Abruptly, before she could release even the tiniest spark, someone grabbed her from behind and yanked her through the gap in the fence. In a crazed fury, she turned on her captor. Sparks crackled between her fingers. A prelude. Every nerve, every instinct screamed *now*.

But it was Junkyard's face that loomed into her dazed vision. Not Monte's. Not Fenrir's. She fought to hold back the power, to pull it back into herself. The fire in her hand guttered and died. She slumped and would have fallen if Junkyard hadn't caught her. He lifted her to her feet and half-dragged her away from the fence. His jaw muscles bunched with worry and anger.

"What the hell's the matter with you?"

"I—I was—" I was about to try my new, god-like powers...

"Never mind." He shoved her toward the train. "Run."

She didn't argue. The power in her hand had fled and the gangbangers were nearly at the fence. She drew a breath and forced her legs to move.

The train had reached walking speed. Soo got to it first and galloped toward the back end, looking for a place to catch on. Lennie and Junkyard tore after her, spurred by the sounds of their pursuers crashing into chain link. Soo shouted over the train noise. "Cain't see no ride. Nothin' but tankers."

Monte's pack found the loose section in the fence and poured through the gap. Three figures peeled away from the rest and ran toward the train's head end. The others charged after their prey, trying to catch them before they boarded. Lennie saw a ladder on the outside of the next tank car and pointed. "Can we get on top?"

"Rather not," Junkyard gasped. "Too easy to pick us off."

The gangbangers' shouts grew closer. Soo swore and tried to pick up the pace, but could only manage an exhausted lope. Lennie wasn't doing much better; a stitch stabbed her side with every breath and her calves ached from running on cinders. She couldn't feel her pinkie toe at all. She was tempted to take her chances hanging off the side of a tanker, but the profile of the oncoming cars changed. Boxcars surged past a moment later.

"There!" Junkyard pointed at an open door in the side of an approaching boxcar. He and Soo stopped abruptly and began running the other way. Caught off guard, Lennie skidded in the cinders. The gangbangers were less than 50 yards away.

Junkyard dropped back, grabbed the door latch, and swung himself up and in. Looked easy when *he* did it.

Soo went next. She pulled Woody's strap over her head and handed the guitar up to Junkyard. Visibly exhausted, she stumbled as she clutched at the door latch. She held on, legs churning, but couldn't get her feet under her to push off. Junkyard tossed Woody inside, caught hold of Soo's wrist, and pulled.

"Dang it, Junkyard!" she yelled between breaths. "Even one—*oof*—scratch—on that guitar—an' yer dog meat!"

He hooked Soo's rope belt with his other hand and tossed her in after Woody. Not waiting to see where she landed, he turned and gestured at Lennie.

Her turn.

The boxcar had pulled ahead of her while she waited for Soo to board. She fought to make her rubbery legs catch up. Junkyard's gestures grew frantic and he pointed, yelling. Two gangbangers were almost on her. Their eyes glinted yellow.

New life pumped into Lennie's muscles. She sprinted, grasped the door latch, and tried to swing aboard like Junkyard. In a nightmarish rerun of the night before, her legs banged into the doorframe and flailed in open air. She screamed, as much afraid of her pursuers as of the grinding wheels. Junkyard's wild-eyed face swung into her vision. He grabbed her arm, ripped her fingers from the latch, and yanked her halfway into the boxcar. The lip of the doorframe cut into her stomach and her legs dangled outside.

Junkyard shouted incoherently and pulled at her arm. Too late. A gangbanger clamped down on one ankle and tore Lennie from Junkyard's grip. She kicked hard, freeing herself, and then she was sliding backward, clawing rust and dirt and metal. The doorframe carved into her underarms and she was flying backward, staring facedown at the rushing ground, her palms skidding across the metal floor.

Junkyard threw himself down and caught her wrists. Her muscles screamed at the jolt of her weight and their eyes met through outstretched arms. Then he heaved, falling on his back. She shot inside and landed hard on top of him.

Soo stuck her head out the door. "That did it. Ah don't see how they're gonna catch us now." She pulled back inside and wrinkled her nose. "Hooo-eee. What kind o' cargo are they shippin'? Smells like somethin' crawled in here to die."

Lennie hadn't noticed the odor. She lay gasping across Junkyard's legs, with his knee in her chest, one wrist still locked in his grip, and her face pressed against the gritty, vibrating floor. Nothing had ever felt so comfortable—or so safe. She closed her eyes and gave in to the tremors running through her body.

"Woody!" Cursing fluently, Soo scrambled over to her discarded guitar. She shot Junkyard a dirty look. "Even one scratch, boy, and yer—"

"Yeah, yeah. I know. Dog meat." He shifted his legs under Lennie. "Uh, could you— move—just a bit."

Lennie moaned. With a weak, "sorry," she rolled off him. The effort sent small, sharp pains through her strained shoulders, but she didn't think she was seriously hurt.

Junkyard rubbed his thigh where her elbow had been. The

inconstant light cast his face in sharp angles and flickering shadows. He looked away when she tried to meet his eyes.

Soo sat cross-legged beside them with the guitar on her lap, examining the battered wood in the moonlight. Lennie couldn't see how she could tell the new scratches from the old. Finally satisfied, Soo began fiddling with the tuning pegs.

No one spoke. Lennie was grateful for that. Her mind was blank, and she liked it that way. No thoughts of loss or pain, fear or death. Just let the rocking boxcar lull her like a cradle and take her somewhere safe.

Junkyard wasn't so content. He fidgeted restlessly and his gaze darted between the dark corners of the boxcar. "It really does stink in here," he said. "That smell's got to be coming from somewhere."

His voice was tense and he rose to his knees. Lennie moaned softly. What now? Couldn't she have just five minutes of peace? Though there definitely was a stench hanging in the air—a mixture of wet dog and rotting meat. Whatever made that smell had to be long dead. Right?

She sighed and sat up. The way her day had gone, the dead just might rise up and come after her. Reluctantly, she peered into the shadows. The boxcar appeared empty except for mounds of debris along the walls.

"Hey y'all, lookee here." Soo set the guitar down, leaned into the shadow to one side of the door, and dragged a battered army-issue pack into the patch of moonlight.

"Maybe some yard worker left it behind," Lennie said.

Soo zipped the pack open and rummaged. "Hmmm, skivvies, socks, some matches, a church key. Oh, here." She pulled out a flashlight. "Ah hope the owner don't mind if we borrow this."

She handed it to Junkyard and went back to sifting through the bag. Junkyard swept the light slowly around the boxcar, highlighting piles of debris, some rumpled packing paper, and a push broom. A television with an old-fashioned, numbered dial listed against one wall, near a corner. No boxes or crates.

"We seem to be the only cargo," Lennie said, relieved.

Junkyard grunted and began a more methodical search of the boxcar's interior. The light trailed slowly around the outline of the other side-door. It appeared to be securely closed.

"Oh, crap," Soo said. Her whole arm was inside the pack. "Ah don't believe it."

From the disgust in her voice, Lennie thought she must have found the source of the odor. But when Soo pulled her arm out of the pack, she was holding something small and silver.

"This has gotta be Hotshot's flask." She shook it. "It's bone dry, too. Dadblasted idiot was skippin' out on us. He prob'ly stashed his pack here and passed out droolin' under some bush." She let loose a few curses and threw the flask angrily into the pack.

"No," Junkyard said slowly. "I think he caught the train."

He knelt, unmoving, with the flashlight directed at something stiff and lumpy at the base of the door panel. A red blanket had been thrown over it. Lennie remembered Hotshot huddled under that same blanket that morning, his eyes shining with fear when she showed him her father's picture.

"Shee-it," Soo said hoarsely. "That's the blanket he got down in Santa Fe, last year. D'ya think he's...?"

"Yeah." Junkyard's lips hardly moved. "Yeah, I do."

He got up and moved closer, steadying himself against the wall when the train hit a bump. For a moment, he just stood over the blanket, studying it, as if reluctant to do anything more. Lennie understood how he felt. Something about the shape, the way the blanket draped over it, made her stomach ache with foreboding. Hardly aware of what she was doing, she crawled closer. Mesmerized, she watched Junkyard's hand reach out, already certain what would happen next. With a rough flick of his wrist, he jerked the blanket aside.

The smell hit her first. She pulled away, her lips curling back from her teeth. Road kill, sewer sludge, freshly turned compost—she couldn't quite name it, but it was worse than any smell she had ever encountered.

Soo had come up behind Lennie. She swore colorfully and turned her head. "Hoooo-eeee. Smells like..."

She fell silent. Lennie covered her mouth and nose with her hand. Ignoring the hysterical warning that babbled deep in her mind, she let her eyes focus on the thing that lay at Junkyard's feet.

At first she thought she was looking at a second blanket, so white that it shimmered in the meager light. Only it wasn't cloth at all. It was thick, white string wound close enough to obscure what lay beneath. But the shape was undeniable. Feet, knees, torso, shoulders. A body. The white string ended just below a bald head.

Petey was all tied up, Jungle Jim had said, *like a bug wrapped up by a spider.*

Junkyard stirred beside her. His voice cracked dryly. "That's Hotshot, all right."

"Shee-it." Soo's voice sounded strangled, like she was fighting tears. "Dadblasted fool—why'd he light out like that, by hisself?"

No one answered her.

Lennie couldn't stop staring at the back of Hotshot Bob's pale head. Veins of red branched across his scalp, so it looked like a great bloodshot eye. His face was turned away, but Lennie could see the protruding handle of a knife. Blood coated his neck and pooled on the floor. Not a drop of red marred the pristine white of his cocoon.

Junkyard gently drew the blanket back over the body and stood over it, head down, his expression grim. "Just what the hell was your

288

father involved in?"

That harsh, ugly voice didn't sound like Junkyard's. Lennie looked up dazedly, an image of blood and death still hovering in her vision. He turned toward her, one hand braced against the wall, the other clenched in a fist. His face had turned hard, eyes distrustful. It was the face of a stranger. And that's all he really was, she realized, feeling suddenly trapped and very alone.

"M-my father had nothing to do with this!" she said desperately, though she knew how it looked. "He was just a simple school teacher. I never wanted any of this to happen. I just want to find him and go home."

"So you say. All I know is that you showed Hotshot that picture and he bolted. And now..." He gestured roughly at the body. Lennie dropped her gaze. She couldn't bear to look at either one of them.

The boxcar rattled abruptly and rocked as though running over uneven track. Lennie swayed with the motion, cast adrift in a dark and violent sea. She had no words to rescue herself. At least, none that he would believe.

"Now, don't be gettin' yer undies all in a bunch, Junkyard." Soo's voice sounded nasally, like she'd been crying. "That killer's been around fer months, an' dead people been showin' up as reg'lar as the moon. Hotshot was just in the wrong place at the wrong time, is all."

"Think so? Let's do a head count of all the friends Lennie has made since last night. Jim is dead. Bones is badly injured, maybe dead. Bill is preoccupied with the police, and now Hotshot is dead. Either someone is working hard to keep Lennie from finding her father...or they're protecting him. Now, tell me, Soo—how did the killer know who to kill?"

"What?" Lennie felt as though Junkyard had plucked the knife from Hotshot and plunged it into her chest. "No! That's not—I didn't—"

She had to tell him the truth. Ramblin' Red, the tattoo, the thing in the shadow, those weird women, Fenrir. Everything. It probably wouldn't help, but she had nothing else to offer.

"I can tell you how the killer knew," she began. His frown deepened. She sensed the violence building in him and added hastily, "It's not what you think. Everything has been so strange. Things keep happening that you don't know about—"

A series of loud thumps rattled the roof. At the same time, she felt the floor jump under her. She twisted around.

A dark figure stood in the doorway, silhouetted against a stream of moonlit buildings. Soo cursed and scrambled away. Junkyard swung the flashlight around. The light hit the intruder full in the face.

It was Monte.

A yellowish cast tinted his unswollen eye. He wiped a trickle of blood from his cheek and grinned.

"Hi. I'm back."

Behind him, two more gangbangers swung inside from the roof and dropped to the floor.

CHAPTER TWENTY TWO

Monte swayed as the train rocked over uneven track. His yellow gaze never wavered from Lennie's face. Hunch-shouldered, blood-spattered, he pursued her like a zombie, oblivious to his deteriorating condition.

An electric charge hummed in Lennie's tattooed hand, hair-raising and worthless. She ignored it and scrambled backward until she bumped into the closed side door. Her legs continued pumping uselessly, pushing her into the solid metal.

The flashlight went out and she lost Junkyard in the dark. Shadows crowded in on her. City lights flickered across gang tattoos, bandanas, and knives. She held her breath against a building scream.

"Lennie—move!"

Move. Right. That made sense. But where? Junkyard's voice had come from the left. She crawled toward it and huddled in the corner, behind the old television. The gangbangers hesitated, losing her in the shadows.

But Monte's yellow eyes followed her in the dark. He started toward her. Shudders rippled through her body. She scrabbled at her pocket and pulled out the switchblade. She fumbled trying to open it and it skittered across the floor. Moaning, she felt around for something, anything, to use as a weapon. Bristles scratched her hand. The push broom. Instinctively, she snatched it up and braced it against the wall just as Monte charged. He crashed into the wide brush and staggered back. Howling, he hurled himself at her again and the broom handle bowed. She hoped he was crazy enough to batter himself senseless before it broke.

She had forgotten that Monte was not alone in his head.

His eyes fired, twin suns in a void. His gaze burned into her eyes before she could look away. Like before, a yellow haze flooded her vision and filled her mind. She clung to the broom, her sole contact with reality. An image coalesced within the haze—a face, hollow-eyed and fear shrunken. Cheeks sagged around its slack mouth. Clumps of hair hung over its haunted eyes. Her father's face? No, too young. Too feminine.

You see? I have made a place for you beside your father.

Horrified, she felt herself shrivel. Her shoulders hunched. Her tattooed hand sparked, but found no kindling. Its power flickered weakly and died. The broom slipped from her fingers. This was her fate, to live as a fear-eaten husk in Fenrir's shadow.

Monte's hot, vile breath puffed in her ear. "Now, bitch, do you see how useless it is to fight El Lobo?"

Discarding the flashlight, Junkyard dropped, rolled, and pulled the knife from his boot in one smooth motion. He crouched low, one hand braced on the wall. The shadows might have hidden him, but his warning shout to Lennie had given his position away. The two gangbangers came after him. Monte went straight for Lennie.

They had all forgotten Too Long Soo. She screamed a rebel yell and leaped on a gangbanger's back. That left one punk for Junkyard. A happy-sad theater mask tattoo leered at him in the unsteady light, and he knew he faced the Ragman.

Then he heard Lennie yell. With a quick glance, he saw Monte's dark form bend over someone huddled next to the television. Lennie.

The Ragman would have to wait.

Junkyard dodged the gangbanger and launched a flying tackle at

Monte, ripping him away from Lennie. They landed hard, with Junkyard on top. The Ragman moved toward them, but Junkyard pinned Monte with a knee on his chest and put a knife to his throat.

"So, Ragman—how much does your El Lobo care about Monte, here?"

Scowling, the Ragman stopped. Monte seemed unaware of the knife. He howled and struggled to reach Lennie, who lay on the floor, retching. He might look like he had been through a meat grinder, but he was strong. Junkyard leaned hard onto Monte's chest and broke his skin with the sharp blade.

Monte stopped struggling. His gaze shifted, casting Junkyard's face in lurid, yellow light. Junkyard drew back, staring. "What the hell?"

The light seemed to invade Junkyard's brain, loosening his already failing control. Repressed emotions eddied through his mind. Rage, a need for violence, desire for revenge...

Soo shrieked. Junkyard blinked and remembered the third gangbanger. Grimacing with effort, he broke from Monte's gaze. The yellow taint faded from his mind.

"No more of that," he growled. Whatever the hell *that* was. He slammed his fist down on Monte's head and left him lying on the floor.

Soo clamped a hand to her face. A dark stain trickled through her fingers. The short gangbanger smiled and charged her. Before Junkyard could intervene, Soo kicked out, driving the pointed toe of her boot into the gangbanger's belly. He doubled over, sucking for air. Then, grimacing, he lunged at her again.

"Aw, hell," Soo said, sounding more disgusted than afraid. She hefted Woody like a baseball bat and swung.

The wood connected with a crack. The gangbanger staggered back and teetered at the lip of the door. He screamed and clutched at the guitar. His fingers tangled in the strings. Cursing, Soo held onto Woody and tried to shake him off.

"Soo! Let go!" Junkyard lunged for her, but he was too far away. The gangbanger's feet slipped and he tumbled into the night, pulling Woody after him. Soo let go too late. She fell forward. Her long frame stretched out the door as if she were trying to catch wind and fly. Then she was gone.

Junkyard charged the door, as if he might somehow bring her back. He caught himself on the doorframe, swinging all but an arm and a leg outside. Battered by the wind, he stared down the track, hoping to see a long, lanky shape pick itself up from the gravel. But it was no use, and he knew it. The train was moving too fast. Tomorrow, someone would find her body. People would shake their heads in pity—just another hobo lying broken next to the tracks.

He pressed his forehead to cold metal and closed his eyes. If Jungle Jim had been his conscience over the last year, Soo and Bones had been his family. He didn't think he had the courage to continue the hunt without them.

"Junkyard! Look out!"

He didn't register Lennie's panicked scream until pain erupted in his hand. His fingers instantly went numb. Somehow, he held on. He tried to pull himself back inside, but the Ragman was there, grinning, his fist raised for another blow, and there was nothing Junkyard could do to stop him.

"Hey! You!" Lennie shouted from inside. "I've got something for you."

Both men looked over the Ragman's shoulder. Lennie faced them, holding a push broom like a ram. Even in the dim light, Junkyard could see her eyes narrow and her lips curl back from her teeth in an ugly snarl.

"Eat this!" she screamed, and she rushed the gangbanger.

The broom caught the Ragman in the back, spinning him around. He stumbled into the open doorway, arms windmilling, his tough-guy scowl wiped away by desperation. His flailing hand brushed Junkyard's arm, then grabbed for him, but Junkyard shook him off. Lennie rammed the gangbanger again. This time, the Ragman caught the broom, and Junkyard feared a replay of Soo's death. But before the Ragman could regain his footing, Lennie gave a last push and let go. The Ragman was gone.

Junkyard imagined he heard the crunch of the gangbanger hitting the cinders above the roar of the wheels. Nodding in grim satisfaction, he pulled himself inside.

"Thanks," he began, "you saved my life."

Lennie's expression stopped him. She was staring out the open door, her hands bunched over her mouth as though she might throw up. Her face looked gaunt and hollow-eyed in the dim light. The angry, vertical line between her eyebrows now seemed out of place in features strained by fear and exhaustion.

"Lennie?"

She lowered her hands and looked at him, her eyes full of self-loathing. "I—I killed him. Didn't I."

"Oh, Lennie." She looked so lost. Despite his doubts about her, he wanted to go to her, to brush the stray curls from her face and somehow make the pain go away. How could he have ever thought she was connected to the Hobo Spider murders? "I'm sorry."

He felt the movement before he saw it, coming from the forward end of the boxcar. Monte exploded from the shadows, eyes burning yellow. Junkyard shoved Lennie out of the way. The crazed gangbanger drove his shoulder into Junkyard's gut, driving him into the boxcar's back end. Junkyard's head cracked against the siding, and the boxcar became a spinning top of pain. Monte roared and rammed into him again, trapping him against the wall.

A face out of a horror movie swam in Junkyard's blurred vision. Blood-caked. Slack and drooling. That unbearable stench. How could it be alive? And those eyes—yellow slits glowing from a bruised and broken skull. As though Monte's head were an empty shell and a bright flame burned within.

Junkyard struggled to fight, to clear his mind, but those eyes. *Those eyes.* Whispering dark tendrils filled his vision, worming into his mind. He felt Monte's hands at his throat, squeezing. He couldn't breathe. The world blurred in a yellow haze. Using every ounce of his fading will, Junkyard wrenched his head and broke eye contact. But he had grown too weak to break Monte's strangling grip.

Beyond Monte's shoulder, Lennie stood as if frozen. Her eyes were fixed, trance-like, on Monte. Junkyard worked his jaw, trying to tell her to do something—anything—but no sound came out. She extended her arm, palm-outward, like she meant to rush Monte and push him out of the car. She'd probably die trying unless Junkyard could help.

He beat feebly on Monte's arms, but his hands didn't seem to work right. His head throbbed. His cheeks felt ready to split. The last of his strength left his body and he sagged. The only thing holding him upright was Monte's grip on his neck.

Do it, Lennie. Do whatever. Now.

But instead of rushing Monte, she flexed her fingers back, a look of hard concentration on her face. Her hair rose from her shoulders, floating as if lightening were about to strike. The air sparked and crackled around her, lighting the boxcar in brief, bright flashes. Startled, Monte let go of Junkyard and swung to face her.

Junkyard collapsed. Air rushed into his lungs. He could only lie gasping as Monte went after Lennie.

But as Monte reached for her, sparks flew from her fingers and swarmed him. With a high-pitched shriek, he whirled and swatted the air. The sparks spun a cocoon of light, solidifying in endless, winding, constricting strings, trapping his arms and legs. He let out an anguished wail and toppled to the floor. The light in his eyes went dark.

Heaving air down his bruised throat, Junkyard rolled to his hands and knees. He blinked and shook his head, but he couldn't clear the yellow haze from his vision. Too weak to stand, he crawled to Monte's side. The gangbanger's eyes stared, unfocused, empty of life. Junkyard remembered the emptiness behind the yellow slits and wondered if Monte had been dead all along.

He touched the substance that covered the body and jerked his hand back, repulsed. It felt unnaturally smooth, almost gelatinous, like dry slime. And it was string.

The body was covered with white string. Just like Hotshot. Just like Tin Can Petey.

Just like his brother.

He looked up at Lennie and saw the way her eyes shone, the exaltation in her face. Who else could have done what she just did?

He struggled to his feet. If he weren't so weak, he knew he would hit her, maybe strangle her as Monte had tried to strangle him. He wanted to punish her for his suffering over the last year, for his brother's horrible death, and for all the other victims. As it was, he could only muster the energy to spit in her face.

Lennie snapped out of her trance and wiped at her cheek. Bemused, she looked at her wet hand, and then saw his expression. The euphoria bled from her eyes.

"Junkyard," she said, looking bewildered, "wh-what's wrong?"

"It's you," he said. "You killed my brother."

CHAPTER TWENTY THREE

"Your brother?"

Lennie stared dazedly at Monte's cocooned body. Monte was Junkyard's brother? That didn't make sense.

All that string. She had done that. But how? And why now?

Junkyard had been about to die. She remembered that much. He had just hung there, limp, with Monte's hands around his neck. She couldn't let him die. But she couldn't fight Monte, either. At least, not physically.

Her hand had been buzzing so badly she'd thought her finger joints might vibrate apart. She had stretched it toward Monte, thinking maybe this time...

When Monte dropped Junkyard to come after her, she'd met those horrible yellow eyes. But instead of locking up and letting that creeping yellow haze overwhelm her, something clicked in her mind. The world seemed to shift, and it all became so obvious, so easy. The power streamed from her fingers.

And it felt good. Better than good. She felt fully alive and strong. Unbeatable. Like approaching the end of a 400-meter race knowing she was well in front and going to win.

And then the power was gone. A beautiful euphoria followed; an endorphin rush like no other. But Monte was wrapped in pristine white string. She hadn't expected that.

Urdie's voice whispered in her mind. *Six threads, twisted into one, bound and knotted.*

Was this what she was expected to do? Use a bunch of thread to bind Fenrir, a man with the soul of a monster? Right. She didn't

298

intend to get that close to him.

The euphoric cloud dissipated, leaving her exhausted and frightened. Junkyard was looking at her like she had committed the worst crime imaginable. She wanted to explain everything, but her thoughts slipped and spun incoherently. "I thought—I thought there would be lightning."

"Lightning?" Junkyard snarled. "What the hell are you talking about?"

"My hand. It's been..."

She stopped, not knowing where to start. The train rumbled on. Light and shadow flickered across the hard angles of Junkyard's face. He looked so angry. If only she had told him everything from the very beginning. But he never would have believed her. He certainly wouldn't believe her now.

He waited for an explanation, fists half-raised. All that anger, directed at her. She averted her eyes, but there was nothing to look at except shadow, discarded junk, Hotshot's body...and Monte, staring at her in accusation. His face was so grey. So still. Why didn't he move? It was like he was—

"Oh, God. Is he—is he dead?"

Junkyard swore. "Don't give me that crap. Of course he's dead. Just like all the others."

She shook her head, feeling sick. He couldn't be dead. No one died of being tied up. Did they? But the way Monte stared, never blinking...

"You don't think he died because...that I...?"

"Got another explanation?"

The accusation in his voice cut through her confusion. "How can you believe I could kill anyone?"

But he did. His expression said so.

She took a step back. "No—"

It was that tattoo. The Valknut, or whatever. That bastard Ramblin' Red had branded it on her. How could she know what it would do? She scratched at the design, drawing blood. She'd burn the thing off if she had to, just to get rid of it. She didn't want that sort of power, to tie people up like that. To kill...

Junkyard closed the gap between them and grabbed her roughly, his face contorted with anger and hatred. "Why'd you do it? He was just a kid, dammit! Not a drifter or some punk criminal. Just a student trying to get home."

"What? Who-who are you talking about?" He couldn't mean Monte. That guy was no student.

A horrible understanding struck her.

"Your brother. Did he die like—" *Like Monte*, she started to say, but he might take it as a confession. "Like Hotshot?"

A yellow spark flickered in his eyes, filling her with dread. She could feel violence building in him. The heat of it radiated from him like an aura. She tried to twist away, but he was so strong. And where would she go? There was no escape, no way to fight him. She didn't *want* to fight Junkyard. She had to make him listen.

The spark in his eyes bloomed into a yellow fire, rooted deep, as though kindled by his soul. The flesh of her tattooed hand prickled in response. But she didn't dare use that weapon on Junkyard. This wasn't his fault. She closed her eyes and twisted her face away from that fiery gaze. His anguished voice rang close to her ear.

"I saw the pictures after they found him, Lennie. I saw what you did to him."

"No, I swear I didn't hurt him. This was the first time! I didn't even know what would happen."

But he wasn't listening. "Who're you gonna kill next? Me?"

He shook her, hard. Her head whipped back and forward. Her teeth snapped down on her tongue. Pain and blood erupted in her mouth. The tattooed hand flared wildly. The urge to use it became unbearable. But she couldn't shake the image of Monte's grey, dead face from her mind. She clenched the hand and pressed it to her stomach.

Junkyard shoved her back, slamming her into the closed door. Air whooshed out of her. Blood from her cut tongue gurgled in her throat when she tried to breathe. She gagged and coughed, gasping air into tortured lungs. Junkyard came at her, an angry silhouette against the moonlit sky—featureless, except for two glowing, yellow eyes.

"Do you know what I planned to do to the guy who killed Austin, once I found him?"

She tried to push him away, but he brushed her arms aside and struck her face. Her head knocked against the solid metal door. Her eyes lost focus. She fought for consciousness, clawing weakly at his arms, at his face, but he wouldn't let go. He meant to kill her.

A long, discordant blast of the locomotive's horn sounded up the line, followed by the screech of tortured metal. Junkyard jerked his head up, listening, and the yellow faded from his eyes. His eyebrows lifted and he blinked at Lennie as though awakening from a deep sleep.

"Lennie?"

The world faded and her legs went slack. Junkyard held her upright, his touch suddenly gentle. "Lennie, I'm so sorry. I didn't mean—"

Airbrakes chuffed violently. The boxcar lurched and rocked on its wheels. The floor tilted crazily, tossing them both. Lennie fell and skidded on her face, caught in a maelstrom of tumbling debris. The television bounced out the open door. She felt herself slide after it and scrambled for a handhold. The boxcar slammed to a stop and the back end flew up. Lennie hurtled forward and smacked into the front wall. Her arm buckled and something snapped in her chest, the crack of breaking bone lost in the cacophony of screeching metal. Helpless, she tumbled and slid. When the boxcar finally stopped, she came to rest in a heap of cardboard and packing paper.

The sounds of a thousand car crashes echoed down the length of the train. Moonlight filtered inside through a cloud of dust and smoke. Blood bubbled in Lennie's lungs and she couldn't draw air. Panicking, she tried to prop herself up. Bones shifted in her arm with an explosion of white-hot pain and she collapsed. Her consciousness fled, leaving only a dim awareness of a warm, gentle pulse radiating from the interlocking triangles on her hand.

The boxcar tossed Junkyard like laundry in a dryer. He hit the floor...a wall...tumbled and tangled with a length of packing paper. Only the white streak of the moon through the open door told him which way was up.

And then it was over, as abruptly as it had started. He lay across the lip of the door, one leg dangling outside. He clutched the doorframe reflexively against a danger that had already passed.

Though the boxcar no longer moved, his vision spun as though his brain rolled in his skull. He probed a walnut-sized bump on his forehead and winced. Funny, he didn't remember hitting his head on anything.

The bucolic smell of clover wafted inside and struck his reeling senses. His stomach churned. He knew he should lie still, but he couldn't. He had to find Lennie.

He hoped she hadn't fallen from the train.

He grimaced and pushed the thought aside. He couldn't face that possibility. Not after what he had almost done to her. He rolled to his knees and a wave of vertigo washed over him. Partially digested hobo coffee rose in his throat. He braced himself and waited, wondering if he would pass out before he had a chance to vomit. A few gasping breaths later, he began to feel better, though his head still ached and sharp points of pain throbbed all over his body. He was certain he had left bits of skin on more than one surface of the boxcar.

At least that damn yellow fog was gone, whatever it was. He might not be thinking well, but his thoughts were his own.

The boxcar listed to one side, derailed. Sounds from a distant highway joined the tick of cooling metal and the last gasp of useless air brakes. Junkyard half crab-walked, half slid down the sloped floor, looking for Lennie by the filtered light of the moon.

His attack on her sickened him. It felt too much like his first days on the iron road, when the rage born of his brother's murder was still fresh and hot. Worse than that. He hadn't tried to kill anyone, back then—just beat up or be beaten. But he could still feel the muscles in Lennie's warm, slender arms under his bruising fingers.

She hadn't told him the whole truth. He knew that. And she had done that weird trick with the string. But it was ludicrous to think she could be the serial killer. She was as shocked as he by what she had done to Monte. Besides, there was something...well, too *nice* about her.

He found her in the rear corner, lying like a broken doll on a pile of debris. Her arm was bent awkwardly, like it had an extra joint. A tangle of curly, caramel hair shrouded her face. His hand shook when he brushed it back. Her skin was so pale. "Lennie?"

She didn't react. Afraid to move her, he pulled open the letter jacket he had given her. Blood had soaked through her t-shirt. Too much blood. Alarmed, he felt her neck. No pulse.

She was dead.

He sat back, choking on a bitterness that had nothing to do with coffee. The wreck had killed her. Something blocking the track, a brake malfunction, human error—it didn't matter. He felt as guilty as if he had done it himself. He took her hand and held it clasped between his own. They were still in the city, only a couple of miles from the train yard. Someone would come soon and take her away. He bowed his head. She would not wait alone.

Briggs watched the squad car pull away, leaving him alone in the train yard. The warehouse was a bust. It had taken the police about five seconds to figure that one out. They hadn't even bothered to go inside.

Bill Sutter had led them there. Once confronted with the evidence, he had opened up like a carton of Chinese food, spilling out an incoherent mixture of fact and devil-made-me-do-it delusions. The warehouse was the only aspect of the story that could be verified. But the place was obviously abandoned. The patches of rust on the siding were so large that he could see them in the dark from fifty yards away. The panel door hung askew, leaving a gap big enough to admit a full-grown man. Not likely a headquarters for the BRR, as Sutter had claimed.

Still, some of Sutter's story had resonated with the weirdness Briggs had been experiencing over the last few hours. Briggs wanted a closer look.

The building gave him the same eerie being-watched sensation he had felt in the woods earlier. He hesitated, reluctant to move closer and feeling intensely stupid about it. Annoyed with himself, he started forward, but froze when a loud tapping rattled the siding.

Heart thudding, he waited for any sign of movement. There was nothing. Then the wind stirred the weeds sprouting from the gravel and sent the door panel tapping against the siding.

Briggs rolled his eyes. "Sheesh. Give me a break."

From now on, Marybeth could keep her theories about the supernatural to herself.

He approached the building from the side, away from the line-of-sight of the door. As he eased close to the doorway, he paused to listen. Nothing. Not even the skitter of rat claws. He leaned his head forward and tried to peer inside.

Absolute darkness.

He couldn't imagine anyone dumping their garbage here, never mind storing weapons and drugs, as Sutter had claimed.

But maybe that was the effect the bad guys were hoping for. Maybe gangbangers waited in the dark, ready to spring out at him like an unwanted surprise party.

And maybe they'd give him a birthday cake and a present with a big, pink bow.

He detached his nightstick from his belt, extended it, and eased into the building. Light struck him the moment he broke the plane of the doorway, as if someone had flicked a switch at that exact moment. Shocked, he blinked to let his eyes adjust. The place was poorly lit; a single bulb dangled from the ceiling by an orange cord. Cluttered metal shelves lined the walls, loaded with an assortment of weapons and drug paraphernalia, just as Sutter had claimed. But there were no signs of whoever had turned on the light.

Then the familiar stench struck him and he spotted the white coil hanging just inside the door. The cord Sutter claimed to have gotten from a guy named El Lobo. As much beast as man, the deranged bull had said. From the stink, Briggs almost believed it. He stepped closer, reaching out, but couldn't bring himself to touch the strands.

Sweat broke out on his forehead. This was getting creepier by the moment. And dangerous. This El Lobo character wouldn't leave this stuff unguarded. Time to go. He turned to leave, pulling his phone out to call for backup.

"You ain't going nowhere, *Amigo.*"

A gangbanger stood in the doorway with a gun pointed at Brigg's chest. He looked like he'd been run over by a train. His once-white tank shirt was torn and streaked with dirt. Scratches and bruises covered his bare arms, and blood flowed freely from a row of stitches that had broken open. He smiled at Briggs, the grin of a wolf. "You won't be makin' no phone calls tonight, so just drop the cell on the floor. The stick, too, man. And that gun under your jacket."

Briggs complied, bending to set the weapon on the floor. He studied the gangbanger covertly, hoping for an opening, but the banger never blinked. Briggs straightened and pointedly looked the punk over. "So, are you the famous El Lobo?"

A sneer twisted the punk's lips. "*Pendejo!* You too stupid to live. El Lobo is no 'banger. But you will see that soon enough. He is coming."

Junkyard lifted his head when he heard the sirens. Someone would take Lennie away, soon. Maybe in a black SUV, like Jim. And then he would…what? Go back to hunting the Hobo Spider? The prospect filled him with emptiness.

Lennie's fingers grew warmer between Junkyard's hands. He found that somehow comforting, as though he could share some of his life with her. But then her hand grew too warm. Hot. Her chest rose hesitantly. A gurgling came from her throat, the sound almost lost in the hissing, clicking aftermath of the wreck.

She was alive.

A thin stream of blood trickled from her nose. Her mouth fell open and the stubborn crease between her eyes deepened with pain. He gaped at her, unbelieving. But then he remembered the night before, on the train, when that unexplained puncture in her side had healed as he watched. Super healing powers weren't any weirder than the ability to spin thread from fingers.

He squeezed her hand and gently laid it across her stomach. Leaning close, he whispered, "I'm going for help. Just hang in there."

He climbed up the sloped floor and paused to survey the wreckage. Their boxcar lay diagonally on the tracks, propped against another boxcar, with the coupler from a third car imbedded in its side.

Voices echoed up the line. Circles of light danced over the cars as the crew checked the damages. Junkyard yelled as loud as he could, "Hey, over here!"

No response. They must be too far away to hear. Frustrated, he contemplated going after them, but he didn't want to leave Lennie. He was about to slide back down to check on her when a man emerged from the shadow of the boxcar.

"Thank God! I thought no one heard me. My friend is hurt and I'm afraid to move her."

The man didn't respond, or even move. Junkyard eyed him uncertainly. He was big. As big as those beet pickers who had nearly taken him apart the day he had met Jim, and a lot more menacing. But Lennie needed help. "You got a cell phone?"

The man lifted his head to look at Junkyard. Yellow eyes flared from the shadowy face. The glow of a cigarette appeared like a third eye.

Shivers rippled Junkyard's skin. "Oh, crap. Not another one."

His instincts screamed at him to flee, but he couldn't leave Lennie. He pulled his knife, but held it, forgotten, when the man smiled, revealing enormous, pointed teeth. Junkyard couldn't move. He could only stare into those piercing, yellow eyes. This was something he couldn't fight.

Jungle Jim's voice seemed to call to Junkyard. A warning. *Look away.*

But a yellow haze pervaded Junkyards thoughts, obscuring the hobo clown and all he represented. The wild, unfocused rage he'd kept battened down so tightly sprang free, seeking a target.

And the thing spoke. "Bring the girl to me."

CHAPTER TWENTY FOUR

Fenrir smiled as Junkyard laid the unconscious girl at his feet. Here was the last obstacle to his chosen destiny. Sirens wailed from all directions, racing toward the buckled train. They foreshadowed the days to come, when the wails of human, Aesir, and Vanir alike would rise with every siren in every city of the world.

It would begin tonight.

Free of interference, free of prophecy, Fenrir would ride the backs of a million souls by morning. He closed his eyes and felt along the threads that his mind held like the reins of a thousand thousand war horses. Each thread restrained one of his minions. Berserkers, poised to fire a weapon, start a fire, collapse a power grid, cripple air traffic control, flood the stock market, riot, lynch, terrorize, destroy, and in one glorious moment, bring down the powers of the world. He lifted his face to the sky.

"The world has never been so ready to die. And it is I—Hrodvitnir—who will rise from the ashes."

Though he did not shout, his words penetrated the soil under his feet and the ground rumbled with their power.

A bit melerdramatic, don't ya think?

That voice!

A thousand thousand. Heck, I cain't even count that high. Careful yer horses don't bolt all at once an' tear you to a thousand thousand pieces.

That nagging little gnat of a voice buzzed at him, sucking the sweetness from his victories. Fenrir shook his head as if to dislodge it from his ear. The inconsequential remains of Angus Cook would not distract him, now. Not on the eve of his greatest battle.

He would begin with the death of the girl. She alone had the power to stop him.

Douglas Harding, the man she called Junkyard, stood over her, unmoving but for the sporadic twitch of his hands. Fenrir could feel the struggle within him, the burgeoning feelings he begrudged himself, his desperate desire to save the girl, the rage at the evil that had taken his brother's life, his confusion over the girl's involvement.

So much emotion. So easy to twist, to bend to one's whim. Fenrir opened his connection to Harding's mind and let his will flow. Harding's eyes began to glow.

Careful, now. The lad ran wild at the end of yer tether, the last time.

"Silence!"

Perhaps the girl's death would quell that irritating voice. It pleased Fenrir to make Harding the instrument of her destruction.

Yer slippin', Fenrir. You couldn't even handle one muddle-headed hobo clown. He tricked ya—an' him with a broken brain.

Fenrir's focus shattered and Harding's eyes faded to dull brown. Rage boiled under Fenrir's skin, urging a different shape, demanding that he tear into his tormentor and rend human flesh from bone. The short hairs bristled and thickened over this pale, weak body. Muscle and sinew strained as Fenrir's true form fought to be free of Angus Cook. But as he crouched, ready to leap from the body, to turn and sink wolf teeth into its offending heart, the reasoning part of his mind heard the laughter of Angus Cook.

At once, his rage hardened into cold anger. This human had nearly provoked him into destroying this form prematurely.

"No," he growled. "Soon, I will discard this body and then you shall truly, most painfully die, but I will not kill you now."

Nor would he kill the girl. Again, he focused on Douglas Harding. "Bring her."

She would join her father in the lair of the BRR. There, as the world began its irredeemable fall into chaos, Fenrir would release this human form to its owner. Angus Cook would live in freedom long enough to see the last of his line die before him. That would be Fenrir's parting gift to his host.

For once, the voice was silent.

Gentle waves lapped the lakeshore just inches from Too Long Soo's head, spraying her face with cool droplets. She didn't respond. Her body lay broken and bleeding at the bottom of a rocky embankment. The sporadic sounds of nighttime highway traffic drifted over the train tracks—rescue just a few dozen yards away. She didn't hear it. Her soul had fled to her deepest core, waiting for the end.

A calm fell over the lake, rendering its dark surface so flawless that the moon seemed to shine from its depths. A loon's call rose in mournful laughter, as if it had met fate and thought it a bitter joke. Then silence. A moment of waiting.

A sigh stirred the opposite shore. A breath sustained beyond human capacity. It found direction and blew, cutting a wake in the lake's smooth surface, shattering the perfect, three-quarter moon.

The living air struck the body on the lake's shore and poured down into nostrils, flooding slack mouth, soaking into skin. Sparks crackled in the straw-like hair. Fingers stretched and splayed. Twisted limbs turned and straightened, drawing life as a thirsty plant draws water. Bruises disappeared, bones healed, bleeding stopped. At last the body lay still and natural, as if sleeping on a bed of rocks.

The one who had become Too Long Soo sat up and clutched her chest as if remembering pain. But there was nothing wrong with this body.

"Fenrir, you silly pup. I tried to tell you it wouldn't work. Maybe I can be changed.

She examined herself. Moonlight highlighted long, bony fingers and a down vest that had torn, spilling its feathery guts. Patched jeans bagged around skinny legs that ended in pointy-toed boots. She frowned. "Oh, dear. I definitely can be changed.

"But I can't be killed."

The air shimmered beside her, solidifying into a grungy canvas bag. "Ah, here we are. I believe I was starting on bright orange."

Rummaging inside, she pulled out a tangle of beige twine and some twigs. She grunted in disgust. "Macramé. It had to be macramé."

Grumbling about pot hangers and owls with button eyes, she tucked the bag under her arm and scrambled up the embankment. Behind her, unnoticed, hung the mangled remains of a guitar, entangled in the branches of a scrawny tree.

Lennie awoke with the side of her face pressed to a gritty cement floor. The smells hit her first—pot, cigarettes, stale beer. Then came memory of noise and chaos, as if the world were shaking apart around her.

And there had been pain. Something had broken in her chest, draining her life away. She should be dead by now. The last thing she remembered was a tingling warmth spreading from the triangles tattooed on her hand.

Well, at least she'd gotten one good thing out of that tattoo.

But where was she? Boxcars didn't have cement floors. She wasn't eager to try moving just yet, but she had to see. She cracked her eyes open. Junkyard sat cross-legged before her, under a familiar bare bulb hanging from an orange cord. She was in the warehouse from her dream.

And Junkyard's eyes glowed yellow.

"She's awake," he said.

Shoes scraped the floor. A dead animal stench wafted over her, overwhelming the others. Lennie's stomach heaved and she swallowed hard. She knew who was there without looking.

"Good," said a deep, coarse voice. "Then we can begin."

The words sent a chill through her that threatened to freeze her to the floor. Gotta get out of here. She rolled to her feet and tried to run, but Junkyard rose and tackled her down. She tried to push him off and wriggle free, but he pinned her easily.

"No, let me go!"

"I think not." Junkyard's voice, but Fenrir's words.

Knife in hand, Junkyard leaned so close that his hair tickled her cheek. An inhuman hatred distorted his features. Hatred so deep that she might not have recognized him but for the long sideburns and the hard angles of his face. His yellow eyes bored into her, unwavering. She refused to meet them. They had become a conduit to Fenrir's mind.

Her skin twitched as the knife drifted toward her. "Junkyard, he's using you. You've got to fight him—"

The knife came at her face. Its tip traced down her cheek as lightly as a lover's touch. A stinging wetness followed its trail. The blade stopped at her throat. Lennie swallowed against its sharp edge. Keeping her eyes averted from Junkyard's face, she flexed her tattooed hand. It burned with all the voltage of a penlight. She doubted there was enough power to net a mouse.

The pressure on the blade increased. Lennie's lips parted. She wanted to scream, but the breath caught in her throat. Then a shadow fell over them both.

"Restrain yourself, Douglas. I am not finished with her, yet."

Shadow oozed over Lennie as if it had physical substance. Shudders wracked her body. She had felt that darkness before—in the parking lot—at the carnival—but not so powerful, so invasive as this. The tendrils of Fenrir's will prodded her mind for weakness, seeking passage like great, poisonous worms. She fought them, gasping with effort, and kept her gaze locked on Junkyard's chin, on the short whiskers that had sprouted since morning—on the cleft that she hadn't noticed until now. Junkyard could play with his knife all he wanted, as long as he stayed between her and Fenrir. But Junkyard released her and stepped back into the shadow.

And Fenrir was there.

Her great-great-whatever grandfather, cigarette and all. Only he wasn't her grandfather. The body was an inadequate mask, too puny to disguise the monstrous evil it contained. Broad-shouldered and enormous, he sat on a battered, over-stuffed chair, holding a staff like a scepter in his hand. The throne of the hobo king. She would have laughed if he weren't so terrifying.

The weight of Fenrir's power fell full upon her with crushing force. Her hand responded, a hornets' nest against an avalanche, barely enough to keep her mind free.

"Do you know," Fenrir said, his voice a low growl, "how long I have waited for this moment?"

Don't look at his eyes. She forced her gaze to Fenrir's shoes, making herself note their high-polished blackness. Against her will, her gaze trailed up his legs, pausing at the rough-carved staff in his hands—the one from Verdandi's vision?

She wasn't allowed to study it. Irresistibly, her eyes traveled upward, along the starched whiteness of his shirt, to his hard, cruel mouth. He plucked the cigarette from thick lips and exhaled. Smoke swirled around him, twining into the shadow. He smiled, unveiling pointed animal teeth. Lennie shuddered. I will *not* meet his eyes.

"For millennia, I waited underground, listening and planning. For a century, I gathered my legions. And now, this night, they will fall like an ax upon the neck of the world. There is only you—" contempt hung from his words, "—to stand in my way."

He snapped his fingers and signaled. "Bring her to me."

There was a note of finality in his voice.

Junkyard stayed beside Fenrir's throne like a guard. When he didn't move, Lennie felt a brief hope that maybe he was fighting Fenrir. Maybe she wasn't alone against the monster. Then strong hands grabbed her from behind and bent her arm back until her tattooed hand touched her shoulder blades. She cried out, tried to twist away, and managed to stomp hard on her captor's foot. He swore and his grip loosened, but before she could escape, a wiry arm snaked around her neck. A voice grunted in her ear. "Hold still, *güerita*, or I will break your arm like a twig."

That voice! It couldn't be...

Then she saw the theater mask tattoo on the arm that held her. Shocked, she stopped struggling. "But—but I—you fell out of the train. You can't be..."

The Ragman laughed, his breath hot on her neck. "Yes, I should be dead. Is one of the perks for working for El Lobo."

"For selling your soul, you mean."

Snarling, he wrenched her arm. Lennie gasped, as much from revulsion at his touch as from pain. Whispered words scorched her ear. "I hope he gives you to me when he has finished."

"Enough! Bring her closer. I would look at the brave warrior who is the Allfather's last hope."

A rabbit's panic struck Lennie. She back-pedaled against the Ragman, fighting with all her strength. Relentless, he wrestled her forward to face Fenrir on his throne. A cloud of malevolence closed around her. She collapsed under its weight, shaking, afraid to move, almost unable to breathe.

How could Ramblin' Red ever think she could handle this monster? His miserable gift couldn't compensate for what she was: an ordinary girl, weak of courage and weak of will. Her father's daughter to the end. She felt herself shrinking, going away—running away—into the recesses of her mind, where Fenrir couldn't reach her.

"On your feet, *jaina.*" The Ragman twisted her arm until her back arched and she cried out. The pain shocked her mind clear of Fenrir's smothering will.

He had almost taken her. Worse, she had rolled belly up in defeat without the slightest struggle. Self-disgust gave her new courage. She nearly met Fenrir's eyes, focused on his broad nose instead. "Nice try, hamburger breath. But it'll take more than parlor tricks to get to me."

Only bluster, and Fenrir knew it, too. He signaled the gangbanger to let her go and leaned back on his throne. "More than tricks, you say."

He curled his fingers one at a time into a fist, popping each knuckle with a crack like breaking bones. His smile grew wider.

Had he looked at her father that way, too? Like a predator toying with its prey?

In that moment, staring at his flaring nose and animal teeth, she swore he wouldn't have her. She would fight him, defy him to the end. If Ramblin' Red's so-called gift was useless, she would kick, hit, claw, and when that no longer worked, she still had her mind. She would shut him out, cling to thought and memory. He couldn't touch her there.

She didn't know him very well.

"I will enjoy your screams," he said. "But first, I would like you to meet someone."

With a wave of his hand, he directed her attention to his flank. Only then did she notice the others in the room. To his left, an old man drooped, unmoving, a crumbling monument to despair. To Fenrir's right, next to Junkyard, another man slumped in a kitchen chair with his arms tied behind him. His head lolled so she couldn't see his face, but she recognized the blue windbreaker of the railroad detective from the poetry reading. He moaned and lifted his head. There was blood on his temple and his eyes were unfocused.

But they were brown.

"Briggs—don't look into their eyes!" He blinked at her stupidly, then his head flopped down and she thought he might pass out again. "Briggs—no—no, you've got to listen to me! Do *not* look into—"

Fingers tangled in her hair and yanked her head to face Fenrir.

"I see you've met our fine detective. A nuisance, of course, but he will prove useful once he's been properly…educated." Fenrir's hands tightened on the arms of the throne and he leaned forward. A predatory smugness infused his voice. "But I would think you'd be more interested in your father. Don't you wish to say hello?"

Somehow, she had known who stood to Fenrir's left. She closed her eyes, not wanting to look, and cursed herself for ever pursuing this quest.

She had once had a father, years ago. A kind man, with a paunch above his belt and the shine of skin through thinning hair. He had doted on his only child, loved his wife, and then he was gone. Lennie should have been content with that. It was more than some people had. But she had gone looking…and now she had found him.

Drawing a breath, she looked full on the human wreckage at Fenrir's side. Bent nearly double, he listed to one side with shoulders hunched and arms dangling. He seemed suspended only by the strings of Fenrir's will.

"Dad?"

Her voice cracked and dried up. She could only stare, trying to find some trace of her father in that ruined face. Once-full cheeks drooped like deflated balloons. His mouth gaped around broken teeth. His hair was gone but for the few greasy, gray strings clinging to his face and neck. His clothing hung in rags, colors faded and lost under layers of dirt. If she had passed him on the street, she would have averted her eyes in disgust, never seeing him as her father.

Fenrir's voice knifed through her horror. "Yes, indeed. He caused me some small inconvenience a few years back, but we've worked out our differences. Haven't we, Jarvis? Why don't you give your daughter a hug?"

Jarvis Cook only stared vacantly at a point somewhere over Lennie's shoulder. A line of drool dripped from his chin. Lennie shuddered. Fenrir frowned at her in mock sympathy. "Odd, I should think he would be more excited to see you than that. But then, he doesn't seem to be seeing much of anything, does he?

"Still, he has served me well, these ten years. A living testament to One-Eye's weakness." He laughed and stroked his carved staff almost lovingly. "To think I once feared the Allfather. Now, he dares not show himself to me."

Lennie wasn't listening. She had found her father buried in the derelict's eyes. Though jaundiced and puffy, their shape was unmistakable. The same eyes, though young and clear, stared from her face in the mirror each morning. But what she saw in her father's eyes terrified her more than anything ever had. Worse than the hatred in Junkyard's eyes, worse than the yellow malevolence in Fenrir's, her father's eyes contained...

...nothing.

No sign of will or life, as blank as a corpse's eyes, set in a face distorted by unfathomable fear.

Her heart burned with the pain of his suffering. What had that beast done to him?

Will he do it to me?

She thrust the thought aside, snarling at her own cowardice. He was her father, and this beast had mangled him beyond human endurance.

Jarvis Cook cringed suddenly and ducked his head, lifting an arm as if to ward off a blow. Just as suddenly, he slumped and resumed his empty stare. Lennie glanced at Fenrir, but the monster showed no sign of noticing. Appalled, she watched her father repeat the entire sequence, and knew it was only a reflex. As his arm blocked empty air, Lennie's gaze fell on his upraised hand.

It bore the same interlocking triangles that Ramblin' Red had branded on her.

The moment seemed to freeze in time—the upraised arm, the fear like a permanent scar on her father's face. The Valknut had doomed him to ten years of torment. Hatred possessed her every bone, tendon, and muscle. Hatred not only against Fenrir, but against Ramblin' Red, who had tried to use such a gentle, innocent man as a weapon.

Her body trembled with emotion. The heat of it flowed to her hand, feeding the tattoo's power. Her hair floated about her head and she felt an exultation she had never known before. She raised her arm and the air crackled around her. Fenrir must never be allowed to do this again. Not to anyone.

Fenrir's eyes widened as he sensed the change in her. She felt his fear and knew she could destroy his plans, maybe even destroy him. He knocked Jarvis Cook's hand down and stepped in front of him, towering over Lennie. Dark tendrils flailed against her mind. She brushed them aside easily and thrust her palm toward Fenrir. Sparks wove between her fingers, ready to burst forth.

And then, because she wanted to see the suffering of the monster that had tormented her father, wanted to see his fear as he was bound, she looked into his eyes.

For a moment, their gazes held. She stared into the feral eyes of the beast and her will held firm. But the mind and the will were Fenrir's domain. A yellow haze flooded Lennie's thoughts. The power hummed in her hand, but she couldn't tap it. She couldn't move, even to lower her arm.

And the warehouse was gone. She was at home—her real home. In the kitchen, with its warm hardwood floors and gingham curtains. Her mother stood at the sink, alive and amazingly young. And her father was there, striding toward her mother. He, too, was young, with a soft build and thinning hair—just the way she remembered him.

"Mom! Dad!"

Her father turned his face toward her. Only it wasn't his face. His eyes were small and mean, and a scowl twisted his mouth. He reached for her mother and yanked her around. She tried to cover her tear-stained face with an arm. One eye was swollen and purpling.

"I'm not finished with you, bitch."

He backhanded her, and her head whipped back. She crumpled to the floor. He leaned over and grabbed her by the hair, fist pulled back to strike. Lennie tried to run to her mother, to stop him, but her feet wouldn't move.

"No! Dad, no!"

"Shut up, kid. Once I'm finished with her, you're next."

But that had never happened. Never. He was kind and gentle. He couldn't hurt anyone. He was too...

The yellow haze deepened and the thought came before she could stop it.

He was too weak.

And the kitchen was gone. She was at a faculty picnic. She remembered it well. There were no other kids her age at the party and so her father had played catch with her. Now she saw it again, from an adult perspective. Saw her father retreat from his coworkers, red-faced and sweating. Saw him mumble to the school principal with his gaze on his feet, and knew he found it easier to play with a child than to speak with adults.

Had it happened that way?

The scene changed and he faced a classroom of kids, out of their chairs and running wild. They screamed and ripped pages from books and threw pencils until he fled the room.

How could she know that?

But it was there, in her memory. He left the picnic, left the classroom, left his job...and he left his family.

Mother drank because he abandoned her.

Was that her own thought? Or Fenrir's? She could no longer tell the difference. But it didn't matter, because it was true. Her mother drank because her father had left, and she died because she drank.

She saw her mother rise from her death bed, skeletal, sallow-skinned, a fifth of bourbon in her bony hand—*Drink, daughter—it's the only way to go*...saw her pathetic coward of a father slink away in the night, slithering through the grassy lawn...saw her teenager self, skinny, friendless, mocked by classmates, working, always working, her childhood stolen.

The old rage rose up in Lennie. Hard, angry hurt boiled in her gut. When her mother had died, Lennie's first thought before she had even called the ambulance was that it should have been *him*.

And she saw him as he was now, all shriveled, a hollow shell with nothing but fear echoing inside, and she felt the injustice of it again.

Fenrir released her body and she let her arm drop, forgotten power crackling in her hand. Her wrist brushed her pocket, across the hard outline of the switchblade. She pulled it out and opened it. The dim light flashed on the metal.

Sharp.

It was not right that Jarvis Cook should live—not after the grief he had caused. She shifted her grip on the knife, holding it as Junkyard had shown her, and walked toward her father. The warehouse fell silent but for the slap of her shoes on the concrete floor.

She stopped before him, hating the decay in his face, despising the lines around his mouth, carved by helpless fear.

Yes, she thought, looking into his vacant eyes. You should die.

It was time.

The human heart pounded in Fenrir's stolen chest, ready to burst. The human skin stretched to hold him, to keep him in this shape, for he had grown too large in all his glory and power. Soon, he would let go and show the world his true form.

Very soon.

But first, he would enjoy dismantling Angus Cook's family, putting an end to their pestiferous ways. The girl's mind was now open to him and her desires conflicted most deliciously. Even now, as she readied the knife to plunge into her father's heart, her own heart cried out for paternal love.

Her act of patricide would be a most satisfying beginning to her suffering.

Brought 'er right back into your lair, eh. You got some kinda death wish, boy?

Fenrir only smiled. Soon that ever-present gnat would be

silenced forever.

Come to witness the end of your family line, human? Watch now.

The girl pulled her arm back, her knuckles white around the knife's handle. Corrupted memories ruptured like abscesses on the surface of her mind. Fenrir held her there, poised on the edge of murder, steeping her in the agony of anticipation, while her father stood before her in imbecilic oblivion.

Don'tcha slip, now. That hand of hers is buzzin' like a trunk full of wasps.

Silence, cow dung! You will not distract me.

That Allfather fella ain't no fool. He musta had some reason fer choosin' that girl.

An image of Fenrir's nemesis burst in his mind, with one eye of glowing ice and a smug curl to his treacherous mouth. Fenrir's eyes flamed. *No fool? You grow as desperate as he. First he sent a weakling, and then a girl. It seems One-Eye needs another drink from the well—his wisdom has grown weak.*

I'm just sayin' there must be somethin' to her, is all.

The thousand thousand souls tethered to Fenrir's will stirred restlessly, straining against his control. Sweat beaded on his brow. *Enough! Your pathetic attempts to interfere will work no more!*

It was time to end this impasse. It was time to begin his true destiny.

Carefully, carefully, he focused his will on the girl. He must release her to allow her to destroy Jarvis Cook, but her hand still radiated the Allfather's power. He must reach into her mind and instill one last compulsion—

Hey! Look! Ain't that the Allfather sittin' on that there rafter?

Startled, Fenrir lifted his gaze.

The color of anger is yellow.

The knife rested heavy in Lennie's hand, deadly, cold, ready to drink warm blood. There was no warehouse, no Junkyard brooding in the shadows, no Briggs, no gangbangers...not even Fenrir, evil incarnated sitting on a hobo throne. There was only her father, the object of longing and hatred so balanced that she couldn't move.

Kill him.

Yes...

Kill him, kill him, kill him kill him kill himkillhimkillhimKILL—

Abruptly, the voice stopped, leaving her alone in her own darkness. She was free to move. Free to kill.

And why not?

She gazed at the slack, tortured face of her father, the question cycling over and over in her mind. Why not? Sweat dripped from the handle of the knife and she still didn't strike.

Because—because—

Something flickered in the emptiness of her father's eyes. Not the terror evident in the lines of his face. Nor the yellow reflection of Fenrir's will. For a moment—just a moment—Lennie saw compassion.

Her knife-hand wavered, stopped by that one look, that single touch of her father's gaze. A fierce, human warmth blossomed in her chest, blasting the darkness from her mind. She spun away from her father, faced Fenrir and met his eyes once again.

"Because," she shouted, hurtling herself at the monster, "he is my father."

And she thrust the blade at his heart.

Her aim was true. His eyes widened, flickering brown and yellow. His body shimmered, outline blurring. As the knife's tip touched his white shirt, he seemed to flow aside, and the blade plunged into the back of the throne.

Momentum carried Lennie into Fenrir. His body swelled, changing shape, as if something huge and terrible writhed under his skin. The reek of corrupted flesh radiated from him. Gagging, Lennie tugged at the knife, but it stuck fast. With a howl, Fenrir lifted her like a child and cast her from the throne. She sprawled, rag-doll helpless, at Junkyard's feet.

"Kill her!" Fury distorted Fenrir's face. He hardly seemed human. "And bring me her hand. I would have the Allfather's mark as a trophy."

Before she could move, Junkyard dropped on her and trapped her to the floor with a forearm across her chest. Her tattooed hand burned almost beyond endurance. Sparks swarmed the air around her, lifting her hair. She flexed her fingers but didn't dare look away from Junkyard to take aim at Fenrir. And she couldn't, even now, turn the power on Junkyard. Eyes blazing, he raised the knife. She caught his wrist and strained to hold it back, knowing it was useless. He was too strong, too quick.

Then his grin faded. With a puzzled expression, Junkyard looked at the knife in his hand and back at Lennie. "What..."

Yellow and brown warred in his eyes. What twisted memories did he see?

"Fight it, Junkyard," she whispered. "Whatever he's showing you, it isn't real."

His knife arm wavered. But how could he fight what he didn't understand? He hadn't had visits from weird sisters or one-eyed hobos, and he didn't have Ramblin' Red's mark on his hand. His eyes bloomed fiery yellow. The knife came down.

Lennie saw the change and twisted free. The blade chinked on the cement behind her. Gathering her legs, she threw herself forward in a sprint start. He dove and caught her ankle, and she hit the floor hard. He was on her in a blur. Straddling her, he knotted his fingers in her hair and yanked her head back against his chest. The cold blade pressed under her chin. She could hear his heart pounding, the harsh rush of breath in his throat. His arm tensed and she closed her eyes.

A new voice called out. "Harding! What the *hell* are you doing?"

Briggs. Lennie had forgotten about him.

"She killed Austin," Junkyard snarled, his voice so strangled with anger that Lennie could hardly understand him. "She's got to die."

"No! That's not true." Briggs's voice cracked hoarsely, then became calm. "It was Bill Sutter—"

"Silence! Kill her now, Douglas."

Lennie sensed the compulsion behind Fenrir's command, but still the knife didn't move, and Briggs kept talking in an even, clipped voice. "Sutter was the Hobo Spider. We found evidence in his house. Let her go."

"Shut up! You lie to protect this bitch." Junkyard's blade bit into Lennie's skin. She gasped, not daring to move.

"We got a confession out of him. He killed them all, Junkyard. It was Bill Sutter, not the girl. He said El Lobo made him do it."

A deep growl shook the metal siding. "I said, be *silent*."

There was a loud thud. Briggs grunted and said no more.

The old rage swelled, unbound, in Junkyard's chest. A clean rage that shredded the yellow-tainted images in his mind of Lennie rising bloody-handed from Austin's corpse. He saw her now as she really was—small, afraid...and beautiful. She hadn't killed those hobos. She hadn't killed Austin. He let go of her hair, feeling the soft curls slide from his fingers.

Briggs said Bill had killed Austin and Tin Can Petey and all the others. But Junkyard didn't believe Bill was any more responsible than Lennie.

El Lobo was the real Hobo Spider.

Junkyard didn't understand how it could be true, or why. It didn't matter. He rose to face El Lobo, leaving Lennie on the warehouse floor. The dark man exuded power, both in his oversized build and in the yellow glow of his eyes. That didn't matter, either. Junkyard hefted the knife in his hand and smiled. The rage that filled him felt more like joy.

Austin's murderer would finally pay.

Lennie felt Junkyard's weight lift from her back. Relieved, she sighed and laid her head on the cool floor. But the moment didn't last. The Ragman rammed into Junkyard, knocking him down onto Lennie. The sudden weight crushed her against the floor. Junkyard rolled off, and the Ragman was on him, smashing a fist down at his head. Junkyard blocked it and threw an awkward punch to the Ragman's ribs.

Winded and gasping, Lennie dragged herself to her feet and looked for a way to help Junkyard. It would be easier to separate a pair of fighting pit bulls. There was only one thing she could do to stop this madness.

She bore the mark. She had the power. She could do what she was sent to do.

Hardly able to control her quaking limbs, Lennie faced Fenrir before his throne. To one side, Briggs hung limp, suspended by the ropes that held him to the chair. His head sagged to his chest and fresh blood dripped from his nose. To the other side, her father stared stupidly over her head.

No help from them. No help anywhere. Nothing but Lennie and

her fickle tattoo to face Fenrir. Though every muscle ached with exhaustion and every nerve twitched with fear, she stretched her palm toward him. Sparks jumped finger to finger. There was still power in that hand.

Fenrir merely grinned. "You are too weak, girl. I will never be bound again."

Lennie ignored him and focused on the tattoo. Power crackled through her body and flowed into her hand. Her spark-filled hair floated around her, and still the power grew, until it seemed her hand would catch fire.

Now, she thought, willing the tattoo to let loose.

Nothing happened.

"Oh, come *on*!" she screamed.

Shadows swirled at Fenrir's feet. He seemed to grow larger, towering over her as he had in the parking lot. Against her will, her legs took her closer to him. His mouth opened in a dog-like grin, saliva dripping from sharp fangs. He took her by the shoulder and pulled her close, and she could do nothing to stop him, though her hand hummed like a high voltage power line.

As she waited for those teeth to sink into her flesh, a bewildered thought fluttered through her mind. But I'm his great-great-whatever-granddaughter. He isn't supposed to be able to kill me! That crazy woman with all the beads—Verdandi, that was her name. She said Fenrir couldn't kill his progeny.

So how come I feel drool running down my neck?

"Because, my dear—" Fenrir answered, though she hadn't spoken out loud, "—I find that I can kill you, after all."

Sharp-toothed jaws clamped onto her throat, puncturing skin, crushing airways. Something tore in her neck...something vital. Blood and saliva soaked her shirt in a hot rain. Her vision distorted, lights flashing at the edges. I'm dying—this can't be happening—I'm really dying…

As the strength drained from her limbs, a black shape swooped at Fenrir's back, croaking her name. Death is a raven? Perhaps she would fly away with it…

And then Fenrir stiffened and threw his head back, his teeth tearing from her flesh. His eyes had gone wide, his blood-smeared mouth stretched in a shocked oval. Lennie slid from his grip and fell to her knees. She clapped her hands to her neck, trying to stop the flood of blood pouring through her numb fingers. She tried to cough, to gasp, anything, but the damage was too great. She would bleed out at Fenrir's feet.

But even as she gave in to despair, she felt the wasp-nest hum in her tattooed hand. A warm tingle ran up her arm and spread through her body. The wounds began to close. Air rushed into her lungs, stinking of cigarettes, blood, and decay, and feeling wonderful.

But Fenrir was still there, towering over her. She scrambled back, expecting another attack. But he was statue still. The staff slipped from his fingers and clattered on cement. His eyes drained to a dull, unfocused brown. With an almost contented sigh, he pitched headlong and crashed to the floor.

Behind him stood Jarvis Cook, a bloodied knife in his upraised hand.

He lowered his arm and blinked groggily, as if awakening from a long nightmare. Then he looked at Lennie and she could see the man who had taken her swimming in the bright sunshine all those years ago.

"Dad!" Her fingers slipped from her bloodied throat, her wounds already closed and forgotten. She ran past Fenrir's body and fell into her father's arms, not caring about the filth that coated him, not noticing the fleshless bones beneath his ragged shirt. He let the knife fall and wrapped his arms around her.

"Lennie!"

That was Junkyard's voice. She should go to him, make sure he was all right. She should check on Briggs, call the police. But for now, she just wanted to feel safe from the world, as she hadn't felt since she was a child in her father's arms.

"Lennie!" Junkyard's voice exploded with urgency. The raven screamed and fluttered at her head. She stirred reluctantly. Then the smell hit her, worse than before—animal filth, rotting flesh, blood in a septic wound. She gagged and turned her head, still clinging to her father.

A dark shadow boiled around Fenrir's body, expanding like a loose second skin. And as the shadow grew, layers of gray fur sprouted in waves along its length. Its head lifted, the curly black hair straightening, thickening, lightening to a silvery gray. The human features remained a moment longer, a mockery of the monster's stolen shape. Then the muzzle elongated and opened, revealing a long red tongue and teeth like railroad spikes.

Lennie's hand began its hornet buzz. Gnat wings against such a monster. Its eyes sprang open, yellow and hate-filled, and Lennie knew the beast was Fenrir in his truest form. A wolf. Impossibly huge, eyeing her with a slathering hunger beyond the need for mere flesh.

But this was no ordinary wolf. She could feel his ancient power, more vast than could be contained in any body. An eater of worlds. He needed no jaws to crush her.

He rose on four slender legs, leaving his human husk broken on the ground. Panic sprang from Lennie's deepest animal core. She stood wild-eyed, waiting for death. Fenrir crouched and licked the drool from his teeth, his muscles tensing to spring.

Then the raven screamed overhead, shocking Lennie from her paralysis. It plunged from the rafters and clawed at Fenrir's face, beating his eyes with its wings. Hackles raised, the wolf snarled and reared at the bird, catching tail feathers in his teeth. The raven squawked and fluttered upwards. Fenrir's eyes returned to Lennie. She avoided his gaze and backed away, crowding Jarvis Cook toward the warehouse door.

"Get out of here, Dad. I-I'll stop him." She didn't believe it. What weapon would work on a monster like that? But she had to try.

Jarvis Cook had a different plan. His scrawny arm caught her from behind and pushed her out of the way. She crashed into a metal shelf, scattering stacked weapons to the floor. She scooped up a gun and whirled to face Fenrir, fumbling at the safety.

Jarvis Cook drew himself straight and thrust his hand at the monster, palm outward. A faint swarm of sparks gathered around it. "You can have me, mongrel, but you can't have her."

His voice sounded rusty, weak. His words were futile. And Lennie loved him for them.

Fenrir panted, wet tongue lolling from his mouth—a laughing dog with rabid eyes. *I can have you both. And I will.*

And the wolf sprang. Lennie pointed the gun and pulled the trigger. Click. Another useless weapon. She flung it at Fenrir and watched helplessly as his front paws drove into her father's chest, knocking him to the ground. Jarvis beat at him with stick-thin arms. Teeth tore at him and he screamed. Then a lean, jean-jacketed figure flew through the air and knocked the wolf aside. Junkyard, with new blood on his face.

He wrapped his legs around the great beast and buried his arms in the fur around his neck. "Run, Lennie!"

Lennie didn't move. Her father lay limp on the floor, his face a bloody mess. She wanted to drag him away, to somehow escape this horror, but Junkyard could never defeat Fenrir. Only she had that power. Whether she wanted to believe it or not, this was no longer about saving her father, or even herself.

This *thing* had caused so many deaths, people she cared about—Bones O'Riley, Too Long Soo. Jungle Jim.

Her mother.

Junkyard would be next, and her father, then Lennie herself. What then? The world? She couldn't let that happen.

Her tattooed hand throbbed painfully. She didn't trust that weapon, but she had no other choice. She lifted her arm, thrust her hand palm outward. If she could just release it, this time.

Junkyard slid his legs off Fenrir's back. He braced himself and twisted the wolf's head, trying to throw him like a calf. A bull-sized calf. It didn't work.

Use it. Use it now.

Concentrating, Lennie gathered the power into her hand. Sparks swarmed the air around her, but she hesitated. She didn't want to encase Junkyard along with Fenrir.

The Wolf bucked his back legs and tossed Junkyard against the wall. Junkyard slid to the floor, landing awkwardly. Before Lennie could loose her power, the wolf whirled and pounced. Junkyard rolled to his feet to meet him. It was like watching a single sand bag stand against a tidal wave. Fenrir crushed Junkyard to the ground. Junkyard strained to hold Fenrir's dripping maw away from his throat.

"No!" Lennie almost dove onto Fenrir's back, but what could she do against such a terrible beast? She looked frantically for a weapon. Some sort of club or knife...a chainsaw would be nice. Stacks of guns lined the shelves. Probably unloaded. Nothing else looked deadly enough.

Then she spotted Fenrir's staff, which had rolled away from the fighting. Only it was not a staff at all. A spear. Like a javelin, but heavy and coarse, with dangling black feathers. The javelin was not her event, but she knew the technique. She snatched it up and hefted it, finding its balance.

Junkyard groaned, his arms giving way to Fenrir's weight. As Lennie lifted the spear to throw, the raven flew at her face, croaking and beating at her with its wings.

You must not kill him! The prophecy...you must bind him.

That voice! She saw the raven's shriveled eye. Its one good eye was blue. Furious, she knocked the bird aside.

Fenrir lifted his head and his gaze riveted on the spear. His eyes flamed. This time, Lennie stared into them, and the power in her hand flared to match. He rose from Junkyard and stalked Lennie, stiff-legged. His hackles raised and muzzle wrinkled in a sharp-toothed snarl. She lifted the spear to her shoulder. Fenrir's voice spoke inside her head.

This is not my time to die. And you will not be my killer.

The dark tendrils of his thoughts beat at her and yellow haze swirled at the edges of her vision, but her palm crackled with power and he couldn't find a hold in her mind.

He stepped closer. *You, however, are not part of the prophecy.*

She could capture him now. Junkyard was a safe distance away.

You can die any time. For example—

She could bind him. She knew it would work, this time. But what was bound could be unbound. Maybe not in her lifetime, but Fenrir would live to kill again.

—you could die now.

In one smooth motion, Fenrir crouched and sprang. Fur and teeth and eyes filled Lennie's vision. She held her breath and threw with all the power of her legs and back. Honest, human power. The spear drove deep into Fenrir's chest.

An ordinary spear would have made Fenrir laugh. He would have plucked the puny thing from his chest and used it to pick her flesh from his teeth. But this was Gungnir, the spear of the Allfather. Nothing could stand before it.

His graceful leap faltered. Yowling, he hurtled out of control. Lennie dove out of the way as he crashed into the stockpile of weapons and drugs. The metal walls rang like a giant bell. Shelves collapsed, bringing down an avalanche of boxes. He writhed in the chaos, biting at the spear. His legs beat the air, running, running, then slowing and falling still. He lifted his head weakly and strained toward Lennie. The light flickered in his eyes. Then, with a long, pleading whine, he let his head fall back and lay still.

Silence filled the warehouse. Lennie watched Fenrir's body warily, looking for signs of life. Her hand still hummed with power, and she held it out, ready. But the pressure she'd felt all day had lifted and the dark tendrils that had pried at her mind were gone.

She pushed herself to her feet and approached Fenrir. He lay awkwardly amid a jumble of boxes and weapons. The odor had somehow changed, becoming less foul and more pathetic, though it still reeked of road kill. She nudged the wolf with her foot, sensing the emptiness in his body. He was dead.

The body began to shimmer and grow transparent. Its features blurred, and then sprouted falcon feathers and a sharp, curved beak. The feathers fell away and a more human visage washed over it—one with dark, curly hair and broad shoulders. Then the wolf returned, now clear as glass. Pure animal, it was beautiful, with a coat like snow under a silver moon.

And then it was gone.

CHAPTER TWENTY FIVE

The spear rattled to the floor and rolled to Lennie's feet. She watched Fenrir's blood evaporate from its bronze tip. She had done it—she had killed the Wolf.

So why didn't it feel like a victory?

The raven cawed above her head and flapped down to the floor where Fenrir had died. It turned its single bright eye to Lennie and croaked. Then it fluffed its feathers, and began to swell, flowing upward into the familiar shape of Ramblin' Red. He brushed the last black feathers from his arms and glared at her.

"You fool—you've ruined everything!" There was no trace of the comfortable drawl in his voice. "I should slaughter you where you stand."

Lennie stared at him, disbelieving. "You've got a hell of a nerve. Fenrir's dead, the world is saved—just what did you expect from me?"

"I *expected* you to follow directions," he said coldly.

Oh, this was too much. She flushed and stepped toward him, remembering her threat to gouge out his one good eye. Her toe bumped the spear. Picking it up, she poked him in the chest with it.

"*You* did this to me. You did this to my father...gave us this bizarre power without even an instruction manual."

She poked him again. "You sicced us on an all-powerful monster that could eat a VW Bug in one bite, all for some damn prophecy that no one except you gives a rat's ass about."

His eye widened, fixed on the spear, and he took a step back. "Now, that's not true. He was going to destroy the world—"

But Lennie wasn't listening. She pressed on, jabbing him in the chest for emphasis. "You destroyed our lives. You took my father away and virtually murdered my mother. Just what gives you the right?"

"I explained all that." He eased the spear aside and rubbed his chest. "You and your father had the best chance of reaching Fenrir unharmed."

"Oh, really. And why couldn't you do it, Mr. I've-Got-Mysterious-Powers?"

"Me?" he all but squeaked. "He could have *killed* me." His gaze never left the spear in Lennie's hand.

She snorted. "Well, I'm not going to kill you."

She tossed the spear to him, cross-wise. He flinched, but caught it out of the air. Relief spread across his face and he began to pump himself up with his usual arrogance. Lennie glared into his one blue eye.

"Killing is too good for you."

She raised her tattooed hand, still coated with her own blood. The unspent power flashed around her fingers, flowing easily this time. Light collected like a snowball in her palm. Ramblin' Red's mouth fell open and he backed away.

"No—you can't!"

But of course she could. Sparks flowed from her hand and swarmed him. He swatted at them, his eye widening in panic. An aura glowed around him like a second skin. It peeled away from his body, taking on the translucent form of a robed, bearded man with one blue eye, a broad-brimmed hat, and a spear in one hand.

Ramblin' Red's true form, Lennie supposed.

The robed figure shot upward, escaping the doomed human body. But the sparks pursued him, spinning strings in the air around him. Though he flailed and twisted and tried to escape, they closed on him, winding ever tighter, encasing him along with the spear. The light of his aura vanished and the cocoon hit the floor with a satisfying thud. The human body collapsed next to it.

Lennie strode over to the cocoon and gave it a solid kick. She heard a faint grunt and it bucked a little. Junkyard limped up behind her and looked over her shoulder.

"Hmm. Kind of like having a tiger by the tail, eh?"

"It's only a problem if I let him go."

Jaw set, she turned from the cocoon. The anger had drained away, leaving her exhausted and vaguely dissatisfied. Heroes saved the world. Heroes got the glory. So how come she felt more like a janitor?

Then she saw her father, who lay motionless where Fenrir had left him. Blood pooled on the floor near his head. "Oh my God—Dad!"

She ran to him. Tooth marks punctured his skin in oozing points of red. Mostly superficial. But one deep, ragged gouge tracked down one cheek and across his neck. The kind of gouge that meant a person would never wake up.

Junkyard came up behind her and put a hand on her shoulder. "Lennie..."

"All I wanted was to find my father." Her throat closed around the words. She drew a ragged breath and sagged to the floor. She lifted her father's hand to her lap. There was no pulse.

How could he be dead? Numb, she could only grasp the unfairness of it. He had saved her, become her father again. And for those few moments, she'd had a family.

She pulled his silver watch from her pocket. It was warm in her hands, as warm as it had been all those years ago, when he'd taken it from his own pocket to let her wind it. She popped it open. The inscription said, *May there always be enough time.*

But he hadn't had the time. Not with her mother, and not with her.

Lennie had wanted to give it back to him, to tell him that her mother...well, she didn't know what she would have told him. She closed it and laid it gently in his hand.

Junkyard squatted beside her and put an arm around her shoulders. "Lennie, I'm so sorry—"

But she wasn't listening. As she touched her father's hand, something tingled under her fingertips—a faint vibration in the wasted bones of his fingers. Her tattoo prickled in answer. Could it be?

She turned his hand over. The Valknut was there. Three interlocking triangles, just like hers. The thing was a curse. She had hated its indelible presence. But it had also saved her life.

Maybe...

Before the thought had fully formed, the vibration faded, as though he was too weak to sustain it. Desperately, she clamped her tattooed hand over his. There was no time to think. No time to doubt. She focused inward, calling on her remaining energy. She was so exhausted.

The power seemed to take forever to build. Then the familiar charge grew in her hand and she let the energy flow.

For a moment, it seemed to work. She felt her father's Valknut awaken under her palm. The air hummed around their clasped hands. Junkyard flinched as sparks flowed in a warm, gentle current over her father's body. But her father remained still and lifeless, and the current faltered.

No! She couldn't let him die. Her heart still beat. She still breathed, moved, thought. There had to be more to give. She reached deeper, and the stream of sparks brightened. At the same time, the room seemed to darken. She swayed, feeling as though her own life were pouring out the end of her arm. Someone moaned—her father? She slumped forward, and still the current flowed into him.

"Lennie." She felt Junkyard's arm around her shoulders, pulling her upright. "That's enough. Stop."

But she couldn't. The power drained out of her, siphoning her life away. Cold spread through her limbs and her heart fluttered against her ribs. Then a boney hand grasped her wrist and pulled her tattooed hand free, breaking the current. The backlash hit her like a defibrillator. She gasped and tried to sit up, but the room spun around her and she had to close her eyes.

"Easy now," Junkyard murmured in her ear. "Take a deep breath—that's right. Now another."

Slowly, the warmth returned to Lennie's limbs. She opened her eyes. The room held still and everything stayed in place. "All right. I—I'm okay."

She looked down at her father, hardly daring to hope. He tried to smile at her, but winced when the movement creased an angry red scar across his cheek—all that was left of his wound. And his eyes—

His eyes looked normal.

"Thank you," he said, and though she was no longer a child and her father had wasted down to skin and bone, his hands remained large enough to cover hers in a warm, reassuring grip. Lennie trembled all over, unable to say anything.

"Uh, hello? A little help, do you think?"

Lennie and Junkyard turned, startled by the sound of Briggs's voice. He blinked at them and strained against his bindings. Junkyard's arm tightened around Lennie's shoulders. "Stay with your father. I'll take care of Briggs."

He hesitated, touching her bloodied cheek. His eyes were full of concern. "Will you be all right?"

She nodded and watched him stride over to Briggs's chair. Her shoulders felt cold where the warmth of his arm had been.

After a moment's search, Junkyard scooped up a blood-crusted knife that had been dropped during the fight. He used it to saw through the ropes holding Briggs to the chair.

"Shit," Briggs said, eyeing the stained knife. "What did I miss?"

Junkyard glanced back at Lennie. "It's complicated. But right now, we need an ambulance."

The ropes fell away. Briggs rubbed his arms and flexed his hands, then pulled out his cell phone. As he made the call, his gaze traveled around the warehouse, first resting on the bleeding body that had once held Fenrir, then lingering on the one-eyed, redheaded man and the cocooned form beside him. Behind them lay the Ragman, who moaned but didn't move. Briggs looked almost relieved to see him.

"Well, I know what I can arrest him for, at least. He's the one who put me in that chair. As for the rest—" He shook his head. "I hate to sound cliché, but how the hell am I going to write this one up? You're gonna have to tell me what happened. Somehow, I don't think I'm going to like it."

Junkyard shrugged. "Not sure what happened, myself, and I was awake through it all."

The man who had been Ramblin' Red sat up and rubbed his neck. "Did I git hit by a train or somethin'?"

Lennie sucked in a breath and checked to make sure the cocoon was still intact. She gave the redheaded man a hard look. "What are you? I mean, who..."

Her voice dwindled. He grinned sheepishly. "Nah, dontcha worry." He tapped his forehead. "Ain't nobody in here but me. Name's Walter Galloway, but you can call me Red."

He stood up, shook out his legs, and patted himself down. "No harm done, neither. If you call bein' locked inside yer own head for a hunnerd years no harm. But my friend Angus, over there, he ain't doin' so good. Might be he could use some help."

He gestured at the body vacated by Fenrir. Blood soaked his back. Lennie had assumed he was dead. Briggs approached the body carefully and felt for a pulse.

"He's right. This guy's still alive. But, to be honest," he fingered his bruised temple where Fenrir had struck him, "I'm not sure how much I want to help him. Know what I mean?"

Jarvis Cook squeezed Lennie's hand. "It's okay, the monster is gone. All that's left is another victim. Go help him." He grinned. "After all, he is your—"

"I know. He's my great-great-whatever-grandfather."

But Junkyard stopped her before she could kneel beside the injured man. He frowned at her, doubt clear in his face. "Are you sure about him? I mean..."

"I'm sure," she said firmly. "That's not Fenrir."

He gave her a long, hard look, then his expression relaxed. "Okay. I'll trust you. I should have trusted you all along. I just wanted so badly to find Austin's killer—"

"Sshhh." She laid a finger over his lips. "It wasn't your fault."

He caught her hand and held it tight. Horror haunted his fatigue-stained eyes. "All this time, a year on the rails...all those murders. And it was Bill Sutter all along." He grimaced and shook his head. "How can you be the bait when the fish knows you're there?"

"You couldn't have known."

"But I should have."

He let go of her hand and stuffed his fists in his pockets. His face twisted in self-torture. Lennie knew that expression. She had worn it for years as her mother committed suicide by inches. "Hey, you didn't kill those people. I don't think Bill Sutter was really responsible, either."

She looked down at Angus Cook, who had begun to stir. "The evil that killed your brother—probably hurt more people than we'll ever know—that evil is gone. It's over. It's time to live your life again."

His shoulders hunched inside his brother's jean jacket. So many of the buttons were now missing. Lines of pain having nothing to do with his bruises etched deeply into his face. He was silent for a long time, unable to meet her eyes.

"I don't think I know how."

Lennie looked around the warehouse at the odd mix of strangers who stared anxiously back. The lost, the homeless...the lonely. "Then we'll figure out how together."

She knelt beside Angus Cook, laid her tattooed hand over his wound, and the sparks began to fly.

ACKNOWLEDGMENTS

Several people have provided support throughout the journey this book has become. Foremost of these, I'd like to thank my parents and my husband, Tom, who got me started by saying, "Good idea. You should write that novel." (Granted, he was referring to an idea I had involving Nostradamus and time travel, but I took it as a blanket endorsement.)

I also thank Cathy Hedge, Mark Rogers, Glenn Sixbury, and Dave Phalen for sharing their writing expertise with me throughout the process. You guys are the best on several levels. Thanks also go to beta readers Lee Killough, Char Simser, Juliana Loughin, and Tammy Mack, and to Hannah Loughin, whose unbridled enthusiasm for the story kept me going when I wondered if it was all worth it.

Thanks for feedback go to Pat, Kim, Stacy and Jean of the unofficially named Mighty Mighty Duct Tape Writers Group of Manhattan. Also, I say an all-encompassing "thank you" to the members of Leonard Bishop's Manhattan group who commented on parts of this book over the years.

Ryan Runyan helped with police procedural and military details. "Chip" the railroad detective and Clifford (Oats) Williams gave me invaluable details about life on the iron road. My thanks go to all of you.

Finally, thanks go to J.W. Manus for her careful proofreading and enlightening discussions about grammar, Jonathan D. Allan for putting together the print version, and Hannah Loughin for final proofreading of the print version. Any error of formatting, grammar, fact, or prose are due to my own, um, poetic license.

ABOUT THE AUTHOR

In the beginning, I liked any book with mice in it. And fairy tales.

But that was elementary school. At some point, mice morphed into SF&F, with detours into horror, mysteries, thrillers, and the occasional classic. And then reading became writing. And editing. And blogging. And eventually a novel, *Valknut: The Binding*. You can also find my short stories *Rose in Winter* at Amazon (or in *Marion Zimmer Bradley's Sword and Sorceress XXI*) and *Hell Hole* at Amazon (or in *Anthology from Hell* from Yard Dog Press).

When I'm not writing, I work as a statistical consultant and teach a technical writing course at a University.

And on Fridays I curl.